OTHER MULTNOMAH TITLES FROM AL AND JOANNA LACY'S HANNAH OF FORT BRIDGER SERIES

Betsy Fordham's husband is captured and killed by Cheyenne Indians, leaving her bitter and fearful. Hannah befriends Betsy and tells her of the help God can provide for overcoming her grief, bitterness, and fear. Although that message is at first rejected, the disappearance of Betsy's two young sons—and their eventual rescue by Shoshone Indians—brings her to the place where she's ready to hear the message that God loves her, and that His perfect love casts out fear.

Hannah of Fort Bridger Series #3

ISBN 1-57673-083-2

With her infant daughter, Julianna LeCroix heads west to begin a new life following her husband's death. Along the way she encounters kind strangers who share the gospel with her, and a desperate drifter named Jack Bower who takes her hostage to conceal his identity. As he travels with Julianna, Jack finds himself falling in love with her. He hires on with a local rancher, becomes a Christian, and eventually asks Julianna to marry him—just before the stagecoach that would separate them forever heads for the horizon!

Hannah of Fort Bridger Series #4

ISBN 1-57673-234-7

THE PERFECT GIFT

BOOK FIVE

AL AND JOANNA LACY

MULTNOMAH PUBLISHERS

THE PERFECT GIFT

© 1999 by Lew A. and JoAnna Lacy

published by Multnomah Publishers, Inc.

Cover design by Left Coast Design

Cover illustration by Frank Ordaz

International Standard Book Number: 1-57673-407-2

Scripture quotations are from *The Holy Bible,* King James Version

Multnomah is a trademark of Multnomah Publishers, Inc.,
and is registered in the U.S. Patent and Trademark Office.

The colophon is a trademark of Multnomah Publishers, Inc.

Printed in the United States of America.

For information:

Multnomah Publishers, Inc., Post Office Box 1720, Sisters, Oregon 97759

Library of Congress Cataloging-in-Publication Data:
Lacy, Al.
    The perfect gift/by Al and JoAnna Lacy.
    p.   cm.—(Hannah of Fort Bridger:5)
    ISBN 1-57673-407-2 (alk. paper)
    I. Lacy, JoAnna.   II.Title.   III.Series: Lacy, Al.
    Fort Bridger series: bk. 5.
    PS3562.A256P47   1999
    813'.54—dc21   99-11742
                                          CIP

99 00 01 02 03 04 05 06 — 10 9 8 7 6 5 4 3 2 1

*This book is fondly dedicated to Jeff Leeland—
my faithful prayer partner and friend.*

*He too knows the anxiety of caring for a gravely ill loved one,
and his tender heart is always willing—
even in the midst of a busy day—
to stop for a moment and pray with me,
helping me to share my burden and to make my day brighter.*

May our precious Lord bless you and yours, Jeff, with just Himself.

In His matchless love,

JOANNA
GALATIANS 6:2

Every good gift and every perfect gift is from above,
and cometh down from the Father of Lights,
with whom is no variableness,
neither shadow of turning.

JAMES 1:17

PREFACE

Historians of America's Western frontier have long probed into the constitution of the women who gave up their homes to journey westward with their husbands in search of a richer and fuller life.

Historian Emerson Hough wrote,

> The chief figure of the American West is not the fringed-legged man riding a rawboned pony, but the gaunt and sad-faced woman sitting in the front seat of the wagon, following her husband where he might lead, her face hidden in the same ragged sunbonnet which had crossed the Missouri long before.
>
> There was the seed of America's wealth! There was the great romance of all America—the woman in the sunbonnet; not the man with the rifle across his saddle horn. Who has written her story? Who has painted her picture?[1]

In an article written in 1857, we found a description of the typical woman in the sunbonnet heading west. She is described as riding on the high seat of an ox-drawn wagon with the reins in one hand. Her husband is on his horse beside the wagon. The woman has household goods packed all around her, with a sack of potatoes to rest her feet upon. In one arm is a child some two or three years old, and in her free hand she holds an umbrella to screen her throbbing head from the oppressive heat of the sun. With her on the seat is a bundle of sundries for which she could find no other place secure from falling overboard from the rocking to and fro of the ponderous wagon.[2]

Author Louise Clappe quotes a Californian describing the

disappearance of women at the end of a Plains journey: "The poor women arrive looking haggard, burnt to the color of hazelnut, the natural gloss of their hair entirely destroyed by alkali, whole plains of which they were compelled to cross on the way."[3] Most of the sunbonnet travelers arrived at their destinations and made new homes for their husbands and children. Some, however, were buried along the trail, while others arrived sick in body and had to endure long months of recovery. Still others arrived whose minds had come unhinged from the horror of Indian attacks—the threat of being captured, molested, and tortured, along with the horror of seeing their husbands and children massacred.

In addition to the Indian danger, there were wild animals to fear, violent thunderstorms, excessive heat, clouds of dust, fatigue, and often the sorrows of having husbands and children become ill or die.

Some of the women whose mental capacities were affected by the strain of the westward move never recovered, and they lived the remainder of their lives with fragmented minds. Others, in time, were able to continue life as normal wives and mothers. Fortunately, the majority of the women who dared the perils of the Western frontier were able to tolerate their afflictions, both physically and mentally.

Historian Dee Brown wrote, "Faith in God was a mighty force always at hand to strengthen the pioneer woman in her sorrows and her struggles against adversities."[4] This comment is underscored by the many references to the sustaining hand of God recorded in the diaries kept by women, both on the trail and over the years that followed, as they settled in the West.

In our series, Hannah of Fort Bridger, JoAnna and I are attempting to write this woman's story, and with words, to paint her picture. We chose Fort Bridger as the central site of the series for a number of reasons. One reason was because during the great migration west, Fort Bridger was on the Oregon Trail and was a favorite place of wagon masters to stop and rest along the wearisome, dusty journey.

Another reason was because the army fort was there, and officers were allowed to bring their wives when they were assigned to the fort. Also, Fort Bridger became a focal spot for stagecoaches, which brought new people to the scene with regularity. The area around the town was also drawing families to establish farms and ranches.

In our novels we seek to tell the stories of these people as their lives come in touch with Hannah Cooper, a strong Christian widow and mother, and proprietor of the town's gathering place, the general store.

In *The Perfect Gift*, book 5 of the Hannah of Fort Bridger series, we shine the spotlight on "the woman in the sunbonnet."

1. Emerson Hough, *The Passing of the Frontier: A Chronicle of the Old West,* Chronicles of America series (New Haven, Conn.: Yale University Press, 1920), 93–94.

2. *Kansas Historical Quarterly,* Vol. XVI 1948.

3. Louise Amelia Clappe, *The Letters of Dame Shirley* (San Francisco: Grabhorn Press, 1922).

4. Dee Brown, *The Gentle Tamers* (Lincoln, Nebr.: University of Nebraska Press, 1981).

PROLOGUE

In *Pillow of Stone,* Hannah of Fort Bridger book 4, heiress Julianna LeCroix had left New Orleans with her infant daughter, Larissa, to begin a new life in Idaho after her husband's death and the theft of her inheritance.

Early in her journey, she encountered kind strangers who shared the gospel with her. While the gospel seeds were taking root in her heart, Julianna and her baby were kidnapped at gunpoint by Jack Bower, a drifter who hoped to trick the hired killers hot on his trail by disguising himself as a family man.

Julianna never dreamed she would be attracted to a gun-toting fugitive, but after she and Jack both became Christians in Fort Bridger and Jack was hired by the town council as a deputy, she found herself deeply in love with him, yet didn't tell him. To complicate matters, although Jack had confessed his love to Julianna, he didn't believe he was good enough for her.

The night before she and Larissa were leaving for Idaho, Julianna made up her mind to tell Jack she loved him when he came to say good-bye at the stage station the next morning...

CHAPTER ONE

Hannah Cooper and several others stood outside the Wells Fargo office as Julianna boarded the stage with eleven-month-old Larissa in her arms.

The beautiful young mother looked stricken as she peered out the stagecoach window.

Hannah met Julianna's gaze, and tears welled up in her eyes as an unspoken question hung between them. Where was Jack?

Stagecoach driver Cal Springer snapped the reins, and the stage rolled out.

Julianna felt as though her heart would break. Why hadn't Jack come to tell her good-bye and ask her to stay? He said he was in love with her, and she had read the truth of it in his eyes.

Dear Lord, help me! she cried inwardly. *Help me!*

Two businessmen sat across from Julianna, riding with their backs to the front of the coach. Wiley Stamm, who had noticed Julianna's tears, asked if she'd had a difficult time saying good-bye to someone special.

Julianna nodded. "You might say that, Mr. Stamm."

They were about ten miles out of Fort Bridger when they

heard a noise above the rumble of pounding hooves and whir of wheels.

Wiley Stamm looked out his window toward the rear of the stage. "Wagon coming up behind us. The driver seems to be in a hurry. Looks like he's going to pass us."

Darrold Conister, the other passenger, leaned close to Stamm, trying to catch a glimpse of the oncoming wagon. "Looks like the man in the wagon is trying to get the driver to stop the stage. He's wearing a badge. Some kind of lawman."

Julianna twisted around and looked back through her window, catching a glimpse of the driver. It was Jack!

Moments later the stage had come to a halt and Wiley Stamm was holding baby Larissa while Jack helped Julianna out of the coach.

When they were standing outside the coach, facing each other, Jack gripped her upper arms as though fearful she might climb back into the stagecoach. "Julianna, I couldn't bring myself to tell you good-bye at the stage office. Just the thought of watching you ride out of my life...I had to come after you."

He gazed intently into her tear-clouded eyes. "You once told me you had strong feelings toward me. I thought if I could get you to stay in Fort Bridger, I'd have a chance to turn strong feelings into love...the marrying kind of love. I—"

"Jack," she cut in, "I'm in love with you! I don't want the style of life I used to have. I want the kind I can have with you."

"If I could only— What...what did you just say? Oh, Julianna, you've made me the happiest man in the world!" He pulled her close and kissed her for a long moment, then realized they had an audience...and a waiting stagecoach.

Jack held on to Julianna's hand while he told the driver he was relieving him of two of his passengers. After loading Julianna's luggage into the borrowed wagon, Jack helped her onto the seat. The stagecoach was rolling away as he placed Larissa into her arms.

When Jack had climbed up into the driver's seat, he bent over and kissed the baby, saying, "I love you, Larissa."

The little girl smiled at him, stuck her thumb in her mouth, and snuggled against her mother's wildly beating heart.

Jack placed a tender hand on Julianna's cheek and kissed the tip of her nose. "I love Larissa's mommy, too."

Julianna gazed back at him, her eyes revealing what was in her heart. "And Larissa's mommy loves you, Deputy Marshal Jack Bower."

A wide smile spread across Jack's face as he snapped the reins and swung the wagon around to head back to Fort Bridger.

An azure sky stretched as far as the eye could see in the wintry morning light as Matt McDermott drove westward across southern Wyoming's rolling hills. The wagon bed was loaded with heavy sacks of grain, and the wheels complained with groans and squeaks of the excessive weight.

It was the third week of November 1870. November was autumn's iron month in Wyoming, paving the way for winter's arrival with its raw, savage winds and heavy snows.

Beside McDermott was his wife, Emily, two years his junior at age twenty-seven. There were deep lines in her brow, at the corners of her eyes, and around her mouth. Strands of gray threaded her dark brown hair that was mostly hidden beneath a heavy scarf.

Six-year-old Holly McDermott sat on her mother's lap bundled in a thick wool blanket and dressed as warmly as possible. Her long auburn hair was braided in pigtails, and the cold morning sun highlighted a smattering of freckles on her nose and cheeks. From time to time, Holly coughed from deep in her chest.

Holly was looking ahead on the trail, waiting for Fort Bridger to come into view. Her eyes focused on a huge dark blot in a shallow valley off to the left. The blot seemed to be alive with motion. "Papa, what's that big dark spot down there?"

"Honey, that's a herd of buffalo."

"Oh! I haven't seen any buffalo since we came to Wyoming!"

"Well, you won't be able to say that anymore."

Emily pulled Holly closer and kissed her forehead. "There's lots more to see in Wyoming, too, honey. You know those soldiers on horses we see riding by our place now and then?"

"Uh-huh."

"Well, today we're going to see the fort where they live."

"That's Fort Bridger, huh."

"Yes."

"Why do they call it Fort Bridger, Mama?"

"It's a long story, honey. But to make it short, many years ago a man named Jim Bridger established a trading post there, on the banks of the Black's Fork of the Green River. He called it Fort Bridger, but it really didn't have any soldiers there. Later, the United States Army built a fort there, so they just named it Fort Bridger. At the same time, a town was growing around the trading post. So now Fort Bridger is both a town and an army fort."

Holly lifted a mittened hand from beneath the blanket and covered her mouth as she coughed hard, a rattle sounding in her throat. She sniffed and coughed again. Emily took a handkerchief from her coat pocket and pressed it to Holly's nose. "Blow, honey."

When Emily had put the handkerchief back into her pocket, she said, "Matt, maybe Holly and I shouldn't have come with you. Being out like this isn't going to make her cold any better."

Matt nodded, then said in a low tone, "But since this trip means staying overnight in Evanston, I just couldn't bring myself to go off and leave you with your nerves still shot like they are, and the nightmares—"

"I know, darling," Emily cut in. "And I appreciate your concern." She was quiet a moment, then said, "We've got her bundled up real warm. I don't think her cold will get any worse."

Holly turned and looked at her mother. "Mama, did you bring some horehound drops?"

"Why, no, honey. Is your throat sore?"

"Not really sore. Just kinda dry."

"Tell you what, sweetheart," Matt said. "When we get to Fort Bridger, we'll pick you up some horehound drops. I'm sure they've got a general store there."

"Thank you, Papa," Holly said, smiling.

She continued to watch the buffalo herd in the valley to the south until they passed from view. Moments later, her line of sight focused on the mountains to the southwest. "Oh, look! Mountains! Do they have a name, Papa?"

"Mm-hmm. They're called the Uintahs. Those are the same mountains we can see from home. They just look bigger and different here because we're closer to them. The Uintah Mountains are mostly in the territory known as Utah."

"They've got snow on their tops," observed the girl.

"They'll have plenty more pretty soon," put in Emily.

"Do they get as much snow here as we did in Kentucky, Papa?"

Matt chuckled. "Honey, what little snow we got in Kentucky isn't anything compared to what they get here. You've already seen some snow here, but the big storms come from December through March. From what they tell me, it can get three and four feet deep at times, and the drifts pile up anywhere from six to eight feet."

"Oooh. You're six feet tall, Papa. That's a lot of snow, but eight feet is even more."

Suddenly the uneven rooftops of the town in the distance caught Holly's eye.

"Oh, look...Mama...Papa! It's a town! Is that Fort Bridger?"

"Sure is," Matt said. "We'll be there in about half an hour."

Holly kept her eyes glued to Fort Bridger, and soon they were riding down its wide main thoroughfare.

They passed residential areas on both sides of the street before reaching the business section that was mostly made up of false-fronted clapboard buildings. One exception was the Uintah Hotel and Glenda's Café, which were actually one frame building, the hotel part being three stories. Other exceptions were the Western Union office, where passengers were boarding a stage as the McDermotts passed, and the livery stable—both were of log construction. The one-room schoolhouse was a white frame building.

Matt read the signs on both sides of the street as they moved along slowly. He noted the gun and hardware store, the bank, and the tonsorial parlor, along with various shops and stores. Finally he saw the shingle outside a white building informing him it was the office of Frank O'Brien, M.D.

Emily kept her arms around Holly and pointed ahead with her chin. "Right up there, Matt...the general store."

As Matt drew rein and brought the wagon to a halt in front of the store, he said, "Look there, Emily, how well kept it is."

"I'll say." She ran her eyes over the clean, well-painted building and sharply lettered sign. "I wish Stewart's General Store in Mountain View was as clean-looking as this one."

Matt grinned as he focused on the sign overhead. "I can tell you real quick why there's a difference. This one's owned by a woman. See? Hannah Cooper, Proprietor. Bill Stewart is an old bachelor. I hate to admit it, but women are just more conscious of such things."

"Well, I'm glad to admit it," said Emily, looking down into her daughter's eyes. "Aren't you, Holly?"

"I guess, Mama. But I'm not a woman yet."

"You will be someday, honey. But you're a female. And we females are just more particular about things being clean and in order than males are."

Holly giggled, looked up at her father, and said, "Men are messy, all right. Like you when you take your bath, Papa. When Mama and I come into the kitchen after your bath, it's always a mess!"

Matt laughed. "I'm outnumbered in this family! What chance do I have?" He jumped down from the wagon. "I'll just be a couple of minutes. Be right back with those horehound drops."

Cooper's General Store was painted a pale green with white trim. Its sparkling clean windows greeted passersby with an array of colors advertising the bounty inside. The boardwalk in front was swept clean, and an air of welcome extended from the glossy varnished door.

When two couples emerged from the store, chatting animatedly, Emily caught the inviting aroma of freshly brewed coffee. She imagined what must await customers inside—a cheery fire in a potbellied stove, plenty of coffee for Hannah Cooper's customers, and an atmosphere where friendly conversations could always be found. She wished it were that way at Bill Stewart's general store.

While snuggling Holly in the warm blanket, Emily smiled at people as they passed by on the boardwalk.

Matt threaded his way through milling customers to the counter, where he saw a large jar of horehound candy. There was a small, thin, silver-haired man behind the counter who was totaling a bill for a middle-aged couple. Next to him was a young woman with a ready smile. "Good morning, sir," she said. "I don't think I've seen you before."

Matt returned the smile. "My family and I are just passing through town. I needed to get some horehound drops for my little girl."

"Certainly. How much do you want?"

"A half pound will do it," said Matt. "Are you Hannah Cooper?"

"Oh, no. I'm just filling in here, helping her assistant, Mr. Kates. My name is Nellie Patterson. I'm a close friend of Hannah. She's at the Wells Fargo office at the moment, seeing someone off."

Matt nodded. "Nice store."

"Hannah keeps it well supplied and in good repair." Nellie lifted the lid from the candy jar and measured out the desired amount. "Where are you folks from?"

"We live the other side of Mountain View a few miles. Know where Mountain View is?"

"Sure do. Farmer?"

"Mmm-hmm."

Matt noticed two older men sitting near the potbellied stove, drinking coffee and enjoying a game of checkers.

"Well, here you are, sir," said Nellie. "One-half pound of horehound for your little girl. That will be fifteen cents."

Matt paid Nellie, thanked her, and nodded a greeting at other customers as he left the store.

Outside once more, Matt rounded the rear of the wagon and climbed up onto the seat. He held out the bag. "Here you go, Holly."

"Thank you, Papa."

Soon they were moving along the street toward the west end of town. Matt was about to point out the stockade walls to

Holly when Emily stiffened and sucked in a sharp breath. "Matt, look! Indians! Get out of here fast! Hurry, Matt!"

Matt's line of sight focused on a small band of Indians, who were waving at the sentries in the tower as they approached the gate on horses. He could tell by the full head-dress of the one in the lead that he was their chief. The warm reception they received from the soldiers told him the Indians were friendly toward whites.

"Ma-a-a-tt!" cried Emily, her voice quavering. "Go! Hurry!"

Holly was sitting straight up on her mother's lap, eyes bulging with fear.

"Honey," said Matt, "those are friendly Indians. Probably Crow. See? They're waving and smiling at the sentries in the tower."

Emily was now frozen in terror and could no longer utter a sound. Her body was rigid, and there was a wheeze in her breath. Matt snapped the reins to speed the horses up. He needed to get Emily where she couldn't see the Indians, as quickly as possible. When they were out of town, he pulled the wagon to the side of the road and took hold of Emily's hand.

"It's all right," he said. "There are no Indians now." As he spoke, he leaned close to her.

Emily's face was devoid of color, and the pounding of her heart caused her to take slow, suffocating gasps.

Matt glanced down at his daughter and touched her cheek. "Holly, there's nothing to be afraid of. Please don't cry. It'll make Mama worse."

The little girl blinked at her tears and nodded. Suddenly she began to cough, which seemed to break Emily's trance. Emily drew the blanket closer around her daughter's face with a trembling hand and shuddered as if to throw off her terror. "Are—are you...all right, honey?"

Holly moved the horehound drop to the other side of her mouth and nodded.

"And how about you, darlin'?" Matt said, squeezing her hand.

Emily swallowed with difficulty and looked back over her shoulder toward Fort Bridger. "Where are they?"

"The Indians?"

"Yes! Where are they?"

"Honey, they're still back there in town. They aren't coming after us. They're not like the Pawnees. They're friendly to white people. I think they're Crow."

Emily looked over her shoulder again. "I hope the army kills them!"

"Honey," Matt said, "didn't you hear what I said? Those aren't hostile Indians. Didn't you see the soldiers in the tower waving to them?"

"M-Matt, wh-why are you s-stopped? We have to g-get away before they attack us!"

He squeezed harder on her hand. "Emily! Look at me!"

She turned and looked directly into his eyes.

"Honey, those Indians in town are not bad Indians. They're on good terms with the military in Fort Bridger, and I'm sure with the townspeople. You mustn't be afraid. Do you understand what I'm saying?"

Emily closed her eyes and swallowed hard, then met his gaze again. The glassy look was gone. Nodding, she said, "Y-yes. I understand."

"Good. Now, honey, we've talked about the hostile Indians in Wyoming: the Cheyenne, Blackfoot, Shoshone, and the Snake. But do you remember those army patrols that ride by our place every few days?"

"Yes."

"Remember I told you that the patrols are from Fort Bridger? The reason they send out those patrols is to keep the hostiles away from this area, and to make sure we are safe. There aren't any bad Indians anywhere near here. The people in Mountain View, and our neighboring farmers, told us that the Fort Bridger patrols cover a radius of forty miles. That takes in our place, and it takes in Evanston, where we're going with this grain."

"B-but, Matt...if hostile Indians really want to attack white people, they can sneak past the army patrols."

"I won't say they can't. But listen to me. They're putting more forts in this part of Wyoming all the time. The hostiles know that if they come in here and cause us trouble, they will pay a heavy penalty for it."

Holly stared into her mother's pallid face. All this talk of wild Indians had set her little heart to fluttering. Ever since those horrible Indians in Kansas did what they did when she and her parents were coming to Wyoming, her mother was prone to fits of weeping. Holly was at a loss as to how to help her mother. The times when Emily wept uncontrollably, Holly thought it must be her fault that her wonderful mother was sad so much of the time. She tried extra hard to be very good.

Emily looked down at Holly and saw the fear in her large blue eyes.

"We'll be fine, Mama," Holly blurted out. "Papa knows 'bout Indians, and he says we shouldn't worry."

Emily let a smile curve her lips as she glanced at Matt. "I'm sorry, darling. I'll be all right. It's just...it's just that the sight of those Indians back there at the fort brought back those awful memories."

Matt caressed his wife's soft cheek. "I know, darlin'. I'm sorry I can't make those memories go away. But you mustn't let them make you afraid. When you do, you can see how it frightens Holly. We came here to be happy and begin a new life."

"Yes," Emily said in a whisper. "I'll do better, I'm sure, as time passes." She drew Holly closer. "I'm sorry, sweetheart.

Mama shouldn't have gone to pieces like that."

Matt put his arms around both of them. "Let's talk to Jesus about it right now."

When Matt had finished praying, he kissed his wife and daughter and took the reins in hand. He ran his gaze over the two most precious females in his life, then set his troubled eyes to the west and put the horses in motion.

"Mama's sorry, honey," Emily said, hugging Holly close. "I didn't mean to frighten you."

Holly reached up a mitten-covered hand and patted her mother's face. "It's all right, Mama. I understand. I know what those Indians did was very hard on your nerves."

The wagon rolled along on the rough road for several feet before Emily turned to Matt and said, "Thank you for being so patient with me, darling."

Matt grinned. "I love you, sweet stuff. I want you to be all right. With the Lord's help we'll get you through this."

Emily patted his arm and looked down the road ahead.

When they were some five miles west of Fort Bridger, she said, "Did Mr. Ralston tell you anything about the hotel in Evanston, darling? Whether it's new or old, or anything like that?"

"Mm-hmm. He said it's fairly new. I hope it's as nice as that hotel we saw back there in Fort Bridger."

Suddenly the rear of the wagon began to sway. When Matt looked back he saw the right rear wheel wobbling its way toward the outside edge of the axle. Suddenly it dropped off, and the wagon came down on that corner with a loud noise, frightening the horses.

Matt gave a hard yank on the reins. "Whoa, boys!"

The horses fought their bits for a brief moment, then settled down.

"Oh, Matt, how could the wheel have come off?" Emily cried, gripping Holly tightly against her.

"I'd say we lost the lug nut."

Mother and daughter watched as Matt climbed down and knelt to examine the axle for a moment. "That's it. The lug nut wasn't stripped off. The threads are fine. It simply came loose. Probably because of this excessive weight."

Frowning, Emily said, "So what now? How will you ever get the wheel back on?"

Matt sighed. "I'll have to unload all the grain sacks, then wait for a man to come along who can put the wheel back on the axle while I lift the corner of the wagon. But first I've got to find the lug nut. Couldn't have been very far back when it came off. You two sit tight; if somebody comes along before I get back, wave them down, will you?"

"I will," said Emily.

Holly cuddled close to her mother, and Emily forced herself to put the Pawnee attacks from her mind. She looked down at her daughter's red hair and thought about what a treasure Holly was to her, and how much she loved her.

With the stillness of the wagon, and her body protected from the cold, the six-year-old girl began to doze.

Emily's thoughts trailed back over the years to the heartaches she and Matt had known. She had miscarried twice before carrying Holly full term and delivering a normal, healthy baby. Then it appeared for some time that the McDermotts would never have any more children. But when Holly was three years old, Emily found that she was expecting another baby. Her pregnancy went well, and she gave birth to little Michael. Tragedy struck, however, when Michael died of a high fever two days after his first birthday.

Emily fought the tears that threatened to surface. If anything ever happened to this precious little girl in her arms...

Movement on the road up ahead drew Emily's attention. Someone was coming their way. Another minute showed her it was a wagon pulled by two horses. She looked back and saw her husband still searching for the lug nut. "Matt! Somebody's coming in a wagon!"

Holly stirred and came awake.

"Sorry, honey," Emily said, "but I had to let Papa know there's a wagon coming."

Holly straightened up, blinking, and looked up the road.

Matt came to stand beside the wagon. "I haven't been able to find the lug nut, honey. Must have come off further back than I figured. The wheel could have stayed on for quite a while after the nut fell off." He focused on the wagon approaching them. "At least here's our chance to get a ride back into Fort Bridger."

Emily nodded. "Maybe we can still make it to Evanston before dark."

"Sure would like to."

Soon they could hear the rattle of the wagon and pounding hooves and could make out a man at the reins and a dark-haired young woman on the seat beside him, cradling a bundle in her arms.

Sunlight glinted off metal on the man's coat.

"Oh, look, Matt! The man's wearing a badge. Certainly a lawman will stop and help us."

CHAPTER TWO

The wagon rocked along the rough old road as Jack Bower guided the team eastward. Morning sunlight had given the air some warmth, and soon the vapor clouds puffing from the mouths and nostrils of the horses disappeared.

The horses topped a gentle rise and dipped down a long slope that bottomed out where a small brook meandered across the plains. As the wagon moved slowly down the rise, Julianna smiled at Jack.

He met her gaze. "I'm so in love with you it hurts, Julianna."

"I don't want to cause you any pain," she said softly.

"Oh, but it hurts so good. I wouldn't want it any other way."

Julianna looked down at the baby in her arms. "We wouldn't either, would we, Larissa?"

The dark-haired baby made a grunting sound in response. Julianna laughed. "See, there, Jack! Larissa wants you to hurt good when you love both of us."

"Be assured my love is for both of you."

There was a short silence between them, then Jack said, "I want you and Larissa to move into the house I rented. I'll find another place to hang my hat until we get married."

"Oh, darling, I don't want to put you out of your house. Surely I can find someplace for Larissa and me to stay."

"No way. The house is small, but it's quite comfortable. I know you and Larissa will find it adequate. I want you to live there. I'll pay the rent and buy all the groceries, household necessities, clothing, and anything else you need. No arguments, all right?"

Julianna was not accustomed to such kindness and concern from a man. Her arranged marriage to Jean-Claude LeCroix had given her a husband who was selfish, self-centered, and eager to please himself. Even when the baby came along, little Larissa received very little attention from her father. Although Julianna had loved Jean-Claude to a degree and had done everything she could to be a good wife to him, she had not been in love with him.

She thought of the last days of his life, when he lay dying at age twenty-nine with cirrhosis of the liver from his vile drinking habit. She was not a Christian then, but when she beheld him in the bed with death's pallor on his face, she felt natural human compassion for him. Though he had brought the deadly illness on himself, it hurt to see him suffer.

Jean-Claude had been her husband for three years, and he was Larissa's father. He had made life miserable for her when the whiskey was in control of him, but when he lay dying, her heart had gone out to him.

Suddenly Julianna was reliving Jean-Claude's last day...

A single candle cast a soft glow over the room where her husband lay. The overpowering odor of Jean-Claude's illness made her feel a bit nauseous. She hesitated at the door, then moved quietly into the room.

Jean-Claude did not stir. She could see the even rise and fall of his chest and knew he was asleep. She wandered about the room, touching the many beautiful pieces of furniture that only the wealthy could buy. She was running her hands along the smooth cherry dresser when she heard the sound of Jean-Claude's bedcovers rustling, followed by a weak moan. Julianna walked toward the bed and sat down in the overstuffed chair beside it. The soft candlelight showed her Jean-Claude's dull eyes.

"Can I get you something?" she asked.

"Water," he said, licking his dry lips.

Julianna poured a cup of water from a pitcher on the bedstand and held it to his mouth. When he had drained it, Jean-Claude reached out a shaky hand and took hers in his weak grasp. He stared at her for a long moment, then said in a feeble whisper, "Julianna…I…"

She leaned closer. "Yes, Jean-Claude?"

"I…I'm sorry for all the misery I've caused you. You've had a hard life with me. I really do love you, and I wish I had treated you better. Can…can you find it in your heart to forgive me?"

Julianna felt tears collect in her eyes. She gently squeezed his hand and said, "I forgive you."

Jean-Claude swallowed hard. "And when Larissa grows up…would you ask her to forgive me for not being a good father to her?"

"I will."

He managed a smile. "Thank you."

Later that day, with Julianna alone at his side, Jean-Claude LeCroix died.

"…arguments, all right?"

Jack's voice penetrated Julianna's thoughts. "Excuse me? What did you say?"

"I said you're not going to give me any arguments about living in the house, are you?"

Julianna gave him a lopsided smile, flashing a dimple. "You talk so tough for such a gentle man, Deputy Marshal Bower. All right. I won't give you any arguments. But I can't speak for Miss Larissa."

Jack reached over and chucked Larissa under her fat chin. "You won't give me any trouble about this, will you, sweetheart?"

Larissa giggled.

"See there, Larissa's mommy? She's not going to give me any trouble."

A serious look captured Julianna's features. "Oh, Jack, I'm so happy! How I praise the Lord for bringing us together and letting us fall in love!"

"Me too," he said, drinking in her beauty with his eyes. "I'm the most blessed man on the face of this earth. I have Jesus in my heart. And the most beautiful and wonderful Christian woman in the world loves me and has consented to become my wife...and I already have the most sweet and beautiful baby daughter."

Julianna shook her head in amazement. "Thank You, Lord," she said, looking toward the sky.

"Ah, Julianna..."

"Yes?"

"Would it be all right if I call myself Daddy to Larissa, even though we're not married yet, and I haven't officially adopted her? No sense confusing her. If I'm Jack for a while, then I'm suddenly Daddy, she might wonder who I really am."

Julianna laughed. "What's she going to do when she hears somebody call you Deputy Bower?"

Jack snickered. "Well, I guess that'll confuse her, too, but we'll cross that bridge when we come to it. How about me being Daddy to her now?"

"I'd love it."

He chucked Larissa under her chin again. "You hear that, sweetheart? I'm Daddy now."

Larissa giggled her approval.

Jack sighed as the wagon neared the top of the draw. He looked back at the baby and leaned close as her bright eyes watched him. "Larissa, I'm Daddy. D-a-a-addy. Can you say it? Da-a-addy."

The baby twisted her tiny face, giving him a strange look.

"Say it, honey. Da-a-addy."

Larissa moved her mouth as if she were going to try, then just stared at him.

"Why don't you try 'Da-da'?" Julianna said. "I think for her eleven-month-old mind it would be simpler."

He leaned close again and said, "Larissa, say Da-da. Da-da. Da-da."

Larissa's dark eyes were fixed on Jack's lips as he formed the words.

"Da-da," Jack said again.

And then it came. The tiny voice said, "Da...da."

"Yes!" Jack shouted. "She said it! She said it!" He leaned over and kissed Larissa's chubby cheek. "You're Daddy's precious baby girl, you are!"

Larissa giggled, knowing she had pleased him.

Julianna sighed. "Oh, Jack, we're going to be so happy together!"

Jack reached over and cupped Julianna's chin in his hand and planted a soft kiss on her lips. "That we are, darlin'. That we are."

They drove on quietly for a few more minutes; then Jack narrowed his eyes against the sun's glare and squinted down the road. "Looks like a wagon in trouble up there."

Julianna focused on the scene ahead. "I think there's a woman on the seat and...a child."

As they drew near, the man standing beside the wagon stepped into the road and lifted a hand.

Jack pulled rein. "Howdy. Looks like you've lost a wheel."

The man nodded. "Lug nut came off. I'm Matt McDermott. This is my wife, Emily, and our daughter, Holly."

"Happy to meet you. I'm Deputy Marshal Jack Bower from Fort Bridger. This is Julianna and Larissa. What can I do to help you?"

"I tried to find the lug nut but wasn't successful. Can you give us a ride into town?"

"Of course."

"When we passed through Fort Bridger, I noticed the hostler's sign says he does wagon repairs. Then we'll need a ride back and help to put the wheel on. I hate to ask—"

Jack cut in. "Maybe your problem is already solved, Mr. McDermott. I borrowed this wagon from Ray Noble, the hostler and wagon repair man. I just remembered there's a tool box in the back. Maybe there'll be some lug nuts in it."

Jack urged the team forward a few feet until the wagon seats were almost side by side, then climbed over into the wagon bed. Matt moved up close and watched as Jack opened the tool box and began rummaging through it. In just a few seconds he held up a lug nut. "Here you go. Got a wrench right here, too."

"Great!" Matt said.

Jack climbed out of the wagon bed. "We'll have to unload those sacks of grain so we can lift the wagon."

"Do you have time to help me?"

"Sure. Let's tackle it."

While the men began unloading the grain, Julianna eyed Holly, who was coughing again. "She had that cold for long?"

"About a week," Emily said as she adjusted the blanket covering Holly.

Holly coughed again, and Emily lightly caressed her forehead then pulled the blanket closer. Julianna noted the protective, almost desperate, gesture. "Is she getting better, Mrs. McDermott?"

"Well, she isn't any worse. I'm hoping she'll start improving soon." She paused, then said in a rush of words, "It was necessary that Holly and I come along with Matt on this trip. At least it has warmed up some the past couple of hours."

"Yes," said Julianna. "I'm glad for that."

Emily glanced at Larissa. "How old is she?"

"Eleven months. She'll be a year old on December 16."

"I'm sorry, what did your husband say the baby's name is?"

"Larissa."

"Yes. Larissa. That's a pretty name."

Julianna cleared her throat. "Ah...Mrs. McDermott, I—"

"Just call me Emily."

"All right. Emily, I need to explain something. Jack is not my husband. We're engaged and will be married in a few months."

"Oh. I'm sorry, Julianna."

"Please don't be. It's not what it looks like. My husband died a few months ago in New Orleans. That's where Larissa and I are from. We came west, intending to live with my deceased husband's parents in Boise, Idaho. But the Lord had a different plan for us. Jack and I met and fell in love. Larissa and I were on a stagecoach just this morning, heading for Boise. It's too detailed to go into now, but Jack borrowed this wagon and came after us. He stopped the stage and asked me to marry him. So...after a proper courtship, we'll be married."

"That's wonderful," said Emily. "I love to see the Lord work in people's lives."

Julianna's eyes brightened. "Are you a Christian, Emily?"

"Yes. So are Matt and Holly. She just received Jesus into her heart three weeks ago."

"Oh, that's marvelous!" Julianna looked at the two men unloading the grain. "Jack," she called, "these people are Christians!"

"I know," he said, pausing with a heavy grain sack in his

hands. "Matt just told me they're born-again, blood-washed children of God."

"It's great to meet others in God's family," said Matt. "Praise the Lord! Emily, Jack just told me that he and this lovely widow are engaged."

"Yes. Julianna told me."

When the men resumed their work, Julianna set kind eyes on Holly. "How old are you, dear?"

"I'm six, ma'am. I took Jesus into my heart two days after my birthday."

"That's wonderful, honey. So now you have two birthdays, don't you?"

"Uh-huh."

Julianna looked at Emily. "Jack and I are new Christians ourselves. But we're already finding out how glorious it is to belong to Jesus and to have Him guiding our lives."

"Nothing like it," said Emily. "What would we do without Him?"

"I can't even imagine it, now that I'm saved."

While the women talked, Matt and Jack continued to pile the sacks of grain on the ground.

"Where do you live, Matt?" Jack asked.

"We have a farm about twelve miles southeast of Lyman. Know where Lyman is?"

"No. I'm fairly new here."

"It's about eight miles east of Fort Bridger. That puts us about twenty miles from Fort Bridger."

"You come into our town much?"

"No, sir. Today is the first time. We do our shopping in Mountain View or in Lyman. We're new here ourselves. Just since August."

"Oh? Where you from?"

"Kentucky. We joined a wagon train in Independence, Missouri, in April. Arrived in Wyoming on August 7."

"Wagon train, eh? How'd the trip go?"

"Rough. We had some pretty frightening lightning storms. One wagon team was hit by a bolt. Killed both horses. The wagon was right in front of ours. That scared Emily pretty bad. We went one long stretch with water pretty scarce, too. Emily was afraid Holly would dehydrate. But those things weren't the worst. Twice in Kansas the train was attacked by Indians. Pawnee."

"Oh, no."

"Yeah. It got plenty bloody. Some of our wagon train people were killed. Others wounded. Pawnees did some other pretty bad things, too. Just about frightened Emily out of her mind. The whole journey really took its toll on her, but the Pawnee atrocities did the most damage to her nerves."

Jack straightened and looked toward the women before turning back to say, "She still having trouble?"

"Yeah." Matt dropped a sack on the pile. "Nightmares, and the effects of them. I was afraid for a while that her mind would go."

"But she's better now?"

"Yes, praise the Lord. But she's a long way from over it."

"Well, I'm glad to hear she's doing better at least. What part of Kentucky did you live in?"

"Our farm was near Lexington. We…ah…came on hard times brought on by a long dry spell. Lost the farm."

"I'm sorry. That had to have been rough on both of you."

"It was." Matt climbed into the wagon to drag some more sacks toward the tailgate. "It took much prayer and a lot of love to keep Emily from falling apart. She really put forth an effort to keep trusting the Lord and finally came to the place where she was able to say she believed everything would work out for us."

"Since I'm so new at knowing the Lord," said Jack, "I'm just beginning to learn about the Christian life. But as I think on it, I can well imagine how losing your farm could tend to shake your faith."

"For sure," said Matt, grunting as he dragged a sack.

"So how did you end up with a farm way out here in Wyoming?"

"The Lord worked it out, even as Emily said He would. Just a few days before we were to vacate the farm, we received word that my bachelor Uncle Louie—brother of my deceased father—had died. He willed his twenty-acre farm near Lyman, Wyoming, to me. Emily and I praised the Lord for providing the farm for us, and quickly made plans to head for Wyoming."

"God is good, isn't He?" said Jack. "Hearing that kind of story encourages me to learn to trust the Lord more."

"Jesus never fails, Jack." Matt hopped down from the tailgate. "Sometimes in our Christian lives it appears that He's going to fail us, but He always comes through. It's not always in the way we thought He would do it, or even should do it, but He never fails."

A few minutes later, all the sacks were out of the wagon. As Matt rolled the wheel up to the axle, Jack said, "Does the farm produce enough for you to live on?"

"No. I do odd jobs in Mountain View and Lyman, and on farms and ranches. Like this grain here. I'm hauling it for a farmer who has several hundred acres. He's paying me to haul it to a customer of his near Evanston."

"I see. Well, it's good that you can pick up the extra work."

"Yes. We do produce enough hay to feed five head of beef cattle and the family cow. We raise vegetables in our garden and have chickens and hogs. We also have several gnarly old apple trees in the front yard. They help supply us with fresh fruit in the summertime and dried fruit in the winter. Emily also cans the vegetables. Combined with all of these things provided by the farm, my odd jobs help us manage to keep our heads above water."

"Thank the Lord for the way He provides," said Jack.

"Amen. Well, I'll lift up the back of the wagon if you'll slip the wheel on the axle."

"Fine," said Jack. "Or if you'd rather, I'll lift the wagon and you put the wheel on."

Matt shrugged. "All right. You lift the wagon." He took hold of the wheel, then said, "You have any idea what a lug nut costs? I want to pay the man."

"I have no idea, but don't worry about it. If Ray wants money for it, I'll take care of it."

"But that's not right. Let me give you—"

"Don't argue with me, or I'll jail you," said Jack, giving him a mock scowl.

Matt looked heavenward and said, "Lord, what do I do with this guy?"

"Obey him," Jack said, chuckling. "Or go to jail."

The wheel was back on the wagon quickly, and the two men began the task of reloading the sacks into the wagon bed.

Emily was just finishing her description of life in Kentucky when Julianna noticed all the grain sacks had been loaded.

After the men had climbed back into their wagons and the McDermotts expressed their thanks, Jack and Julianna extended an invitation to come visit them sometime in Fort Bridger.

Julianna said good-bye to little Holly and wished her a quick recovery; then Matt McDermott snapped the reins and put his team into motion.

"Nice folks," said Jack, taking up the reins of his own team. "They've had some hard knocks in life. I hope things go better for them here in Wyoming. She tell you about losing their farm in Kentucky?"

"Yes. Must've been plenty hard to take."

Jack urged the horses down the road, his eyes fixed on the spot where he would soon see the fort's tower and the roof of the Uintah Hotel in Fort Bridger outlined against the sky.

Julianna turned on the seat and looked back at the McDermott wagon. Emily was homesick and unhappy, but she was carrying something else inside that was eating at her. And what about Holly? That cough sounded like it came from awfully deep in her chest.

When she righted herself on the seat, with a sleeping Larissa in her arms, Jack said, "Concerned about Emily, aren't you."

"Yes. There's more than the loss of their farm bothering her."

"She didn't tell you about the Indian attacks in Kansas?"

"No."

"Well, let me tell you what Matt told me."

When Jack had finished relating the events of the McDermotts' wagon train journey, Julianna shook her head in amazement and said, "No wonder."

"No wonder what?"

"She has that haunted look in her eyes. I knew there had to be some deep wound inside. Apparently the wound hasn't healed."

Jack nodded. "Matt even told me he feared that Emily might crack up mentally, but she's doing better now, though she's still a long way from being over it."

"That's evident," said Julianna. "But I'm glad she's better than she was."

They rode in silence for a few minutes, then Julianna said, "Jack, did you notice how much little Holly McDermott looks like Patty Ruth Cooper? Not so much in the face—though there is a slight resemblance there—but they both have that deep red hair, long pigtails, and light sprinkling of reddish brown freckles on their noses and cheeks."

Jack chuckled. "Funny. I was about to bring that up to you. They're almost exactly the same size, too."

CHAPTER THREE

Hannah wiped tears from her cheeks and sniffled. When the stage carrying Julianna and Larissa turned a corner and vanished from view, Hannah looked at her best friend and said, "I don't understand why Jack isn't here, Glenda. Why wouldn't he come and tell Julianna good-bye? I know he's in love with her. Poor little thing. She's heart-broken."

Wells Fargo agent Judy Charley Wesson smacked her lips and put a hand on her bony hip. "Shore is a mystery to me, gals. I cain't understand young folks today. Why'd Jack let 'er go in the first place? An' second…why didn't Julianna hang around a little longer so's Jack could work up his courage to ast her to marry him?"

"Yeah," said Curly Wesson. "Shore seems to me they shoulda tol' each other how they really feel, an' let thet thar romance develop."

Patty Ruth giggled, twisted slightly in Curly's arms so she could look him in the eye, and said, "Uncle Curly, how come you talk funny? Why did you call it 'thet thar' romance? It should be that there romance."

"Patty Ruth," Hannah said, "haven't we talked about this?"

Curly winked at Hannah. "It's all right if this little redhead wants to go on in error." Then he said to the child, "You see, Patty Ruth, it ain't me an' Aunt Judy Charley who talk funny. It's

41

the rest of the world...includin' you! Mebbe one o' these here now days, you'll pick up our jargon an' learn to talk right."

Patty Ruth frowned. "Jargon? What's jargon?"

"See thar! You don't even know 'bout jargon. Why, child, jargon is the way people talks. Aunt Judy Charley an' Uncle Curly talks properly, an' you don't!"

Patty Ruth giggled again. "You're funny, Uncle Curly," she said, wrapping her arms around his neck. "But I love you anyway!"

Curly held her tight and kissed her cheek. "You're the funny one, little girl. But I love you anyway!"

Hannah stared down the street where she had last seen the stage and sighed. She silently placed Jack and Julianna's future in God's hands, asking Him to do what had to be done in order to bring them together. She then turned to the Wessons and said, "Patty Ruth and I have to get back to the store. Nellie's filling in for me, but she needs to get home."

"I'll go with you, Hannah," said Glenda. "I have to get a few groceries."

Curly put Patty Ruth down. "See you later, sweetie pie!"

Patty Ruth hugged his neck and echoed, "See you later, sweetie pie!"

Patty Ruth then hugged and kissed Judy Charley and joined her mother.

Hannah pulled her coat snugly over her protruding midsection, and as she and Glenda moved down the street with Patty Ruth between them, Hannah looked down and said, "Oh, Glenda, I'm starting to waddle."

"Well, honey, you're coming up on your sixth month. Most of us mothers begin to waddle about this time."

Traffic was picking up on Fort Bridger's Main Street as the town's stores and other businesses opened. As Hannah moved slowly along the boardwalk, she said, "Glenda, it bothers me that Jack let Julianna go without coming to the stage depot to see her off. It more than bothered her."

Glenda nodded. "About a week ago, Gary and Jack happened to be alone for a few minutes on the street, and they got to talking about Julianna. Gary said Jack told him that until he landed this job as deputy marshal, he'd been nothing but a drifter. Gary said that in the same breath Jack mentioned the times he'd been forced into quick-draw gunfights simply because in protecting himself years ago, he proved to be fast."

"I get it," said Hannah. "He was comparing his background to Julianna's background of refinement, high society, and riches. Jack must feel he's not good enough for her."

"That was Gary's assessment. And with him not showing up to tell her good-bye this morning, I think that in Jack's mind he's doing Julianna a favor by staying out of her life. It has to be tearing his heart out to do it."

Hannah nodded. "Mm-hmm, and loving her as he most surely does, he couldn't bring himself to come and tell her good-bye."

"That's how it adds up, as I see it."

"That's too bad. I don't think Julianna has told him how much she loves him. That girl would marry him if he asked her. The hurt she felt when he didn't show up was quite evident in her eyes."

"Yes. I saw it too."

"Tell you what," said Hannah. "God is able to work it out between them, and I'm already praying that He will do it soon."

"Gary and I will pray that way, too," Glenda assured her.

Patty Ruth looked up at her mother. "Mama, will Miss Julianna and Larissa ever come back to see us?"

"I'm sure going to pray that they do," Hannah said.

"I wish they would live here. When Larissa gets older, she could play with me an' Belinda."

"Belinda and me," said Hannah.

Patty Ruth eyed her carefully. "Huh? You? You an' Belinda

would play with Larissa? Couldn't I play with Larissa, too?"

Hannah gently yanked one of Patty Ruth's pigtails. "You know what I'm saying, you little stinker!"

Patty Ruth giggled. "I love you, Mama."

Hannah tugged on the pigtail again. "I love you, too, little stinker."

As the trio continued along the boardwalk they heard someone say, "Well, good morning, Heidi. How's my wife's favorite dressmaker?"

"Just fine, sir."

Hannah, Patty Ruth, and Glenda looked back, and Heidi smiled at them, hurrying to catch up. The women greeted each other; then Heidi squeezed Patty Ruth's cheek between thumb and forefinger and said, "Good morning, Miss Cooper!"

The child giggled. "Good morning, Miss Heidi."

The town's dressmaker pointed up the boardwalk and said, "Time to get Heidi's Dress Shop opened up."

"From what I'm able to observe, Heidi," said Hannah, "your business is doing well."

"Yes, praise the Lord. One of these days I'm going to have to hire a seamstress to help me keep up with it."

"I'll help you, Miss Heidi," spoke up Patty Ruth. "I helped Mary Beth sew a border on the cloth for the nightstand in our room."

Above Patty Ruth's head, Hannah rolled her eyes, and Glenda covered her mouth to stifle a smile.

Heidi bent low, looked Patty Ruth in the eye, and said, "You're a little young to make dresses, honey. Besides, you'll be going to school next fall, and you wouldn't have time to make dresses, too. And let me tell you something. My sister is very much looking forward to having you in school."

"Really?"

"Really. Sundi loves your brothers and Mary Beth, and she loves you, too. Just like everybody in Fort Bridger does."

Patty Ruth's lips curved upward. "I love Miss Sundi, an' I love you, too, Miss Heidi. An' when I get bigger, I'll make dresses. Would you let me make dresses for you when I get bigger?"

"Of course, sweetheart."

Patty Ruth clapped her mittened hands. "Oh boy! Did you hear that, Mama? When I get big, Miss Heidi will give me a job makin' dresses! Can I practice sewin', Mama?"

"We'll see, honey."

Patty Ruth ran her gaze back to Heidi. "It'll happen, Miss Heidi. It always does when Mama says 'We'll see.'"

Heidi laughed. "Guess I'd better keep moving. Got to get the shop open."

As the women walked along, Heidi said to Hannah and Glenda, "I heard that Julianna was going to take the morning stage to Evanston, then go on to Boise. Did she actually do it?"

"Yes," said Glenda. "We just saw her off."

"Jack didn't try to persuade her to stay in Fort Bridger?"

There was a brief moment of silence, then Patty Ruth said, "Mr. Deputy Jack didn' come to tell her good-bye."

Heidi looked startled.

"That's right," said Hannah.

"I don't understand. I know that man is head over heels for Julianna And she is for him, too."

"We're going to pray the Lord will work it out, even though she's going to Idaho," said Glenda. "Boise's not so far away."

"Well, I'll just put them on my prayer list, too," Heidi said.

Hannah widened her eyes meaningfully as she looked at Heidi. "While we're on the subject of romance, Heidi, it's no secret that you and our esteemed town marshal have a strong liking for each other. We understand why you keep your guard up…but is Lance showing any interest in being saved?"

"I've talked to him about it many times," Heidi said.

"What does he say?"

"Lance lives a clean, moral life, as you know. Clean mouth, no tobacco, no liquor."

"Mm-hmm."

"He says since he lives clean, he doesn't need salvation. I've tried to show him what the Bible says about the new birth, and that he's dead spiritually no matter how clean he lives, but he just won't let it sink in."

"He's such a delight to know," said Hannah. "Pleasant man, especially since he has to deal with the low side of life in his work. You really feel something for him, don't you, Heidi?"

"I won't deny it. There's much about Lance to love. What I feel for him could develop into the marrying kind of love, but like you said, Hannah, I have to keep a guard on my heart. It would be against the Word of God for me to marry an unsaved man."

"I've known Christians," said Glenda, "who have let themselves fall in love with an unsaved person and expected God to save that person later."

"Seldom happens," said Hannah. "The marriage that starts out in defiance of God's Word is doomed for misery and disaster. The Holy Spirit had Paul write so plainly in 2 Corinthians, chapter 6, that believers are not to be unequally yoked to unbelievers, and when that commandment is violated it always brings heartache."

Heidi nodded. "Both of you please keep Lance in your prayers. I want him to be saved, primarily because of his lost condition, but also because I do have a love for him. He's told me that he loves me. Something beautiful could develop between us if Lance knew the Lord."

"We'll keep him before the Throne," said Glenda.

"For sure," Hannah said, patting Heidi's arm.

When they drew up in front of the dress shop, Heidi took a key from her purse and inserted it in the door. "Well, nice talking to you, ladies...and little lady."

Hannah and Glenda continued on toward the general store with Patty Ruth hurrying alongside them.

"Speaking of someone who needs to be saved," said Glenda, "my heart is heavy for Jacob."

Hannah sighed. "Mine, too. He's such a dear man. He's doing a wonderful job as my assistant. You remember how I had you and Gary pray that the Lord would send me someone with merchandising experience?"

"Yes."

"With this baby coming, I really needed someone full time who could lift the load from me. I have no doubt that Jacob came to Fort Bridger as an answer to prayer."

"He's comfortable living in the back of the store, isn't he?"

"He really likes it. Of course we have him for supper three or four nights a week. Once in a while I have him come up for breakfast. But never on Saturday mornings, because he observes his Sabbath on Saturdays. Keep him in prayer, will you, Glenda? I have faith that the Lord will one day show Jacob that Jesus is the true Messiah, and he will open his heart to Him."

When they stepped up on the boardwalk, Patty Ruth pointed down the block and exclaimed, "Mama! The In'ians are at the store!"

In front of Hannah's store were several pinto ponies and the white-faced bay stallion belonging to Chief Two Moons.

Hannah traded groceries with the Crows for deer and antelope skin products, which in turn she sold in order to come out even.

When they reached the store, the door opened and several Crow braves filed out, carrying boxes of groceries. They spoke in a friendly manner to Hannah and Glenda. Behind them was the stalwart Chief Two Moons and his lovely squaw, Sweet Blossom.

Hannah flashed the chief a smile, greeting him, then

opened her arms to Sweet Blossom. The two women had become close friends, and Two Moons looked on with pleasure as they held a long embrace.

Sweet Blossom then spoke warmly to Glenda and embraced her, then Patty Ruth.

Hannah glanced at the braves as they wrapped the groceries in buffalo hides and tied the bundles on travois that were crisscrossed over the withers of three horses. She turned back to Two Moons. "Did you get everything you needed, Chief?"

He nodded. "Hannah Cooper's man, Jacob Kates, much generous in trade."

Hannah smiled. "I told him to be generous whenever you come in. Your deer and antelope products sell quite well. Especially to the mountain men who come into town from time to time."

"Good," said the chief. "Two Moons would not want Hannah Cooper to—how does white man say?—to come out on short end of stick."

Hannah laughed. "I appreciate that, Chief, but our business deal is doing well."

"Two Moons glad," he said, a smile tugging at the corners of his mouth.

None of the group in front of the store noticed three drifters clad in dirty buffalo hide coats who stood on the boardwalk across the street. The three men watched the scene, mumbling to one another.

Sweet Blossom patted the little redhead's freckled cheek. "Patty Ruth Cooper must come Crow village sometime when sister, Mary Beth Cooper, come with Sundi Lindgren."

Patty Ruth looked up at her mother. "Can I, Mama?"

"Of course, honey, but probably not until spring when the weather is warmer."

Sweet Blossom smiled and nodded. "Hokay. Patty Ruth Cooper come Crow village when snow gone."

It pleased Patty Ruth to receive the invitation. She had secretly envied her big sister's trips to Two Moons's village every Saturday with Sundi Lindgren to assist the schoolmarm in teaching the Indian children.

Two Moons set soft, dark eyes on Hannah. "Chief Two Moons and his people so glad for Mary Beth Cooper to come with Sundi Lindgren. Children learn much. Speak English better than Two Moons!"

Hannah laughed.

Sweet Blossom's eyes sparkled as she said, "Count better than chief, too!"

Hannah thought the chief's skin darkened a shade and wondered what Sweet Blossom was referring to, but left it alone.

"I'm glad you and Jacob get along so well when I'm not in the store," Hannah said to the chief.

Two Moons nodded. "Jacob Kates good man. Like him very much. Just one problem."

Hannah's eyebrows arched. "Oh? What's that?"

"Two Moons have hard time understand Jacob Kates's words."

Hannah laughed. "You mean he talks too fast?"

"Um. And words have different sound."

"Oh. That's what we call an accent, Chief. New Yorkers talk different than folks who live farther west. They also talk very fast."

"Um. Fast."

"But you and Jacob did get everything worked out on the trade?"

"Um. Worked out hokay. Just take longer than when Two Moons does business with Hannah Cooper."

Two Moons checked to see if his braves had the travois loaded and ready to go. When he saw they were quietly waiting for him and his squaw, he said, "Time go, Sweet Blossom."

The three drifters across the street were watching the scene intently.

The chief and his squaw bid Hannah, Glenda, and Patty Ruth good-bye and mounted their horses. They waved, and Two Moons led the pintos out with Sweet Blossom at his side.

Hannah was about to enter the store when Regina Samuels came from her husband's barbershop directly across the street.

"Hannah!" called Regina. "Just wanted to ask you a question."

The trio of drifters across the street waited till Regina stepped up on the boardwalk before following.

"Yes, Regina?" said Hannah.

"I was just wondering about Julianna. Did she get on the stage?"

"I'm sorry to say she did."

"Oh. I was so hoping she and Deputy Bower would get together."

"Me too. But she's gone."

"How did he take it?"

"Well, he wasn't there to see her off, so I can't really tell you."

"Hmm. Cade and I both figured he'd ask her to stay and...well, you know..."

"Hannah and I were hoping it would be that way, too," said Glenda, "but it didn't happen."

"Well, maybe—"

"Excuse us, ma'am," said the biggest of the smelly drifters to Hannah, "but we couldn't help notice that you were treatin' those filthy Indians like human bein's."

Regina stepped out of their way, blinking in amazement, while Glenda laid a hand on Patty Ruth's shoulder and pulled her close to her side.

Hannah's creamy skin flushed and a glint of anger captured her brown eyes. "I don't know who you are, mister, but those Indians *are* human beings, and they're my friends."

She started to turn toward the door but halted when the bearded man said, "Anybody who'd be a friend to one of them filthy red animals oughtta be tarred and feathered and run outta town."

Hannah Cooper, who was ordinarily a sweet and docile person, saw red at hearing this hairy man's words. "Look who's calling who animals!" she snapped. "You'd make a sweaty buffalo smell good! In case you don't know it, you're standing on the stretch of boardwalk that I own. Remove yourselves from my property right now, or I'll send for the marshal!"

"You don't have to send for me, Hannah," came the familiar voice of Lance Mangum as he threaded his way through the crowd gathering on both sides of the store. "I'm here."

The big drifter scowled as the marshal moved up close to him and said, "What's your beef with Mrs. Cooper, mister?"

Hannah spoke first. "He jumped me for being kind to Chief Two Moons and his people, Marshal. Called them filthy red animals, and said I should be tarred and feathered and run out of town for befriending them."

Mangum stepped closer to the big man, his voice sounding like flint on steel as he growled, "Those Indians are good people, mister. They're friends of everybody in this town, and in the fort. They are not animals, and they're not filthy. You and your pals have horses, I assume?"

The drifter's bearded face was like stone. "Yeah."

"Then you find them, mount up, and ride. I don't care which direction...just ride. Troublemakers are not welcome in this town. Especially ones like you who would dare speak to a lady like you just did. Ride. Now!"

The drifter ran his gaze up and down the marshal, whom he outweighed by at least seventy pounds, then showed him a grin that went no deeper than his tobacco-stained teeth. "You talk awfully tough for a tinhorn badge-toter. Take that badge off, and let's see if we have to ride."

With hands faster than summer lightning, Lance Mangum batted the man's dirty hat from his head, grabbed a handful of hair, and slammed his fist into the man's nose. The drifter's massive body fell back against his two friends, knocking them backward. All three fell in a heap.

The big man lay in the street, his eyes glazed and blood running from his nose. When his two friends managed to get to their feet, Mangum said, "I gave your pal an order a few moments ago, and I meant it. Now pick up your pal, put him on his horse, and plant yourselves in your own saddles." When they stood there staring at him, he said, "Do I have to say it again?"

"No, sir, Marshal," replied one, fear evident in his eyes. "C'mon, Bart."

Mangum pointed to the boardwalk. "Don't forget his hat."

They jammed the dirty hat on the bleeding man's head, and the crowd watched as they crossed the street to the hitch rail. They struggled to get the big man on his horse but finally had him in his saddle; then they mounted up and rode south out of town.

The people cheered and applauded their marshal, and the crowd dispersed except for Heidi Lindgren, who stood nearby on the boardwalk.

Hannah smiled at Mangum. "Thank you, Marshal."

"My pleasure, Hannah."

Heidi stepped up. "Beautifully done, Lance."

There was love light in Mangum's eyes as he said, "You call bloodying a man's nose beautiful?"

"Yes. He had it coming. You do beautiful work."

Mangum chuckled, shaking his head. "Whatever you say, Heidi. May I walk you back to the shop?"

"Of course."

"Thank you, again, Marshal," Hannah said.

He gave her a small wave and walked away with Heidi.

When Hannah, Glenda, and Patty Ruth entered the store, they found Pastor Andy Kelly and Rebecca at the counter. Jacob was stuffing groceries into a paper bag, and Nellie Patterson was helping him.

"I suppose you took in the excitement outside," Hannah said.

"Sure did," said Jacob. "I like that marshal."

"He's good at his job," commented Kelly.

"Are you all right, Hannah?" Rebecca asked, moving to her side.

"I'm fine, thank you."

"We heard what you told that guy, Hannah," said Nellie. "You put him in his place right and proper."

Hannah grinned sheepishly and dipped her head as she ran a finger across the bridge of her nose. "I don't get mad often, but that man rubbed my temper the wrong way."

"I can understand why some people don't like the hostile-type Indians," said Glenda. "But before they shoot off their mouths like that bully did, they should find out just which kind of Indians they're talking about."

"I agree," put in Jacob, sliding two stuffed paper bags across the counter to Kelly. "There you go, Reverend."

Kelly smiled at the little man. "Thank you, Jacob. And as I was saying before the excitement started, we'd sure love to have you visit our services."

"Well, like I've told you before," said Jacob, "I'll just do it sometime."

Patty Ruth moved close to the counter, looked up at Jacob, and said, "Pastor Kelly is the best preacher in all the world, Uncle Jacob."

The little Jewish man chuckled. "I don't doubt that for a minute, honey."

"I need to be going, Hannah," Nellie said, removing her apron and laying it on a chair behind the counter.

"I'm sorry for the delay," Hannah said in apology.

"Oh, that's all right." Nellie shrugged into her coat. "I still have plenty of time to get everything done at home."

As Nellie went out the door, Kelly laid adoring eyes on Patty Ruth, bent down so he could look her straight in the eye, and said, "Know what? I found out something about you from B.J."

Patty Ruth frowned, looking a little anxious. "Yes, sir?"

"He told me that your birthday is next month...Friday, December 30. Is that right?"

She nodded.

"And B.J. said you're going to be four years old. Is that right?"

The child giggled. "B.J. is always wrong about stuff. I'll be six years old!"

Kelly laughed. "I was only kidding, honey. B.J. didn't really say that."

Patty Ruth lifted her small shoulders and let them down. "He does dumb stuff like that, though."

Hannah stepped close to her little daughter, laid a hand on her head, and said, "I'm going to give Patty Ruth a big birthday party, and among others I'll be inviting, I want to invite you, Jacob, and you, Pastor Kelly and Rebecca, and Glenda."

Each person said they would plan to be there.

Patty Ruth looked up at Hannah. "Uncle Gary can come, too, can't he, Mama?"

Hannah winked at Glenda, then said, "He's too naughty, honey."

"Mama, Uncle Gary isn't naughty!"

"Sometimes he is, honey," said Glenda, chuckling. "But if Uncle Gary is a good boy between now and then, I'll bring him to the party with me."

When the Kellys left, and Glenda started picking up the things she needed, Hannah moved behind the counter and took off her coat, replacing it with an apron.

Patty Ruth hung up her coat, stocking cap, and scarf on her own peg, and moved behind the counter where she would be in her usual position to "help" her mother and Jacob.

Soon Glenda left, too, and customers continued to come and go. After a while, when a lull came in business, Hannah was filling the candy jars on the counter while Jacob was sorting through the records of the morning's sales. Patty Ruth stood on a stool, watching him.

Jacob gave Patty Ruth a sidelong glance and said, "So you're going to turn six years old next month, eh?"

"Yes, I am," Patty Ruth said proudly.

"Looks like you're getting to be an old woman. Six years! That's really old."

Hannah sent a furtive glance at her daughter, waiting for her comeback.

The child thought on it a moment while Jacob went back to his work. Then she tapped him on the shoulder. "Uncle Jacob?"

"Yes, old woman?" he replied, grinning from ear to ear.

"Did Moses wear a beard?"

"I don't know."

Patty Ruth giggled. "Well, you should know."

"And why's that?"

She giggled again, crinkling her freckled nose at him. "You were travelin' with him in the wilderness, weren't you? You should have paid attention!"

CHAPTER FOUR

P atty Ruth grinned triumphantly, and Jacob Kates threw back his head and laughed all the way to his belly. Hannah ducked her head and stifled a snicker.

At that moment, the front door opened and the little bell above the door jingled. Patty Ruth saw her best friend, Belinda Fordham, enter with her parents behind her.

"Belinda!" she cried, scrambling down from the stool. She ran around the end of the counter and darted toward her friend.

"Hi, Patty Ruth!" came Belinda's happy reply.

Bringing his laughter under control, Jacob turned to Hannah and said, "I have to admit that was a good one. She really got me! How did she ever come up with it?"

"She heard her father use that 'Moses' line on a friend of his back in Missouri, about a year ago."

"A year ago! I'm amazed! What a memory!"

"Let me tell you, Jacob, that child never ceases to amaze me in one way or another, every day."

Army Captain John Fordham and his wife, Betsy, approached the counter. Hannah and Jacob greeted them as the two five-year-old girls moved about the store, talking rapidly. Patty Ruth was telling Belinda about the big ugly man who talked bad to her mother and got punched by Marshal Mangum.

Hannah rounded the end of the counter and embraced Betsy as the tall, handsome captain glanced at the girls and said to Jacob, "We just heard about the incident a few minutes ago. I guess those fellas will steer clear of Fort Bridger from now on."

"If they know what's good for them, they will," said Jacob.

The Fordhams moved down one of the long aisles of shelves and began their grocery shopping. Other customers came in, and while they shopped and Hannah and Jacob took care of them, Patty Ruth and Belinda could be heard from all over the store, giggling and enjoying each other's company.

When it came time for the Fordhams to have their bill totaled, Hannah waited on them while Jacob took care of the other customers. Betsy called to Belinda, and the girls came from the rear of the store and stood close by.

As Jacob's last customer left the store, Patty Ruth stood in front of the counter beside her friend. "Mama?"

Hannah looked up from her paperwork briefly. "I'm busy, honey. I'll talk to you after Belinda and her parents leave."

"But I wanted to ask you somethin' with them here."

"Oh. All right. What is it, sweetheart?"

"Are you going to invite Belinda and her mother and father to my birthday party?"

"Why, of course," said Hannah, running her gaze to Belinda, then her parents. "We couldn't have the birthday party without your best friend and her parents there, could we?"

"That's what I was thinkin'. I sure want 'em there."

"Well, we'll be there, honey," said the captain. "You can count on it."

Betsy stood over Patty Ruth. "I recall that your birthday is in December, sweetie, but I don't know what day."

Patty Ruth blinked, then said, "Uh…it's uh…five days after Christmas."

"The thirtieth?"

The little girl's eyes lit up. "Yes, ma'am! Mm-hmm. The thirtieth. It's on a Friday."

"We'll buy Patty Ruth a present, won't we, Mother?" spoke up Belinda, who strongly resembled Betsy in facial features and coloring.

"Of course we will, honey. We'll talk about it later, and maybe you can help choose what we get her."

The door opened, and more people from the fort came in.

Later, after lunch, things were quiet in the store. Patty Ruth was helping Jacob stock shelves near the counter where Hannah sat on a stool. Hannah could feel the baby kicking and wondered at God's miraculous way of allowing a woman to feel the life within her long before the baby was born.

She watched Patty Ruth and Jacob working together, and smiled to herself. The dear man was so patient with her little girl, allowing her to hand him various goods to put on the shelves—a job he could do quicker and easier by himself.

Setting his kind eyes on the child, Jacob said, "So you were born five days after Christmas, eh?"

"Mm-hmm." Patty Ruth handed him a box of prunes. "An' you know what?"

"What?"

"Even though I was born five days after Christmas, my papa an' mama always said I was their very special Christmas gift."

Jacob smiled down at her. "Well, such a beautiful little girl had to have been the perfect gift to Solomon and Hannah Cooper."

Hannah's ears picked up on Jacob's words. "Well put, Jacob," she said. "Patty Ruth was indeed God's perfect gift to Solomon and me in December of 1864. But the Bible tells us that God's most wonderful and absolutely perfect gift to the world is His precious virgin-born Son, the Lord Jesus Christ. In the book of James, it says, 'Every good gift and every perfect gift is from above, and cometh down from the Father of lights.'"

Jacob looked relieved when the door opened and three people entered the store. He greeted them, as did Hannah, and he was spared from commenting on her words.

As he headed for the counter to take care of the customers, Jacob admitted to himself that he was impressed with the joy and peace he saw in the lives of Fort Bridger's Christian people. They definitely had something that made them different from everyone else.

Moments later, the door opened again, and Hannah looked up to see a smiling Justin Powell, owner of Powell's Hardware and Gun Shop, come in.

"Hello, Justin," she called.

"Hello to you, too, Hannah. Heard about the trouble. Glad those dudes are gone."

"Me, too."

"Hi, Mr. Justin!" Patty Ruth ran to him.

He picked her up, saying, "How's my favorite five-year-old girl in all the world?"

"Jis' fine. Where's Miss Julie, an' Casey, an' Carrie?"

"They're at our store, honey. Miss Julie's watching the store while I pick up some groceries for her."

Justin hugged Patty Ruth and set her down. "Well, I have to hurry."

The door opened again, and Mandy Carver came in. "Hello, everybody," she said, giving them a wide smile.

Patty Ruth ran to her and lifted her arms. "Hi, Miss Mandy!"

The town blacksmith's wife bent over, hugged the little girl, and said, "Hello, sugar! I sho' do love you!"

"An' I love you, too, Miss Mandy," said Patty Ruth, kissing her cheek. "I've been helpin' Uncle Jacob put stuff on the shelves."

"That's a good girl, honey." Mandy moved to the counter and said to Hannah, "I heard about that big fella givin' you trouble over bein' nice to Chief Two Moons an' his folks."

"Well, as I'm sure you also heard," said Hannah, "Marshal Mangum took care of the problem."

"Yes'm. He sho' nuff is one good lawman." She turned toward a row of shelves and said, "I guess I'd better git what I need an' head fo' the house."

Julianna LeCroix sat close to Jack Bower with a sleeping Larissa in her arms. Jack had his right arm around her and drove the team with one hand. It was just past noon, and the brilliant Wyoming sun shone down on Fort Bridger in the distance.

"This is going to surprise some people in town, Jack."

"That it will," he replied, letting his eyes roam over the rolling hills before them. "Only one person knows that I was chasing down the stage. And that's my boss. But I asked him not to say anything to anyone. You know, in case you turned me down and went on to Boise."

She smiled at him. "Did you really have any doubts?"

"Well-l-l-l…"

"I understand. I should have told you in plainer terms how I feel about you."

Jack shrugged. "Doesn't matter now." He pulled her tighter against him.

"You didn't tell Ray Noble why you were borrowing his wagon?"

"Nope. All I told him was that I needed it for a while. He didn't ask why, and I didn't volunteer the information."

The flags on the poles at the fort tower were visible now.

"Hannah's going to be very glad when she finds out about us," said Julianna, "and so is Glenda. They both have proven to be such wonderful friends to me. Neither one said anything when you didn't show up to tell me good-bye, but I saw it in their faces. Oh, Jack, I'm so glad you love me and want me!"

He kissed her cheek. "And that goes double for me."

Julie Powell was finishing a sale when Justin entered the store with a bag of groceries in one arm. He recognized the customer at the counter as a rancher who came to town periodically. "Howdy, Clete. How's everything?"

"Just fine, Justin," responded Cletus Froggate. He thanked Julie and left with his merchandise.

The sound of children playing came from the back room.

Justin set the bag on the counter. "Here's your groceries, honey."

"Thank you, sweetheart." Julie closed the cash drawer. "Looks like sales have been good all morning."

"Real good."

Moving around the end of the counter, she said, "I did about two hundred dollars just while you were at Hannah's." She turned toward the rear or the building and called, "Casey! Carrie! Put your coats and caps on! Time to go home!"

Justin kissed his wife good-bye and watched her pull their five-year-old son and three-year-old daughter down the boardwalk in their toy wagon with the grocery bag between them.

In the next fifteen minutes he had four customers; then things got quiet.

Justin took advantage of the lull in business to carry some boxes out of the storeroom and begin stocking shelves in the hardware side of the store. He was standing on a stepladder rearranging some items when he heard the little bell above the front door jingle. Two strangers went toward the gun and ammunition side of the store. They were both in their early twenties and wore their guns low on their hips. Both were raw-boned, but one was a few inches taller than the other.

"Gentlemen," Justin said with a nod, an uneasy feeling settling in his stomach. "What can I do for you?"

The shorter one said, "I'm lookin' for a new revolver. Want to stay with a .44 or a .45 caliber."

Justin climbed down from the ladder and slipped behind the long glass case that displayed a large assortment of hand-guns. "I can show you several kinds, sir."

The two men eyed the display as Justin slid the case open. "Let's see, here. We'll start with these."

Justin took three revolvers out and laid them on cloth squares on top of the case. "My favorite of these three is this Colt .45 Peacemaker. Six-shot. It's the latest model—1870. Seven-groove rifling. Seven-inch barrel."

"Looks good," said the prospective buyer. "How much?"

"Forty-seven dollars."

The man nodded, then looked at the next one.

"This is a good gun here," said Justin. "Adams Dragoon. 1869 model. It's a heavier caliber, but I thought I'd show it to you. It's a .49 caliber, five-shot. Seven-inch barrel. Packs a real wallop."

The short man glanced at his partner. "Almost as potent as a buffalo gun."

"Yeah," the tall man said, grinning.

"Because of the higher caliber," said Justin, "it has solid-frame construction, which is different from the Colts. You'll notice the ringed hammer, which is a new idea; gives it the luxury of double action. It has three-groove rifling."

"Mm-hmm," said the shorter man. "How much?"

"Seventy-five."

He raised his eyebrows. "Mm-hmm," he said again, then went to the third gun.

"Colt again," said Justin. "Seven-groove rifling, .44 caliber.

Single action. 1870 model. Six-shot. It's used by a lot of army officers. Barrel's seven-and-a-half inches."

"How much?"

"Fifty. Now, if none of these suit you, I've got plenty more."

The man looked at his partner, then back at Justin. "I kinda like this .49 caliber cannon here. I'll take it."

"Fine," said Justin, picking up his pad of sales slips and a pencil.

The partner whipped out his gun and cocked the hammer in one smooth move, lining it on Justin's chest. "He didn't say he was gonna buy it, pal. He said he would take it. We'll just take all three, and plenty of cartridges, too. While we're at it, we'll empty out the till."

Justin's features tinted with anger, but he didn't make a move. While he was held at gunpoint by one man, the other man stuffed three revolvers under his belt, then moved behind the glass case and helped himself to several boxes of cartridges for each gun.

He grinned wickedly and went to the cash drawer, which was behind the counter on the hardware side of the store. "Woo-ee! Look what we got here, Len!"

The taller man glanced toward the bank of windows behind him. "Hurry up, Tony, before somebody comes in!"

"Yeah, yeah, yeah," Tony said, stuffing wads of currency in his pockets. "Looks like we came in at the right time. This drawer is loaded!"

Len kept his gun lined on Justin as he looked toward his partner. "That's good, but hurry up!"

Justin saw Marshal Mangum ride by on his horse. *Look this way, Lance,* he said inwardly.

Len's tension showed in his tone as he said, "Tony, you ready to go?"

"Hold on!" Tony jammed money in his jacket pocket. "No

sense leavin' this stuff. It'll spend for us just as good as him."

A few seconds later Tony left the cash drawer hanging open and picked up the cartridge boxes. "Let's go."

Len sneered at Justin. "Guess we ought to tie you up and gag you, so you won't alert the law before we're outta town. But we don't have time for that, so..." He swung the barrel of his gun in an arc and cracked Justin on the side of the head.

Justin crumpled to the floor behind the glass. He was dazed but conscious. He pulled his knees under him and reached up to grip the edge of the case, shaking his head in an attempt to clear away the dizziness, then pulled himself upright and looked out the front windows. Len and Tony were casually untying their horses from the hitching rail.

Justin watched them swing into their saddles and slowly ride away from the front of the store. He staggered to the door and moved out onto the boardwalk, using the outside wall to support himself as he scanned the street in both directions. The robbers were just passing the front of the marshal's office where Lance Mangum was tying his horse to the hitching rail and talking to a couple of men.

"Marshal!" Justin shouted. He pointed at the two riders. "Those two on the piebald and the gray roan! They just robbed me!"

Mangum pivoted and saw the robbers putting spurs to their mounts. He untied his horse and was about to mount when he saw the robbers angling for the closest intersection to the west. At the same instant, Mangum saw Jack Bower at the reins of a wagon with Julianna LeCroix sitting next to him.

Mangum stepped into the street and shouted at the top of his lungs, "Jack! Those two riders! Robbers!"

As the riders bore down on the intersection, Jack's thoughts tumbled around each other. He must put Julianna and Larissa out of danger. Rather than use the wagon to block the robbers' progress, he quickly pulled it to the side of the street and set the brake. As he jumped groundward, he said, "Julianna, get down on the floor of the wagon!"

Julianna cuddled Larissa to her breast and squeezed down between the seat and the wagon front. The horses whinnied nervously. When she had Larissa as low as possible, Julianna couldn't help but rise up enough to watch Jack. The riders were bearing down on him.

Jack planted his feet in the middle of the street, cocked his Colt .45, and pointed it at the two robbers, who were coming at a full gallop. "Stop!" he shouted.

When they gave no indication they would obey, Jack aimed at the man who sat tallest in the saddle and dropped the hammer. The Colt roared, and Len rocked back in the saddle and fell sideways.

Tony swore and aimed his horse straight at the man with the smoking gun.

There was no time for Jack to get off another shot. He heard Julianna's shriek as he leaped aside in the nick of time, rolling in the dust.

Marshal Mangum thundered by on his horse in pursuit of the fleeing robber.

The other robber's horse trotted down the street and came to a halt. Jack's eyes went to the man he had shot and saw him gritting his teeth in pain, but he had his gun out of its holster and was taking aim.

Jack rolled, and the bullet missed him, striking dirt and raising a small cloud of dust. Still rolling, Jack fired at the robber but missed.

Julianna clutched little Larissa to her chest, bending as low as she could in the wagon to shield the baby and herself from flying bullets. Larissa, frightened by the noise of the gunfire, was shrieking at the top of her tiny lungs.

"Please, Lord," breathed Julianna, her pulse pounding so hard she could feel it throb in her temples. "Please! We just found each other. Don't let him be taken from me now!" Hot tears brimmed in her eyes and spilled over.

She heard two more shots; then the gunfire stopped as suddenly as it had started.

Julianna cautiously raised her head until she could peek over the front of the wagon between the horses. She breathed a sigh of relief when she saw Jack's dust-covered form walking toward the robber. Tiny tendrils of smoke rose from the muzzle of his revolver. The dead robber was sprawled on his back, his gun still clutched in his hand.

Men were moving off the boardwalks toward the spot where Jack was standing.

Larissa was still crying, and now she squirmed to be free of her mother's protective hold. Assessing the scene before her, Julianna loosened her grip on the baby and raised up onto the seat. She spoke quietly to her little girl, calming her fears.

Larissa looked around the crowded street with wide eyes still brimming with unshed tears. She wiggled her fat little hand free, popped her beloved thumb in her mouth, and settled quietly against her mother.

At the western edge of Fort Bridger, Lance Mangum bent low over his gelding's neck, driving the horse as fast as he could go.

The robber's horse was making little dust puffs on the road as he reached the outskirts of town. Its rider used the reins to whip the animal into more speed. When he saw the lawman gaining on him, he turned around in the saddle and fired.

Mangum felt a bullet pluck at his sleeve and returned fire.

The robber jerked, straightened up for a second or two, then peeled out of the saddle head first. When he hit the ground, the momentum carried him over in a limp cartwheel. Then he lay still.

Mangum gently drew rein and slowed his gelding to a trot until he came on the spot where the dead man lay.

With the danger over, Julianna hurried to where Jack stood over the dead body with townsmen circled around him. Justin Powell stood beside Jack, holding a bloodied bandanna to his head.

"Pardon me, gentlemen. Pardon me, please."

The men quickly made room for Julianna to pass.

Jack heard her voice and looked around. He opened his arms as she threw herself into them. Holding mother and baby in a close embrace, he said, "It's all right, darlin'. This part, at least, is over. I hope Marshal Mangum has caught the other one by now. Justin was just telling me what happened. Those two men robbed him at gunpoint, hit him on the head, and took off."

Julianna turned her gaze on Justin. "Are you hurt bad?"

"I don't think so, but I'll have Doc O'Brien look at my head as soon as I unload my guns and money from this guy." He bent down and began pulling the stolen bills from the man's pockets.

Jack and Julianna looked into each other's eyes, and Julianna sighed. "Darling, I'm so glad you're all right."

With baby Larissa cradled between them and the crowd looking on, the couple put their foreheads together and breathed a silent prayer of thanks to the Lord.

Suddenly Julianna heard a familiar voice behind her.

"You're back! Oh, praise the Lord! You're back!"

Hannah Cooper was hurrying down the middle of the street as fast as her extra load would let her. She had Patty Ruth by the hand.

Everyone heard the little redhead cry out, "And look, Mama! Mr. Jack has his arm around her!"

CHAPTER FIVE

Hannah embraced Julianna. "Oh, honey, I'm so glad you're back!"

"Thank you, Hannah." Julianna lowered her voice. "Jack and I will come to the store and see you as soon as all this excitement is over. We have something to tell you."

Hannah gave her a squeeze. "He came after you, didn't he?"

Jack was busy talking to Fort Bridger's mayor and barber, Cade Samuels, but he overheard Hannah's question and said, "Yes I did, Hannah. I went after her because I'm so in love with her I can't live without her."

"I'm glad to hear that, Jack. Both of you please come and see me as soon as you can. I want to hear all about it." Hannah hugged Julianna again, then turned to her daughter. "Come on, Patty Ruth. We need to get back to the store."

As she took Patty Ruth's hand and turned to leave, she saw Justin bending over the dead robber, taking back his stolen property.

"That looks like some cut, Justin. You need to let Doc O'Brien tend it."

Justin looked up at Hannah while stuffing the third stolen revolver under his belt. He took a bloody bandanna from his hip pocket and dabbed at the trickle of blood running down the side of his face. "I will, Hannah. Just needed to collect what this guy stole from me."

"Are you all right?"

"Sure. When this guy's partner hit me with his gun barrel, it dazed me some, but I'm fine."

"Would you like me to let Julie know about this?"

"Thank you, Hannah, but I'll do that after I see Doc."

"All right. Can I carry those cartridge boxes for you?"

"Hannah Marie Cooper, you are absolutely the most kind and caring person I have ever met. You need to go back to the store and sit down. Thank you, but I can handle the boxes."

"All right, but you get that cut tended to, you hear?"

"Yes, Mother," he said, chuckling.

Hannah laughed and started across the street with Patty Ruth. Just then she saw Dr. O'Brien hurrying toward the crowd collected around the dead man.

"Doc!" she called, waving him down.

The short, pudgy Irishman drew up with his black medical bag in hand. "I was stitching up a bad cut on a child's arm and couldn't leave him till it was done. I heard the gunfire. Am I needed, or—"

"Deputy Bower killed a robber, Doc, and Marshal Mangum has gone after the other one. They robbed Justin at his store, and one of them gave him a bad gash on the head. He needs your attention. He's in the circle over there."

"Thanks," said Doc and made a beeline for the circle of men.

Justin had risen to his feet, his arms loaded with cartridge boxes. A fresh trickle of blood ran down his face.

"Hold it, Justin," said Doc. "Let me take a look at that cut."

Powell grinned. "Oh, hi, Doc. I was going to come and see you as soon as I took these stolen goods back to my store."

"Well, from what I see, I think you'll need stitches."

As O'Brien took a closer look at the cut, somebody shouted, "Here comes the marshal!"

Lance Mangum rode in, leading another horse with a body draped over the saddle.

When Heidi Lindgren saw Lance's blood-soaked sleeve, she stepped off the boardwalk and rushed toward him.

"Good work, Marshal!" Cade Samuels called out.

Heidi's tremulous voice cut through the rumblings of the crowd. "Oh, Lance! You've been shot!"

"It's only a scratch." Mangum swung from the saddle and touched ground, giving her a lopsided grin.

"It's more than a scratch. Dr. O'Brien's right here. Let him look at it."

Doc turned from Justin and eyed the bloody sleeve. "I want you to come to my office right now, Marshal. These no-goods put a gash in Justin's head when they robbed him. Both of you need attention right now."

"Doc," said Justin, "I've got to go put a Closed sign in the store window and lock up. I'll be there in a couple of minutes."

"All right, but don't dillydally."

Justin chuckled. "Doc, you're an old grandma."

O'Brien's eyes glinted. "Well, I became one from doctorin' kids like you!"

Dan Bledsoe, owner of Bledsoe's Clothing Store, stepped up. "Justin, I can carry those cartridge boxes and the revolvers to the store for you. I'll hang your sign in the window and lock the door. You go on with Doc and get that cut stitched up."

"Good for you, Dan," said Doc. He turned to Justin. "Let's go. You, too, Marshal."

"I'll tie your horse to the hitch rail in front of your office, Lance," said Heidi. "Go on with Doc."

Because Fort Bridger did not yet have an undertaker, Dr. Frank O'Brien served in that capacity. "Cade," O'Brien said to the mayor, "have some of these men take the bodies to the small building behind my office. I'll hire my usual outlaw buryin' crew to put them in the ground tomorrow."

Samuels nodded. "Right, Doc."

As Heidi took the reins of Mangum's horse, she said, "I'm so thankful that bullet didn't hit you a few inches to the left."

He gave her a weak grin. "Heidi, being vulnerable to outlaws' bullets is part of my job. But…ah…I'm glad it's just my arm, too."

Cade Samuels lifted his voice and said, "Everybody give our two lawmen a big cheer! They handily took care of these outlaws!"

When the applause died down, Doc O'Brien guided his two patients down the street toward his office.

One of the women in the crowd standing around Jack and Julianna spoke up. "Julianna, someone told me you left town on the stage this morning. That you were going to Idaho to live."

Julianna ran her gaze over the faces in the crowd and smiled demurely as she said, "I did leave, folks. But for reasons that will become public later, I have returned."

"Miss Julianna," said Curly, "I shore am right proud that you came back. You an' the new deppity hyar gonna hitch up?"

A sharp elbow rammed Curly's ribs. "Ow!" He winced and rubbed his rib cage and shot a questioning look at his wife.

"Honey pot," said Judy Charley, showing her single snaggletooth in a grin, "you shouldn't ast Julianna sich a question! Mebbe they gotta talk 'bout thet kind o' stuff afore they come to a agreement!"

"Oh! I'm sorry, Miss Julianna," said Curly. "I jist was hopin' everthang was gonna be all right between yuh!"

Jack leaned close and said in a low tone, "Tell you what— we'll make it public pretty soon, but for your information, Julianna and I got formally engaged this morning."

Curly slapped his leg. "Wal, don't that beat all! I shore am glad to hyar it, kids!"

"Me, too!" chimed in Judy Charley.

Curly gave Judy a hurt look, still rubbing his ribs. "Now it's ol' Curly who's gotta see Doc…fer a half-dozen busted ribs!"

The skinny woman cackled and said, "Shore, honey bun, I really poked yuh a good one, didn't I?"

Curly broke into laughter. "Wal, if'n you had hit me much harder, they'd be broke!"

Dr. O'Brien worked on Justin's gash while his wife, Edie, held a compress on Lance's arm to keep it from bleeding until her husband could see to it.

Doc was putting the third stitch in Justin's head when there was a rapid knock at the door to the outer office and waiting room.

"Edie!" came Julie Powell's voice. "It's Julie! May I come in?"

"Uh-oh," said Justin. "She's found out."

"Sure, honey, come in!" Edie said.

Julie rushed to the table where Justin was lying while Doc tied up the final stitch. "Oh, darling! Are you all right? How bad is it, Doc?"

"I'm fine, honey," Justin said. "I was going to come home and tell you about it when Doc finished up here."

"He'll be all right, Julie," said Doc. "As you can see, he's got a pretty good knot on his head, but the cut only took three stitches. He's lost some blood, but there's nothing to worry about."

"Thank the Lord!" She turned her attention to Mangum, who sat on an adjoining table with Edie at his side. "How about you, Marshal? Is it bad?"

"Just a scratch. I'll be fine."

Ten minutes later, Justin and Julie left together with some headache powders for Justin to use when the dose Dr. O'Brien had given him wore off.

The doctor moved to the next table, looked down at the marshal, and said, "Well, let's see what we have here."

"I think it'll take about three stitches, Frank," Edie said as she removed the compress.

Doc looked at the wound. "Mm-hmm. Three is about right, honey. Let's get it done."

While Doc was cleaning the wound with antiseptic solution, Lance gritted his teeth against the stinging and said, "I'm sure glad it wasn't my gun arm that got hit, Doc."

O'Brien, like so many of the Christians in Fort Bridger, was burdened for the soul of Lance Mangum. "I'm glad, too, Marshal. But what were Heidi's words a little while ago? 'I'm so thankful the bullet didn't hit you a few inches to the left.'"

"Or I'd be dead?"

"Yes, sir, and you'd be in eternity now."

"And you're going to say that my eternal place would be hell."

Edie was working at the other table, cleaning up from the work her husband had done on Justin Powell. She continued what she was doing but watched the marshal out of the corner of her eye.

O'Brien arched his bushy gray eyebrows. "Well...?"

"Doc, the way I see it, I've got as good a chance of going to heaven as anyone else."

"Son, nobody goes to heaven by chance. They go there by the blood of Jesus Christ or they don't go at all. Only the blood can wash away our sins, and this can't happen until we repent of our sin, open our hearts to Him by faith, and ask Him to save us, cleanse us, and forgive us for all of our transgressions against Him."

When Lance Mangum remained silent, Doc and Edie exchanged glances but said no more.

When the stitches were in place and the arm bandaged, Doc said, "Maybe you ought to take the rest of the day off,

Doc said, "Maybe you ought to take the rest of the day off, Marshal. Give your strength a chance to come back."

Lance sat up and pulled what was left of his bloody sleeve down over the bandage. "Too much to do, Doc. Besides, I don't really feel weak. I'll be fine. What do I owe you?"

The chubby Irishman grinned. "It's on the house."

Mangum shook his head. "No, Doc. You have to make a living just like the rest of us. How much?"

"I don't have to make a living from the man who wears the badge in this town and puts his life on the line for me every day."

Mangum reached in his pocket, took out a ten-dollar gold piece, and laid it on the table. "Lawmen should pay their bills like everybody else, Doc. Thanks for fixing me up."

O'Brien frowned. "Pick it up, Marshal. Let Edie and me do this for you."

Mangum turned and headed for the door as if he had not heard him.

"I need to see the wound in three days," Doc called out.

Pausing at the door, Mangum said, "I'll drop in and let you look at it. Thanks again."

Mangum passed into the outer office and beheld a lovely blonde sitting in the waiting room.

"Heidi," he said softly, "who's watching your shop?"

"Nobody. I'll go back in a minute. I just had to see if you're all right." She stood up as she spoke.

"Fit as a fiddle," he said, moving close to her and looking down into her blue eyes. "Doc put three stitches in my arm and wrapped it up good. Come on. I'll walk you back to the shop."

As they moved down the boardwalk toward the dress shop, Heidi said, "Lance, I praise the Lord that you weren't killed."

"Yeah. Me, too."

Things on Fort Bridger's Main Street had settled back to normal when Jack and Julianna stepped through the door of Cooper's General Store. Jack was carrying Larissa, who was fascinated with the little bell that jingled above the door as they entered.

Hannah and Jacob were busy behind the counter, but Patty Ruth left her stool, rounded the end of the counter, and said, "Mr. Jack, could I give Larissa a hug?"

"Of course." He grinned at the little redhead and eased down to her height.

Hannah paused while totaling her customer's bill and said, "How's the marshal, Jack?"

"He's all right. On the job already. When he got back from Doc's office, I asked him if I could have a little time so Julianna and I could talk to you."

Jacob sent a glance to his employer. "I can handle the store if you want to talk in private."

Hannah smiled at the little man. "Thank you, Jacob." Then she said to Jack and Julianna, "As soon as I'm finished with Mrs. Conway's bill, we'll go upstairs to the apartment. I want to hear all about it."

The door opened and Marshal Mangum came in and headed directly to his deputy, who was still bent down so Patty Ruth could hug Larissa. "Jack," he said, "I know you came here to talk to Hannah, but I need you to come back to the office with me."

"Sure, boss. What's up?"

"I was going through my Wanted file and came across those men we killed today. Your man's name is Tony Welton, and mine is Leonard Case. Both were wanted by the federal government on train robbery charges, so both of us have to fill out a report, and we have to send it in immediately. I'm sorry to take you away right now."

Jack handed Larissa to Julianna. "I'll be back as soon as I can, honey," he said.

"Tell you what, Jack," said Hannah, "I'm sure Julianna would like you present when we talk. I'll take her upstairs to the apartment and let her rest and care for Larissa. You and Julianna plan to have supper with us this evening. We can talk then."

"We don't want to impose, Hannah," said Jack. "How about if I take all of you out to Glenda's Café for supper?"

"That's very nice of you, but I've already got beef stew slowly simmering on the stove. Let's plan to eat and talk at my table tonight."

"Don't pass it up, Jack," put in Jacob. "I eat about four meals a week with my boss and her kids. You won't find better cooking anywhere on this planet. Miss Hannah's beef stew is world famous."

Hannah laughed. "That might be stretching it a bit, Jacob."

"Not at all. I'm the man who knows. Take my word for it, Jack. Don't miss that world-famous beef stew."

Jack grinned. "All right, Hannah, we'll see you for supper."

Hannah led Julianna into her sunny kitchen, where the ever-present teakettle was staying warm on the back of the stove. Julianna took a deep whiff of the savory aroma in the air. "Your world-famous beef stew sure smells good; I can hardly wait for supper!"

Hannah chuckled. "I hope you won't be disappointed."

"I'm sure Jacob's appraisal of your cooking is quite accurate."

Hannah took Julianna's coat and the baby's wrap, then led mother and baby into her bedroom where she left Julianna to change and feed Larissa. After tossing a couple of logs onto the dwindling fire in the parlor, Hannah returned to the kitchen to prepare tea.

When Julianna reappeared, the fireplace was crackling and giving off welcome heat.

Hannah turned from the stove. "Go on in by the fireplace, honey," she said. "Baby asleep?"

"Yes." Julianna moved into the parlor area and saw that Hannah had placed cups and saucers on the small coffee table near the fireplace.

Hannah came in with the steaming teakettle and poured hot tea into the cups. "Sit down, honey. I'll be right back."

After placing the teakettle back on the stove, Hannah returned to the parlor. Julianna was seated on the couch, her hands clasped tightly. She was trembling.

"Julianna, what's wrong?"

Suddenly the young woman burst into tears, her entire body quaking. Hannah sat down beside her. "Honey, what is it?"

Julianna drew a shuddering breath. "It just hit me! That awful shoot-out today! I...I was down on the floor of the wagon, holding Larissa close to me, and I kept raising my head to see if—to see if Jack was...was—"

Julianna broke into uncontrollable sobs. Hannah held her tight and patted her soothingly. "Go ahead, honey. Cry it out."

Julianna sobbed for several minutes; then the tears became much lighter and intermittent. She accepted a handkerchief from Hannah and drew a deep breath, making a gulping sound. "I...I'm sorry. I don't know what came over me. What did I do that for?"

"Sweetie, it's called delayed reaction. You are very much in love with Jack, right?"

"Oh yes!"

"Today, not only were you and Larissa in danger, but you saw the man you love facing death at the hands of that outlaw. One bullet could have snuffed out Jack's life, and you knew it. Delayed reaction often happens when a person witnesses the kind of violence that you did today, especially when someone you love is a potential victim. Once the danger is over, you sort of fall apart from the relief of it all."

Julianna nodded. "I see what you're saying. Instead of falling apart at the scene, it took a while for the horror of it to register in my brain."

"Something like that."

Julianna touched Hannah's hand. "Thank you for understanding."

"I understand, honey, because I've been there. Solomon fought in the Civil War. He went through some terrible battles and was seriously wounded twice, and not so seriously a couple other times. And...I lost him to a violent death a few months ago when he gave his life to save mine and the lives of our children."

"Yes," said Julianna patting her hand again.

"Our tea is cold. Let me get some more."

Hannah poured out the cold tea and returned with the cups steaming again. As they sipped, Julianna said, "You know, thinking back on that awful scene today, I felt as if someone was there. I...I mean, I know the Lord was, and I remember asking Him to keep Jack from getting killed. But there was something—someone...oh, I don't know how to say it."

Hannah reached for a Bible on the small table at the end of the couch. "Let me show you something." She flipped to the first chapter of the book of Hebrews. "Here, honey. Look at verses 6 and 7. In verse 6 we see that God told all the angels to worship the first begotten, who is His Son, Jesus Christ. In verse 7, God says He made His angels spirits. See that?"

"Mm-hmm."

"Now, look at verse 13. He speaks of the angels here. See that?"

"Yes."

"Now look at what the Bible says in verse 14 about God's angels. 'Are they not all ministering spirits, sent forth to minister for them who shall be heirs of salvation?'"

Julianna blinked in amazement. "Are you telling me—"

"Yes! God has sent forth His angels to minister to God's born-again people. Angels have corporeal bodies, of course. They have been seen in physical bodies right here on earth. The Bible tells of it over and over. But they can also function as spirits. That is, in a nonmaterial fashion. That's why they can be right here with us and we can't see them. They are ministering spirits. God has given them to us to minister to us when we're in need. That's why you sensed something you can't really describe. Scripture indicates that each of God's born-again children has at least one angel who watches over him or her at all times."

Julianna's eyes were wide. "Guardian angels!"

"Yes."

"And I have one with me at all times?"

"At least one."

Julianna popped her hands together. "Isn't that just about the most wonderful thing you ever heard of? My very own angel. It's…it's almost more than I can take, after what happened today."

"Yes, honey. God has so graciously provided for our every need."

The two women talked for several minutes of how good the Lord was to His children.

After a while, Hannah rose from the couch and said, "Well, honey, I need to get back down to the store. You stretch out here on the couch and rest while Larissa allows it. There are logs right here by the fireplace. Throw one on anytime the fire starts to dwindle."

"I'll do it," said Julianna, rising from the couch. "And thank you, dear Hannah, for being such a help to me."

"My pleasure."

Julianna watched as Hannah put on her coat. "Would you like me to walk down the stairs with you, Hannah?"

"I'll be all right, thank you. Lie down now and get some rest." Hannah stopped at the door. "May I ask you something?"

"Certainly."

"Would you mind if Jacob came for supper tonight while we talk?"

"Of course not. What we're going to tell you will be common knowledge soon, anyway. We just wanted to tell you and your children first. Jacob's presence won't be a problem at all."

"You don't think Jack will mind?"

"Of course not."

Hannah beamed a smile and said, "Jacob ate with us just last night and was planning to fix his own supper in his room downstairs tonight. But after his compliment on my 'world-famous' beef stew, I feel he should get his share tonight."

Julianna laughed. "Well, I should say so! Jack and I will love having him here as we tell what's happened between us."

That evening, Hannah, her children, and her guests sat down to a simple but delicious meal that she and Mary Beth had prepared, with Patty Ruth's help.

When Jack smelled the savory, spicy stew he said, "Julianna and I will tell you our story after we eat. This looks too good to delay getting it to my stomach!"

When everybody at the table had their fill of the luscious stew and golden brown cornbread, thickly spread with creamy butter and slathered with honey or strawberry jam, they leaned back and made themselves comfortable.

The adults enjoyed hot coffee as Jack told the little group of his decision to remove himself from Julianna's life because he felt he wasn't good enough for her. The stage had been gone only a little while when he knew he loved her too much to let her go.

Julianna told of how ecstatic she had been to see him pull alongside the stage and tell the driver to stop.

The precious looks that passed between the young couple as they told their stories brought joy to the little company gathered around the table.

"This is so wonderful!" exclaimed Mary Beth. "It's so romantic!"

While the others were making similar comments to the young couple, a small stab of pain pierced Hannah's gentle heart, and a fresh longing for Solomon stole over her. Memories of him flashed through her mind.

She forced her thoughts back to the present and was rewarded with a soft kick from the babe she carried beneath her heart. *Thank You, Lord, for Your sufficiency and Your tender mercies,* she thought. A smile graced her lips as she said, "Julianna...Jack...I'm so happy for you."

Patty Ruth spoke up. "Mr. Jack...Miss Julianna...can I come to your house when you get married, so I can spend some time with Larissa?"

"Patty Ruth Cooper," said Hannah, mildly scolding her, "haven't I taught you better than that? You don't invite yourself to someone's home."

The child blushed and dipped her head, then looked at her mother from the tops of her eyes. "I'm sorry, Mama."

Julianna cleared her throat and said, "Would it be all right if I invite her?"

Hannah tilted her head, sent a glance at Patty Ruth, and looked back at Julianna. "Yes. Of course."

Julianna gave the child a tender look and said softly, "Patty Ruth, Mr. Jack and I will be happy to have you come and visit Larissa."

Chris and B.J. exchanged glances, then looked at the ceiling and rolled their eyes.

Mary Beth said, "Patty Ruth loves babies, and she's so cute with them."

The Cooper brothers stole another glance at each other and looked at the ceiling again.

"Tell you what," spoke up Jack, "the whole Cooper family will be welcome at our house anytime, and so will Jacob."

Jacob smiled, as did everyone in the Cooper family.

Speaking of our house," said Jack, "I've already established that Julianna and Larissa are going to move into the house that I've rented. I'll find someplace else to live until we get married."

"Tell you what, Jack," said Jacob. "You can live in my quarters with me like you did before you were hired as deputy marshal and rented the house."

A wide smile captured Jack's handsome face. "Well, thank you, Jacob. I'll just take you up on it."

"Be glad to have you," said the little man.

There was a knock at the door.

"I'll get it," said Chris, shoving back his chair.

Patty Ruth giggled. "Oh, Chris! It isn't Abby Turner. She doesn't go calling this time of night!"

Chris's face tinted slightly as he gave his little sister a cold, steely look and headed for the door.

Pastor and Mrs. Andy Kelly were on the porch. They had been out of town since early that morning and had returned about an hour ago. While eating supper at Glenda's Café, they had heard about the shootings and that Jack had gone after Julianna and brought her back. They wanted to hear all about it.

The four Cooper children immediately offered to clean up

the table and the kitchen, and the adults made their way into the parlor where a cheery fire glowed, warming the room.

Hannah prepared a tray of warm gingerbread and hot coffee. When everyone was served, she joined them to listen as Jack and Julianna told their story to the Kellys. When they announced they would marry in a few months, the pastor told them he would be glad to perform the ceremony.

When the evening came to a close, Hannah invited Julianna and Larissa to stay the night. Jack said that tomorrow he would move into Jacob's quarters with him, and Julianna and the baby could move into his house.

The Kellys left, and moments later Jacob excused himself and went downstairs to his quarters.

As Jack was telling Julianna and Larissa good night, Hannah looked at them with delight. Tears misted her eyes as she praised the Lord in her heart for His perfect way.

CHAPTER SIX

Whooping, yapping Pawnees came in waves toward the circle of wagons. The thunder of horses' hooves rolled across the hot Kansas plains like the fire of heavy artillery.

Rifles barked and spit fire back and forth, and gun smoke hung in the breezeless air like the pall of death.

Emily McDermott held little Holly close to her as they lay flat beneath the family wagon. She glanced up ahead and saw Matt kneeling by the tailgate of wagon master Hank Dekins's wagon, then spoke against Holly's ear, telling her everything would be all right, even though she wasn't sure of that herself.

She looked toward Matt again and watched him and Hank Dekins take careful aim and fire their rifles. Each time she saw an Indian peel off his horse, she rejoiced inside.

Pawnee bullets chewed the ground all around the wagons and ripped into canvas tops and wagon beds. When a bullet plowed the ground in front of Emily and Holly and scattered dirt particles in their faces, Holly screamed, "Mama! Make those Indians go away! Please, Mama! Please!"

Emily tried to keep the quaver out of her voice as she said, "They'll go away pretty soon, honey. Just keep your eyes closed!"

She heard a Pawnee bullet rip through the canvas top of their wagon, and another one splintered wood near the tailgate. "Dear Lord," she whispered, "please make them go away! Please don't let Holly or Matt get hit!"

Emily watched wide-eyed as Matt fired at a yapping Pawnee who was off his horse and running toward the wagon circle, attempting to get between the McDermott wagon and the one behind it. Matt's bullet caught the Indian dead center in the chest.

"Yes!" Emily shouted, shaking her fist in jubilation.

Suddenly she felt hands like steel bands clamp down on her ankles, and she was dragged from under the wagon with Holly wrapped in one arm. She kicked and screamed, trying to get a grip on the prairie grass with her free hand, but it was no use. She twisted about and saw a big Pawnee with war paint striped across his nose and cheeks, and a demonic look in his eyes.

She shrieked the word "No!" struggling to free herself from the Indian's grasp. Through the curtain of her terror she heard Holly scream.

The Indian made a grunting sound, let go of Emily's ankles, and seized her free arm. He yanked Holly from her grasp and threw the little girl under the wagon where she let out a howl when her body struck a wagon wheel.

Emily looked toward her husband, who was busy shooting at Pawnees, the roar of battle filling his ears. "Ma-a-a-att!"

The Indian lifted her off the ground and draped her over his shoulder. She caught a glimpse of Holly scrambling out from under the wagon, terror etched on her small face. "Mama-a-a!"

The Indian carried Emily toward the rear of the McDermott wagon, bent on taking her outside the circle with him.

"Ma-a-a-a-tt! Ma-a-a-a—"

"Emily? Emily! Wake up, honey! Wake up! You're having a nightmare!"

She drew a ragged breath and lurched up in the bed. When she opened her eyes, moonlight was streaming through the windows of the bedroom. Cold sweat lay on her brow, and her whole body shook.

"It's all right, honey," Matt said, folding her into his arms. "It's all right. You're safe. Were…were you dreaming about—"

"The Pawnees? Yes!" She clung to him, digging her fingernails into his back. "Oh, Matt! That savage would have had me if you hadn't—"

"It's all over, Emily. You're safe in your home in Wyoming. You're not in Kansas. There are no Pawnees here. It was only a nightmare."

They heard a cough and looked toward the doorway. They could see Holly's small form standing in the doorway. She was rubbing her sleepy eyes. "Mama, what's wrong?"

Matt walked over and swept her up in his arms. "Honey, Mama just had a bad dream. She's all right now."

"Did she dream about those awful Indians, Papa?"

"Yes, honey. Her dream was about the Pawnees."

"I'm fine now, Holly," Emily said, forcing her voice to sound steady.

"I want to hug her, Papa."

Matt carried Holly to the bed and put her in Emily's arms. After a moment Emily drew back and looked into Holly's eyes. "I want you to get back to bed now, sweetheart. I'm sorry I woke you up."

"That's all right, Mama. I love you, Mama."

"I love you, too, sweetheart. You get back to sleep now."

Moonlight filled the room with its silvery hue as Matt laid his little girl in her bed and pulled the blankets up snugly under her chin. He sat down on the edge of the bed and caressed her face with his big hand, gently wiping the tears from her cheeks. "Holly, darlin', Mama's going to be fine. Please don't cry."

Holly's lips quivered. "But…but…"

"But what?"

"I'm afraid, Papa."

"Of what, honey?"

"Maybe those bad Indians who tried to take Mama will come here and take her away."

"That won't happen, Holly. You don't have to be afraid. Remember the soldiers from Fort Bridger who patrol around here?"

"Yes."

"They'll keep the bad Indians away."

"Promise?"

"Promise."

Holly studied her father's eyes in the pale light. "Then why's Mama afraid?"

"She's not, honey. If she hadn't had the nightmare, she wouldn't have been crying out in her sleep. And she wouldn't have awakened you." He bent over and kissed her forehead. "You go back to sleep now."

"Yes, Papa." She looked around. "Where's Dolly?"

Matt spotted the rag doll on the floor where Holly had dropped it when she got out of bed. "Here she is," he said, picking it up. He lifted the covers and placed the doll in the curve of Holly's arm. "Eyes closed now. Off to dreamland."

A ragged cough captured her for a moment; then she closed her eyes and hugged her beloved rag doll close.

Matt sat there for a few minutes, letting Holly feel his presence. She coughed lightly once, then her eyes grew drowsy.

Soon her droopy eyelids closed and she was breathing evenly.

Matt rose from the bed and stood over his precious sleeping daughter. His own thoughts went back to that hot day in Kansas when the Pawnee warrior almost got away with Emily. He thanked the Lord for sparing her life.

When Matt returned to the bedroom, Emily pretended to be sleeping. She felt him kiss the back of her neck, then turn over. In a matter of moments he was asleep.

Emily's thoughts trailed back to Kentucky. She had dearly loved their farm in bluegrass country. Though the house was old and weathered, it was their first home. They had labored hard to fix it up, work the fields, and tend the animals.

She had sewn her own curtains and tablecloths and had scrubbed and painted and polished until the little farmhouse was warm and welcoming. Matt worked from predawn until dusk around the house and farm, and they had enjoyed seeing the fruits of their labor.

But as with all farms, they were vulnerable to the natural elements. The skies had been dry and cloudless for too long. With nothing put aside for a bad crop year, the McDermotts found themselves on the brink of foreclosure. The bank was breathing down their necks, demanding payments they could not possibly make.

Although their home held many precious memories, and to lose it would be devastating, Matt and Emily were well grounded in the Word of God and they knew the Lord was in control of their lives.

When the bank foreclosed and gave them two weeks to vacate the premises, a letter arrived from Uncle Louie McDermott's attorney in Rock Springs, Wyoming. Although they were sad to hear of Matt's uncle's death, the Lord had given them a twenty-acre farm in Wyoming.

Many tears were shed the day they left family and friends. Both Matt and Emily had lived all their lives near Lexington, Kentucky, and knew everyone for miles around. They had grown up on neighboring farms and attended the same one-room school and the same church. And now they were leaving all that was familiar and loved for the unknown.

On the day before they left for Wyoming, Matt and Emily had gone to the little country cemetary where Michael was buried and spent a few minutes weeping over the tiny grave. Emily remembered the emotional pain she had felt the day they pulled away in the old covered wagon and headed due west for Missouri. Matt was on his horse, and she drove the ox team with Holly at her side. Indeed, leaving home, family, friends, and church in Woodford County, Kentucky, to go west to Wyoming Territory was the hardest thing Emily McDermott had ever done. But Matthew was the love of her life, and she would go to the ends of the earth with him…or for him.

A few weeks later, the McDermotts arrived at Independence, Missouri, where they signed up with a wagon train led by Hank Dekins, a grizzled, silver-haired man in his midsixties. They were glad to be with Dekins because he was an experienced wagon master.

Lying there in the moonlit room with Matt asleep beside her, Emily let her mind trail back to the night around the campfire on the east bank of the Missouri River when Dekins gave instructions for the journey ahead…

The flickering light of the campfire danced across Hank Dekins's face while he answered questions, most of them coming from the men.

Matt and Emily stood next to a family named Conners, with Holly between them.

When a break came in questions, Cliff Conners raised his hand.

"Mr. Dekins, we've talked about weather, the different kinds of terrain we'll be crossing, water sources, and how much ground we expect to cover daily on level ground and in the mountains along the Oregon Trail. All of this is very important, but there's a subject that hasn't come up yet—the Indian danger. None of us relish the idea, but we've come with guns and plenty of ammunition to face the inevitable. Would you talk to us about this danger?"

Hank grinned, showing a mouthful of buck teeth. "If no one had brought it up, sir, I would have talked about it, believe me."

Matt felt Emily reach around Holly to touch his arm. He knew she had a deathly fear of having to endure hostile Indian attacks on the trail. They had talked about it at length while traveling from Kentucky. Gently he took her hand.

Hank ran his gaze over the faces in the half circle. "Now, folks, I'm not gonna beat around the bush. The possibility of an Indian attack is the greatest danger we will face. I wanted to wait till all of you were here in Independence before going into it, so now is the time.

"Since we don't pull out until day after tomorrow, I will give instructions on what all of us are to do in the event of an Indian attack. But I need daylight to show you how to form a circle with the wagons when we see hostiles coming at us, and how to position yourselves for the best protection. In the morning we'll actually practice forming a circle so you can get the feel of it.

"I'll say it now and repeat it tomorrow: In the event of an attack, I want the women and children to lie belly-down under the wagons. Even the women who are going to be using rifles. This is for your protection. You're hardest to hit from a galloping horse when you're down there."

A young mother's hand went up.

"Yes, Mrs. Amstutz?"

"Mr. Dekins, wouldn't the women and children be safer inside the wagons, lying flat on the floor?"

"No, ma'am. I've been leading wagon trains across Indian country for nigh onto twenty years. I've been through more Indian attacks than I care to count. Believe me, you're safer underneath the wagons."

Bernice Amstutz shook her head. "But underneath the wagons we'll be right out in the open, where the Indians can see us. Certainly it would be better if we were inside where they couldn't see us. And we would also have the sides of the wagons to protect us."

"Not so, ma'am. When Indians are firing at a wagon train, they will purposely fire directly into the wagon beds and through the canvas covers, hoping to kill someone taking refuge in there. Even the boards from which the wagon beds are made can be easily punctured by rifle bullets. Like I said, the safest place to be when the wagons are in a circle and fighting off Indians is underneath the wagons. It's hard for a mounted hostile to get the proper angle to aim his rifle at ground level. Makes it hard to be accurate."

Mrs. Amstutz looked to another woman close by and shrugged. The woman smiled weakly and nodded.

When Emily squeezed Matt's hand, he whispered, "Don't be afraid, honey. Hank has gotten through many an Indian attack. If we have them, we'll get through them, too."

Holly looked up at her father. "Promise, Papa?" she whispered.

"Promise," said Matt, giving her an assuring smile.

"Now let me explain something about the Indians we

might face," said Dekins. "In eastern and central Kansas, our greatest threat of attack is from the Pawnee. As we head northwest into Nebraska, the enemies become Cheyenne, Arapaho, and Sioux. In Wyoming, it'll be these last three, plus Blackfoot, Shoshone, and Snake. Once we're in Idaho, and we head northwest toward Oregon, the Indian threat pretty well drops off. Now, of all these tribes I have named, the Pawnee is the worst because of one specific reason—what his religion teaches about white women."

There were audible gasps and some murmuring that quickly trailed off.

"Let me explain," said Dekins. "When Pawnees attack wagon trains, they will do their best to get their hands on the white women, whom they will abduct in the midst of the dust, smoke, and excitement of battle. They take the captured women to their village. The warriors who are not married will molest them; then they will be offered by the entire village as sacrifices to their gods. In their religion, they believe the gods will smile upon them when they offer white women as sacrifices and will ensure the success of their crops and their hunting."

The wagon master's vivid explanation of the Pawnee atrocities against white women put a slight nausea in Emily's stomach and a feeling of needles pricking her spinal column. She felt that a too-tight collar was choking her, and a brassy taste rose in her mouth.

Matt leaned close. "I guarantee you, honey, if we have to fight the Pawnees, there'll never be one get near you. I'll always stay close by."

Emily bit down hard on her lower lip and nodded. Her throat was so tight she couldn't speak.

On the first day out, the wagon train crossed the Missouri. Matt rode his horse beside Emily, speaking words of comfort and encouragement to her as she drove the ox team through the four-foot depth of water.

They traveled four days, making between fifteen and eighteen miles a day without incident.

On the fifth day out, Matt was riding beside the wagon, directly behind the lead wagon driven by Hank Dekins. Hank periodically switched off from wagon seat to horseback with young Clancy O'Rourke, who had been traveling with him for some four years. At the moment, Clancy was somewhere up ahead, riding point.

It was midmorning, and the blazing sun bore down from a cloudless sky. Even though Emily and Holly wore sunbonnets, their faces were red and sweating.

Emily's hands were blistered from holding the reins mile after mile for four days. She glanced sideways at Matt and said, "I didn't know Kansas was so flat. I think I can see into next month."

Matt chuckled. "Well, from what Hank told me, it'll stay this flat even when we angle into Nebraska and all the way into Wyoming, until we reach the foothills of the Rocky Mountains. And then, we'll have some mountain passes to—"

Matt stopped speaking.

"What is it?" Emily said, leaning forward in an attempt to see around the Dekins wagon.

"It's Clancy. He's coming in a hurry. I hope—I hope he hasn't spotted Indians."

Emily's neck hairs lifted, sending a sizzling chill down her backbone. She put an arm around Holly and pulled her close.

Matt trotted up beside the lead wagon. Hank was pulling rein as he watched Clancy thunder in.

"Pawnees, Hank!" Clancy shouted. "They're waitin' for us in a dry riverbed up ahead!"

"They're not waiting now," said Matt, looking past horse and rider.

The Indians were coming like a horde of low-flying killer

bees. Hank stood up in the wagon, signaled for the wagons to form a circle, and shouted for them to hurry.

Once the wagons were in a circle, Matt hurried to get his wife and daughter under the wagon, then rushed to join Hank at the rear of the Dekins wagon, rifle ready. Down on one knee beside the wagon master, Matt glanced at Emily and Holly. They lay flat side by side, and he could tell that Emily was talking to Holly, trying to calm her. He moved his lips in silent prayer, asking God to protect them.

The Pawnee warriors were now strung out in three sinuous lines and came boiling in, yapping and barking like dogs, and ejecting war whoops. Matt and Hank fired simultaneously, each dropping a painted warrior from his horse. Both men let out their own war whoops.

The air came alive to the menacing slap and whisper of hot lead. Pawnee bullets plowed ground, ripped at canvas wagon covers, and splintered wagon beds. As the second wave came in, Emily heard Hank shout something to Matt about repeater rifles, and the words "stolen them from the U.S. Army" reached her ears.

The battle had been going on for about twenty minutes when the Pawnees came in a double wave. Hank and Matt blasted away, firing at the attackers as fast and accurately as possible. Some of the Indians were on foot, trying to make their way inside the circle. Some were being cut down, others were giving it up and dashing back to their horses. A few were not giving up.

Matt later told Emily that rage had flared through him like a windblown fire when he heard her scream his name and saw the Pawnee carrying her over his shoulder. In one smooth move Matt had whipped the Indian's knife from its sheath and rammed the blade full-haft into his back. He caught Emily as the Indian started to fall. She was still screaming when Matt laid her gently on the ground. He pulled the knife from the back of the grunting Indian and rolled him over, then drove the knife through his heart.

Emily was babbling incoherently when Matt placed her beneath the wagon and said to Holly, "Stay with Mama, honey. I need to get my rifle. I'll be right back."

Seconds later, Matt was with his family, firing at the Pawnees with his Remington .44 caliber repeater rifle from underneath the wagon.

Soon the Pawnees gathered their wounded and rode away, leaving their dead to pick up later.

Matt had finally gotten through to Emily, and when she realized what he had done to save her from the Indian, she wrapped her arms around him and wept with relief.

Hank Dekins returned to their wagon after checking all around the circle of wagons. Emily listened in horror as Dekins told Matt they had two men and a woman dead, six people wounded, and one seventeen-year-old girl missing.

Everyone gathered inside the circle to mourn their dead and care for the wounded. The parents of the missing girl were in deep grief, knowing there was no way ever to get their daughter back. Hank pointed out that even if they could find the Pawnee camp or village, it would be suicide to go in and try to rescue her. They would be vastly outnumbered.

The dead were buried before sundown. The next morning, the wagon train pulled out, leaving behind graves and dead Indians sprawled on the ground around the site.

In the days that followed, the missing girl's mother went out of her mind, unable to cope with the knowledge that her daughter had been sacrificed to the Pawnee gods. The heartbroken father took his wife and their other children and headed back to Illinois, where they had come from. Even as the wagon pulled away, Emily could hear the poor mother babbling insanely.

That night, Emily's nightmares began. She woke up screaming night after night, reliving the horrible moment when the Pawnee warrior had snatched her from under the wagon and carried her away. She couldn't ask Matt to take her and Holly back to Kentucky. They had no home to go to. They must go on to Wyoming.

Chapter Seven

Julianna LeCroix awakened early and looked toward the crib where Larissa was sleeping soundly. She stretched lazily and smiled to herself as she remembered Jack bringing her back to the house after moving his personal things to Jacob Kates's quarters. He had let her discover the brand-new crib next to the bed. And in the kitchen was a high chair. Both items he had purchased at Hannah Cooper's store.

Julianna smiled as she said out loud, "Good morning, Lord Jesus. Thank You for another day of life. Thank You for my wonderful salvation, and for bringing Jack into my life. I'm so...comfortable...with him, Lord. Something I never had with Jean-Claude, as You well know."

She steeled herself for the initial shock of cold air outside the warm bed, then threw back the covers and slid her feet into slippers before hurrying to the wool robe draped over the wooden chair in front of the dresser. She tossed her black tresses outside the collar of the robe and cinched the sash around her slender waist, then moved to the crib and looked at her precious little daughter, who was under a thick cover of small blankets. Dark hair, a button nose, and chubby cheeks showed from under the nightcap Larissa wore. Her sweet little mouth reminded Julianna of a soft spring flower.

When she glanced toward the windows, she could see the

sky was gray and heavily clouded. She crossed the bedroom to peer out a slightly frosted pane and could see a fresh coating of snow on the ground and on the roofs of neighboring houses. Evergreens and naked-limbed cottonwoods, elms, and oaks were coated with snow. Gray squirrels hopped through the yard, playing happily.

Julianna shivered slightly, then hurried to the parlor where she removed the lid on the potbellied stove and built a fire. When it was popping, she returned to the bedroom and stood over her sleeping baby, looking down at her with a heart full of love.

"Thank You, Lord," she said, "for this sweet little doll. She is such a delight."

Larissa moved her head slightly, took a short breath, and settled quietly in slumber again.

Barely moving her lips, Julianna whispered, "Larissa, darling, God has been good to you, too. Da-da loves you in a big way. I know he will be a good daddy to you. We'll be very happy with him. Jesus lives in Mommy's heart and in your new daddy's heart, and this will make for a beautiful home."

The baby stirred again, then settled down once more.

"And honey," Julianna whispered, leaning down a little closer, "someday when you get old enough to understand about God and about sin, you will open your heart to Jesus, for you will be raised in a Christian home like Pastor Kelly preached about last Sunday night. I'm so thankful that Jesus' blood keeps you safe while you're little like this. Mommy doesn't want anything ever to happen to you, but if it did, I know you would be waiting for Daddy and me in heaven."

Warmth from the potbellied stove began to creep through the house as Julianna quietly brushed her hair before the mirror at the dresser. Electricity in her hair made little snapping noises.

Suddenly there was a knock at the front door.

She smiled at herself in the mirror and laid down the hair-brush. This early-morning visit had become Jack's ritual since the first day.

She pulled the neck of her robe up tight under her chin and hurried to open the door. "Good morning, Deputy Marshal Bower! Do come in out of the cold."

Jack's breath whitened the air. "Thank you, ma'am."

He closed the door and ran his gaze over her face and hair. "Are you always this beautiful so early in the morning?"

"Aren't you kind," she said, laughing. "I'm glad I look that way to you, and I hope I always will."

"No doubt about it. I'm on my way to the office, as usual. Just wanted to see if you and Larissa are all right, and if you need anything."

"We're fine, and at this point we have everything we need."

"She awake yet?"

"No."

Jack snapped his fingers. "Missed again. Oh, well, I'll get my hug and kiss later."

"I talk to her sometimes when she's asleep."

"You do?"

"Mm-hmm. I was telling her a little while ago how happy we're going to be when her mommy marries the man she's learning to call Da-da, and he adopts her as his own little girl."

Jack moved close to Julianna and enfolded her in his arms. She responded by wrapping her arms around him and laying her head against his muscular chest.

"Sweetheart," Jack said, inhaling deeply and letting it out in a slow sigh, "it's so wonderful to know you really love me and are going to marry me. God has been so good to this ol' ex-drifter."

Julianna hugged him tight. "He's been awfully good to this

ex-rich girl and widow, too. I still feel like I'm dreaming. Oh, darling, we're going to be so happy when God makes us husband and wife!"

Jack kissed her soundly and said, "I'd better get to work on time, or Marshal Mangum may be looking for another deputy!"

Lance Mangum was putting a coffeepot on the potbellied stove in his office when he heard the familiar sound of boots stomping off snow. Then the door opened and his deputy stepped inside.

"Good morning, Jack," said Mangum with a smile. "I'll have the coffee hot in a few minutes. Had breakfast?"

"Yes, sir." Jack removed his mackinaw and hung it on a peg by the door and topped it with his hat. "Had a good breakfast with Jacob Kates. Between the two of us, we made it edible. Scrambled eggs and biscuits with cream gravy. Of course, in a few months I'll be eating Julianna's cooking. I'm sure it'll be better than what Jacob and I throw together. So what did you have for breakfast?"

"Haven't had it yet, but I'm about to."

Jack moved closer to the stove. Noting only the coffeepot, he said, "You mean you're having coffee and nothing else for breakfast?"

"That's about the size of it."

Jack frowned. "I don't get it. I've been upstairs in that apartment of yours. You've got cupboards with food in them and a nice stove to cook your meals on."

Lance shrugged his wide shoulders. "I don't do a whole lot of cooking. About half the time I eat at Glenda's Café. Sure would be great to have a good cook commanding that kitchen upstairs."

Jack chuckled. "Well, then, go to work on it."

Lance shook his head. "Good women are hard to find. I'm sure glad for you, Jack. It's easy to see that Julianna is the right woman for you, and I wish you all the happiness possible."

Jack grinned. "Thanks, boss. Julianna's a wonderful little lady. Truly I've been blessed. I don't deserve her, but I'm sure going to keep her."

Lance gave him a droll look and said, "That was some way to meet the woman of your dreams, I'll give you that. She's traveling with her baby to Idaho, you kidnap her to protect your own hide, and you end up marrying her."

"That wasn't my doing, boss. That was God's doing. Only He can take chaos and make order of it. And my life was total chaos."

Lance nodded.

"While we're talking about women," said Jack, "I overheard someone say that you're sweet on Heidi Lindgren. Is there anything to it?"

Mangum moved away from the stove and sat down at his desk. He picked up a pencil and toyed with it for a few seconds, then said, "Since you're my deputy and we're good friends, Jack, I'll give you a straight answer. Yes, there's something to it. I'm so in love with Heidi that it hurts."

"I see. And how does she feel about you?"

"Well ...she's very nice to me. But that's where it ends. A few weeks ago she even took the time in the midst of her busy schedule to make me a nice shirt. In fact, I'm wearing it."

"Hmm! So just out of the blue, Heidi up and made a shirt for you."

"Right. And believe me, it was a sacrifice of her time. Her business at that dress shop is booming. She's making dresses for the women of the town, the fort, and all around the Fort Bridger area. I know for a fact that she often works fourteen, fifteen hours a day."

Jack moved his head slowly back and forth. "Well, I'd say with a schedule like that, making the shirt for you shows that she likes you a lot."

"I drew the same conclusion." Lance toyed nervously with the pencil. "But when I've tried to romance her, she sort of pulls into a shell."

Jack sat down in a chair near the desk. "Tell me why you think that is. You bathe regularly. Your breath doesn't smell. You certainly aren't ugly."

Lance chuckled at his deputy's stab at humor. "I figure it's because Heidi's quite involved in the church, and I don't even attend. She doesn't want to get involved with me on anything more than a friendship basis."

"You have something against the church?"

"Oh no. They're all nice people. Pastor Kelly and Rebecca are top drawer. It's just that..."

"What?"

"Well, this business about being saved. I just don't cotton to it. Sort of fringes on fanaticism. I know you're a member of the church, Jack, and I don't mean any offense."

Jack nodded without comment.

Mangum nervously adjusted his position on the chair. "Heidi has talked to me about this salvation business, but I've told her that if I live a decent life, I figure it'll be all right when I die and stand before God."

"Boss, I've only been a Christian for a few weeks, and I don't consider myself qualified to give you all the proper answers. But let me ask you to ponder one question."

"What's that?"

"If you could be all right before God when you face Him at the end of this life just because you lived decently, why did Jesus Christ bother to leave heaven, take on human flesh, die on the cross, and raise Himself from the grave? Why did He do all of that if you could live good enough to go to heaven?"

Lance swallowed hard. "I...I haven't really looked at it from that point of view."

"Think about it, will you?"

Mangum nodded.

The coffeepot on the stove was giving off a bubbling sound. Lance rose from the chair. "I'll pour my breakfast now. Want some?"

"'Bout half a cup will be fine."

Lance handed Jack his cup and sat down again behind the desk.

"You do make good coffee, boss," Jack said. "You're going to make some gal a good wife."

The marshal scowled. "You're cute, you know that?"

Jack shrugged. "So what can I do about it? If you're cute, you're cute. Seriously, Marshal, I think I might know why you can't get any further with Heidi. Recently, Pastor Kelly taught a Sunday school lesson on marriage, and he brought up that God's Word warns against Christians marrying non-Christians. The pastor gave examples of Christians he knew who had disregarded God's warning and married unbelievers. The results were disastrous."

Lance kept his gaze on his deputy while sipping coffee.

"You see, boss, when a person is born again, he has a hunger for the Word and a desire to hear it taught and preached, and he wants to be in church to fellowship with other Christians. Born-again people are not perfect, and they can even get out of fellowship with the Lord at times, but they won't stay there. Jesus said His sheep follow Him. They are going the same direction He is, and they can't be happy and contented living out of fellowship with Him.

"When a Christian is married to a person who isn't going the same direction he or she is and doesn't have the same desires, it makes the marriage very difficult. And when children come along, they're pulled in two directions. Pastor Kelly's lesson really made sense to me."

Lance nodded. "Thanks for telling me. That helps me understand why Heidi doesn't let me get close to her. She's a sweet girl, Jack, but there's a wall between us."

"Yes. And according to what Pastor Kelly taught on the subject, the wall is there because Heidi knows what the Bible says on the subject."

They heard feet stomping on the boardwalk outside the door; then the door opened. When Jack saw light come into Lance's eyes, he pivoted on the chair to see who had come in. Both men rose to their feet at Heidi's entrance.

"Good morning, gentlemen," she said, closing the door and moving across the room. There was a package in her gloved hands.

"Little present for you, Marshal," she said, moving up to the desk.

Lance blinked. "Heidi, it's not my birthday, and Christmas isn't till next month. What's this?"

"Open it and see."

Jack watched with interest as his boss opened the package and pulled out a beautiful black-and-white Western-cut shirt.

"Oh, Heidi! I really like this! But you shouldn't have done it. I know how busy you are."

Heidi smiled. "I'm not too busy to make a shirt for my favorite town marshal. Actually, Lance, this shirt is to replace the one you were wearing in the shoot-out. I couldn't have you short on shirts now, could I?"

Lance gave her a tender look. "Thank you, Heidi. I'll treasure this shirt just as I do the one I'm wearing right now."

"I'm glad for that," she said with a smile. "Well, I have to get going."

As she turned toward the door, Lance said, "Ah...Heidi?

Could you and I have a private little talk sometime soon?"

She turned around to face him. "I could make time right now, if you wish. I don't have to open the shop for about twenty minutes."

Jack headed for his coat and hat. "Tell you what, Marshal, I'll go out and patrol the town a bit."

"The town does need patrolling," Mangum said, a slanted grin capturing his mouth.

Jack put on his hat and mackinaw. "See you both later."

When the door closed, Heidi moved toward the desk where Lance stood feasting his eyes on her beauty.

"Please sit down," he said. When Heidi was seated, Lance sat down behind the desk. "Jack just explained something to me, Heidi."

"What was that?"

"That Christians are told in the Bible not to marry non-Christians. Is that why you haven't let me get close to you?"

She closed her eyes, silently asked the Lord to give her wisdom, then said, "Yes, Lance. I haven't talked to you along this line because...well, because you've told me that you're in love with me. If...if I told you that I was in love with you, and explained what God says about believers not being unequally yoked to unbelievers, I feared that you might make a false profession of faith in Jesus Christ just so you could win me to yourself. Your eternal soul is in the balance, and your profession of faith needs to be real."

Lance stared at the desktop for a moment, then raised his eyes to meet her gaze. "I appreciate your concern for me, Heidi, believing what you do, but—"

"But you don't believe that you need salvation." Compassion showed in Heidi's eyes. "Lance, you need to hear the preaching of God's Word. You've said that you would come to church sometime. Will you come and listen with an open heart and mind?"

Lance wrestled with the idea for a moment, then looked her in the eye and said, "I will, Heidi. I'll come to church sometime soon."

The sun was lowering in the sky when Heidi heard the little bell jingle above her shop door. She left the sewing table in the back room and moved past the dress forms of various sizes that lined the narrow hallway.

"Hello, Julianna. What can I do for you?"

"I wanted to buy some fabric. You stock your own materials, don't you, Heidi?"

"Yes. I buy them through catalogs from the manufacturers back east. Did you want a dress made?"

"Ah…no. Jack came by the house at noon to check on Larissa and me. He was telling me about the shirts you made for Marshal Mangum. I'd like to make Jack a couple of shirts myself."

Heidi's eyes lit up. "Really? You're a seamstress?"

"Well, I never did it professionally, but I used to make shirts for Jean-Claude. Those were dress shirts, of course, but I believe I could make the Western style like the men wear here. Could you sell me some material?"

"Well, of course, honey. Let's go look at some in the back room."

As they made their way down the narrow hallway, Heidi said, "Will you let me see those shirts when you finish them?"

"Certainly. But why?"

"Deputy marshals don't make a lot of money, do they?"

"No."

"I'm looking for a seamstress to hire. She wouldn't have to work here in the store at all. She could do the work at home. I assume you've made dresses."

"Lots of them. Even though I was raised in a wealthy family, I still made a lot of my own dresses. I just love to sew, and I like to work on patterns I've made up myself."

They stopped at a long row of shelves loaded with bolts of cloth.

Heidi set her soft gaze on Julianna. "Would you be interested in sewing for me if I find your work acceptable?"

"I sure would. Of course, I'd have to ask Jack first, but I'm sure he would agree that I should do it. I'd just love it, Heidi!"

"All right. When you've finished the first shirt, bring it to me and let me see it."

"Certainly. And I have some dresses that I made in New Orleans. Would you like to see those?"

"Of course. Tell you what—why don't I drop by and look at them even before you make the first shirt?"

"Come on by the house. You're welcome anytime."

It was just the Cooper family at the dinner table that evening. Jack Bower and Jacob Kates were eating Julianna's cooking at Jack's house.

While feasting on the delicious meal of fried chicken, canned corn, mashed potatoes, and chicken gravy, the Cooper children talked about Christmas only a month away.

Patty Ruth furtively gave Biggie a bite of chicken beneath the table while chewing a mouthful of mashed potatoes. She ran her gaze over the faces of her family and spoke around the food in her mouth. "I hobe eb'rybody 'mebers thad nex' mumf is my b'thday."

"Patty Ruth!" said Hannah. "Haven't I told you not to talk with food in your mouth?"

"Well, B.J. dub." Biggie was licking the little redhead's

fingers beneath the table and wagging his tail with delight.

"I don' neither!" objected the eight-year-old.

Hannah cleared her throat gently. "B.J., I've had the same problem with you, too. It just hasn't happened as often as with your little sister. Am I correct?"

"Yes, ma'am," B.J. said.

Patty Ruth swallowed the entire mouthful as quickly as possible.

"Get it all down?" Hannah said, a mild frown on her face.

Patty Ruth nodded. "Yes, ma'am."

"Did Biggie get all of his down?"

Patty Ruth's face turned crimson. There was no sense denying it. Her mother not only had eyes in the back of her head, she also had supersensitive hearing. "Um…yes, ma'am."

"All right," said Hannah, "now what was it you were try-ing to say when your mouth was full?"

"Oh. I was sayin' that I hoped ever'body remembers that nex' month is my birthday."

"How could we forget?" Chris said. "You start reminding us two days after you've just had the last one."

"Yeah," said B.J. "How could we forget?"

An indignant look captured the little redhead's face. "Well when we lived in Missouri, both of you boys gave me Christmas presents, an' the tags said, 'Merry Christmas an' Happy Birthday.' I wanna be sure that don't happen this year. Nobody else in this fam'ly gets the same present for Christmas that they do for their birthday!"

Chris snickered. "Well, that happens, P.R., because you're so naughty. You really shouldn't get any presents at all."

Patty Ruth's blue eyes widened. "Oh yeah? I'm not naughty! You boys are the ones who are naughty! How 'bout las' week when Mama tol' you to be sure an' let Biggie out before bedtime, an' you didn' do it? Huh? How 'bout that? If you'd put him out like Mama tol' you, he wouldn' have…have…did what he did on the floor!"

"Oh?" said B.J. "Well, that's not as bad as you settin' the curtains on fire in yours and Mary Beth's room! You're the one that's naughty!"

"I didn' do that on purpose! You an' Chris were so lazy, you didn' let Biggie out on purpose!"

"Yeah, sure," said B.J. "You set those curtains on fire 'cause—"

"Patty Ruth was carrying the candleholder for me that night, B.J.," cut in Mary Beth. "She did not touch the flame to the curtains deliberately!"

"That's enough!" said Hannah, a flinty look in her eye. "No more arguing! You boys are older than your baby sister. You shouldn't be picking on her."

"We were only kidding, Mama," Chris said.

"Yeah," said B.J. "We were just kiddin'."

"All right, then, you boys apologize to Patty Ruth and tell her you were only kidding. And you ask her forgiveness for saying what you did, even though you were only kidding."

When she saw a hint of rebellion in her sons' faces, she said, "I'm waiting."

Still, they remained silent.

Hannah's back arched. "All right. Chris, kiss your little sister!"

The fourteen-year-old knew better than to refuse. He had been through this exercise before. He shoved back his chair and rounded the table to where Patty Ruth sat.

"Kiss her and tell her you didn't mean what you said about her being naughty," said Hannah. "Apologize and ask her forgiveness."

Chris bent down to Patty Ruth's level and looked her in the eye. "I really didn't mean what I said about you being naughty, P.R. I'm sorry." He planted a kiss on her cheek. "Do you forgive me?"

Little sister studied his face, then said, "All right, Chris. I forgive you."

B.J. was next.

When the deed was done, Hannah said, "Now that harmony is once again restored to the Cooper household, we can talk about Christmas. Of course we will all remember that Patty Ruth's birthday is five days after Christmas, and that will be a separate occasion...even when it comes to presents."

When she had gone to bed, Hannah thought back to the conversation at the supper table. This would be the most difficult Christmas she had ever encountered, and she knew it would be equally as hard on her children. Solomon had dearly loved this most precious holiday and had always gone out of his way to make it special for each of them.

Tears spilled from her eyes as she thought of last Christmas, when Solomon was with them. "Oh, Lord, I miss him more with each passing day. I need Your comforting presence right now."

Suddenly Hannah thought about Christmas a year from now. The baby would be some nine months in age—old enough to notice the candles and popcorn strings on the tree. A small smile captured her lips, and she nestled into her pillow.

CHAPTER EIGHT

The iron gray sky was spitting snow as Matt McDermott finished repairing the barn door. It worked perfectly when he slid it in the metal grooves, and he smiled to himself as he placed his tools in the toolbox. He stepped outside and slid the big door shut.

The wind was picking up, peppering his face with snowflakes as he walked toward the old farmhouse. When he drew near, the back door opened and elderly Chester Neely shuffled out onto the porch, leaning on his cane.

"The door's working fine now, Mr. Neely," Matt said, brushing snowflakes from his eyelashes. "If we don't get a blizzard tonight, I'll be back in the morning to work on that broken stanchion. Should be able to fix it by noon; then I'll start replacing those bad floorboards in the hayloft."

Neely reached a gnarled hand into the bib pocket of his overalls and pulled out a wad of money. Peeling off three one-dollar bills, he extended them to Matt, saying in his aged voice, "I sure do appreciate gettin' all these repairs done in the barn. I've just gotten too crippled up with this arthritis to do that kind of work anymore."

"Well, Mr. Neely, I appreciate getting the work."

Neely grinned, showing near-toothless gums. "You be careful ridin' home, Matt. Snow's comin' harder every minute."

"I will, sir. It's only five miles home. I'll be there before it gets totally dark. And if this doesn't turn into a blizzard, I'll be back in the morning."

The storm was increasing in intensity, and darkness was blanketing the land as Matt drew near his farm. Through the swirling snow he could make out the outlines of the house and outbuildings. Lantern light in the farmhouse windows sent out a welcome.

He turned into the yard and trotted the horse toward the barn, glancing at Holly's window as he passed. She had kept him and Emily awake a good part of the night with her fits of coughing, and she'd been feverish that morning when he left for the Neely place.

Matt guided the horse inside the barn and removed saddle and bridle, then pitched an ample supply of hay in the feed trough along with an oat-barley mixture and pumped water into the small tank.

Emily was at the stove preparing supper when Matt entered the kitchen. She left her steaming skillet and moved toward him as he slipped out of his sheepskin coat.

Matt quickly hung up his coat and hat on pegs, then folded Emily into his arms and kissed her. "How is she?"

"Not good. She's coughing more than when you left for work. The congestion in her chest sounds deeper, and I think her fever is higher."

Matt clenched his teeth. "Let's go take a look at her."

As they walked toward the child's room, Emily said, "I put the mild mustard plasters on her chest three times today and did the towel and steam treatment twice, but it just hasn't seemed to help her. I'll try it some more after supper."

Holly was coughing when her parents entered her bedroom. Her face was as white as the sheet tucked under her chin.

"Hi, sweet baby," Matt said as he kissed her forehead. "Not feeling so good, huh?"

Holly tried to speak, but the effort made her cough and she choked on the fluid deep in her throat. Matt eased her up and patted her back till the strangling sound stopped and she drew a rattling breath.

Matt placed the back of his hand against Holly's flushed cheek. "Emily, I think her fever is definitely higher than it was this morning. I know you've done everything you could, so I'm going to ride to Mountain View right now and bring Dr. Garberson. I'll be back as soon as I can."

"Supper's almost ready, Matt. You've worked hard all day, and you've got to be hungry."

"Supper will have to wait, honey. Holly needs Dr. Garberson's attention right now."

Emily nodded.

The wind was howling around the eaves of the house, slapping snow against the window panes.

Worry lined Emily's brow. "The storm's getting worse, Matt. You'll have to hurry."

"I will." He bent down and stroked Holly's fevered brow. "Papa's going after the doctor, Holly. I'll be back with him as soon as I can. I love you."

"Love you." The words emerged as a hacking whisper.

Emily felt panic rise in her as she followed her husband to the kitchen. While Matt was putting on his coat and his hat she said, "Honey, I'm really worried about this storm. I know Holly needs Dr. Garberson, but it's turning into a blizzard out there. You could get caught in it and freeze to death. Let me go ahead and put more mustard packs on her and do some more steaming. The storm will probably be over by morning. Then you can go after the doctor. I can't stand the thought of you in that blizzard."

Matt gave her a quick hug. "I can make it to town, honey. Our little girl's life is at stake."

"I know, but so is yours if you go out there. Matt, I love

you, and I can't stand the thought of losing you."

"I'll be fine. If Holly has pneumonia, she could die without Dr. Garberson's help."

"But—"

"I have to go, Emily." He kissed her soundly, then turned and opened the door. "I'll be back with the doctor in a little while. I love you."

Emily went to the kitchen window and peered out into the wind-driven snow. The lantern lights in the windows gave her a vague view of her husband as he passed close to the house and waved then was swallowed instantly by the storm.

Her own appetite gone, Emily took the skillet and pans off the stove and put on a pan of water to heat. She poured another pan half full of cold water, picked up a washcloth, and hurried to Holly's room.

While she bathed Holly's face, neck, and wrists in an effort to reduce the fever, a hacking cough seized the little girl. After nearly a half hour of laboring to bring Holly's temperature down, Emily wrapped her in a heavy blanket and carried her to the kitchen table. She held Holly on her lap and bent her forward over the steaming pan of water while holding a large towel over her head to get as much of the steam in her lungs as possible.

As she sat there, Emily thought back to the day when she first learned she had another baby in her womb. A wan smile graced her lips as she recalled the day her precious little Holly was born strong and healthy. What a joyous day! She recalled singing praises to the Lord until she was totally exhausted.

And then…miracle of miracles, she had given birth to a second full-term, healthy baby. Michael had been such a blessing to their Kentucky home, and Holly was fascinated with him. Matt and Emily had great dreams for their two children.

Then little Michael died.

Ever since losing him, Emily had clung to Holly. Her precious daughter gave so much love that it eased the pain of Michael's absence.

While Holly drew deep breaths of steam, Emily thought about her wonderful, loving husband who was out in the howling storm.

Oh, Lord, thought Emily, *I love them both so much. Please keep Matt safe in the storm, and please never let anything happen to take Holly from my arms.*

Soon the water cooled, ceasing to give off steam. "All right, sweetheart," Emily said, "back to bed now."

Holly held tightly to her mother's neck as she struggled to breathe through the congestion in her chest.

Emily laid her in the bed and pulled the covers up under her chin. "You haven't had anything for your tummy since I gave you the broth this afternoon, honey. Do you want something?"

"I'm not hungry, Mama," Holly wheezed. "Could I just have some water?"

"Of course."

When Holly had taken a few sips, Emily said, "You go to sleep now. Doing the steam treatment is hard for you. I know you're tired."

The child nodded, coughing again. The rattle in her chest sounded deeper every time she coughed.

Emily blinked against tears and caressed her daughter's cheek. "I'll be back to look in on you in a little while. You go to sleep."

As soon as Emily reached the hallway, she hurried to the kitchen and sat down at the table to weep. "Oh, dear Lord," she sobbed, "please don't take my little girl! She's sick, Lord. Very sick! I beg You to bring Matt and the doctor safely through the storm. Please, God! Please let Dr. Garberson make her better!"

She drew a shuddering breath. "Dear Lord, You took two babies from my womb dead, and You took little Michael from my arms when he was barely a year old. I'm not bitter toward You, Lord. You know my heart. I know You don't make mistakes. In Your great wisdom You saw fit to take them from me, and I know they're in heaven with You. But now my little Holly is so very sick. I couldn't stand to lose her, Lord. Please make her well."

Emily felt sudden nausea as the stark memory of the second Pawnee attack on the wagon train flooded her mind. She had almost lost Holly then...

It was just past noon, and there was no shelter from the fierce sun on the treeless Nebraska prairie. The women were putting the lunch dishes and utensils away, preparing to resume their westward trek.

At the McDermott wagon, Matt was using buckets to water the oxen while Emily was inside the wagon, making little clattering and tinkling noises as she put things away. Holly was talking to two children beside the wagon—Maryanne Whicker and Bobby Thompson.

"Would you ask your mom, Holly?" Maryanne asked.

"Sure. She won't care, I know."

Holly went to the rear of the wagon and lifted a foot onto the first of three steps her father had built to help her climb in.

"Mama..."

Emily shut the lid on a wooden box and looked at her daughter. "Yes, honey?"

"Could Bobby and Maryanne ride in our wagon so we can play together?"

"It's fine with me, honey." Emily moved to the rear of the wagon so she could see the other two children. "Bobby...Maryanne...we'd love to have you ride in our wagon this afternoon, if it's all right with your parents. Go ask them, will you?"

"Sure will, Mrs. McDermott!" said Bobby, hurrying away.

"Be right back to ride with you, Holly," said Maryanne. Then she dashed toward her parents' wagon.

"You're the best mama in all the world," Holly told Emily.

"Why do you say that, sweetheart?"

"'Cause lots of the mamas in the wagon train won't let children ride with their kids in their wagons."

"I know, honey, but I don't see why. I know that riding in the wagons hour after hour, all day long, gets boring. If you have someone to play with, it helps make the trip better. Right?"

"Uh-huh. It's lots more fun."

Matt was hanging a couple of buckets on the side of the wagon next to the water barrel when he saw the Thompsons and the Whickers coming his way. Bobby Thompson and Maryanne Whicker were running ahead of their parents.

The children reached Matt first. "Mr. McDermott," Bobby said, "me and Maryanne are gonna ride in your wagon this afternoon with Holly."

"Oh? Well, that sounds like a good idea to me."

"Holly asked me if it would be all right, Matt," said Emily as she climbed down from the rear of the wagon. "I told Bobby and Maryanne to ask their parents."

Matt nodded, then turned to the parents as they drew up.

"Emily," Darla Thompson said, "the kids told us you gave them permission to ride in your wagon with Holly this afternoon. We thought we'd best ask you."

"I sure did," said Emily.

"You sure you can stand the giggling?" Burt Whicker said. "You know how little girls giggle."

"Especially when boys tease them, which I know my son will do," said Rex Thompson.

"I think I can stand it," Emily replied. "I'd love to have them."

The parents lectured their children about being good in the McDermott wagon and minding Holly's mother. Both children promised to be good and happily climbed into the bed of the wagon with Holly.

An hour later, Matt was riding beside the wagon, talking with Emily about their future life in Wyoming. The three five-year-olds were laughing and squealing and having a good time in the back of the wagon.

"Just a minute," Matt said and tugged slightly at the reins to let the wagon move ahead so he could guide his horse to the rear of the wagon.

Holly stopped giggling when she saw Matt looking in on them. "Papa, Bobby's teasing us. He says boys are smarter than girls. Tell him they aren't."

"Well, how can I do that, honey? It's the truth. Boys are smarter than girls."

"Mr. McDermott!" said Maryanne. "How can you say that?"

Matt laughed. "It's easy. Listen. Boys are smarter than girls."

"Papa! You're supposed to be on my side!"

"Oh no," said Matt. "Us boys have to stick together!"

Bobby giggled and flipped one of Holly's pigtails. "See there? I knew your papa would say boys are smarter!"

"Yeah?" challenged Holly. "My mama wouldn't! I'll just go up front and ask her!"

Even as Holly spoke, the air was filled with Hank Dekins's voice, shouting, "Indians!"

Hank was on his horse beside the lead wagon driven by Clancy O'Rourke.

The Pawnees came at a gallop from a gully where they had been hiding.

"Too late to form a circle!" Hank shouted. "Go, Clancy!"

O'Rourke put the ox team to a run as Hank rode swiftly

alongside the train, telling the drivers there was no time to form a circle; they must keep up with the lead wagon. Hank shouted for everyone with guns to open fire on the Indians as soon as they were within range.

Matt shouted for the children in his wagon to lay flat on the floor and stay there. Emily had the oxen moving as fast as they could go and was keeping up with Clancy. As Matt pulled his rifle from the saddleboot, he heard Emily call back to the children and ask if they were flat on the floor.

The Indians began shooting first, and the men and women in the wagons and the men on horseback returned fire while the wagons raced across the grassy prairie.

Bullets ripped into the wagons, some ricocheting and whining like angry bees.

After a short time, the Pawnees ran low on ammunition and galloped away, leaving their dead and wounded behind.

When the Indians were out of sight, Hank Dekins rode to the front of the fast-moving train and signaled for the wagons to stop.

Matt drew up close to his wagon as Emily halted the oxen, her hands trembling. He noted the bullet holes in the sides of the wagon and rips in the canvas top where Pawnee slugs had struck the top.

Emily turned on the seat to look into the wagon, but boxes, blankets, and articles of clothing had fallen from their places during the bumpy ride and obstructed her view.

"Holly!" she called. "Holly, are you kids all right? Bobby? Maryanne?"

As Matt headed toward the rear of the wagon with his heart in his throat, Emily leaned from the seat and said shakily, "Ma-a-a-att, I can't get an answer from the children!"

Hank Dekins passed by as Matt flipped the latches on the tailgate. "Matt, everything all right?"

"I'm not sure yet."

"Be back after I see about the others," Hank said.

Matt hopped up on the tailgate and began throwing aside boxes, clothing, and whatever else was in his way. "Holly! Hey, kids, you okay?"

He threw aside the last blankets that were on top of the children and felt his heart lurch at the sight of blood.

Emily's scream shredded the air as the parents of Bobby and Maryanne reached the wagon.

Naomi Whicker dashed up beside Emily, her eyes probing the interior of the wagon as Matt dropped to his knees, unable to get a breath. "Maryanne!" she wailed.

Darla Thompson screamed when she saw the three children crumpled in a tight heap and their blood-soaked clothing.

Matt lifted the limp form of Bobby Thompson and slowly turned to hand the boy to Rex Thompson. Other people were collecting at the rear of the McDermott wagon as Darla Thompson screamed Bobby's name and then fell to the ground in a dead faint.

Matt lifted Maryanne Whicker off of Holly and handed her body to her father.

"No-o-o-o!" wailed the little girl's mother. "My baby-y-y-y! No-o-o-o!"

Hank Dekins was off his horse now and pressing through the crowd.

Emily stood frozen as she watched Matt bend over Holly. She sucked in a sharp breath when she heard Holly whimper.

Matt carefully examined his daughter, trying to find the wounds that had soaked her dress with blood. It took only seconds to realized the blood was that of her two little friends. Holly was unscathed.

There was weeping and wailing among the travelers while the McDermotts held their little girl in their arms, thankful she was still alive.

In addition, two women and another child had been killed, and three men wounded.

That night, as the people sat around the big campfire, mourning their dead, Emily held Holly close to her breast and sobbed with a combination of relief that she still had her child and grief for the others who had been killed, especially the children riding in her wagon.

When everyone returned to their wagons, Holly was put to bed and Emily fell apart. Matt tried to soothe her, but all she could say was she wanted to go back to Kentucky where there were no bloodthirsty Indians.

Matt held her in his arms as he talked to her. "Honey, listen to me. We have no home in Kentucky. You know we're low on money. We have no choice. We've got to go on to Wyoming."

She looked up at him by the light of the nearby fire and stared for a long moment. There was a strange look in her eyes akin to the look Matt had seen there when little Michael died.

"Emily," he said softly, "everything's going to be all right. We'll have a happy life in Wyoming."

"If we ever get to Wyoming," she said in a broken voice.

The next morning, after a sleepless night, Emily moved like a zombie while cooking breakfast for her family. Matt gave Holly a spit bath to get the blood out of her hair and off her skin. While he helped her into a clean dress, he noticed the acrid smell of burning food.

When he climbed out of the wagon, he found Emily sitting by the fire, staring at the burned bacon and pancakes in the skillet without seeing them. He removed the skillet from the fire, then bent over his wife and looked into her eyes. There was no sign that she knew he was there.

For the next week, Emily was unable to drive the wagon. Matt tied his horse to the tailgate and drove while Emily sat on the seat beside him, holding Holly in her arms and staring blankly into space. Over and over she mumbled about lost babies.

When the Rocky Mountains came into view, Emily was lucid for the first time in seven days.

Holding Holly as usual, she turned to Matt and said, "Where are we now?"

Matt smiled. "We're in Wyoming, sweetheart. See the Rockies out there?"

Emily turned her glassy gaze westward. "Uh-huh."

A minute or so passed, then she said, "If Holly is ever taken from me, I won't be able to stand it."

Matt put an arm around her and said softly, "Nothing is going to happen to Holly. The Lord will take care of her, and you will be fine."

Emily's eyes slowly gained focus, and she turned to Matt. "Yes, darling. Yes. You are right. The Lord won't let anything happen to my sweet little Holly. He took our other babies, but He will never take Holly. She will always be with me, and I'll be fine."

CHAPTER NINE

Emily got up from the table and moved like a sleepwalker toward the parlor window. She pressed her face to the frosty glass and saw what appeared to be the snowy equivalent of a waterfall, as countless flakes poured down in churning wind-driven currents and piled up on the porch.

When she turned from the window and looked down the hall toward Holly's room, her attention was drawn to a daguerreotype of Matt, Holly, and herself on a small table next to a softly glowing lantern. She walked to it slowly, then picked it up and looked into Matt's eyes, speaking to him as if he were in the room.

"Yes, darling. You are right. The Lord won't let anything happen to my sweet little Holly. He took our other babies, but He will never take Holly."

Emily didn't seem to notice that the fire had died out in the fireplace, leaving only ashes and some red coals.

Still moving like a sleepwalker, she went to Holly's room and found her asleep. She touched her daughter's hot, moist brow. "Mama will put some cold water on you again, honey."

Holly coughed in her sleep, the rattle coming from deep in her chest.

"Papa will be here with Dr. Garberson pretty soon, sweetheart," Emily whispered.

She could hear the wind whining through the eaves as she

went to the kitchen and returned with a pan of cold water and a washcloth and towel.

Holly didn't stir while Emily repeatedly bathed her forehead, temples, neck, and wrists.

Some time later Emily tucked the covers under Holly's chin and said, "Sleep on, honey. Mama will be back in a little while."

She shuffled to the kitchen and set the pan of water on the cupboard without emptying it. A violent trembling seized her at the sudden memory of the second Pawnee attack. She raised a shaky hand to her mouth and began to weep as she relived the horror of the moment when Matt had found the children and lifted the blood-soaked little bodies out of the wagon.

As visions of that terrible day flooded her mind, Emily lost all track of time. When her tears finally subsided, she heard the sound of chimes from the grandfather clock in the parlor. She sat up with a start and moved her lips silently with each chime. Ten o'clock, and Matt had not yet returned with Dr. Garberson.

The wind shrieked around the house, rattling the windows, and Emily could hear icy snow crystals pelting the panes. She turned unseeing eyes toward the kitchen window and said in a hollow monotone, "They'll be here soon. Matt always keeps his word. They'll be here. It's just the storm slowing them down."

She headed for Holly's room, talking to Matt as if he could hear her. "I know, honey, I know. You're late because of the storm. But it's all right. Holly and I are okay."

She paused at the door to Holly's room and gazed on the small form beneath the covers, focusing on the auburn hair and pretty face with the dusting of freckles.

"Yes, darling. You're right," she said in a thin whisper. "The Lord won't let anything happen to my sweet little Holly."

She moved toward the bed like a shadow, and what she

saw brought a smile to her lips. "You're sleeping good now, sweetheart. You're not coughing, and that's wonderful. This time the steam treatment helped, didn't it? Oh, yes…that's really wonderful!"

She touched Holly's brow, and a broad smile spread across her face. "Well, isn't that something! Your fever's broken. You're going to get well, honey!"

There was a folded blanket at the foot of Holly's bed. Emily picked it up, let it fall open to its full length, and laid it on the chair. Then she lifted Holly's covers, saying in little more than a whisper, "I know you're sleeping well, honey, but Mama wants to hold you. I'll try not to wake you up. We'll go into the parlor so I can tell Papa and Dr. Garberson how much better you are."

She lifted Holly into her arms. "My, you are relaxed, aren't you? You feel extra heavy. I guess it's because you're sleeping so soundly."

As she carried Holly down the hall toward the parlor, she continued to talk to her. "It's so wonderful that you're not coughing anymore, honey. Won't Papa and Dr. Garberson be surprised?"

Emily sat down in her favorite rocking chair, taking no notice of the chill in the room, and adjusted Holly's limp form on her lap as she tucked the blanket around her.

She snuggled her little girl close and leaned over to press an ear to her chest. She listened intently for a long moment, then another smile spread over her lips. "Isn't this something, Holly? I can't even hear a rattle in your chest anymore. Papa is going to be so happy! You just rest now."

Earlier that evening, Dr. William Garberson and his wife had been settling down in front of their parlor fireplace when they heard a horse whinny.

"Someone's here," said Alma Garberson, rising from the chair.

Dr. Garberson set aside the book he had just picked up. "I'll go, dear."

Even as he spoke, there was a loud knock on the door.

Alma followed him.

When the doctor opened the door, a blast of cold air blew snow into the hallway. He quickly stepped aside, motioning for the man to enter, then pushed the door closed against the force of the wind.

"Matt! Whatever brings you here must be something mighty serious to come out on a night like this."

Matt's clothing and hat were caked with snow. "Evening, Mrs. Garberson," he said with a nod. Then he said to the doctor, "Yes, sir. Mighty serious. It's Holly."

Alma gasped. "Has she gotten worse?"

"Yes. I wouldn't bother you, Doctor, especially on such a night, but Holly's lungs are full of congestion. She coughs incessantly, and her fever is high…maybe higher than it has ever been. I…I really hate to ask you to go out in the storm, but Holly needs you desperately."

Garberson glanced at his wife, then said, "Storm or no storm, Matt, you don't need to feel bad about asking me to come to your little daughter at this time of night. I'll gladly do anything I can to help her."

"Thank you, Doctor."

"Now you go in there by the fireplace and warm yourself while I bundle up and get my medical bag."

The two men pushed their way through the blizzard as the wind snatched at their breath and covered them and their horses in a thickening layer of ice and snow. Dr. Garberson was following

Matt McDermott single file through the blinding storm.

Matt had to stop periodically to get his bearings. There was no way he could make out where the road was, so he would stop and wait until he recognized a landmark, then motion for the doctor to follow.

He led Garberson across farm fields and ranch pastures, trying to take as many shortcuts as possible. Several times they strayed the wrong direction and had to backtrack to get on course.

At one point, Matt had come to the edge of a deep gulch and saw it just in time. He pulled rein and Garberson's horse bumped into the rear of his.

"What's the matter?" the doctor shouted, but his words were swept away by the wind.

Matt raised a gloved hand and waved him back, then turned his mount about and moved as close to Garberson as he could and shouted, "Gulch! Too deep!"

The doctor raised a hand to tell him he understood.

Matt took the lead again and rode through a field of snow-laden haystacks, weaving among their hulking forms.

Finally the two men rode into the McDermott yard. The farmhouse windows were aglow with lantern light. Matt led the doctor past the house and inside the barn.

"It's a good thing we told Alma that I'd be staying the night," Garberson said. "I know I'd get lost trying to ride home in this storm. I appreciate your putting me up."

"Least I could do, Doctor," said Matt. "You'll like our guest room, I assure you. Nice big feather bed."

They attended their horses as fast as their frozen fingers would allow; then Matt and the doctor bent into the wind and headed toward the house through the thick curtain of snow. They entered the back door and paused just inside the kitchen to stomp snow from their boots and remove their snow-caked hats and coats.

Matt frowned as he felt the chill of the room. He hung up his coat on a peg beside the door and topped it with his hat.

"Should it be this chilly in here, Matt?" Dr. Garberson asked.

"No. Even though the wind is driving cold air through any cracks it can find, it shouldn't be this cold." He stepped into the hallway with the doctor on his heels and called out, "Emily!"

There was no response.

A few steps took them to Holly's bedroom. Pausing there, they saw that the covers were thrown back and the bed was empty.

"Emily!" Matt called again, heading up the hall. There was a lantern burning in the master bedroom, but it was unoccupied.

Matt hurried toward the front of the house and the parlor. He noted that the fire in the fireplace had gone out. The lantern on the small table burned brightly, showing them Emily rocking back and forth with Holly on her lap.

Not wanting to wake Holly, Matt whispered, "Honey, Dr. Garberson's here. Aren't you about to freeze to death? You've let the fire go out."

When Emily didn't respond, Matt leaned down to look her in the eye. "Emily…"

She kept rocking as if she had not heard him. Her face was creased by lines of strain, and she had a vacant, faraway look in her eyes.

The rafters creaked and windows rattled as the wind lashed the house fitfully.

Matt stepped directly into Emily's line of sight as the doctor moved closer. "Emily, I'm home. Dr. Garberson is with me. He wants to examine Holly."

Emily blinked, and her eyes focused slightly. She studied Matt's face, then said in a slurred voice, "Oh. You're home, Matt. Is it still snowing?"

"Yes, it's still snowing. Dr. Garberson's here to look at Holly. I hate to wake her, but it's necessary." He extended his hands. "Here, honey, let me have her. I'll carry her to her room. You've let the fire go out. I'll get another one going in a minute. Come on. Let me have her, so Dr. Garberson can get started on her."

Emily shook her head. "No need, Matt, darling. Holly's fever is gone, and she's not coughing anymore. There isn't even a sign of a rattle in her chest."

Dr. Garberson leaned down beside Matt. "Emily," he said softly, "I know you're tired, and you've been under a lot of strain with Holly so sick. I'll take her back to her room and examine her. Matt can stay here with you."

Emily squinted at him, then smiled. "Oh, hello, Dr. Garberson. You can go home now. Holly's fine. I did a steam treatment on her after Matt left, and I bathed her in cold water. She isn't coughing anymore, and her fever's gone. She's well now."

"I'll start a fire," said Matt, heading for the fireplace. "You go ahead and look at Holly, Doctor."

Garberson nodded, then drew closer to the little girl. His features tightened as he looked at her pallid face and laid a palm on her brow. He moved his hand from her brow to her chest. After a few seconds, he pulled down a corner of the blanket and closed his fingers gently on the child's wrist.

Emily was studying the doctor with glazed eyes. The only sounds in the room were Matt's fire-building and the howl and whine of the wind. Garberson closed his eyes for a moment, then let go of Holly's wrist and stood with his head down while Emily continued to rock.

A few minutes passed.

When the fire was finally crackling and giving out warmth, Matt turned from the fireplace and noted the physician's stance. "What's the matter, Doctor?" he asked.

Garberson glanced at Matt and said, "I have to take Holly to her room and examine her."

Emily bristled, her mouth turning down. "No, Doctor. It isn't necessary. She's well now. Matt will pay you for coming, but you can go home."

A sick feeling surged within Matt, and he reached out a hand to Holly's brow. It was cold to the touch. He looked at her more closely. His mouth went dry and his heart began to thud in his chest. "Doctor, she...she doesn't seem to be breathing."

Emily shook her head. "She's breathing, Matt, darling. She's just worn out from being so sick."

"Emily, let me have Holly." Matt's breath was coming in short gasps. "Dr. Garberson needs to examine her."

"No!" Emily stiffened and clutched Holly tighter to her breast. "She's well. She doesn't need to be examined."

Garberson laid a hand on Matt's shoulder. "Let's go into the kitchen and talk. We'll be back in a few minutes, Emily," the doctor said.

Emily stared blankly into space as she caressed Holly's hair. "We'll be here," she said. "Holly and me. She's sleeping so peacefully, isn't she?"

Garberson took Matt by the arm and nodded toward the hallway. At the parlor door, Matt looked back for an instant. Emily was rocking slowly, still caressing Holly's hair and talking to her in a low tone.

The doctor guided Matt to the kitchen table and pulled out a chair for him. Suddenly Matt's knees gave way and he sank onto the seat. Garberson eased onto the chair beside him and said, "Holly's been dead for at least a couple of hours. I...I'm so sorry, Matt."

At hearing the doctor's dreaded words, Matt felt a pain stab his heart, and a cry tore from his throat. "No! No, Doctor! This can't be happening! My little girl! No!"

Garberson laid a hand on Matt's arm. "Without question it was pneumonia."

Matt's face twisted. "The storm. If only we could have gotten here sooner."

"It wouldn't have helped," Garberson said softly.

Matt closed his eyes, and for a moment his face was wrenched into a mask of grief and agony. When he finally looked at Garberson through a wall of tears, he moaned, "My precious Holly can't be gone! She can't be!"

The doctor kept his hand on Matt's shoulder as he said, "I'm so sorry. I—"

"Emily will never survive this, Doctor. You saw her in there. She's on the verge of totally losing her mind." Tears slipped down his cheeks and dripped off his chin. "How am I ever going to endure the pain of losing my daughter and watching my wife crack up?"

Matt buried his face in his hands and wept. Suddenly he gulped and stood up. "Excuse me, Doctor," he said, and dashed into the hall.

The doctor followed and saw him enter the master bedroom and close the door.

Inside the master bedroom, the grieving father fell on his knees beside the bed and sobbed. When he was able to bring his emotions under control, he said, "Lord, I come to You because You are 'the friend that sticketh closer than a brother.' You are the only one who has all the answers. At this moment, I need the comfort that only You can give."

Scripture after Scripture began flooding his mind, and when he had the "peace of God which passeth all understanding" in his heart, he prayed earnestly for Emily, asking the Lord to work in her disturbed mind and to give her the same peace.

"Lord," he said, slowly rising to his feet, "I don't understand why You've taken Holly, but I will trust You in spite of it because I know You never make a mistake."

He dried his cheeks with a handkerchief and stepped out into the hallway. Garberson was just coming out of the parlor.

"She's no better, Matt," Garberson said. "I can't get through to her. It's like she's detached from reality. If she were fully present, she would comprehend that Holly is dead."

"What can I do, Doctor? I can't bring my precious little daughter back, but I have to do whatever I can to save Emily from this devastation threatening to claim her."

Garberson rubbed his jaw. "Matt, there is no such thing as a hospital in Wyoming, or even a clinic this side of Cheyenne City that can care for mental patients. If Emily can grasp reality and face the fact that Holly is gone, after a while she may snap out of it. Until that time, when you're working away from home, you'll need to have someone here to look after her."

Matt digested this information silently.

"Of course," said Garberson, "we have to consider the possibility that Emily may never come back to reality. I'll see that you have plenty of sedative powders for her, and I'll explain how and when to use them, but as for the rest, we'll just have to take this one step at a time."

"What's the first step?"

"To make her acknowledge reality. If she's going to get well, she has to do that. The quicker she sees the facts, the quicker she can learn to live with them and start on the road to recovery. Even then it's going to take a mountain of love and care from you."

"I've got more than a mountain of that," said Matt.

"Then let's start right there. You talk to her. Try to make her understand that Holly is dead."

"All right, here goes."

Garberson followed Matt to the parlor.

Emily was still rocking Holly's lifeless body when Matt knelt down in front of her.

Her eyes were glassy, but she managed to focus on his face. "Is Dr. Garberson gone?"

"Ah...no. He's still here." Matt took hold of her hand. "Honey, I need to explain something to you. You know I love you with all my heart, don't you?"

"Of course." Her eyes seemed to look right through him. Then she looked down at Holly. "We know Papa loves us with all of his heart, don't we, Holly?"

Matt clenched his teeth and squeezed back the tears as he said, "Because I love you with all my heart, Emily, I wouldn't lie to you, would I?"

"Of course not."

"All right. Are you listening to me?"

"Mm-hmm."

"All right," he said, squeezing her hand. "You need to understand that Holly is dead, honey. Jesus took her to heaven to be with Him."

Emily looked at him and smiled. "Yes, darling. Yes. You are right. The Lord won't let anything happen to my sweet Holly. He took our other babies, but He will never take Holly. She will always be with me, and I'll be fine."

Matt recalled the moment on the Kansas plains when he had heard those same words come from Emily's lips.

Dr. Garberson touched Matt's shoulder and bent down before the blank-eyed mother. "Emily," he said, "I would like to give you a sedative. You need to go to bed and get a good night's sleep. Matt will take care of Holly."

The words seemed to sink in. Slowly, Emily brought her gaze to Matt. "I should do what Doctor says, shouldn't I?"

"Yes, honey. You need your rest."

Her eyes were a bit clearer as she turned them on

Garberson. "All right, Doctor. I'll take the sedative." Then looking at her husband, she said, "Matt, you will see that Holly has
something to eat, won't you?"

Matt nodded. "I'll take care of her, honey."

Emily relinquished the limp body of her daughter to Matt.
Dr. Garberson helped Emily out of the rocking chair and guided
her down the hall toward the master bedroom. He sat her down
on a chair in the bedroom and said, "I'll be right back."

Emily nodded.

Moments later, Matt entered the bedroom as Dr.
Garberson was helping Emily drink a large glass of sedative
mixed with water.

When she had drained the glass, Garberson said, "That's a
good girl, Emily. Now I'll leave the room so Matt can help you
undress and get into bed."

While Matt was helping Emily into her nightgown, she
said, "Darling, did Holly get enough to eat?"

"Ah…yes."

"Good. Did you put her to bed?"

"Yes. She's in bed."

"She'll sleep good, now that she's well. No more coughing
in her sleep."

"Mm-hmm. Let's get you tucked in now."

As Matt pulled the covers up to Emily's chin, she smiled
and said, "Tell my little girl Mama loves her, won't you?"

Matt swallowed a hot lump. "I…I'll tell her, honey."

"Know what I want to make Holly for Christmas, darling?"

"What?

"A new red dress. Red is her favorite color."

"Yes. She loves red. You close your eyes now and get to
sleep."

Emily reached out from under the covers and took his
hand. Though her eyes were somewhat vacant, she set her gaze

on him and said, "I love you, darling."

"I love you, too, sweetheart." He bent down and kissed her forehead. "See you in the morning."

Matt turned the lantern low and headed for the door. He paused in the doorway and looked back just as Emily said, "Yes, darling. Yes. You're right. The Lord won't let anything happen to my sweet Holly. He took our other babies, but He will never take Holly. She will always be with me, and I'll be fine."

Tears filled Matt's eyes as he stepped into the hall.

CHAPTER TEN

D r. Garberson was turning the logs and poking at the fire when Matt came into the parlor. He could hear the wind whining at the top of the chimney as sparks rushed up from the blazing logs to meet it.

The doctor leaned the poker against the stone fireplace. "I'm sure glad Alma isn't expecting me back tonight. I'd never make it."

Matt nodded "If this storm lasts into or through tomorrow, I guess we've got a doctor in the house."

Garberson moved to one of the overstuffed chairs facing the fireplace and sat down. Matt eased into the other one and stared at the fire.

"While you were putting Emily to bed I examined Holly's body. She definitely had pneumonia."

Matt tried not to give in to the tears that felt hot against his eyelids but couldn't stop them. When he had gotten control he apologized.

Garberson smiled thinly. "You don't have to apologize for being human, my friend. This has been plenty tough on you, as well as on Emily."

Matt blew his nose then stuffed his bandanna back into his hip pocket.

"This mental problem of Emily's," said the doctor, "do you know what might have brought it on?"

"Oh yes. She's shown signs of it before, but Holly's sickness these past few days brought it completely to the surface."

"Tell me about it."

"Well, it's a long story."

The doctor settled back in the chair. "I'm not going anywhere."

While the storm raged on, Matt told Dr. Garberson the whole story of Emily's miscarriages and the loss of their little son; of losing the farm in Kentucky; of the difficult journey to Wyoming in the wagon train and particularly the two Pawnee attacks. He explained the details of the attacks and what they did to Emily, including the nightmares she had suffered ever since.

Garberson listened intently, nodding and making small sounds of sympathy. When Matt had brought him up to the moment, the doctor said, "I understand now. From what I observed tonight, I can tell you that Emily's mind has been fragmented like broken glass. Her mind has sustained some powerful blows, and each blow has further weakened her mental fiber. There's a possibility this all started with some serious mental wound when she was a child, which would leave her somewhat weakened as other misfortune happened through the years."

"Why do you say that, Doctor?"

"Because you and Emily read the Word every day and have a daily prayer time. A close walk with the Lord will often fend off mental breakdowns that would otherwise overcome us when we're under undue pressure, but not always. Sometimes there are wounds in the mind that are as real as wounds in the body. But remember this, Matt: just because a person is a Christian doesn't keep him or her from suffering physical problems...and so it is with mental problems.

"What I'm saying is, just because Emily's mind has been fragmented by all that has come upon her is no sign she's a weak Christian. You must emphasize this to her when she gets better."

"I see, Doctor. I'll remember to do that."

"With God's help, along with much love and care from you, Emily could recover and be normal once more. I emphasize *could* recover. There are no guarantees. Another thing I did while you were putting Emily to bed was write down the instructions for using the sedatives. I'm leaving you a big supply. I'll come by and see Emily as often as I can, but the main thing is that she get plenty of rest at night. The sedatives will help."

Matt nodded.

"Is there someone who might come and stay with Emily when you're doing your odd jobs?"

Matt shook his head. "We haven't lived here long enough, Doctor. We don't know anyone well enough to ask for that kind of help. I'll just have to stay home with her until she gets better. I'm trusting the Lord to bring her back to her right mind, and very soon."

Garberson nodded. "I want you to know right now, there won't be any charge for my services through this entire situation."

Matt's face pinched. "I can't let you do that, Dr. Garberson. You have to make a living just like the rest of us."

"I'll be fine, Matt. End of discussion."

"But—"

"End of discussion."

"I don't know how to thank you…"

"It will be thanks enough if I can see Emily get well. Now, new subject of discussion."

"Yes, sir?"

"Holly's funeral."

A stricken look came into Matt's eyes. "Oh. Yes. The funeral. What am I going to do? There's no preacher."

"Closest one is in Fort Bridger. Pastor Andy Kelly. Good man. Preaches the Word straight from the shoulder. But with the amount of snowfall, it would be asking a lot for him to come this far. If you'd like, I could read Scripture at the graveside and bring a brief message."

Matt's eyes brightened. "I'd appreciate that very much."

"All right. It's settled. Now, whenever I'm able to leave here, if you'll let me use your team and wagon, I'll take Holly's body to the undertaker in Mountain View. Have you met Clayton Minter?"

"No, but I thought he was a carpenter and cabinet maker."

"He is, but he's also the only undertaker this side of Rock Springs. Builds his own coffins."

"I see." Matt rubbed the back of his neck. "Do you have any idea what he charges for his services and for a coffin?"

"I'd say both would total about forty dollars. If you don't have it, I'll—"

"No, you won't, Doctor. I can pay him twenty right off. I'll have to make arrangements to pay the rest of it as soon as I can go back to my odd jobs. He'll work with me on that, won't he?"

"I'm sure he will."

A pensive look came into Matt's eyes.

Garberson studied him. "What are you thinking, Matt?"

"Emily…"

"Yes?"

"I'll need to get someone to stay with her the day of the funeral."

The doctor shook his head. "I think she should attend the funeral, Matt."

"But in her present state of mind it could really throw her for a loop."

"I don't think so. It might be the very thing to bring her to reality about Holly's death."

"Hmm. You may be right."

"Like I've already said, Matt, we need to get her to see the facts as soon as possible. The sooner she does, the sooner she can begin to heal."

"All right then. Emily will attend the funeral. Will she need to be sedated for it?"

"No. I want her mind clear so the truth of Holly's death can get through. Since I'll be right there, I can sedate her if needed. I'll—" He broke off.

"What is it, Doctor?"

"Listen!"

"What do you hear?"

"The silence. The wind has stopped blowing."

Both men stepped outside onto the porch. It was no longer snowing, and there was only a slight breeze.

"Look up at the sky," Matt said, his breath puffing out from his mouth. "See up there to the west? Stars!"

Garberson noted the slight break in the heavy night sky, where the clouds were coming apart. A few stars twinkled like beacons. The blizzard was over.

They moved back inside, and Garberson said, "The snow's about twenty inches deep, Matt. If I can use your wagon, I'll take Holly's body to town with me in the morning. I'll send someone back with the wagon who can bring my horse back to me. That all right?"

"Sure. Question is, should I let Emily see the body in the morning? Should I let her watch you drive away with it?"

Garberson thought on it for a moment. "Probably be best that she not see me drive away with the body. She'll think I'm just taking a sleeping Holly with me and no doubt will want to go along or will resist my taking her altogether. I'll sedate her in the morning."

"And what do I do when Emily wakes up and wants to see Holly?"

"First thing you do is tell her that Holly died, and the

body has been taken to the undertaker in town. If you get through to her, all the better. Once she's over the shock, give her more sedative and let her sleep. But if you don't get through to her, you'll have to play it by ear until the day of the funeral, which will probably be day after tomorrow. I'll send a message about that with the person who returns your wagon."

"All right, Doctor."

"Now, you'd better see if you can get some sleep, Matt. How about I give you a light sedative?"

"Well, sir, how about you get to bed in the guest room, and I spend a little time with my daughter's body? I...I want to fix her up a little before the undertaker sees her."

Garberson frowned. "Well, all right. You want a light sedative to take after you're finished?"

"Maybe. I'll see."

"I'll mix it and leave it on the kitchen cupboard."

"Fine. You get some sleep, Doctor."

Matt carried a pan of warm water along with a washcloth and towel into Holly's room and closed the door. The warm air from the fireplace had heated up the house, and the room was comfortable.

He set the pan on the small table beside the bed and wept as he looked at Holly. After a few minutes he began to tenderly wash her face, thinking of how small and beautiful she was.

Emily had undone Holly's braids earlier in the day, and now her long auburn hair was matted and tangled. He picked up Holly's hairbrush from the dresser and slowly ran it through the shiny hair, smoothing it back from her forehead. He kept his eyes on her face the whole time, trying to memorize each dear feature.

Matt's thoughts went back to the happy day Holly had

been born, and he thought of how from that moment on, she was such a special joy to him.

"Dear Lord," he said in a low tone, "Holly's not in this earthly shell, I know. She's with You now, in Your loving hands. Shower her with Your love till I come to heaven and can shower her with mine."

Morning came with brilliant sunshine reflecting off the thick mantle of snow on the ground. Drifts were piled over six feet high around the back of the house, the barn, and the outbuildings.

While Matt prepared a hot breakfast for Dr. Garberson, the physician attended a groggy Emily, administering an additional sedative. She was soon back to sleep.

When breakfast was over, Matt trudged through the deep snow to the barn, harnessed the team, and drove the wagon to the front porch where the drifts weren't so high.

While Garberson was looking in on Emily once again, Matt went to Holly's room. Her lifeless form lay on the pink quilt he had chosen as her shroud. He placed her adored rag doll in her arms and leaned over to place a last, loving kiss on her cold cheek.

Then he wrapped her so her face was covered and held her close to his chest, feeling anew that his heart was going to break into a million pieces. He carried her to the front of the house, where Garberson was waiting at the front door.

"Emily's sleeping peacefully, Matt," Dr. Garberson said. "I wish you had taken the sedative I fixed for you."

"I did all right, Doctor. Got a little sleep, anyhow."

Outside, the naked tree limbs sang a creaking song in the arctic breeze, and a lone hawk rode the currents high above the white ground, his wings spread proudly.

Matt tenderly placed Holly on a bed of straw, then stepped back and bit down on his quivering lips.

Dr. Garberson put his arm around Matt's shoulder and silently prayed for God's matchless grace to fall on this broken man.

"Thank you, Doctor…for everything," Matt said through a tight throat as unshed tears filled his eyes.

Garberson hugged him, all the while patting his back, then turned and climbed aboard the wagon. As he took up the reins, he said, "Someone will be back with the team and wagon and have word from the undertaker for you."

Matt watched the doctor pull away, the horses snorting white puffs of air as they hauled the wagon through the deep snow. He watched until the wagon rounded a bend in the road and passed from view. Then he mentally gave himself a shake and went inside. The sudden warmth made his face tingle.

He put more logs on the fire and went to the kitchen to remove his hat and coat. The fire in the kitchen stove was still going strong. He poured himself a steaming cup of the strong coffee he had made for breakfast and sat down at the table.

As he sipped the hot liquid, he stared out the window at the bright world of white. He pictured Holly, nestled in the arms of Jesus in heaven. Almost unbidden, precious, comforting Scriptures found their way into his numb consciousness— verses and lines that in the process of time he had hidden in his heart:

"He healeth the broken in heart, and bindeth up their wounds."

"From the end of the earth will I cry unto thee, when my heart is overwhelmed: lead me to the rock that is higher than I."

"Weeping may endure for a night, but joy cometh in the morning."

"Then shalt thou call, and the LORD shall answer; thou shalt cry, and he shall say, Here I am."

As the Scriptures penetrated his weary mind and sore heart, and God's wonderful peace stole its way into his being, Matt wept, saying, "Thank You, Lord! Yes, You are right here with me! Thank You! I can feel Your precious, comforting presence, and Your sweet peace is flooding my soul!"

He walked down the hall to the master bedroom and stood at the door, watching his wife sleep. He prayed for his darling Emily, asking God to restore her mentally, and thanked Him that He would do it in His own time.

Back in the kitchen he heated a large kettle of water and washed the dishes. With the rest of the hot water, as David of old when his infant son died, Matt washed himself and made ready for the new day—a day that the Lord had made, and by the grace of God he would rejoice and be glad in it.

Emily was still under the heavy sedative Dr. Garberson had given her that morning when a young man in his early twenties returned Matt's team and wagon. There was a note from Clayton Minter, saying that the total bill for the funeral and the coffin would be thirty-five dollars, and Matt could pay him as he was able. Minter added that unless there was a major storm in the next two days, the funeral would be held at the Mountain View cemetery on Saturday morning, December 3, at eleven o'clock.

The young man mounted the doctor's horse and rode back to town with a message from Matt to the undertaker that he and Emily would be there at eleven o'clock Saturday morning for the graveside service, which would be conducted by Dr. William Garberson.

When Matt checked on Emily again, he found her still sleeping. He went back to the parlor and added more logs to the fire, then sat down with his Bible in hand. He read passage after passage, and because he had slept very little last night, his eyes grew heavy and he dropped off to sleep.

When he awoke, the house was cool. He sat up with a start and thought of Emily. Quickly he stoked the fire, got it burning well, then hurried down the hall. She was awake.

When he sat down on the edge of the bed she continued to stare vacantly at the ceiling. He caressed her cheek. "Emily…"

She did not respond.

He patted her shoulder and leaned into her line of sight. "Honey, it's Matt. Can you see me? Can you hear me?"

She blinked slightly and moved her lips, then tried to focus on his face. "M-Matt," she said thickly.

"Yes, honey. It's me."

"Matt…"

"Are you hungry? Thirsty?"

Her focus sharpened. "Where's my little girl? She's all well now. Where's Holly?"

"Honey, she's—well, she's—"

"Have her come in so I can see her."

Matt prayed for wisdom. He recalled Dr. Garberson's insistence that she see the fact of Holly's death as soon as possible. "Emily, darlin'…Holly isn't here anymore. She's in heaven with Jesus."

Emily frowned. "Jesus is with her?"

"Well, yes, because she's in heaven."

"She's all well, isn't she?"

"That's right, honey. She's all well now."

"No more fever?"

"No more fever."

"And she's not coughing?"

"Not at all."

"But Jesus is with her?"

"To be more precise, Emily, Holly is with Jesus in His home above the stars. She's in heaven with Him. And…and

Michael is there with her. And both of our other babies are there, too. Holly is having a wonderful time with them. They're so happy, and they're waiting for the day you and I come to see them. Now, in a couple of days we have to have Holly's funeral. Do you understand?"

Emily blinked and her features showed that she was trying to comprehend what Matt was saying. A slow smile worked its way across her lips. "Jesus can sleep in the guest room, Matt. The children can sleep in Holly's room. We'll buy some extra beds in town, won't we? I want them to be comfortable. Bring them in now, please. I want to see them."

Matt's heart felt like cold lead. He stroked her cheek lovingly and said, "Sweetheart, you must be hungry. Can I get you something?"

Emily's eyes were glassing over again. She didn't look at him as she replied, "I'll eat with Jesus and you and the children."

Another storm came the next night, piling up more snow.

Saturday was a clear, cold day, and as Matt helped Emily into the wagon, she kept looking back at the house, asking why Holly wasn't coming to town with them.

As Matt drove the wagon toward Mountain View he prayed silently, asking God to bring Emily back to her normal mind. He was thankful he had been able to get food down her, though she kept asking why Holly wasn't at the table to eat with them.

Matt had allowed enough time so he could stop by the Neely place and inform the aging farmer why he had not been back to work on his barn. Neely wept when he learned that Matt's little girl had died. Matt explained about having to stay home with Emily until she was better, saying he would get back as soon as he could to do the rest of the repairs.

When they arrived at the cemetery, Dr. Garberson was standing at the open grave with Alma beside him. Clayton Minter was there, standing with the small coffin. He had made a wreath of pine boughs and put it on top of the lid.

Matt helped Emily down from the wagon, and Alma stepped up to greet her.

"Hello, Emily. I'm sorry about Holly. Are you all right?"

Emily seemed to look right through her as she replied, "Holly is well. She will always be with me, and I'll be fine."

Alma glanced at her husband to see if he was watching, and he nodded.

Matt shook hands with Minter, thanked him for his services, and placed two ten-dollar gold pieces in his hand, saying he would pay him the rest as soon as he could.

The service began, and Alma Garberson stood beside Emily and Matt as the doctor read Scripture concerning death and the resurrection. He spoke a few words about Holly and about heaven, noting Emily's empty stare all the while.

When it was time to leave before the undertaker lowered the coffin into the ground and covered it up, Matt turned to the Garbersons and thanked them for their help, then assisted Emily into the wagon.

As he guided the horses out of the cemetery, Emily said, "Dr. Garberson and that lady seemed so sad. Did something bad happen to them?"

"No, honey. Something very sad happened to someone they know."

"Oh." She turned vacant eyes on him. "I'm so sorry." She set her face forward once again. "We need to hurry home now, honey. Holly's waiting for us. We don't want to make her worry, do we?"

CHAPTER ELEVEN

O n the day Holly McDermott was buried at Mountain View, Fort Bridger's Main Street bustled with movement, in spite of the deep snow.

It was business as usual at Cooper's General Store, with the farmers and ranchers in town for their weekly stocking up on groceries and supplies. Saturday drew in more customers than any other day of the week.

Because Jacob Kates didn't work on the Sabbath, Sylvia Bateman and Mandy Carver were behind the counter with Hannah.

Patty Ruth was there, too, helping her mother and the two women. The older Cooper children were upstairs in the apartment. Chris and B.J. were sweeping and dusting while Mary Beth did the washing.

About an hour after the store opened, Sylvia and Mandy noticed Hannah pressing her fist against the small of her back.

"Miz Hannah," Mandy said, "you sit down on this chair back heah and rest yo' sweet self, y'heah?"

When Hannah started to protest, Sylvia said, "Ah, ah, ah-h-h! No argument, lady. Mandy and I have both carried babies, and we know what it's like in the sixth month. Now plant yourself on the chair next to Patty Ruth, or we'll carry you upstairs and tie you in bed."

Mandy nodded. "Yes'm, we will!"

"That's telling her," spoke up one of the female customers who stood next in Hannah's line. "Now, Hannah, nobody's going to fall apart out here if it takes a little longer to get waited on."

Hannah shook her head in mock exasperation. "All right, all right. I'll sit down for a while."

Patty Ruth, who was already sitting down, said, "Mama, when I get a little bigger, I'll wait on customers for you." She held up her prized bear. "An' Tony will help me."

"Mm-hmm. When you get a little bigger." Hannah glanced at the stuffed bear, who was Patty Ruth's constant companion. "I know you'll be a big help to her then, Tony," she said.

Patty Ruth held Tony closer to Hannah and made his head bob as she spoke in a low voice, "Yes, ma'am, Mrs. Cooper. I will be a big help to the cute little girl."

"Patty Ruth," said Mandy, "you can put these few groceries in the sack fo' Miz Wilson while I add up her bill."

The child promptly climbed up on a stool and began placing the items in a paper sack as she had learned to do.

Hannah pressed a fist to the small of her back and leaned against it in the chair to get as much pressure as she could. She recalled this same discomfort when she had carried her other children. But somehow this pregnancy was different.

As she pondered it, she decided it was because she was alone with this baby. Everyone around her was kind and solicitous, but nothing could make up for the loss of Solomon and not being able to share this special time with him.

Hannah glanced at Patty Ruth and thought of the other three children upstairs. They were all such precious gifts from the Lord, and although the child she now carried beneath her heart would never know his or her father, Hannah determined to make Solomon very much a part of the child's life. She would speak of him often and show the child his photographs time and again as the years passed. She already had a name in mind if this child was a boy.

As though the baby knew what she was thinking, Hannah felt a soft kick. A smile graced her lips as she absently patted her rounded tummy.

By midmorning, Hannah's back pain had eased, and with the growing number of customers entering the store, she took up her position at the counter once again and began waiting on customers.

Patty Ruth was helping Sylvia bag groceries when she heard the little bell above the front door and casually glanced that direction. When she saw Curly Wesson enter with some mail in hand, she excused herself to Sylvia and climbed down from her stool.

The U.S. mail was carried across Wyoming by the Wells Fargo stagecoaches from the railroad in Cheyenne City, and the people of town and fort picked up their mail at the Fargo office. But Curly had been hand-delivering Hannah's mail for the past several weeks.

Patty Ruth grinned up at Curly, her big blue eyes sparkling with anticipation.

People in the store looked around when they heard the pitter-patter of the little redhead's feet as she hurriedly rounded the counter to see her Uncle Curly. The townspeople always found it a joy to behold the customary interaction that took place between Curly and Patty Ruth.

Curly gasped as if surprised to see her and said, "Wal, now lookee here whut I found! A cute little girl with long pigtails an' freckles on her face!"

Patty Ruth giggled.

Curly bent down to look her in the eye and said, "Haddy, little girl."

Giggling some more, she said, "Howdy, big man." The fact that Curly was quite small and very thin made no difference to Patty Ruth, for he was a big man in her eyes.

"Whut's yore name, little girl?"

"Patty Ruth."

Curly sucked in a sharp breath. "Patty Ruth? Yore name's Patty Ruth?"

"Mm-hmm."

"An' how old are you?"

"Five. But I'll be six on December 30."

Curly gasped again. "Yo're five, an' yuh'll be six on December 30?"

"Mm-hmm."

"Wal, do you know whut I do when I meet a little girl an' her name is Patty Ruth, an' she's five years old, and she's gonna be six on December 30? Do you know whut I do?"

"No."

Opening his bony arms wide, Curly grinned and said, "I hug 'er!"

All the people who had been watching this well-established greeting between Curly and Patty Ruth applauded while the two hugged each other.

When Patty Ruth had climbed back on her stool, satisfied that she was still Uncle Curly's favorite little girl, Curly stepped up to the counter. "Hyar's yore mail, Miss Hannah. I'll see you all later." He winked at Patty Ruth and went out the door, leaving the little bell jingling.

Hannah laid the mail aside to take care of two women customers from the fort.

It was almost noon before business slacked off, as it ordinarily did at lunchtime. Hannah took advantage of the lull to begin sifting through her mail. Patty Ruth stood close by with Tony in her arms.

"Oh, praise the Lord!" Hannah said.

Sylvia and Mandy, who were stocking shelves, looked up. "What is it?" Sylvia asked.

"A letter from my parents." Hannah tore the envelope open. "I've written them three times over the past month and haven't had a reply. I was getting concerned."

Mandy and Sylvia watched Hannah read. When she sighed, Sylvia said, "Everything all right?"

"Yes. Mother and Daddy have been on a trip to Cincinnati, Ohio, to visit Sol's brother, Adam, and his family. They're back home in Independence now and are doing fine."

Hannah went on reading the letter, which had been written by her mother.

Esther Singleton had written descriptions of what she'd made for Chris, Mary Beth, B.J., and Patty Ruth for Christmas. She and Hannah's father, Ben, had shipped the presents—including Hannah's—by rail three days before Esther mailed the letter, and should reach Fort Bridger well before Christmas.

Patty Ruth watched her mother place the letter back in its envelope. "Did Grandma and Grandpa say they're gonna come an' see us, Mama?"

"No, honey. I'm hoping they will come next summer, but we'll have to wait and see."

Patty Ruth nodded. "Sure hope they will. I miss 'em."

"Me, too."

The door opened with the familiar jingle, and Hannah looked up to see Julianna LeCroix enter with a bundled-up Larissa in her arms.

Patty Ruth made a dash around the end of the counter, shouting, "Larissa! Larissa!"

Julianna smiled as the child approached. "Look, Larissa, it's your friend, Patty Ruth." She lowered the baby to Patty Ruth's eye level.

Hannah looked on with pleasure while her little girl tickled Larissa's chubby cheeks and talked to her in loving tones.

"Hannah," Julianna said as she stepped up to the counter with Patty Ruth at her side, "I know you don't usually eat lunch till about one o'clock, but I've got some vegetable soup simmering on the stove. Would you and your children like to come to lunch at my house?"

Hannah saw Patty Ruth's eyes light up. "Well, I guess we could do that. I was going to go upstairs in a few minutes and help Mary Beth fix us a lunch, but we'd love to come to your house."

"Good! I have a couple of other reasons I'd like you to come. One is...since it's warmed up some, I thought maybe the children would like to build a snowman in my yard."

Patty Ruth danced up and down, clapping her hands. "Oh boy! Can we build a snowman, Mama? Can we?"

"All right," Hannah said, laughing. "Go upstairs and tell your sister and brothers we're going to Miss Julianna's house for lunch right now, and the four of you are going to build a snowman in her yard after lunch."

Patty Ruth ran toward the back door but skidded to a halt when her mother called her name. "Yes, Mama?"

"Put your coat and stocking cap on. It hasn't warmed up that much."

"Oh. Okay."

When Patty Ruth dashed out the door clad in coat and knit stocking cap, Hannah said, "So what's the other reason you want us to come?"

"Well, right now it's a secret. But after lunch, when the children are making their snowman, I'll show you."

After lunch, the Cooper children bundled up to go outside. Larissa was in the bedroom, asleep in her crib.

Julianna handed Chris two chunks of coal and produced a length of red material. "Here's coal for his eyes," she said, "and a scarf for his neck."

Chris smiled. "Thank you, Miss Julianna! This'll really be neat!"

When Julianna closed the door behind the children, she peered through the window and laughed.

"What's so funny?" Hannah asked.

"Your youngest son."

"What's he doing?"

"First thing he did was lie down on his back, swing his arms in the snow, and make an angel."

"He's done that ever since he was five years old."

Still looking out the window, Julianna laughed again.

"Now what?"

"Patty Ruth just made a snowball and hit Chris with it."

Hannah rolled her eyes. "Now why doesn't that surprise me?"

Gleeful laughter could be heard from the front yard.

"So who's winning the snowball fight?" Hannah said.

"Well, I'd say the girls are, but only because the boys are letting them."

"Sounds like my boys. They like to tease their sisters a lot, but when it comes right down to it, they watch over them like mother hens."

Julianna turned away from the window and rejoined Hannah at the table.

"I appreciate your inviting us over so they can play, Julianna," Hannah said. "We don't have a yard, and it's hard for them to build a snowman in the alley, though they've done it a couple of times."

"As far as I'm concerned, they can come here and build a snowman anytime they want. And I know Jack feels the same way. You have four wonderful children, Hannah. Each one is special in his or her own way."

A warm smile curved Hannah's lips. "Thank you."

"And I'm sure the one you're carrying will be special just like the others."

"There's not a doubt in my mind about that. So, tell me what this big secret is."

"All right. Follow me."

Hannah stayed on Julianna's heels as they walked toward the rear of the house. Julianna paused at the door across from the main bedroom and put her hand on the doorknob. She turned and said, "I have a new career."

Hannah's eyebrows arched. "Oh, really?"

"Take a look!" Julianna swung the door open.

Hannah saw four different sizes of dress forms standing by one wall, several bolts of material in a corner, and a large table with thread spools, needles, thimbles, scissors, and a partially made dress with a paper pattern next to it.

"Julianna! This is wonderful! I didn't know you were a seamstress!"

"I made many of my own dresses from my teen years and up, just because I wanted to. I also made shirts for Jean-Claude. A few days ago I went into Heidi's dress shop to buy some material to make Jack a shirt. Heidi told me she's been looking for a seamstress to help her keep up with business. When I told her I'd be interested in making dresses at home, she came by the house to see some dresses I had made. She liked them and hired me."

"Well, praise the Lord!" Hannah said, giving Julianna a hug. "I'm sure this will help with the finances when you and Jack get married."

"It sure will. I'm so excited about it. And so is Jack. He liked the shirt I made him, too. In fact, he wants me to make him some more."

At that moment, Larissa woke up and began fussing.

"Uh-oh. Time for Larissa's lunch. I'll feed her in the bedroom."

"Tell you what," said Hannah. "While you're nursing the baby, I'll go outside and see how it's going with Mr. Snowman."

Julianna nodded. "I'll be out to see for myself when Larissa's tummy is full."

Hannah donned her heavy coat, wrapped her wool scarf about her neck, and stepped out onto the porch. The sun was peeking between some drifting clouds, and a slight breeze toyed with the skeletal branches of the cottonwoods. There were several small boulders scattered about the yard, their tops crusted with snow.

"Look, Mama!" cried Patty Ruth. "We're gettin' the bottom part of his body made!"

"Sure enough, honey. Looks like it's going to be a good one."

"Wanna help, Mama?" asked B.J.

"Thanks, B.J.," she said, "but I think I'll just find me one of those boulders to sit on, and watch."

"You made snowmen in Missouri when you were a girl, didn't you, Mama?" said Mary Beth.

"Sure did. Lots of them."

Chris, who loved to tease, said, "Really, Mama? I didn't know they had snow back when you were a girl!"

Hannah pointed a stiff finger at him. "That's enough about your dear mother being old, young man!"

Chris laughed.

Hannah made her way across the yard to a boulder beside a snow-laden evergreen and brushed some of the snow from its top before sitting down. She waved to a man and woman who rode by in a wagon, then put her attention on the children as they worked together on the snowman.

After a few minutes, Patty Ruth trudged through the snow, her face screwed tight and on the verge of tears. "Mama, they won't let me help 'em anymore."

Hannah took Patty Ruth in her arms. "Why not?"

"Chris and B.J. said I'm too short to help, now that they've got the top part of the snowman on."

"Chris!" Hannah called.

"Yes, Mama?"

"Come here a minute!"

Chris ran to her. "Yes, Mama?"

"Your little sister tells me that you and B.J. won't let her work on the snowman anymore…that she's too short."

"That's right. When we put the second ball on, she can't reach it to help pack more snow so there'll be plenty to set the head on. We didn't mean to hurt her feelings, but she's just too short." He looked at the pout on his little sister's face and said, "I'm sorry, Patty Ruth. You can't help it that you're five years old."

Patty Ruth stiffened. "I'll be six pretty soon!"

"I know," Chris said, "but when you can't reach the spot where we're packing snow, there's nothing we can do about it."

"Well, isn't there something else she can do?" Hannah asked.

Chris thought on it, and suddenly his eyes lit up. "Yes! When we get the head on, I'll lift her up and let her put the coals in for the eyes, and she can put the scarf around his neck!"

Patty Ruth's pout disappeared, and a smile replaced it.

"Will that be all right?" Chris asked.

"Sure!"

"Okay, I'll holler for you when we're ready."

"Thank you, son," said Hannah.

Chris smiled at her and ran back to join Mary Beth and B.J.

A short time later, Chris called for Patty Ruth, and Hannah watched the little girl put coal eyes in place while Chris held her up. Mary Beth helped Patty Ruth tie the scarf around the snowman's thick neck.

"He looks good, kids," Julianna said as she stepped outside donned in hat and coat to view the finished snowman. She descended the stairs and moved toward them.

Patty Ruth ran toward Julianna, shouting, "I put the eyes in and the scarf on!"

Julianna ran her gaze over the children's happy faces and said, "I think that's the best snowman I've ever seen."

B.J. put an impish look on his face. "That's because it was me who made it so good, Miss Julianna."

Chris playfully disagreed, saying it was his expert work that produced such a good one.

Mary Beth chuckled. "Well, I think the best parts of the snowman are the eyes and the scarf that were put in place by my baby sister."

Patty Ruth's eyes brightened. She strutted toward them, hands on hips, saying, "See there, boys? You're not so hot after all!"

"Oh yeah?" gusted B.J., bending over and forming a snowball. "I'll show you, Patty Ruth!"

"B.J.!" came Hannah's stern voice as she joined the group. "Put it down."

The boy dropped the partially formed snowball and grinned. "I wasn't really gonna throw it at her, Mama."

Hannah gave him a skeptical look, then turned to Julianna. "We need to be going. Thank you so much for lunch, and for letting the children use your snow to make the man."

"My pleasure," said Julianna. "And I want you kids to come over and see your snowman anytime you want."

Both women started to say something at the same time. "Go ahead," Hannah said.

Julianna smiled. "Friday, December 16, is Larissa's first birthday."

"My sixth birthday is five days after Christmas," put in Patty Ruth.

"I know, honey," said Julianna. "Six years old! Anyway,

Hannah, I'm having a party for Larissa on her birthday, and I would like for you and the children to come. I've invited Jack, of course, and Jacob, and Pastor and Mrs. Kelly. The party will be at seven o'clock that evening. Will you come?"

"We'd love to. But only if you'll let me bake Larissa's birthday cake."

Julianna frowned. "But I don't want to put you to that work. I—"

"It's not that much work. Mary Beth will help me."

"Sure will," said the girl.

"Well, all right."

"Tell you what," said Hannah, "Patty Ruth and I will bring the cake over that afternoon and help you get ready for the party."

Julianna gave Hannah a quick hug and said, "You are such a good friend. Thank you. Now, what were you going to say a moment ago?"

Hannah laughed. "I was going to invite you, Larissa, and Jack to Patty Ruth's birthday party. It's on a Friday, too."

"We'd be honored to come."

"Wonderful! I'll give you more details later."

That evening, after Jack and Jacob had eaten supper at the Cooper apartment and returned to their quarters, Chris said, "Mama, I need to meet in private with Mary Beth, B.J., and Patty Ruth."

"Oh?" Hannah teased. "You have some kind of secret you can't share with your mother?"

"Yes, Mama, I do." He grinned mischievously. "And if you'll think what big day is coming up later this month, you'll know what it's about."

"Oh! You mean Patty Ruth's birthday!"

The children laughed, then Chris said, "This is a different big day, Mama."

"Could it be Christmas?"

"Mm-hmm."

"All right. I need to write to Grandma and Grandpa Singleton, so while you have your secret meeting, I'll do that."

Huddled together in the girls' room with his younger siblings, Chris kept his voice low and said, "When we lived in Missouri and Papa was alive, he always got us to working early on what each of us would give Mama for Christmas. Well, since Papa has gone to heaven, and I'm the man of the house, I'll spearhead the project."

B.J. stiffened. "What makes you the man of the house, Chris? I'm here, too."

"I know," said big brother, "but since I'll be fifteen next February, and you won't even be nine till March, I figure that qualifies me as man of the house. Any questions?"

B.J. stuck out his lower lip but remained silent.

"How about you girls?"

"Who can argue with seniority?" said Mary Beth.

Chris's eyebrows arched. "Wow! Where'd you learn that word?"

"I pay attention in school," she said dryly.

"So what's seen your ority?" Patty Ruth asked.

"No, honey," said Mary Beth. "It's one word. *Seniority*. It means that Chris is the oldest of us four."

"Oh, well, I'll be six five days after Christmas!"

"But you're still the youngest," said Chris. "Now, let me explain about Christmas for Mama. I've made arrangements with Mr. and Mrs. Bledsoe to let each of us buy a Christmas present at their store, to be paid after Christmas when I tell Mama how much we need to pay the bill."

"That's nice of them," put in Mary Beth.

Chris nodded. "So, here's what we'll do. On Monday after

school we'll go next door and each of us pick out what we want to buy Mama for Christmas…"

CHAPTER TWELVE

On Monday afternoon, Hannah Cooper sat by the pot-bellied stove in the store, talking to Ruth Blayney, wife of the fort's physician. Patty Ruth sat in a chair beside her mother, holding her stuffed bear.

Jacob Kates was behind the counter, adding up a bill for a rancher and his wife.

When the front door opened, Patty Ruth spotted her siblings and slipped out of her chair. She held up Tony, wiggling his head as if he were speaking, and said, "Hello, Mary Beth Cooper, Christopher Adam Cooper, and Brett Jonathan Cooper. Did you learn anything in school today?"

Mary Beth snickered. "Well, Tony Marie Cooper, I did. I don't know about my brothers."

"Did I hear you right, Mary Beth?" Ruth Blayney asked. "Tony's middle name is Marie?"

Patty Ruth nodded energetically and answered for her sister. "I named him Tony Marie after Mama. Her name is Hannah Marie Cooper."

Ruth slanted a smile at Hannah, who shrugged and said, "She also gave our little rat terrier a middle name."

"Oh?"

"His name is Biggie Marie Cooper."

"His name's really Big Enough Marie Cooper," announced

Patty Ruth, "but we call him Biggie for short."

Ruth Blayney laughed. "Patty Ruth, you never cease to amaze me!"

"This whole family could say that," said Hannah with a chuckle.

"But we won't say in what way," put in Chris, a sly look on his face.

"Yeah!" B.J. said.

Mary Beth gave her brothers a stern look. "You boys stop picking on my little sister."

"You tell 'em, Mary Beth!" came Tony's deep voice, his head moving with pressure from Patty Ruth's hand.

"Mama," Chris said, "we need to go somewhere for a little while. May we go now?"

Hannah cocked her head sideways. "We? Who's we?"

"Your four darling children."

"And you need to go where?"

"Can't tell you."

"And why not?"

"Has to do with our secret little meeting last night."

A knowing smile captured Hannah's lips. "Oh! Of course. Don't be gone too long."

"Just long enough," said Mary Beth, smiling impishly.

Patty Ruth hurried to where her coat and cap hung on a peg behind the counter, laid Tony down on a chair, and then rushed back to the others. Mary Beth helped her button the coat and don her cap.

When the Cooper children entered Bledsoe's Clothing Store, Dan and Carlene Bledsoe were waiting on customers at the counter but took time to greet the four.

"We're here for you-know-what," said Chris.

Dan nodded. "You just go ahead and look around, kids."

The girls went one direction and the boys another.

Mary Beth led her little sister toward the rear of the store.

"Do you still want to get Mama a pretty hankie, honey?"

"Uh-huh. She likes pretty hankies. What are you gonna get her?"

"Well, you know my secret watercolor painting that I'm doing of our old house in Missouri?"

"Uh-huh. An' I haven't told Mama, either, like I tol' you I wouldn'."

"That's good. Anyway, that's what I'm giving Mama for Christmas. She'll like it, and it won't cost her any money when it comes time to pay Mr. and Mrs. Bledsoe for the gifts."

"Oh. Maybe I should just paint a picture for her, too."

Mary Beth grinned. "I'd say you should wait till you're quite a bit older before you do that."

"Oh. Okay. Look, Mary Beth! Here's some pretty hankies!"

It took the five-year-old several minutes to choose, but finally she put her finger on a white handkerchief with the print design of a bouquet of flowers in the center. "I wanna get her this one."

"Oh, that is pretty, honey," said Mary Beth. "But it would be prettier if it had a lace border around it, don't you think?"

"Yes. Mama would like that."

As Mary Beth was running her fingers lightly through the handkerchiefs, Carlene Bledsoe stepped up. "Finding what you want, girls?"

"Do you have one of these hankies, but with a lace border, Mrs. Bledsoe?" Mary Beth asked.

"No, I'm sorry. Not like this one. Let me show you some that do."

Carlene pulled out several handkerchiefs, but Patty Ruth didn't like the design like the other one, and said so.

"Well, honey, if you're set on this one," said Carlene, "I can sell you some lace border material, and you could have some-one sew it on for you. Maybe you could get Heidi Lindgren to do it for you."

Mary Beth looked down at her little sister. "What do you think about that, Patty Ruth?"

The little redhead pondered the idea for a moment, then said, "How about if I sew it on myself? Mama would like it better if she knew I sewed it."

Carlene and Mary Beth exchanged meaningful glances.

"Ah…maybe you could let Mary Beth help you sew it on, honey," said Carlene.

"Okay. But I'll do most of it, 'cause it's my present for Mama."

Mary Beth smiled, looked at Carlene, and said, "We'll take the hankie and the lace to go with it, Mrs. Bledsoe."

A couple of aisles away, B.J. watched as his big brother picked up a pair of leather fleece-lined slippers. "What do you think of these, B.J.? You know how Mama's feet are always swollen by evening. These would be warm and comfortable for her."

"Sure would," agreed little brother. "She'd really like those."

"All right. That's what I'll get her."

Chris picked up the box of slippers he wanted and tucked it under his arm. "Now, what have you got in mind?"

Pointing back to a table they had passed a few minutes earlier, B.J. said, "I'd like to get her that wooden box over there."

Chris followed the direction B.J. was pointing and walked to the table. The box was made of a reddish wood and had a cameo on the lid. It was a carving of a woman's head with the hair styled like Hannah often wore hers. "This box, B.J.?"

"Yeah. Really pretty, isn't it? And that lady on it looks like Mama, don't you think?"

"Mm-hmm. She does." Chris opened the lid and looked at its hollow interior. "But what would Mama do with it?"

"I don't know, but she'd like it 'cause the lady looks like her, and the box is really pretty."

"Help you, boys?" came a male voice.

They looked up to see Mr. Bledsoe towering over them.

"B.J. wants to get this box for Mama for Christmas, Mr. Bledsoe," said Chris. "He thinks the lady on the lid looks like her."

Dan looked at the cameo over his half-moon glasses. "Well, I declare, she does!"

"But what's the box for, sir?"

"Oh, it can have many uses. Jewelry box. Small keep-sakes. Photographs."

"It's pretty wood," said B.J.

"Yes," said Bledsoe. "It's cherry wood."

B.J. nodded. He had never heard of cherry wood before. "Mama would really like it, I know."

Dan Bledsoe smiled. "I don't know a lady who wouldn't like it, son."

"How much is it, Mr. Bledsoe?" Chris asked.

"There's a tag on the inside of the lid, son."

Chris opened the box again. His eyes widened. "Five dollars! We can't afford it, B.J. You'll have to find a present that doesn't cost so much."

B.J.'s countenance fell. "But it's so pretty. And the lady looks like Mama."

"I know, but it's too expensive. Mama has to pay for these presents after Christmas, and she really wouldn't want us to spend that much on one present."

B.J.'s mouth turned down and a hint of tears showed in his eyes. "But...but she'd really like it."

Touched by the eight-year-old's sincere desire to give his mother such a present, Bledsoe said, "Chris, how much are you allowing B.J. to spend?"

"Has to be about two or three dollars, sir. No more. I'm buying these slippers for Mama, and they're $2.49."

The tall, slender man rubbed his chin thoughtfully, looked down at B.J., and said, "You really want to give this box to your mother, don't you?"

"Yes, sir. It's real nice, like somethin' Papa would buy for her if...if he was here."

"Well, listen, B.J.," Bledsoe said, "I'll just drop the price to $2.49...the same as these slippers Chris has picked out."

B.J. shook his head. "Oh no, Mr. Bledsoe. That wouldn't be right."

"He's right, sir," said Chris. "We can't let you do that. I'm sure the box cost you more than that. B.J. will just have to pick out something else."

Dan Bledsoe was pleased at their attitude and said, "Boys, I'd really like your mother to have the box. Especially after what B.J. said about—well, you know. About your father. Please let me drop the price so she can have it."

B.J.'s eyes brightened. "Mr. Bledsoe, I have an idea."

"Yes?"

"Could I do some work here in the store for you and earn the part above $2.49?"

Dan touched the boy's shoulder and said, "You sure can. How about sweeping the floor for me at closing time for the next three days?"

"Oh, thank you, Mr. Bledsoe!"

Dan extended his hand and B.J. met his grip. "It's a deal," said the store owner.

The Cooper children made their purchases at the counter with Dan and Carlene. As Dan was writing it up, Carlene could see they were all excited about Christmas, but there was a sadness in their eyes. She quessed it was because their father would be greatly missed.

Snow fell intermittently for the next four days. In the evenings at the Cooper apartment, Mary Beth and Patty Ruth spent time in their room while big sister worked on her painting and little sister worked at sewing the lace border on the handkerchief. Patty Ruth had decided she would do the sewing all by herself rather than have help.

Both the handkerchief and the painting were done by the fourth evening.

On the following Saturday afternoon, Marshal Lance Mangum and Deputy Jack Bower were in the office when they heard gunshots. They dashed outside and saw a couple of the town's older men standing in the snow-covered street in front of the Rusty Lantern, Fort Bridger's only saloon.

One of the men pointed toward the saloon. "Shootin' goin' on in there, Marshal!"

Angry shouts filtered outside, followed by two more gunshots and a loud crash.

The lawmen bounded across the boardwalk with their guns drawn and pushed through the bat-wing doors.

The place was thick with gun smoke. Marshal Mangum saw two strangers with smoking revolvers in hand standing over a glass chandelier that lay shattered on the floor. With Deputy Bower at his side, Mangum pointed his gun at the two men and commanded, "Drop the guns! Now!"

The strangers let the guns slip from their fingers. As the guns clattered to the floor, saloon owner and barkeep Lester Coggins stepped around the end of the bar, saying, "Marshal,

I'm sure glad you got here! These two drifters accused me of watering down the whiskey. When I told them it wasn't so, they got mad and started shootin' at the chandelier, trying to bring it down. As you can see, they did."

There were only a few customers in the saloon. All of them stayed put, looking on with interest.

Mangum kept his eyes on the drifters. "Kick those guns over here."

When the revolvers had skidded to a spot near Mangum's feet, Jack holstered his gun, picked up the guns, and laid them on a nearby table. He took his former position and kept a close eye on the drifters as the marshal moved within a few feet of them. Mangum holstered his gun and said, "Names."

The drifters exchanged glances.

"Don't even think of lying to me," Mangum said, a steely look coming into his eyes.

"Lloyd Hurtz," the taller one said.

"H-U-R-T-Z?"

"Yeah."

The shorter one licked his lips nervously. "A.C. Kellogg."

"How long you been in town?"

"Since Tuesday," said Hurtz. "We got this far in that day's snowstorm and took a room in the hotel. Decided we'd just stay a few days."

Mangum looked at the shattered chandelier, then eyed the ceiling. Turning to Coggins, he said, "Lester, what'll it cost to replace the chandelier?"

"'Bout two hundred dollars, Marshal. That'll include the cost to have one shipped from Chicago."

Mangum nodded. "I can see three bullet holes in the ceiling. What's it going to cost to plug them?"

"I'm not sure. Be fifteen or twenty dollars, I'd say."

Mangum turned back to Hurtz and Kellogg. "You're going to do three days in jail for this little escapade, and it looks like you two boys owe Lester 250 dollars."

Kellogg protested. "Hey! What he just told you don't add up to 250 dollars! It'd only be 215, the most 220! What's the other thirty dollars for?"

"Nuisance fee. Pay the man."

Again, the drifters looked at each other.

"We ain't got that much between us," said Kellogg.

"I don't believe you," growled Mangum. "Cough it up."

"He ain't kiddin' you, Marshal," said Hurtz. "We don't carry that kind of money."

The marshal sighed. "Well, I guess I'll have to do a body search. If I find that you're lying, I'll—"

"Okay, okay," cut in Hurtz. "We'll pay it."

"Good. Let's have it."

Hurtz mumbled a string of profanity as he dug his fingers into his hip pocket. Mangum stepped closer to him, his eyes fixed on the man.

A.C. Kellogg's hair-trigger temper flared, and he reached behind his back, gripped the small knife he carried in a sheath, and lunged at Mangum.

Jack Bower, who had been keeping a close watch on the two men, made his own lunge toward Kellogg, shouting, "Marshal, look out!"

Mangum did a quick side step, and the blade barely missed him. At the same time, Jack seized Kellogg's knife hand at the wrist and brought his knee up as he rammed the arm down against it. There was a loud cracking noise, and Kellogg howled. His knife hit the floor and skittered toward a nearby table. One of the customers leaned over and picked it up.

"You broke my arm! You broke my arm!" Kellogg wailed at Bower. He was bent over with pain and looked up sideways at the deputy.

Hurtz swore. "You didn't have to do that! You didn't have to break his arm!"

"Just be glad that's all I broke," Jack said coolly.

"I want Lester paid right now," said Mangum after flicking a smile at his deputy.

When the proper amount of money had been extracted from Kellogg's pocket and collected from Hurtz, Mangum handed it to the saloon owner then turned back to the drifters. "You boys seem to carry quite a bit of cash with you. Looks like while you're doing thirty days in my jail, I'll have to see if I can dig up anything on you being wanted for bank robbery."

"Thirty days!" Kellogg said, holding his broken arm close to his body. "Why thirty days?"

"Because you tried to knife me, and your pal mouthed off about it."

"You ain't gonna find us on any wanted list, Marshal," said Hurtz, scowling at him. "We won that money in poker games."

"We'll see," said Mangum. "Jack, you take Mr. Hurtz here and lock him up. I'll take Mr. Kellogg to Doc O'Brien."

An hour later, Deputy Bower looked up from his desk as the marshal came in with a wan-faced A.C. Kellogg, whose arm was in a cast supported by a sling. Kellogg gave the deputy a sour look as Mangum said, "You can put him in the same cell with his pal, Jack. I'm going to see if I can find anything on them."

When Jack returned from the cell block, Mangum was shuffling through a stack of wanted posters.

"Find anything?"

"Not yet."

"Maybe they were telling the truth."

"Maybe."

As Jack headed for his own desk, Lance rose to his feet

and stuck out his hand. "Thank you, Jack."

"For what?"

"You know for what. If he'd put that knife blade in my neck, it could have been fatal. Thank God and Jack Bower, he missed."

Jack smiled. "I'm glad you put it in that order, boss. You can really thank God you're still here."

Lance nodded.

As he turned toward his own desk, Jack said, "Uh, boss...maybe...maybe this incident was a warning from God."

"What do you mean?"

"Well, you've been promising Miss Heidi you'd come to church. You still haven't done it."

Lance's face tinted slightly. "Tell you what. If you'll pick up where I left off on the wanted posters, I'll go over to the dress shop right now and tell Heidi I'm going to church with her tomorrow morning."

"Be glad to," Jack said, picking up the stack of posters from his boss's desk.

Lance shrugged into his coat, clapped on his hat, and went out the door.

Jack smiled as he watched him go.

Pastor Andy Kelly and Rebecca were pleased to see Marshal Lance Mangum enter the church building on Sunday morning with Heidi Lindgren and her sister, Sundi. The Kellys greeted the trio, making the marshal feel especially welcome.

Lance Mangum got through the pastor's Sunday school class without too much discomfort, but when Kelly bore down hard about sin, death, and hell during the sermon, the marshal was in a cold sweat. He endured the sermon and was able to stay in the pew at invitation time. Inwardly, he was very much relieved when the service was over.

Pastor Kelly had seen the conviction on Mangum's face and asked if he could come by Lance's apartment and talk sometime that week. Mangum hedged, telling the pastor he was too busy for a visit right now but would come back to church soon.

Kelly came back with an invitation to attend the service that night.

When Lance glanced down at Heidi and saw the yearning in her eyes, he forced a smile and told the pastor he would be back that night.

Mangum kept his promise. Again he was visibly eaten up with conviction but stood like a statue during the invitation, though others responded and came for salvation.

At the door, Mangum commented to Kelly that his sermon was powerful and had stimulated his thoughts about the gospel.

Kelly drew Lance aside, leaving Heidi and Sundi to talk to Rebecca, and said, "Marshal, I want you to think hard on what you've heard today, and remember what Jack said to you when that knife barely missed your neck yesterday. It could be a warning from God. Think on that. I want to see you saved."

Lance nodded.

"Marshal, will you come back next Sunday?"

"I...I'll see, Pastor."

Kelly was silent for a moment, then said, "Keep Jack's words in mind, okay?"

Mangum nodded and turned away to rejoin Heidi and Sundi. There was little conversation as he walked the Lindgren sisters to their house.

Heidi and Sundi stood at the parlor window and watched Lance move down the street and disappear into the night.

"He's one miserable man right now," Heidi said with a sigh.

Sundi was smiling. "Mm-hmm. That's good. We know the Spirit is dealing with him. Why don't we pray for him right now, Heidi."

They went to Heidi's room, knelt down beside the bed, and prayed for the salvation of Fort Bridger's marshal.

Lance Mangum lay awake for a long time that night. Words from both of Pastor Kelly's sermons burned through his mind like brands of fire. Kelly had spent part of the evening sermon on the judgment at the great white throne, from Revelation chapter 20. As he tossed and turned, Mangum couldn't get that awful scene out of his mind.

Over and over he saw himself standing before God with the guilt of his sins on him, and the fiery eyes of a holy God boring into his guilty soul. He was finally able to shake off the horror of it and fall asleep an hour or so before dawn.

Chapter Thirteen

L ance Mangum stood before the mirror, noting his blood-
shot eyes as he drew the straight-edged razor carefully
over his face. He paused for a moment to yawn, wishing
he had been able to sleep better, and soon finished the job of
scraping off whiskers and shaving soap.

When he went outside, wearing a sheepskin coat, his
breath caught at the coldness of the air. He turned up his collar
and adjusted his hat.

The sun was just above the eastern horizon, shining down
from a cold, clear sky. It had snowed sometime in the night,
and the mantle of snow glowed pearly white in the brilliant
early-morning sunlight. The naked limbs of the trees were soft-
ened by white cushions of snow.

Smoke tendrils lifted from chimneys as Mangum made his
way toward Main Street. Except for the crunching of his boots
and the sound of his own breathing, he moved through a world
of silence.

As soon as he turned onto Main Street, the sounds of
squeaking wagon wheels, tinkling harness, blowing horses, and
muffled hoofbeats met his ears.

He entered Glenda's Café and inhaled the tempting aroma
of hot food coming from the kitchen. A waitress carrying a tray
of steaming plates and coffee cups to a far table greeted him as
he sat down at the closest unoccupied table. The place was

quite full, and Mangum didn't notice a pair of dark eyes glaring at him from a table halfway across the room to his right.

A couple of men spoke to him, saying they'd heard about the trouble at the Rusty Lantern on Saturday, and they were glad he hadn't been hurt. Mangum thanked them and they moved on.

Gary Williams came out of the kitchen, wearing an apron. His smile reached all the way to his ears. "Good morning, Marshal. Special's ham and eggs with hash browns. Want some?"

"Sounds good," Mangum said. "But what are you doing waiting on tables? I thought the hotel was your domain."

"It is," said Gary, his eyes twinkling, "unless we get short-handed here in the café. Then Glenda bosses me around and tells me to get over here and help. We've got a waitress down with a cold, so my desk clerk is running the hotel today, and I'm waiting tables."

"So Glenda bosses you around, eh?"

Gary chuckled. "Well, you know how wives are. They let us male types think we're the boss, but they have a way of getting what they want."

Lance's mind went to the woman he loved. *I wish I had Heidi to boss me around like that.* Out loud he said, "I've heard how wives are. But I've yet to experience it."

"Well, one of these days you'll get trapped by a female and get your ball and chain."

"I heard that!" came a feminine voice. "Ball and chain, eh?" Glenda had a mischievous look in her big blue eyes. "I'll deal with you when we get home, Mr. Williams!"

"Yeah," said Gary. "She'll lock me in my room, Marshal, and won't let me go out to play with the other kids for a whole week!"

Mangum chuckled.

"Hey, Marshal," Glenda said, "it sure was good to see you

in church at both ends of the day yesterday."

"Sure was," said Gary. "We're glad you came. Will we be seeing you there again?"

Lance suppressed the sudden rise of panic and said, "I'm sure you will. Well, Gary, I'll have that special."

When Mangum left Glenda's Café and headed up the street toward the center of town, traffic was picking up. He looked into the next block and saw his deputy on the boardwalk in front of the office, talking to a couple of men. Someone called to Mangum from horseback, and when he turned back to look toward his office, Jack was going inside.

Lance crossed the street into the next block and came to the blacksmith shop, where Abe Carver was unlocking the door from the inside, having entered the shop from the alley. The muscular blacksmith opened the door slightly to look out and saw Mangum.

"Mo'nin', Marshal."

"Good morning, Abe."

"I finished the horseshoes. Would you like to see 'em?"

"Sure."

Abe widened the door to allow Mangum inside, then closed it. He led him to a shelf near the fire pit and showed him four brand-new iron shoes. "Right heah, Marshal."

"Those look good, Abe," Mangum said, smiling.

"I can put 'em on yo' horse whenever you can bring him by and leave him fo' about an hour."

"All right. How about this afternoon, say, three o'clock?"

"That'll be fine."

"See you then," said the lawman, heading for the door.

Mangum stepped out into the nippy air and turned to head up the boardwalk. He stopped abruptly when he saw a wide-shouldered man in a mackinaw blocking his path. It took him a second or two to realize the face was familiar.

The man stood spread-legged, his hand hovering over the butt of his low-slung revolver. The bottom of the mackinaw had been tucked behind the holster to allow free access to the gun. The man glowered at Mangum with hate-filled eyes and said, "Remember me, Mangum?"

Lance felt a tightness crawl down his back. *Vin Maltz!*

While he'd been deputy marshal of Cheyenne City some five years earlier, Lance had trailed this outlaw and gunslinger across the Wyoming plains toward Nebraska and caught up to him at a corral in the small town of Hillsdale. Maltz had taken refuge in a barn, blasting away at his pursuer. A fierce gun battle took place until both men ran out of ammunition.

Maltz made a run for it, but Mangum pursued him and brought him down with a flying tackle. Maltz went to trial for his crimes and was sentenced to five years in Wyoming Territorial Prison at Rawlins.

A frown hardened Mangum's gaze. Without a blink he said through barely parted teeth, "Yeah, Maltz. I remember you. Served your time, eh?"

"Yeah. Thanks to you. Five years cut out of my life while I rotted in a dirty prison cell." His right hand remained in a hovering position over the butt of his holstered revolver.

Lance smiled wryly and shook his head. "What is it with you outlaws? You commit the crimes, knowing you're breaking the law, but when you're captured by a man with a badge on his chest and sent to prison, you blame the man who arrested you. Can't you figure out that you went to prison because you broke the law? That makes it your fault, Maltz, not mine."

Ignoring Mangum's reasoning, Maltz spat out, "I've lived for one thing since the day I was locked up in that prison, Mangum…to get out and kill you! And that's what I'm gonna do right now! Took me a while to find you, but at last my day has come!" His breath puffed out in little vaporous clouds as he spoke.

Mangum's lips were a hard, unrelenting line as he growled, "I don't want to kill you, Maltz. Don't force me to do it."

People were beginning to gather in the cold sunlight to watch.

Maltz laughed. "You can't buffalo me, lawman. Go for your gun. I want all these nice people to witness that I gave you a sportin' chance."

Tense and ready, Mangum said, "Do you understand that by forcing a lawman into a gunfight—if somehow I'm able to take you down without killing you—it'll mean you'll go back to prison?"

"That don't worry me. I'm gonna kill you, and I'll be long gone from this town in a matter of minutes. Go for your gun."

Jack Bower looked up from his desk when Abe Carver burst through the door.

"Deputy Jack!" Abe gasped. "There's trouble out heah on the street! Some mean-lookin' gunslick stopped Marshal Mangum, and it looks like he's gonna force him into a quick draw!"

Jack was on his feet in a flash, gun in hand.

"Maltz," Lance Mangum said, "I'm giving you one more chance. Find your horse and ride, and I'll forget this ever happened."

Eyes blazing, Maltz said, "Draw, you coward!" then went for his gun.

Mangum's Colt .45 was out, cocked, and leveled on the

gunfighter's chest before Maltz could clear leather. Maltz's hand froze with the weapon halfway out of the holster, waiting for Mangum's hammer to snap down and send a slug into his heart.

Mangum started toward him, saying, "Nice and easy, Maltz. Unbuckle your gun belt and let it drop. You're under arrest."

Suddenly a shot rang out from the boardwalk behind Mangum. He felt the impact of the bullet in his back and found himself helplessly going down. His face hit the hard wood with a jolt. He was aware of more gunshots and a voice shouting.

There were many loud voices as Lance fought to remain conscious. The pain in his back that had started like a small hot orb covered with thorns began to grow, stretching out with spiny arms to fill his entire body. The spines became spears of flame burning through him. He felt himself being lifted up by strong hands, and distant voices were saying something he couldn't understand as a black curtain descended.

Some thirty minutes before Marshal Mangum was accosted on the street by Vin Maltz, Dr. Frank O'Brien sat at his desk in his office, preparing to write a check for medical supplies that had arrived on Friday from Chicago. He would mail it at the Wells Fargo office when he went to pick up the mail later in the day.

Edie was in the examining room, placing the new medicines into the glass cabinet.

O'Brien dipped his pen into the inkwell, glanced at the calendar and noted that it was December 12, then dated the check and signed it. After blotting the ink, he placed the check in the envelope provided by the company, along with a copy of the invoice, and sealed it.

The doorknob rattled, and he looked up to see Curly

Wesson come in with a small box in hand, along with a handful of mail.

"Haddy, Doc."

"Morning, Curly."

"Early stage got in on time with the mail. I noticed there was this hyar box from a drug company in New York. It's got the word *urgent* on hyar, so I thought I'd better brang it on over for yuh."

"Oh yes. That's medicine I ordered for a patient. She's been waiting for it to get here. Thank you for bringing it over."

"Yo're welcome. Figgered as long as I was comin', I'd brang the rest of yore mail, so's yuh wouldn' have to come after it." As he spoke, Curly laid the small bundle on the desk.

Doc thanked him again, and the wiry little man left.

Doc began sifting through the bundle but stopped when he came to a letter from Chicago with his son's name and address in the corner. "Edie! Edie!"

His wife opened the door of the surgery and entered the office. "Yes, dear?"

"Curly just brought the mail by. We have a letter here from Patrick!"

A touch of fear showed in her eyes as Frank slit open the letter. She moved around the desk to stand beside her husband and watched as he took the single page out of the envelope and flattened it on the desktop so they could both read it.

Edie sucked in a sharp breath and made a tiny mewing sound.

"Oh no," Doc said, slumping in the chair.

They finished reading the letter, and Doc's fingers trembled as he folded the letter and tucked it back into the envelope. "What are we going to do, hon?"

Edie squeezed his shoulder. "I don't know, other than write him a firm letter." Tears welled up in her eyes.

The outer door opened, and Rebecca Kelly entered with

her coat collar clasped tightly under her chin and a heavy scarf wrapped around her throat. Doc and Edie glanced through the window and saw the pastor pulling away from the boardwalk in the family buggy.

"Don't tell me that cold's not better," Doc said.

"I think it's getting worse." Rebecca's voice had a nasal quality. "And I'm about out of my prescription cough medicine. Pastor will be back to pick me up in a little while. He has a call to make on a ranch west of town."

"Let's take her in the back room, Edie," Doc said. "I'm going to treat her with that new elixir that came in Friday. We've got to stop this cold before it gets any worse."

Edie seated Rebecca on a chair, then went over to stand beside her husband as he mixed the medicine and heated it. As Doc carried it to his patient, he said, "This is plenty hot, dear, so just sip it slow."

Rebecca nodded, took the first sip, and made a face. "Ugh-h-h! Why can't they make medicine taste good?"

"Maybe someday they will."

She sipped again, then ran her gaze over the faces of the two gentle Irish people. "Doc...Edie..."

"Yes?" said Edie.

"I couldn't help but notice when I came in that there's a touch of sadness on both of your faces. I don't mean to pry, but...is something wrong?"

Edie's lower lip began to quiver.

Rebecca waited, taking another sip of the bitter medicine.

"Well, yes," said Doc. "Something is wrong. We've told you about our son, Patrick Michael, who is a physician and surgeon in Chicago."

"Yes. If I remember correctly, when Pastor and I first came here last August you told us you had been an army doctor until leaving the army to set up your practice here in early 1867. You said your big dream was to have Patrick come to Fort Bridger and work with you for a while, then take over the practice when you retire."

"That's right," said Doc. "You've got a good memory."

"Has something happened—"

Rebecca's words were cut off by the sound of a gunshot up the street.

She started to speak again, but there were more gunshots.

"Can't be those two guys who shot up the saloon the other day," said Doc. "They're still behind bars."

They could hear some shouts, but when there was no more gunfire, Rebecca said, "I started to ask if something's happened concerning your son."

"Yes," said Doc. "When we first wrote to Patrick about coming to take over the practice, he replied quickly, saying it looked like a great opportunity and he would give it a lot of prayer and thoughtful consideration. A short time later, another letter came. He said he had prayed about it and had decided that the Lord wanted him to come and work with me, and ultimately take over the practice. That was six months ago."

Rebecca swallowed more of the elixir. "But something's happened to those plans, I take it?"

"Yes. We were expecting him to be here sometime this next spring, but a few weeks ago we got a letter that hit us pretty hard. He said he wasn't so sure he should come. That things had changed there in Chicago, and he might just stay."

Edie spoke up. "We could tell by the tone of his letter that Patrick's heart was cold toward the Lord."

Rebecca closed her eyes. "Oh no."

Doc nodded. "We wrote him back, asking what had changed his mind. The next letter was vague, but in it he mentioned a young woman. Her name is Lois Trent. He didn't say it in so many words, but Edie and I have a strong feeling that this Lois Trent isn't a Christian. We could see that she's having an influence on Patrick, and it definitely is not a good influence."

"Oh, I'm so sorry."

"We just got a letter from Patrick today," said Edie. "That's why we're upset. In this letter, Patrick says he has decided not to come to Fort Bridger. That his father will have to find someone else to take over the practice when he retires."

"When Pastor comes to get me," Rebecca said, "you need to tell him about this. He'll want to hear it from you. I—"

She was interrupted when the door burst open, and four men came in carrying Marshal Lance Mangum, who was unconscious.

When the black curtain began to lift, Lance became aware that he was lying facedown on a hard surface. There was a stinging sensation in the upper left side of his back, and he could feel something moving against it.

He opened his eyes against a bright blur and heard a feminine voice say, "He's coming around."

Lance closed his eyes against the light.

"No more chloroform," Doc O'Brien said. "I'm almost finished."

Then it hit Mangum's mind like the crack of a whip. Vin Maltz! He was holding his .45 on Maltz, telling him to drop his gun belt, when— What was it? A sharp blow on his back and the sensation of falling.

The fog was slowly lifting from his brain, and Lance recognized the voices. He was at Doc O'Brien's office. Doc and Edie were working on him.

He opened his eyes and this time focused on Edie's plump face.

"Marshal…" said Edie. "Can you see me? Hear me?"

Lance ran a dry tongue over equally dry lips. "I…water. Please." His tongue felt thick and numb.

"Just another minute on the water, Lance," said the doctor. "I need to finish putting this bandage on. Then we can roll you over and give you a drink."

The minute seemed like a year, but finally they carefully and gently rolled him over. The bandaged wound lay against a small pillow, but there was still some pain.

Edie gave Lance a few sips of water, which helped relieve the dryness in his mouth. He squinted to bring the room into focus and said, "Doc, I'm shot in the back, right?"

"Yes. You were about to arrest an outlaw. Do you remember?"

"Yeah. Vin Maltz. I had the drop on him. I told him to unbuckle his gun belt, and...and that's when a slug hit me in the back."

"Yes. Maltz had an accomplice positioned behind you as a backup. When you put Maltz under arrest, the accomplice shot you. Abe Carver saw what was going on and ran to your office to let Jack know. Jack got there just as the accomplice shot you in the back. He shot the accomplice and put a bullet through Maltz's heart. Both men are dead."

Lance moved slightly and grimaced. "Jack's all right then?"

"Yes. He's out in the waiting room. He wants to see you when I say he can."

The marshal closed his eyes and swallowed hard, then said warily, "Doc, how bad is my wound?"

O'Brien turned away, carrying surgical tools to Edie, who was cleaning up at the cupboard.

Fear scratched at Lance's mind. "Doc, how bad is the wound? Did you get the slug out?"

O'Brien laid the surgical tools on the counter, pivoted slowly, and said in a somber tone, "Yes. I got it out."

"Well?"

Lance took the doctor's reluctance to speak as confirmation that he was in danger of dying. The Holy Spirit had done

His work, and Lance said, "Doc, I…I've been a fool for putting off salvation."

Doc was praising the Lord in his heart that the marshal had brought up the subject. Aloud he said, "Anybody who hears the gospel and rejects Christ is a fool. What's been your problem? Having trouble believing that Jesus died on the cross and rose again to provide you salvation?"

"No. I believe it. I just didn't want to be considered a fanatic."

Doc raised his bushy gray eyebrows. "Did you say 'didn't'?"

"Yes."

"You mean the fear of being called a fanatic if you got saved is no longer there?"

"No. I don't care. The fear of God is what's on me. I don't want to go to hell."

"Afraid of dying lost, eh?"

"Yes."

"Well, let me explain your condition. It was a .45 slug. It lodged in the upper left side of your back. I thought at first that it had hit your lung, but when I cut in there, I saw it missed the lung by about a half inch. If it had ripped into the lung, I probably couldn't have saved you. But thank God, you're going to be all right. You'll be off your feet for a few weeks, but you'll be back on the job by the second week of January, I'd say."

Mangum nodded, relief showing on his rugged features.

Doc leaned down close and looked him straight in the eye. "Now that you know you're not in danger of dying from this wound, do you still want to be saved?"

Mangum nodded. "Yes, I do. Like I said, I've been a fool to put off salvation. Will you help me?"

Doc smiled. "Most gladly." Turning to Edie, he said, "Hon, will you see that we're not disturbed?"

Tears misted Edie's eyes. "I sure will." She went out the door into the waiting room.

Doc O'Brien kept a Bible in the office and one in the examining room. He went to the medicine cupboard and pulled the Bible from a drawer. "Let's go over some Scriptures. I want to be sure you clearly understand."

Lance nodded.

Flipping pages, Doc stopped at the opening of the book of Mark and said, "I'm going to read you words that came from the lips of the Lord Jesus Christ Himself. He said in Mark 1:15, 'Repent ye, and believe the gospel.' You've got to understand those two words, *repent* and *believe*.

Lance nodded.

"Do you understand that without repentance of your sin you cannot be saved?"

"Yes. Pastor Kelly made that very clear in both sermons on Sunday."

"And do you understand what it means to repent?"

"Yes. Repentance is a change of mind that results in a change of direction. I am to change my mind about my sin, about trying to make it to heaven on how well I live, about whatever religion I have, and turn around from the direction I'm going and call on Jesus for salvation."

Doc smiled. "You were listening, weren't you?"

"Others have talked to me about this before, too. Heidi, Hannah Cooper, you, and more recently, my deputy, who's a new Christian."

"All right, Lance, you've got the handle on repentance. Now let me show you something about this gospel you have to believe in order to be saved."

O'Brien flipped pages until he was in the first chapter of Romans. "Romans 1:16 says, 'For I am not ashamed of the gospel of Christ: for it is the power of God unto salvation to every one that believeth....' Now, the apostle Paul made it clear in his inspired writings that there are false gospels that are preached by religious systems, but those gospels will not save. It must be the true gospel of Jesus Christ that we believe.

"Listen as I read you God's definition of the gospel." Quickly finding 1 Corinthians 15, Doc said, "Here it is. Paul, under the inspiration of the Holy Spirit, wrote, 'Brethren, I declare unto you the gospel...how that Christ died for our sins according to the scriptures; and that he was buried, and that he rose again the third day according to the scriptures.' There it is, Lance. When Jesus died on that cross, He shed His precious blood for our sins.

"God's definition of the gospel is three things: Christ's death, burial, and resurrection. There are no human works in the gospel, no religious rites, and no one else but Jesus. The Bible says, 'Whosoever shall call upon the name of the Lord shall be saved.'"

Tears were visible in Lance Mangum's eyes.

"Are you willing to turn to Jesus in true repentance, Lance? To call on Him, ask Him to forgive you of all your sins, and receive Him into your heart?"

The tears spilled over onto Lance's cheeks. "Yes, Doc. Yes!"

After Lance had called on the Lord to save him, Doc said, "Is it all right if I let Jack come in and see you now?"

"Of course."

"I can only let him stay a minute, then you're going to have to rest."

"Yes, sir."

Lance heard low murmurs; then Doc came back with Edie and Jack. The O'Briens looked on as Jack gently gripped his boss's hand and said, "Doc just told me, Marshal. I'm so glad for you!"

"Yes!" said Edie. "Praise the Lord!"

Lance looked up at Jack and said, "I'm proud of you for taking out those two outlaws."

"Just doing my job, boss."

"And doing it well, I might say."

Doc touched Jack's arm. "He's got to rest."

"Okay, Doc, but he's got another visitor who wants to see him."

Lance's brow furrowed. "Who?"

"A lovely blonde," Jack said, his eyes twinkling.

"Heidi?"

"That's right," said Doc. "She came in while you and I were going over the Scriptures."

"So she knows?"

"Mm-hmm."

"I'd like to see her alone."

"Of course. But only for a few minutes. You've got to rest." The O'Briens and Deputy Bower left the room, and before the office door closed, Heidi Lindgren was moving toward the table where Lance lay. Tears were already on her cheeks as she said, "Oh, Lance, I'm so happy that Jesus now lives in your heart!"

He took her hand in his. "I am, too. I was such a fool to keep turning Him away."

Heidi wiped tears with a hankie. "I've prayed for you to be saved for so long."

He still had her hand in his as he said, "I know the next thing for me to do is to be baptized and unite with the church. I intend to do it as soon as possible."

"That's wonderful, Lance! I...I don't like to make this visit so short, but Doc says—"

"I know. Will you come back again soon?"

"Of course," she said, giving his hand a squeeze. "Bye for now."

She paused at the door and gave a tiny wave, then was gone.

Moments later, Doc returned with Pastor Andy Kelly. Lance told him of his desire to be baptized, and Kelly said he would baptize him as soon as Doc said it could be done. Kelly led in prayer; then Doc put his foot down and said no more visitors that day.

By the end of the day, word had spread through the town and the fort about the shooting, and that Marshal Lance Mangum had been injured but would be fine in a few weeks.

The O'Briens kept Lance at the office for a few days, allowing only a few visitors—mostly Heidi Lindgren, the pastor, and Jack Bower.

On the third day after the shooting, Sundi Lindgren came with Heidi to see Lance, and when they left, she smiled to herself. Though Lance and Heidi did not openly say or do anything sentimental, Sundi had seen definite signs that romance was blooming.

CHAPTER FOURTEEN

I n the days that followed Holly McDermott's funeral, Emily
was given sedatives to keep her calm and to make her sleep
much of the time. Dr. Garberson came by every other day
to make sure Matt had plenty of sedatives on hand and to see
how Emily was doing. By Wednesday following the funeral
there was still no change.

"Don't give up, Matt," Dr. Garberson said. "She didn't get
this way overnight and she's not going to get over it overnight,
either."

Matt drew a deep breath and let it out slowly. "If I could
only get a small glimmer of hope."

"You will. Just keep talking to her as much as you can,
and do your best to get her to understand that Holly is gone.
Like I've said before, the quicker she can grasp that fact, the
quicker she'll get well. Even the shock that sets in when reality
hits her will serve to make her mind function properly."

Matt rubbed the back of his neck. "I'll do my best, Doctor.
Thanks for coming out again. I wish you'd let me pay you."

Garberson squinted at him and said, "How much did you
make today on your odd job?"

"Nothing. You know that. I can't leave Emily to do my
odd jobs."

"Well, nothing is what it'll cost you for me to make this
house call."

The doctor put on his coat and picked up his medical bag from the small table. He patted Matt's shoulder. "Keep your eyes on the Lord. He'll see you through this."

"I know," said Matt. "He has blessed us in so many ways. My old flesh wants to doubt Him, but in my heart I know it's going to turn out all right. God bless you, Doctor."

"And God bless you too, my friend. I'll be back Friday."

As Matt went to open the door, the doctor furtively laid something on the small table by the coat rack and rushed past him into the cold air.

Matt watched the doctor drive away in his buggy, then went to the fireplace, threw a couple of logs onto the fire, and sat down in his overstuffed chair. He picked up his Bible and held it a moment without opening it. Several verses of comfort he had memorized passed through his mind. When Isaiah 58:9 came to mind, he opened the Bible to that page and let his eyes fall on the words that had given him strength during the past few days: "Then shalt thou call, and the LORD shall answer; thou shalt cry, and he shall say, Here I am."

Tears spilled down Matt's cheeks and dropped on the sacred page. "Oh, Lord," he said, "I need You close to me. Please help me to lay claim this truth. I don't expect to hear it with my ears, but please let me hear Your voice in my heart. Here I am…Here I am…Here I am…"

Matt broke into sobs, and it wasn't until some time later that he could dry his tears and say, "Thank You, Lord. I know You are right here with me. Please give me wisdom as I try to deal with Emily. And please reach down and heal her mind. Dr. Garberson says that when she understands Holly is gone, she'll get better. Please help me get through to her."

After praying for a few more minutes, Matt went to the bedroom and found Emily awake. When he sat down on the edge of the bed, she looked at him with vacuous eyes.

"I love you, sweetheart," he said, taking her hand.

Emily frowned and tried to bring him into focus. Her eyes cleared somewhat, and she said, "I love you too, Matt." She blinked again. "When are you going to let Holly come in and see me?"

Matt reached over and grasped her other hand. Pressing them together within his, he said, "Emily, don't you remember what I told you about Holly?"

She closed her eyes and shook her head slightly.

"Jesus took Holly to be with Him in heaven, honey. Remember? I've told you that several times."

She looked at him and said, "But she's back now, isn't she? It's cold outside. She shouldn't be out in the cold very much or she'll catch pneumonia again."

Matt lifted her hands to his lips and kissed them. "You rest, honey. I'll be back to check on you a little later."

A hint of fear showed in Emily's glazed eyes as she said, "When will Holly be home?"

He patted her cheek and rose from the bed. "You rest now."

Emily was staring into space when he paused at the door and looked back.

Matt went to the kitchen and opened the pantry door. The shelves were almost bare. Soon he was going to have no choice. He would have to sedate Emily in the mornings so she would sleep while he went to work. Then he could buy groceries.

There was still Chester Neely's barn to finish repairing, and he had other odd jobs waiting for him. He moved to the kitchen window. Snow blanketed the land at a depth of some fourteen or fifteen inches. The sun was playing hide-and-seek behind some high, wind-driven clouds.

Movement caught his eye near the barn. A jackrabbit!

He rushed down the hall to the small vestibule and took his Winchester .44 rifle off its rack, worked the lever to make sure it was loaded, and quickly donned hat and coat. Hurrying to the rear of the house, he eased his way out the back door. The jackrabbit was hopping leisurely alongside the barn.

As Matt trudged through the snow toward the house, carrying the dead jackrabbit by the ears, he saw a shadowed face at the kitchen window.

He left his kill on the back porch and entered the kitchen, rifle in hand. Still at the window, clad only in her flannel nightgown, Emily turned slowly toward him. Her face was expressionless as she said, "I heard a gunshot."

"Jackrabbit," said Matt. "I'll skin him. We'll have him for supper tonight."

A faint smile curved her lips. "Holly likes rabbit. She's not in her room. Will she be home in time for supper?"

Matt laid his rifle on the table and gently took hold of her arm. "You need to get back in bed, honey. Look, you have goose bumps."

Emily said no more until she was covered up. As Matt tucked the covers under her chin, she said, "Will she? Will Holly be back in time for supper?"

"Back from where?" Matt said.

A blank look captured her eyes. "Wh-wherever you said she went."

"I told you that Holly went to heaven to be with Jesus."

Emily seemed to be thinking. After a moment, she said, "Well, that's just down the road. She ought to be home by suppertime."

Matt gave Emily more sedative and stayed with her until she drifted off to sleep, then went outside to skin the jackrabbit. As he did so, he felt a bit of encouragement. Although Emily still wasn't grasping what he was trying to get across about Holly, she at least had remembered that Holly loved to eat rabbit. He thanked the Lord for that much.

He returned to the house with the skinned jackrabbit in hand and placed it in the skillet for later, then carried his rifle to the front of the house and placed it on its rack. He took off coat and hat, hung them on the coat rack, and started to turn away when something shiny caught his eye.

He squinted in disbelief at the two twenty-dollar gold pieces on the hall table. A hot lump rose in his throat as he picked them up. "Dr. Garberson," he whispered. "Not only do you refuse payment for your services, but now you do this." He closed his eyes. "Bless him for this, Lord. Give him back a hundredfold."

That evening, while Emily sat up in bed and ate the fried rabbit dinner Matt had prepared, she kept looking toward the bedroom door.

When she finished eating and Matt picked up her tray, she looked at the door again. "Matt…"

"Yes, honey?"

"Did Holly like the rabbit? Why doesn't she come in and see me?"

Feeling the weight of his continual sorrow, Matt set the tray on the dresser, sat down on the edge of the bed, and took both of Emily's hands in his. "Honey, look at me. I want to ask you something. Do you remember what the word *dead* means?"

Emily studied his face for a long moment. "Mm-hmm. The jackrabbit is dead. You shot him dead so we could eat him."

"Right. Now listen closely. Holly isn't with us anymore. Holly is dead. She died of pneumonia. We buried her body at the cemetery in Mountain View. Her soul has gone to heaven. She's there with Jesus now, and we won't see her again until we go to heaven. Do you understand?"

She cocked her head, squinted, and replied, "Heaven must be a very beautiful place, darling."

Matt's heart quickened pace. He gripped her hands tighter. "Yes, honey. Heaven is a very beautiful place. And that's where Holly has gone. She died. Do you understand?"

Her eyes clouded and seemed to lose their focus as she said, "I hope Holly liked the rabbit as much as I did. Will she come in and see me now?"

Matt's heart sank. Then he shook himself mentally and moved his lips soundlessly. "Forgive me, Lord. I realize I'm expecting too much too soon. She's better. Thank You for that. Please help me to be patient about it."

The next morning, Matt explained to Emily that he had to drive the wagon to Mountain View and buy groceries, which she seemed to comprehend. He gave her a heavy dose of seda-tive, hoping she would sleep until he returned.

After purchasing the groceries in town, Matt stopped by Dr. Garberson's office and expressed his deep gratitude for the money the doctor had left on the table. From there, he drove to Chester Neely's ranch and explained why he had not been back to finish the repairs on the barn. Feeling confident that he could sedate Emily sufficiently in the mornings, he told Neely he would do the work half a day at a time until it was finished.

On Friday morning, Matt did as planned and accom-plished a great deal of the needed repairs on Neely's barn. He would finish it at this rate in about a week.

With a half day's wages in his pocket, Matt guided the wagon through the gate to his farm. His head bobbed in shock when he saw Emily coming out of the barn, wearing only her flannel nightgown. He snapped the reins and urged the horses toward her.

Emily stood barefoot in the calf-deep snow, her body

trembling, and stared at him with bulging eyes as he jumped from the wagon.

"Where's Holly?" she demanded.

Matt lifted her up in his arms and headed toward the house. "Emily, you shouldn't be out like this. You'll have pneumonia."

"Where's Holly, Matt? What have you done with her?"

Matt hurried inside and sat her on a chair in front of the fireplace, which still had a good fire burning. He dashed to the bedroom, took some blankets out of the closet, and hurried back to her. She was trembling all over, and her teeth were chattering.

After wrapping her in the blankets, he stoked the fire and added more logs. "Emily," he scolded mildly, "you mustn't leave the house, do you hear me? You could freeze to death out there."

She set scornful eyes on him. "You mean like Holly is doing? She's not in the barn, Matt, so you must have her in the toolshed. Please bring her in before she catches pneumonia again. Why do you make her stay out there?"

The sound of a horse blowing came from outside. Emily looked that direction as Matt went to the window.

"It's Dr. Garberson," he said.

Emily smiled.

Matt opened the door as the doctor stepped up on the porch, medical bag in hand.

"Matt." Garberson nodded. "How's our girl doing?"

As he closed the door, Matt said, "Little episode today. Not good. She's in the parlor."

Garberson gave him a curious look as they moved toward the parlor. "What kind of episode?"

"I'll explain in front of her. Maybe it'll help."

Emily was looking at the floor when they entered the parlor.

Raising her dull eyes, she flicked her husband a petulant look and said, "I'm glad you came, Dr. Garberson. I need your help."

He placed his bag on a small table. "What kind of help?"

"I need you to make Matthew bring Holly in the house. He's got her out there in that cold, dirty toolshed."

Garberson glanced at Matt then said, "Emily, did you go outside to look for her?"

"Yes. That's why I'm bundled up here by the fire now. I woke up while Matt was gone somewhere and went to Holly's room. She wasn't there. I looked through the whole house, even the cellar, and couldn't find her. So I figured Matt had her out in the barn. But I looked in the barn. She wasn't there, either. So she has to be in the toolshed. Matt came home before I could look in the toolshed. He brought me inside. Please go get Holly out of the toolshed, Doctor. Bring her in here to me."

Garberson patted her shoulder and said, "I need to talk to Matt in private for a few minutes, Emily. You wait right here."

The men went into the hall and moved far enough from the parlor door so Emily couldn't overhear them.

"Tell me when she started being more alert and talking as clearly as she is now," Garberson said.

Matt explained the change that had come over Emily in the past two days. He told him about trying to get Holly's death across to her again and again, but how it seemed Emily put up a wall when the subject was broached. He also explained about going to work that morning at Chester Neely's ranch, thinking he had given Emily enough sedative to keep her asleep until he got home.

Garberson nodded. "All right if I try again to get through to her?"

"Sure."

"Let me go in alone."

"Anything you say, Doctor. I'll be in the kitchen."

Matt had been sitting at the kitchen table some twenty

minutes when he heard Garberson coming down the hall.

"I couldn't get through, either, Matt. It's just going to take more time. I know you have to work, and you have no one to stay with Emily, so I'm leaving a stronger sedative. Not much stronger, please understand, but maybe she'll sleep until you get home in early afternoon. Keep telling her about Holly's death. Sooner or later you'll break through."

"I'll keep trying," said Matt, the strain of it all showing on his features.

"I'm encouraged because of her present alertness, Matt. Maybe we're closer than it seems. She told me she's having some headaches, so I'm leaving a couple of envelopes of salicylic acid for you to mix with water and give to her. The directions are on the envelopes. Hide them where she can't find them. I don't want her taking too much. Don't let her have any to prevent headaches…only let her have it when she has one."

"All right. Do you think the headaches are related to her problem?"

"It's possible. Has she told you about the headaches?"

"No. But she hasn't been this clear until today. And as you can see, she's miffed at me right now."

"Not now, she isn't. She talked very sweetly about you to me. From what I know about mental problems like this, mood swings sometimes go with it. I have to leave now, Matt. Get her back in bed as soon as her chills let up."

When the doctor was gone, Matt returned to the parlor to find Emily smiling at him, her eyes glazed more than when he had last talked to her. As he walked her to the bedroom, she held on to his hand and said, "I love you, Matt."

"And I love you, honey."

As he tucked her under the covers, Emily said, "I know you're keeping Holly from me because you don't want her to see me in this pathetic condition. Right?"

Matt closed his eyes, praying for wisdom.

"Right?" she pressed him.

"I…I really wouldn't want Holly to see you like this, honey. That is correct."

Emily put fingers to her temples. "I have a headache, Matt. Dr. Garberson said he left some powders. Would you mix some for me?"

When Matt returned with the mixture, and Emily had downed it, she handed him the cup and said, "Won't you tell me where you're keeping Holly until I get better?"

"I can tell you this much, sweetheart…she's in good hands."

Emily gritted her teeth in pain and rubbed her temples. Occupied with the headache, she didn't press him to tell her just where Holly was.

The next day when Matt arrived home after working the morning at the Neely ranch, he was surprised to see Emily standing in the kitchen when he came in from the barn. She had her robe and slippers on. Her arms were folded across her chest in an indignant manner. "Tell me where Holly is!"

"Emily, I—"

"I didn't look in the toolshed because you told me Holly's staying with someone. I want to know where she is."

Matt sighed. "Will you sit down here at the table and listen real close as I tell you?"

"I don't want to sit down! Just tell me!"

As Matt started speaking, telling Emily that Holly had died with pneumonia and had been buried in the cemetery at Mountain View, Emily blinked and put both hands to her temples. Another headache was coming on. Lights seemed to be glowing in the corners of her eyes, and she could feel pressure building behind her eyes as if black water were being pumped into her head.

Tenderly, Matt said, "Another headache?"

She gritted her teeth without answering.

"Sit down, honey. I'll make you another salicylic acid mixture."

Suddenly her eyes went wild. Shaking her fists at him, she screamed, "If you'd bring Holly home to me, I wouldn't have these headaches. I never had them until you took Holly away from me! I want her back right now!"

"Please sit down, honey. I'll—"

"Don't tell me to sit down! Just go get my daughter and bring her home! Where is she? With a neighbor? In Mountain View? Lyman? Green River? Where, Matt? Where are you keeping my baby?" At that point she went into a wild tirade, screaming at him incoherently.

In desperation, Matt gripped her shoulders. "Emily, listen to me!"

But the screaming went on.

Gripping harder, he said, "Will you stop screaming?"

She stopped long enough to take another breath, and he shook her enough to get her attention, then said in a low, even tone, "Will you listen to me?"

The wildness was still in her eyes, but she stared at him silently.

"Emily, I've told you repeatedly that Holly died. She is dead. Do you understand? She died of pneumonia over a week ago. She won't be coming home. She's in heaven. Do you understand?"

Emily batted her eyelids, and the wildness suddenly left her eyes. She reached up and put her arms around Matt's neck, hugged him, then kissed his lips. As she eased back, her voice was soft and pleasant. "Yes, darling. Yes. You are right. The Lord won't let anything happen to my sweet Holly. He took our other babies, but He will never take Holly. She will always be with me, and I'll be fine."

While Emily was calm, Matt gave her a salicylic acid mixture and was able to get her to eat a small amount of lunch.

Afterward, he gave her a sedative. As they moved down the hall toward the bedroom, she clung to him and said sweetly, "Yes, darling. Yes. You are right. The Lord won't let anything happen to my sweet Holly. He took our other babies, but He will never take Holly. She will always be with me, and I'll be fine."

Soon Emily was asleep. Matt stood over her and wept, begging God to bring her out of it.

He could think of no other way. He had to work at least half days, so he gave Emily the stronger sedative for the next three days, and when he returned home just after noon each day, she was still asleep.

The strain was taking its toll on him, however. He had been spending the nights on the old sagging couch in the parlor but was getting very little sleep. His body was as tired as his mind, and his once handsome face was drawn. Deep lines of worry had formed on his brow. He had to work to keep money coming in, but each day he was in a constant state of concern when he had to leave Emily alone.

Matt wasn't much of a cook, but he did his best to provide something warm at breakfast, lunch, and supper. He encouraged Emily to eat, but he could only force her to take a few bites each meal, sometimes between clenched teeth. She was rapidly losing weight, and he realized he wasn't doing much better. His own appetite was sadly lacking.

There was a continuous prayer on his lips for guidance as he went about his daily routine. Each morning he placed his heavy burden in God's merciful hands, knowing that only the great Physician could heal Emily's mind and give her peace.

On Wednesday, December 14, Matt was delayed while buying groceries in Mountain View and arrived home just after one o'clock to find Emily in Holly's room, pacing back and forth, wringing her hands and wailing loudly. Tears glistened her face.

When she turned and saw him standing at the door, she blared, "This will not go on any longer, Matthew! I want to know where my daughter is!"

Matt's whole body sagged. "Emily, Holly is dead. She died of pneumonia almost two weeks ago. You must face that fact and let the Lord give you peace about it."

"Holly is not dead! Why would you tell me that? I don't care what kind of condition I'm in. I want to see my daughter! Where are you hiding her, Matthew? Where?"

Matt stepped into the room, and Emily backed away from him until she bumped into the bed.

Remaining where he was, Matt said, "Sweetheart, I'm not hiding Holly from you. She's in heaven with Jesus."

"No! No! Holly would not leave her mother! She loves me! You tell me where you're hiding her or I'm going on a search for her. I can't stand living without her! Do you hear me? I'll find her myself if you don't bring her home!"

Matt took her in his arms. "Let me feed you some lunch."

"I'm not hungry, Matthew! I'll never eat another morsel until you bring my daughter home to me! I don't want to live without Holly! I can't stand it! If you don't bring Holly home to me, I want to die!"

"Please don't talk that way, sweetheart. I love you, and I need you."

The mood swing came suddenly. Emily nestled herself comfortably in her husband's arms and said softly, "I love you, too, darling. We have such a happy home, don't we? Just the three of us. Holly will be home soon, won't she?"

Later, when Emily was asleep, Matt went to the small vestibule at the front of the house, took his rifle down, and went to the barn. Emily's talk about wanting to die if she couldn't get Holly back had him frightened. After hiding the rifle in the hayloft, he told himself he would also have to hide his revolver when he came home each day.

CHAPTER FIFTEEN

After shaving the next morning, Matt entered the bedroom to find Emily wide awake. She smiled up at him and said, "Good morning, darling."

"Good morning, sweetheart." He leaned over to plant a kiss on her forehead. "I'll have breakfast ready in a few minutes. I'll bring it as soon as it's ready."

"Oh, Matt, could I come to the kitchen and eat breakfast with you?"

Encouraged by her clearness of mind, Matt said, "Of course. I'll come get you as soon as it's ready."

At breakfast Emily talked of the old days in Kentucky. She seemed to comprehend everything Matt said, and her memory of the old days was clear. But she only talked of the time before any of the children were conceived, and not once did she bring up Holly's name.

Matt was encouraged as he rode out of the yard. Emily had eaten a good breakfast, which had stirred him to do the same. Now under the influence of the sedative, she was sleeping soundly.

When he returned home that afternoon, Emily was still sleeping. When he checked on her about an hour later, she was out of bed and sitting in the overstuffed chair in the bedroom. They talked for a while, and Matt was surprised but pleased that she did not bring up Holly in the conversation.

The next morning, Matt awakened in the parlor to the sweet aroma of hot coffee, bacon, and pancakes. When he entered the kitchen, Emily was standing at the cupboard, dressed and wearing an apron. Her hair was brushed and combed into an upsweep.

"Well, what's this?" he said, smiling.

"I decided it was time I was doing my wifely duties. You still have time to shave if you want to. Breakfast will be ready in about ten minutes."

With each scrape of the razor Matt spoke to the Lord, thanking Him for this sudden change in Emily.

They ate breakfast companionably. Emily talked of the weather, remarking that it was cold enough to keep the snow from melting but she was glad it hadn't snowed for several days. She made no mention of Holly, and Matt was beginning to wonder if she had finally found a way to deal with the truth.

As they were finishing breakfast, Matt said, "Honey, I'm working at one of the stores in Lyman, and I might be a little later getting home this afternoon. I have a shelf job to finish, and I won't get paid unless I finish it. You seem much better. If you wake up and I'm not here, will you be all right?"

"Of course, darling. I really don't think I'll need to take the sedative today. I feel pretty good."

"I'm glad you feel better, but I really don't want you to go off the sedative without talking to Dr. Garberson first. If he doesn't make it today, he'll be here tomorrow. Let's wait and talk to him. Okay?"

"Of course," she said, nodding. "I'll take it after I clean up the kitchen and wash the dishes; then I'll lie down."

"There's no need for you to do the cleaning up, honey. I can do it before I go to work. You just take the sedative and lie down."

"Oh no. Not as long as I'm feeling better. It's my job, and I want to do it."

Matt sighed in relief. "Oh, it's so good to see you like this. Praise the Lord!"

"Yes, praise the Lord," she echoed. "It's good to feel this way."

Emily stood at the parlor window and watched Matt ride away. Then she turned and made her way to the kitchen to start the cleanup job. When she was finished, she went to the bedroom. As she stood in front of the mirror, deciding what task she would tackle next, she looked at her reflection, and a deep frown creased her brow. "Why, Emily?" she said out loud. "Why is Matt lying to you about Holly? Your little girl is out there somewhere. Why should she be staying in someone else's home when she could be here with her mother?"

Her hands formed into tight fists, and her voice was firm as she told her reflection, "The time has come to find her."

Emily opened the closet door and took out her high lace-up boots. There was at least a foot of snow on the ground, and the boots would keep her feet dry. When she had exchanged the boots with the shoes she had put on that morning, she went to the small vestibule at the front of the house and took out her heavy coat and put it on. She tied a wool scarf over her head and went out the back door toward the barn.

"You horses are going to help me find Holly today," she said while harnessing the team to the wagon. "We'll all be much happier when she's home with us, won't we? And so will she."

Breath steamed from the horses' mouths and nostrils as they pulled the wagon out of the yard and started down the snow-laden road. Emily pointed the team north toward Lyman. "Since Matt's been working of late in Lyman," she told the horses, "he must have Holly staying there. Holly always liked to play out in the snow when we lived in Kentucky. I'm sure she'll be playing outside today, wherever Matt has her staying. Certainly whoever has her would let her outside to play, even if they watched her every minute."

When Emily reached Lyman, she began a methodical search, driving along every street and through every alley, looking for her daughter. She saw children playing and longed for the sound of Holly's merry laughter. Twice she saw children building snowmen and recalled how on their Kentucky farm, Holly often persuaded her father to help her build one.

It was late morning when Emily had searched the small town, with no sign of Holly. She was about to give up when she said to the horses, "Maybe Holly's with Matt. I'll find him and just see."

She drove through the business section, looking for Matt's horse. It took her only a few minutes to spot the animal tied at the hitch rail in front of Mitchell's Hardware Store. When she stepped inside, Emily could hear the muffled sound of hammering from somewhere at the back of the store. A glance toward the counter showed her Wayne Mitchell waiting on a customer with two more standing in line. She was glad Mitchell was occupied.

The door leading to the storeroom was closed. Emily glanced over her shoulder, then slipped through the door. Moving stealthily, she approached the open door of a large room from which the sound of hammering was coming. When the hammering stopped suddenly, she froze. Her heart thudded against her rib cage. There were a few taps; then the loud pounding started again.

She moved up to the edge of the door and peeked in. Matt was putting in new shelves, and his back was toward her. She quickly scanned the room, but there was no sign of Holly. There was another room across the narrow hall. She moved swiftly and opened the door. There were all kinds of hardware goods piled on shelves, and boxes stacked haphazardly around, but no Holly.

Consternation welled up in Emily. Where was her little girl? She could feel pressure building inside her head. She sneaked past the door to the room where Matt was building shelves and reentered the store, then hurried out the front door.

Emily was muttering to herself as she drove the wagon south. "Where is she, Matthew? Who has my daughter?" She began to weep as the wagon reached the outskirts of Lyman.

Matt had done a lot of work in Green River. That was it! Green River was farther away than Lyman, or even Mountain View. Holly was staying with somebody Matt knew in Green River! Anger filled her. *Wherever Holly was being kept, it had to be against her will.*

The more Emily thought about it, the angrier she became. She kept picturing Holly locked in a room somewhere, begging to go home. Emily thought she could even hear Holly crying out in terror, frantically pulling on a doorknob, trying to escape.

When she drew up to the road that ran east and west, Emily was so caught up in her visions of Holly as prisoner that, without realizing it, she turned west toward Fort Bridger instead of east toward Green River.

Heidi Lindgren and Doc O'Brien went ahead of Jack Bower, who carried Marshal Lance Mangum up the stairs to his apartment.

When Doc and Heidi reached the landing, Lance said, "Door's not locked. The landlord built a fire in my kitchen stove to warm up the apartment."

Doc opened the door and gestured for Heidi to enter.

As Jack carried Lance through the door, Doc said, "Carry him on into the bedroom, Jack, and put him on the bed."

"Not right now, Doc," Lance protested. "Let me lie on the couch here in the parlor. I can get myself to bed when I'm ready. Come to think of it, let me sit at the table there in the kitchen. Heidi's going to fix lunch for me."

"Don't you need to get back to your shop?" Jack said to Heidi as he placed Lance on a chair.

"I always close it from noon until one o'clock," she replied. "If I hurry, I can feed your boss and make it back to the shop by one."

"But what about your own lunch?" Doc asked.

Heidi laughed. "It won't hurt me to skip it."

"You can eat some of whatever you fix for me," Lance said.

"Fine. Let's see what you've got in the cupboard."

Mangum looked at the two men heading toward the door. "Thank you, Doc," he said, "for the good care. I'm going to be as good as new because of how well you've taken care of me."

"Hah! Just wait till you get my bill!"

Lance turned his gaze to his deputy. "Thanks for carrying me up here, Jack."

"All in a day's work, boss. And—whew!—it was work. What a load!"

Mangum laughed. "All muscle...and don't you forget it!"

"How could I? My back won't let me!"

When Jack and the doctor had gone, Heidi stood at the cupboard and said, "How about beef broth, Marshal Mangum?"

"Sounds good, Seamstress Lindgren."

Heidi giggled. "You are definitely feeling better."

"How could a man not feel better with such a pretty lady to attend to him?"

Heidi blushed and turned away to prepare lunch.

While they ate together, Heidi could feel Lance's eyes on her throughout the meal. It pleased her, but she didn't let on. When they were almost finished, she looked at the clock on the wall and pushed back her chair. "Oh my! It's five minutes to one! I've got to get these dishes cleaned up and hurry back to the shop."

"No need," said Lance. "My landlady has already said she would keep the apartment cleaned up for me until I'm back on my feet. She'll be up in a little while."

"Who's going to cook your meals?"

"She'll do that, too. It's all set. Would…ah…would you like to come for supper this evening?"

"Oh, I can't. I'm helping Mandy Carver make some Christmas decorations at her house this evening. Supper is included."

"Then another night, okay?"

"Sure. We'll just do that." Heidi carried the dishes to the cupboard and said, "You're sure Mrs. Cartwright is coming to clean up?"

"Positive."

"All right. So you're going to lie on the couch for now?"

Lance grinned. "Yes. Would you help me get over there?"

Heidi frowned at him. "You told Doc you could get to the bedroom by yourself, but you can't get to the couch?"

"Well, it'll be difficult, but I'll make it. I thought as long as you were here, I'd let you help me to the couch."

"All right, Marshal Mangum. Let's get it done. I've got to leave."

Heidi leaned close to Lance and said, "Put your arm on my shoulder, and I'll help you get out of the chair." Their faces were only inches apart now, and Heidi paused when their eyes met. For just a moment, two hearts seemed to beat in rhythm, and their lips came very close to touching.

Heidi broke the spell by saying, "Here we go. Hang on and give me all the help you can. You're a big man, Marshal Mangum."

His heart was racing. "And you're a beautiful woman, Seamstress Lindgren."

At Cooper's General Store, Patty Ruth Cooper was helping Jacob Kates unload boxes in the storeroom while her mother sat behind the counter. Leah Morley, wife of farmer David Morley, worked with Hannah behind the counter.

Leah was adding up the bill when Hannah heard the bell jingle at the front door and saw Curly Wesson enter. "Mail delivery boy reportin' in, ma'am!" he said, laying a small bundle of mail on the counter.

Hannah laughed. "Well, thank you, boy!"

Looking around, Curly said, "An' jist whar is that cute little redhead, Miss Hannah?"

"Right here!" came the voice of Hannah's youngest. She came out of the storeroom.

Curly's eyes lit up as he set them on the little girl. "Wal, I declare! Whut a cute little thang you are!"

He looked down at the bright-eyed child and said, "Whut's yore name, little girl?"

Hannah leaned close to Leah and whispered. "I love this act, but I could repeat it backwards."

Leah laughed, and both women looked on, enjoying the exchange between Curly and Patty Ruth, which ended with them hugging each other.

When Curly had gone and Patty Ruth had returned to the storeroom, Leah turned her attention to a lieutenant and his wife from the fort and began adding up their bill.

Hannah was about to look through her mail when the door opened and bank president Lloyd Dawson and his wife, Lois, come in, followed by Mayor Cade Samuels. The three were carrying on a conversation they must have started outside. They waved a greeting at Hannah and Leah, then started down the aisles still talking.

Hannah sifted through the envelopes and smiled when she saw a letter from Mr. and Mrs. Adam Cooper of Cincinnati, Ohio. She quickly opened it and read. There were tears in her eyes when she finished the letter and put it back into the envelope.

"Bad news, Hannah?" Leah asked.

"Oh no. Just sentimentality. The letter is from my late husband's brother, Adam, and his wife. They live in Cincinnati, Ohio. I just miss them very much."

"How long has it been since you've seen them?"

Hannah thought a moment. "It'll soon be a year. They came to Independence to see us in February last year. We write back and forth quite often."

"It's good that you can keep in touch."

Hannah nodded. "We've never been together for very long at a time...especially since Adam married Theresa. But we developed a deep love for each other in a hurry. They have a little boy. Seth. He's six. And they just told me in the letter that Theresa is expecting another child."

Leah nodded. "I assume Adam is younger than...than his brother."

"Mm-hmm. Solomon was thirty-six when he died. Adam is thirty-four. And quite successful for his age, I might add."

"Oh?"

"He is editor-in-chief of the *Cincinnati Post,* the city's leading newspaper."

Leah's eyebrows raised. "Mmm! He's quite young to be editor-in-chief of a large newspaper. I know about the *Post.*"

"So do I," said Lloyd Dawson, who had overheard the conversation as he was passing by. "Did I hear correctly, Hannah? This is your brother-in-law who's editor-in-chief?"

"Yes."

Cade Samuels drew up with two small items and laid them in front of Leah. Looking at Hannah, he said, *"Cincinnati Post,* eh?"

"Mm-hmm. Adam may be young, but he's sharp and resourceful. His big dream is to have his own newspaper someday. I have no doubt he'll do it. He's mentioned a few times that he might like to come west when he starts his paper. Of course, capital will be a problem. He doesn't have the kind of money it takes to start a newspaper...you know, a building, presses, office furniture and equipment..."

Cade Samuels paid Leah for his purchase, looked at Dawson, and said, "I'd love to see a newspaper started in our town. We have to wait for the stagecoaches to bring us the Cheyenne City paper, or the little one from Rawlins, to find out what's going on in the world...and then the news is always several days old."

Dawson glanced at his wife as she came with several items in her arms and laid them on the counter in front of Leah. He nodded his head in agreement and said, "I think this whole town would love to have its own newspaper."

"It would do well, Lloyd," Cade said. "The town is growing, and more farmers and ranchers are moving into the area all the time."

Jacob and Patty Ruth had come from the storeroom, and having heard the conversation, Jacob spoke up. "As a former big-city man, I can tell you that a newspaper would do well here. Small towns love to have their own paper."

Dawson fixed his gaze on Hannah. "Tell you what, Hannah. When you write to Adam, I want you to tell him the mayor and I talked to you about this newspaper idea for Fort Bridger. We'd like to see him come here and start his paper. Tell him the Fort Bridger Bank will seriously consider extending him a loan if he needs it to establish the paper. If he's interested, tell him to write me, and I'll communicate with him so we can get down to some details."

"I'll sure tell him, Mr. Dawson," said Hannah. "And I appreciate your willingness to consider helping him."

Patty Ruth stood behind the counter, taking it all in. "Mama..."

"Yes, honey?"

"Are you talkin' 'bout Uncle Adam?"

"Yes, honey."

"Are Uncle Adam, Aunt Theresa, and Seth gonna move here?"

"Maybe, honey. But nothing's for sure. We'll just have to see if it works out someday."

She clapped her hands and jumped up and down. "Oh boy! It sure would be neat if they moved here! I really love Uncle Adam, an' Aunt Theresa, an' Seth, too! Seth's my— What's the word?"

"Cousin, honey. Seth's your cousin."

"Oh yeah. Cussin'! I love my cussin' Seth."

Hannah shook her head, looked up at the ceiling, and sighed. "It's cousin, Patty Ruth. Cousin."

"Yeah! I sure hope my cussin' Seth moves here."

Shaking her head again, Hannah said, "Well, Patty Ruth, it's time for you and me to go to Miss Julianna's house and help her get ready for Larissa's party tonight."

They arrived at Julianna's house at three o'clock. Hannah was carrying a birthday cake, and they walked slowly and carefully down West Street, the town's last street on the west side.

As they drew near Julianna's yard, Patty Ruth eyeballed the snowman she and her siblings had built. The scarf was still in place, as were the coal eyes, but a few warm days had caused him to sag a bit, and there were spots where chunks of snow had fallen off.

"Mama," Patty Ruth said, "could I stay outside and play with Mr. Snowman? He's got some sore spots in some places. Especially on this side. Could I, huh? Please? I'll fix the places I can reach."

Hannah glanced at the front door of the house and saw Julianna looking out at them. "All right, honey. I'll let you stay outside for a little while. Half an hour at the most, though, because it's too cold to stay out any longer."

"Okay, Mama! You hear that, Mr. Snowman? I gotta fix you up in a half hour!"

"You come when I call, won't you, honey?" said Hannah. "No arguments?"

"Yes, ma'am."

"Promise?"

"Yes, ma'am."

"All right. You'd better get busy. A half hour isn't very long. And don't take your mittens off."

"Yes, ma'am."

Hannah drew up to the porch and Julianna moved down the steps to meet her. "Here, Hannah, let me take the cake."

As they moved inside, Julianna looked over her shoulder at the little girl in the red coat and scarf, and said, "I assume Miss Patty Ruth is going to do some repair work on Mr. Snowman."

Hannah chuckled. "You assume correctly. I think it's the motherly instinct in her. She spotted some 'sore spots' that need healing."

Julianna laughed. "Bless her sweet little self."

"I told her she can only stay out there half an hour."

"Probably long enough to get his sore spots healed, I'd say."

"The ones she can reach, anyway."

Patty Ruth waved at them and called, "I love you, Mama!"

The two women went to the kitchen, where Julianna began to delegate some birthday tasks to Hannah.

In the yard, Patty Ruth looked up at the snowman that stood much taller than she and said, "Well, Mr. Snowman! 'Member me? I'm Patty Ruth. I came back to see you. An' I'm gonna fix your sore spots so they don't hurt no more."

CHAPTER SIXTEEN

As Emily McDermott guided the wagon into the ruts others had made in the snow, hope welled within her that she would find Holly in Green River. The nagging question tormenting her was why Matt would keep Holly from her. Yes, she had been disturbed some lately, but didn't he understand that it was because Holly was so very ill?

And then Holly got well. As soon as Holly got well, Matt took her out of the house and put her somewhere else. He should know that no one could take care of Holly like her own mother.

Pressure was building in Emily's head again. "Dear God, please don't let me have one of those awful headaches. Please. I need to find my little girl. If my head has that terrible pain—"

Her eyes fell on the uneven rooftops of the town ahead of her. "Oh! It's Green River! Please, God, let me find Holly. She needs me, Lord."

The pressure inside her head lessened somewhat, and she sat up straight, saying to the horses, "We're going to find my sweet little girl, boys! I just know it!"

Emily's head bobbed as her eyes caught sight of the large flag waving in the breeze above the tower at the fort. "Whoa, boys!" she said, pulling rein.

She blinked in confusion as she gazed all around her. "Why, this is Fort Bridger! How did I—" She pivoted on the

seat and looked behind her. "What's happened here? I—
How—"

Facing forward again, she looked at the flag once more
and said, "Boys, I don't know how we came this way instead of
going to Green River, but maybe this is where Matt put Holly. I
can't think of anybody he knows here, but he could have found
someone who takes care of children. Let's go on into town and
see if she's here."

She snapped the reins and put the team in motion again.

In less than an hour, Emily had driven down every snowy
street and alley on the east side of Main Street, including making a circle around the perimeter of the fort and passing by the
town's schoolhouse. Each time children came into view, her
heart picked up its pace, but as she studied them, there was no
sign of Holly.

After driving Main Street and still not finding her daughter, Emily determined to cover the west side just as carefully. It
was after three o'clock when she reached the north end of West
Street and headed south. "This is the last street, boys," she said
to the horses. "If we don't find Holly on this one, we'll go
home. Then tomorrow, after Matt goes to work, you can take
me to Green River. We can't give up. We've just got to find her."

Emily's eyes searched the yards on both sides of the street.
There were no children playing in them at all. Moments later,
as she reached the south end of the street, she felt a pang of
despair. Tears filled her eyes. "Why, Lord? Why would Matt do
this to me? Why would he do it to Holly? He knows how much
we love each other and how much we need each oth—"

She yanked back on the reins, bringing the horses to a
sudden stop.

What Emily's eyes beheld sent shivers of excitement within
her. She forced herself to take deep, even breaths, then said in a
whisper, "Holly! Holly, it—it's you!"

Emily could hardly believe her eyes. Though she was on a

quest to find her daughter, it seemed almost unreal that she had actually found her. But there she was, doing what she loved to do so much—building a snowman. Whoever the people were in the house, they had bought Holly a new red coat and red cap to match. But it was Holly, all right. The little girl was exactly Holly's size, and had long auburn pigtails.

"All right, boys," Emily said to the horses, "let's take Holly home."

Emily's heart was pounding as she drew the wagon to a halt at the edge of the yard and climbed down. She trudged through the snow where many footprints had already been made. Tears filled her eyes as she approached the child, crying, "Holly, darling! I've found you!"

The little redheaded girl jumped with a start and wheeled about. Patty Ruth stared at the strange woman who opened her arms and bent low.

"Sweetheart, aren't you going to give Mama a hug? I've missed you so very much!"

When Patty Ruth took a step back, Emily said, "Holly, give Mama a hug."

"My name isn't Holly, ma'am. I'm Patty Ruth Cooper."

Cocking her head to one side, Emily said, "Holly, haven't you missed me? Why won't you give me a hug?"

"I'm not Holly, ma'am," Patty Ruth said emphatically. She had no fear of this woman. In fact, the woman's strange, sad eyes made Patty Ruth feel sorry for her.

Emily looked toward the house and said, "Did those people tell you something bad about me, honey? Something that would keep you from loving me?"

When Patty Ruth saw tears fill the woman's eyes, it made her feel even more sorry for her. She told herself it wouldn't hurt anything if she hugged the poor, sad woman. Moving into Emily's outstretched arms, she said, "I'll hug you, ma'am, even if I'm not your little girl."

Emily held her close, tears streaming down her cheeks. "Oh, Holly, I love you so much! How I've missed you!"

Patty Ruth gave her a good squeeze but did not comment.

Emily held her at arm's length and said, "We need to head for home now, Holly. Let's go."

Patty Ruth stiffened in her grasp. "Please, ma'am. I'm not your little girl. I already have a home."

The look in Emily's eyes grew more vacant. "That's right, Holly. I knew the Lord wouldn't let anything happen to you. He took my other babies, but He would never take you. You will always be with me, and I'll be fine."

Relaxing a bit, Patty Ruth said, "You had babies who died?"

Emily nodded. "I've told you about them. And you remember your little brother Michael. You were four years old when he died. I know you remember. We've talked about it lots of times."

Patty Ruth shook her head. "No, we haven't, ma'am. I'm not Holly. My name's Patty Ruth Cooper."

"Honey, we need to be going now. I want us to be home when Papa gets there."

Patty Ruth stiffened again. "My papa's gone to heaven. He doesn't live with us at home anymore. I have to stay here. I'm workin' on Mr. Snowman. Mama's gonna call me in pretty soon."

"I've been so lonely for you, Holly," Emily said, making a sad face. "Would you just climb up in the wagon and sit with me for a few minutes?"

Patty Ruth's heart went out to the poor lady. "All right," she said. "I'll sit up there with you for a few minutes."

Emily picked her up and placed her on the seat, then went around to the other side and hoisted her dress enough to get a foothold on the metal step and climb up beside the little girl with the long pigtails. "We're going home now, Holly." As she spoke, Emily snapped the reins and put the horses in motion.

At once, Patty Ruth knew she was in trouble. Her features went white with fear. "No! Stop the wagon! I'm not going home with you! Mama wants me to come in the house!"

"Holly, don't you sass me!"

Patty Ruth stood up on the floor of the box and looked back toward Julianna's house. Bursting into tears, she cried, "I want to go to Mama!"

"Holly, you're being naughty! Stop that crying! What will people think when they hear you cry like that?"

Sobbing, Patty Ruth yelled, "I want my mama!"

In desperation, Emily threw an arm around Patty Ruth and clamped her mouth shut, pulling her down on the seat.

Patty Ruth pressed a scream against Emily's strong hand and tried to wriggle loose, but found herself helpless in the woman's grasp.

There was no one on the street to see the wagon turn the corner and head out of town.

Hannah Cooper sat at Julianna's kitchen table, entertaining Larissa, who was in her high chair. Julianna was taking dishes from the cupboard, preparing to carry them into the small dining room to accompany the silverware she had just placed on the table.

Hannah entertained Larissa by squeezing her fat little fist and shaking it. As the baby giggled, she glanced up at the clock on the wall and jumped to see the time. "Oh my! It's been almost forty-five minutes since I left Patty Ruth in the yard. I'll go call her in."

"You just stay seated," said Julianna, picking up the small stack of plates. "I'll go call her in."

"I'm not an invalid, you know," Hannah called after her.

"Of course you're not," Julianna said over her shoulder as she entered the dining room and laid the plates on the table. "But I know what it's like to be going on my seventh month. You and Larissa keep each other occupied. I'll be back in a minute."

Hannah smiled in Julianna's direction and said, "Larissa, your mommy is a stubborn one."

As if she understood, the baby threw her head back and giggled.

Julianna felt the sting of cold air on her face as she stepped out onto the porch. She looked toward the snowman and frowned, then ran her gaze all around the area. When she couldn't see Patty Ruth, she moved off the porch and slogged through the snow, looking right and left for a sign of the little redhead.

The snowman showed signs of repair on the lower parts of his body. Julianna ran her gaze up and down the street, then across to the other side.

No Patty Ruth.

There were so many footprints in the snow throughout the yard that it was impossible to tell if the little redhead had gone around the house. Rubbing her arms briskly, Julianna trudged alongside the house to the backyard and scanned the area, but the only movement was the horses in the small corral.

The barn, maybe, thought Julianna. She threw the latch and stepped inside the barn. "Patty Ruth! Are you in here?"

Silence.

Julianna pulled the door shut and dropped the latch in place. She saw Hannah step out onto the back porch from the kitchen, a quizzical look on her face.

"Something wrong?" Hannah called.

"I can't find Patty Ruth."

"She's not out front with the snowman?"

"No. I'll put my coat on and check with the neighbors. Mrs. Peabody loves children. She might have invited Patty Ruth into her house for some hot cocoa and cookies or something."

"I'll go with you."

"No need," said Julianna. "You shouldn't walk on ice and snow any more than you have to."

"I came all the way over here from the store on it."

"I know," said Julianna, moving up on the porch, "but there's no reason for you to walk next door with me. If Patty Ruth's with Mrs. Peabody, we'll know she's okay."

Julianna left the house in a hurry. Hannah waited at the kitchen table. Moments later, she heard the front door open and close, and Julianna entered the kitchen, looking worried.

"She's not there, Hannah. Mrs. Peabody lies down for a little while most afternoons about three o'clock. She said she saw Patty Ruth playing with the snowman just before she lay down, but hasn't looked outside since she got up a few minutes ago."

A quiver of uneasiness came to life under Hannah's rib cage. Rising to her feet, she said, "I'm going to look for her. First thing is to check with everybody in this block. Maybe she saw a dog or something that interested her. She might be in somebody's house or yard."

"*We* are going to look for her," said Julianna. "I'll take Larissa next door to Mrs. Peabody."

Hannah and Julianna went door to door. By the end of the block they had found no one who had seen Patty Ruth. They crossed the street and started up the other side. When they had canvassed the last house, Hannah drew a shuddering breath. "Where could she have gone, Julianna? It isn't like Patty Ruth to just leave on her own and wander off. If she wanted to go somewhere, she would have come in the house and asked permission."

They were crossing the street, heading for Julianna's house. "I agree. It just doesn't make sense, Hannah. She knew you were going to be calling her in pretty soon."

"The only thing I can think of is that school lets out at three-thirty. Chris, Mary Beth, and B.J. knew Patty Ruth and I were going to be at your house at three. Maybe they came by and took her over to the schoolhouse. She loves to go there, and it's not very far away." She paused. "But I can't imagine them taking her without checking with me first."

"Well, it's worth a try. Let's go tell Mrs. Peabody we'll be a little longer."

It took the women a few minutes to walk to the schoolhouse. There were no children on the playground as they made their way to the schoolhouse porch.

When they stepped inside, Sundi Lindgren was at her desk at the front of the large room, grading papers. She raised her head and smiled. "Hello, Hannah...Julianna. What can I do for you?"

Hannah's voice carried a tremor as she said, "We've got a little girl missing, Sundi. Patty Ruth has disappeared."

"What! Disappeared? From where? When?"

The two women told Sundi the story, then Hannah explained why they had come to the school.

"Your children left with everybody else, Hannah, and I haven't seen them since. I'm sure they're home by now."

Hannah looked at Julianna. "I'm going home. Maybe for some reason Patty Ruth—oh, I don't know!" She pressed a hand to her temple.

"I'm going with you," Julianna said, putting an arm around Hannah

Already on her feet, Sundi said, "I'm going with you, too. I want to know if Patty Ruth is there."

Ten minutes brought them to Main Street. The boardwalks had been shoveled, and they could move faster once they had dry footing beneath them. They met townspeople along the way, but they spoke only a greeting and kept moving.

When they reached the store, Major Clint Barker and his wife Alice were coming out, carrying grocery sacks.

"Hello, ladies," said the major, his brow furrowing at the look on their faces. "Something wrong?"

"We're not sure," said Hannah. "Is Patty Ruth in the store?"

"We didn't see her," said Alice. "Mary Beth and Chris are in there."

Hannah's expression tightened.

"What is it, Hannah?" Barker asked.

"If Patty Ruth isn't here, and her sister and brothers haven't seen her, I'm afraid she's missing, Major."

The major and his wife followed the women inside. There were other customers moving about, and Leah Morley was waiting on a farmer and his wife. Mary Beth was behind the counter, standing next to Leah and observing the transaction. When she raised her eyes and saw the look on her mother's face, she rounded the end of the counter and hurried to her.

"Mama, are you sick?"

"Honey, have you seen Patty Ruth?"

Mary Beth frowned. "Weren't you and Patty Ruth together at Miss Julianna's house? Hello, Miss Julianna...Miss Lindgren."

"We were," said Hannah, "but something's happened. She vanished into thin air."

"What? Mama, what do you mean?"

"Where are your brothers?"

"Chris is in the storeroom with Uncle Jacob. B.J. is next door at Bledsoe's."

As Leah was collecting money from her customers, she looked past them and said, "Hannah, where was she last seen?"

"In my front yard," Julianna said. "She was working on the snowman she and her siblings built several days ago."

Jacob and Chris came out of the storeroom.

Chris immediately went to his mother's side. "Did we hear right? Patty Ruth's missing?"

Hannah could feel hysteria welling up in her chest. "Yes. She's gone. We can't find her."

Chris put his arms around Hannah. "Come, Mama. Sit down." With loving hands he guided her to one of the chairs near the potbellied stove.

Mary Beth moved close and laid a comforting hand on her mother's shoulder.

The rest of the customers in the store gathered around as Julianna told the story again.

"We need to cover the whole town before it gets dark," said Major Barker. "I'll inform Colonel Bateman of this. We'll be back with some men shortly."

"I'll go tell Jack," said Julianna. "We've got to get as many people searching as possible."

The Barkers rushed toward the door with Julianna on their heels. When Julianna reached the door, she looked back and said, "Hannah...let's consider the birthday party canceled. None of us are going to be in a partying mood."

Hannah nodded. Involuntarily her hand went to her mouth. "She...she's got to be found before dark. If she's out there alone and lost somewhere, she'll freeze to death."

Julianna's eyes misted. "We can't let that happen. I'll be back with Jack shortly."

When Julianna was gone, Hannah looked up at her oldest son and said, "Chris, would you go over to Bledsoe's and bring B.J., please? He needs to know about this."

"Sure, Mama. Shall I tell him about it, or do you want to?"

"You can tell him, honey."

"Be back in a minute," he said, bending over and kissing his mother's cheek. "We'll find her, Mama."

Hannah tried to smile as she patted his arm.

As soon as Chris moved away, Sundi took his place beside Mary Beth and laid her hand on Hannah's shoulder. "Chris is right, Hannah," she said softly. "We'll find Patty Ruth."

"Jesus won't let anything happen to her, Mama," said Mary Beth. "He knows where she is, and He will bring her home to us."

Hannah's lips quivered, and tears filled her eyes. She took hold of Mary Beth's hand and squeezed hard.

Chris and B.J. were at their mother's side when Julianna returned with Deputy Marshal Jack Bower. Jack knelt in front of Hannah and said, "I'm going to organize a search party right now, Hannah. I've already got a few men out asking others to join us. The first thing we're going to do is knock on every door in town. Patty Ruth just might have been seen by someone after she left Julianna's yard."

"Marshal Jack…" said Chris.

"Yes?"

"Could I help you? I could ride Buster and move pretty fast."

"I can use you, son," said Jack.

"Okay. I'll go saddle him right now."

At the same time Chris went out the back door, Major Clint Barker entered with Colonel Ross Bateman behind him. They spotted Hannah and made a beeline for her.

"Hannah," Colonel Bateman said, "I'm so sorry to learn about this, but I want you to know you've got some help here. Major Barker and I have twenty men on horseback outside who will help search for Patty Ruth."

Hannah swallowed hard. "Thank you, Colonel. And please thank those men for me."

"I will. And I want you to know that as the troopers come in from their patrols, the sentries at the gate will tell them to join us." The colonel turned to Bower. "Deputy, we should organize between us, so we'll be as effective as possible."

"I agree, Colonel."

"Good. Let's go outside. We need to talk to everybody in town in case somebody saw Patty Ruth, not realizing she was straying. And we need to get it done before dark."

"That's for sure," said Jack. "Let's move."

"Deputy," said Leah, "if someone would ride out to our farm, I know David would join the search."

"I'll see that he's contacted right away," said Jack.

The male customers in the store volunteered immediately. Jacob also volunteered, but Hannah told him she needed him at the store since her mind wasn't working too well at the moment. Jacob deferred to her wishes.

Jack Bower had reached the front door when Hannah called to him.

"Yes, Hannah?"

"Chris is out there now. Would you tell him to go let Pastor Kelly know about this? Then he can join you."

"I sure will." His eyes fell on Julianna. "See you later, sweetheart."

Sundi Lindgren stayed close to Hannah, as did Mary Beth and B.J. After speaking all the encouraging words she could think of, Sundi fell quiet and held Hannah's hand.

Fifteen minutes had passed before Pastor Andy Kelly and Rebecca came to the store. Rebecca threw her arms around Hannah and said, "Don't you despair, sweet Hannah. They'll find Patty Ruth."

Hannah clung to her, letting tears roll.

"We saw Deputy Bower on the street," Pastor Kelly said. "They've got men—army and civilian—going up and down every street and knocking on every door, asking if anyone has seen Patty Ruth. Let's ask the Lord to keep His hand on that precious little girl. He knows where she is. Let's ask Him to keep her safe and bring her home unharmed."

There wasn't a dry eye in the store as Andy Kelly led them in prayer, pouring out his heart to the Lord for Patty Ruth's safe and soon return. When he finished, he told Hannah he would leave Rebecca with her till he returned. He was going to join the search party. With that, he hurried out the door to put wings to his prayer.

Rebecca stood next to Hannah and said, "None of us want a thing like this to happen, dear Hannah, but since it has, I believe you are going to see just how much you and your family are loved in this town."

Hannah sniffed, used a hankie on her nose, and said, "I'm already seeing it, Rebecca."

The little bell above the door jingled, and three more women entered—Glenda Williams, Julie Powell, and Mandy Carver. Their husbands had joined the search party.

A few minutes later, Nellie Patterson came in and told Hannah that both her husband and fifteen-year-old son had joined the search.

Hannah looked around at her circle of close friends and said, "This means more to me than I can ever find the words to say."

Nellie hugged her. "We love you and your children, Hannah. Don't ever forget it."

"How could I? All of you are so wonderful."

The door opened again, and Heidi Lindgren came in, accompanied by Edie O'Brien. The newcomers threaded their way through the group to embrace Hannah and speak their comfort and encouragement.

Managing a weak smile, Hannah said, "Edie, does your presence here indicate that your husband has joined the searchers?"

"It sure does."

"I appreciate that, but shouldn't he stay at the office in case someone needs his care?"

"Oh, he's caring for one particular patient at the moment."

"I don't understand."

Edie glanced at Heidi. "Tell her, honey."

"Dr. O'Brien probably would have gone on the search anyway, but when Marshal Mangum insisted on going, Doc told him he was still too weak to be out riding a horse. The marshal said he was going whether Doc liked it or not."

Hannah shook her head. "Heidi, is Lance out there searching for Patty Ruth right now?"

"He sure is. And Doc is right there with him in case he has any problems."

"Some kind of man, that Mangum," sighed Hannah.

"Don't I know it," said Heidi.

Sundi winked at her sister.

Soon the sun began to drop behind the western horizon.

Hannah glanced toward the large front windows and said, "It'll be dark soon. Nobody's come back yet, which means they haven't found my baby girl."

Rebecca Kelly knelt down in front of Hannah. "Let's pray some more."

Rebecca prayed fervently for Patty Ruth's safe return and asked the Lord to be especially close to Hannah and her other children in the trial that had come upon them.

Just as Rebecca was saying her amen, Chris Cooper came through the door. Every eye watched him as he walked to his mother and said, "Mama, we haven't found her yet, but Deputy Jack asked me to come and tell you that we've covered every house in town, and nobody's seen Patty Ruth. The men are going home and to the fort for lanterns. They're going to keep up the search, even after dark."

Hannah nodded. "I appreciate that so much." Her eyes strayed to the large window again. It was almost dark.

Somewhere out there in the vast Wyoming dusk, her little girl was in trouble.

As the darkness began to deepen, so did Hannah's dismay.

CHAPTER SEVENTEEN

The sun had gone down and was giving off a spray of orange light over the Uintah Mountains as Matt McDermott guided his horse up the gentle rise that would bring his place into view. The temperature was dropping fast, and with the gathering cold came the wind, its icy fingers stinging his face and stabbing through his clothes.

Matt smiled to himself and patted his chest where the money lay that Wayne Mitchell had paid him for the shelves. Mitchell had added ten dollars as a Christmas gift. And to top it off, his wife, Ethel, had asked Matt to come to the house and do some repair work on her kitchen cabinets, saying that she would pay him as generously for his labor as her husband had if he could do the work tomorrow.

Matt chuckled. He liked the Mitchells very much and would have put off his next job by one day to do the work for Ethel, even without the ten-dollar bonus. So tomorrow he would be back in Lyman to do the work at the Mitchell house.

Horse and rider topped the snowy crest, and the horse whinnied at the sight of the McDermott place.

Matt's attention was drawn to the windows of the house, for every one of them was flickering with lantern light. This was the way Emily had always welcomed him home from a day's work before Holly died. His heart leaped for joy at the sight.

As he rode into the yard, he noticed wagon tracks in the snow leading toward the barn. This puzzled him. The wagon had not been out from under its lean-to shelter on the other side of the barn since the last snowfall.

Matt dismounted and led his horse inside the dark barn. Moving to the wall just inside the door, his experienced fingers found the lantern that hung on a large nail. Matches lay beside it on a small shelf. He scratched a match against the wall and lit the lantern. Raising the wick to shed a broad circle of light, he hung the lantern back in place, then removed the saddle from the horse's back and placed it on a nearby sawhorse with the saddle blanket. He took off the bridle and hung it on a peg beside the harness and bridles of the wagon team.

At the back of the barn he opened the door and let the other two horses in. After pouring grain into the feed trough and pitching hay down from the loft, he pumped water into the tank that stood just inside the back door.

As Matt left the barn and headed for the house, the gleaming windows made a pleasant sight. He opened the kitchen door to the smell of supper cooking, and there was Emily, standing at the cupboard, cutting hot bread. She laid down the knife and rushed to him with open arms.

"Welcome home, darling!" she said.

Matt received the longest kiss he'd had since Holly died and was thrilled to see his wife once again so demonstrative. They kissed a second time; then Matt held her at arm's length and ran his gaze over her. She had her hair done in the style he liked best, and had even put on a little powder and rouge, something else he hadn't seen since Holly's death. Not to mention her freshly ironed dress and starched white apron.

"You look wonderful, sweetheart," he said, then kissed the tip of her nose.

Matt was about to ask about the wagon tracks in the yard when Emily suddenly backed away from him, her face lit up like a child's on Christmas morning. "I found her, darling!"

She was so excited she was bouncing on her toes. "I found her! Oh, I'm so happy to have her home! You don't need to keep her in Fort Bridger anymore. I'm fine now. I can take care of her again."

The lines in Matt's face deepened. "Honey, what are you talking about? Who was I keeping in Fort Bridger?"

Emily threw her head back and laughed, then rushed to him and kissed him again. "You know who!" She clapped her hands. "Oh, it's just so wonderful to have her back!"

Matt took hold of her shoulders. "Emily, what's going on? Who is back?"

"Why, Holly, of course. I found her and brought her home!"

"Holly?"

"Yes!"

Matt felt as if he had been socked in the stomach. He had been so happy to see Emily so much like her old self. What new tricks was her mind playing on her now? He made a snap decision to go along with the conversation.

He removed his hat and coat and said, "Where did you find Holly?"

"In Fort Bridger, where you hid her. Who are those people you put her with?"

Fearing her mind was totally coming apart on her, Matt looked at the kitchen table and stared at a third place setting, right where Holly always sat. There was a glass for her milk and the smaller utensils for her use.

Oh, dear Lord, he thought. *Help her! Something has gone terribly wrong with her mind!*

Emily studied him, then followed his line of sight to the table. "What's wrong, darling?"

Matt wasn't sure what to do now. He dare not let this fantasy go too far. "Emily, I—"

"Is there something wrong with the way I set Holly's place at the table?"

Feeling numb all over, Matt said, "No, honey. There's nothing wrong with the way you set it, but—"

"But what?"

"Well, you…you…" Matt closed his eyes and shook his head. "Nothing. Nothing, Emily."

With heavy heart he turned to hang up his coat and hat, and froze at the sight of the small red coat and stocking cap that hung on the peg next to his.

His shoulders sagged. "Oh, Emily, where did you get these? Who do they belong to?"

"They're Holly's, darling. Those people you put her with must have bought them for her."

Matt thought about the wagon tracks in the yard. Facing Emily, he said, "Somebody was here with a wagon today. I saw the tracks in the snow. Who was it?"

"Nobody was here, darling," she said, batting her eyelids. "The tracks were made by our wagon."

"Our wagon?"

"Of course. You took Holly away from me right after she got better. I know you did it because you thought it would be better for me, and I understand. I knew you were hiding her with somebody, but I had no idea who, or where. I thought it might be in Lyman, since you know so many people there, and you work there a lot. So I hitched up the team after you left for work and drove to Lyman."

Matt scrubbed a palm over his face. "Oh, Emily."

"I searched all over town for her, but of course, she wasn't there. I even went into Mitchell's Hardware and went to the back of the building. I thought you might have Holly with you, so I took a look. I saw you working on those shelves, but Holly wasn't there, either."

Despair and confusion flooded Matt's mind. Emily was

worse than ever. And where had she laid hands on the coat and stocking cap?

"So when I didn't find Holly in Lyman," Emily went on, "I decided you had put her with somebody in Green River. I drove out of Lyman, intending to go to Green River, but somehow I made the wrong turn. I went west instead of east and ended up in Fort Bridger."

"Fort Bridger," Matt echoed, knowing he had to talk to Dr. Garberson about getting Emily to the mental clinic in Cheyenne City as soon as possible. Maybe they had a mental hospital in Denver.

"Mm-hmm. And now I know why. God knew where Holly was, and He led me right to her."

Grasping both of her hands in his, Matt said in a gentle tone, "Honey, right after supper I'm going to ride to Mountain View and bring Dr. Garberson. He needs to see you, and I need to talk to him."

"Dr. Garberson? Why? I'm fine, and so is Holly. What do we need him for? Those people you had taking care of Holly let her outside to play with her snowman. They could tell she was all well. She doesn't have a cold at all."

"Snowman? You found Holly playing with a snowman in somebody's yard in Fort Bridger?"

"Yes. The Lord led me right down that street, and there she was! I saw those long red pigtails first. Who could mistake them? I got Holly to climb in the wagon and brought her home."

Cold sweat beaded Matt's brow. Cautiously, he said, "Emily...where is Holly now?"

"In her bedroom. I had to lock her in, because for some reason she keeps crying and saying she wants to go home."

Matt wheeled about and dashed down the narrow hall to Holly's room. The skeleton key was in the keyhole. His blood went cold when he heard the sobbing of a child inside the room.

His fingers were trembling so much he could barely get the key turned, but finally he pushed the door open. His breath hitched in his chest. What he saw sent a mind-numbing wave through his brain. Chills gripped him. For a second or two, it was like seeing a ghost.

Holly!

No...no. But the little girl who was on her knees in the middle of Holly's bed was the same size as his dead daughter. Her hair was exactly the same color, and she wore long braids just like Holly's. She even slightly resembled Holly with her sky blue eyes and the light sprinkle of freckles on her nose and cheeks.

Her terror-filled eyes were swollen by the tears she had shed. Her body was trembling as she inched backward at the sight of the man, and she sobbed in short, jerky breaths.

"See?" Emily said, drawing up behind him. "I told you I found Holly and brought her home!" Pushing her way past Matt, she stopped in front of him. "Holly, stop crying, honey. Say hello to Papa and give him a big hug like you always do when he comes home from work."

Patty Ruth Cooper's forlorn voice said, "My papa's dead. This man isn't my papa. I want to go home."

Matt took hold of Emily's arm and said, "Honey, go back to the kitchen and get supper ready. I want to talk to her alone."

Emily looked at him with eyes that now had a slight trancelike quality to them. "All right, Matt." Then she said to the child, "Papa will bring you to supper, sweetheart. It's so wonderful to have you home again."

Matt felt nauseated but forced a smile to his lips as Emily squeezed past him through the doorway.

"Supper will be ready in about ten minutes," she said, then went to the kitchen.

Matt closed the door softly and stepped toward the bed. His heart went out to this little girl whose eyes revealed cold terror. She had stopped sobbing now but was squeezing her tiny hands together until the knuckles were white.

Matt kept his hands at his sides as he bent down to her eye level and said, "Honey, please don't be afraid. I'm not going to hurt you, and neither is my wife."

Patty Ruth swallowed hard as she listened warily.

"My name is Matt McDermott, and my wife's name is Emily. What's your name, sweetie?"

She drew a shuddering breath. "Patty Ruth Cooper."

"Cooper?"

She nodded.

"And you live in Fort Bridger?"

She nodded again.

"There's a lady in Fort Bridger who owns the Cooper General Store. Would that be your mother?"

Patty Ruth sniffed and nodded again, her eyes glued to his face.

"If I remember right, her name is Anna."

Patty Ruth shook her head. "Hmp-mm. Hannah."

"Oh, that's right. Hannah."

"I want to go home."

"Patty Ruth, I need to tell you something. No one is going to harm you. You are perfectly safe here. I can't explain why at the moment, but I can't take you home tonight. We will feed you well and take good care of you while you're here."

Patty Ruth's lower lip trembled. "I want to go home now. My mama will be very worried about me."

Matt felt a pang of guilt. Certainly Hannah Cooper would be horribly worried, but he had to sort some things out. He had Emily's sanity to consider. He couldn't take the child away from Emily until he had figured out how to do it correctly.

"Patty Ruth, Emily is going to have supper ready in a few minutes. I don't know if I can make you understand, but she is a very troubled person right now. I promise that we are not going to hurt you. We can talk some more after supper—just you and I—but I need you to do me a favor right now. Would you help me?"

Patty Ruth sniffed again and rubbed her nose but did not reply.

Since she hadn't refused, Matt said, "Would you go along with being Holly in front of Emily for me, while we eat supper? And would you not cry?"

Patty Ruth thought on it. For some reason she trusted him. "Okay."

Matt stood to full height and offered his hand. Patty Ruth hesitated briefly, then placed her hand in his. He helped her off the bed and led her to the kitchen.

Emily was pouring milk into Holly's glass as Matt and her daughter came into the kitchen. She smiled at Patty Ruth and said, "Come on, Holly. Mama's got a nice supper fixed for you."

When they were seated at the table, one thing struck a chord with Patty Ruth. The man and woman bowed their heads, and the man prayed, thanking the Lord for the food. He closed the prayer in Jesus' name.

When the amen came from Matt's lips, Emily kept her head bowed and said, "And Lord, thank You that we have our precious little Holly back home with us."

Matt's face tinted as he ran his gaze from Emily to Patty Ruth.

As they began eating, Matt said, "Emily, I don't want you taking the wagon out by yourself anymore. It's best that a woman not be out driving alone."

Emily smiled. "Isn't it wonderful how the Lord led me to Holly today? Oh, it's so good to have her home."

Patty Ruth glanced at Emily in disbelief, then quickly looked away. She thought of her family. Her lonesomeness for them, combined with the strange situation in this house, had stolen her appetite.

"Holly," said Emily. "Sit up and eat, honey. You must eat to keep up your strength. You know how sick you were. You don't want to get sick like that again, do you?"

Patty Ruth looked at Matt. He smiled at her and gave her the nod to play along. Looking back at Emily, she said, "No, ma'am. I don't want to get sick again."

She turned her focus to the food and ate her meal.

Emily looked at the child dreamily while she ate. "I'm so glad to have my baby girl home. I almost had a headache earlier today, but you know what? I haven't had a headache or even that awful pressure in my head since I found Holly. Isn't that great?"

"Sure is," said Matt, his mind going to Hannah Cooper. He wondered what kind of pressure she was feeling at the moment.

When supper was over, Matt told Emily he wanted to talk to Holly again while she was doing the dishes. Emily smiled and readily agreed.

When Matt and Patty Ruth entered Holly's room, he closed the door and told Patty Ruth to climb on the bed and sit. Pulling a chair up before her, he sat down and said, "Thank you, sweetie, for doing what I asked, and acting as if you were Holly."

She nodded without comment.

"You aren't afraid anymore, are you?"

It took her a moment to reply. "No. But I want to go home. Will you take me home now? Mama is very worried, I know. And so are Chris and Mary Beth and B.J. and Biggie. Please, sir. Will you take me home?"

"Chris, Mary Beth, B.J., and Biggie are your brothers and sisters?"

"Chris and B.J. are my brothers. Mary Beth is my sister. Biggie is our little boy dog."

"How old are your brothers?"

"Chris is fourteen. B.J. is eight. An' Mary Beth is thirteen. I don' know how old Biggie is."

"You said earlier that your papa is dead."

"Mm-hmm. He went to heaven to be with Jesus."

"I see." The child's words intrigued him. "Does your family talk a lot about Jesus?"

"Mm-hmm. We pray to Jesus jus' like you did before we ate supper, and we pray to Him lots more times every day."

"And I suppose the Bible is read in your home?"

"Uh-huh. Papa used to read it to us before breakfast and at night. Mama does now."

"Does your family go to church?"

"Yes. Pastor Kelly preaches to us, an' Mrs. Carver is my Sunday school teacher."

Matt had heard about the church in Fort Bridger. He knew that Andy Kelly preached the true gospel of Jesus Christ. Were it not for the distance, he and Emily would be attending there.

The sick feeling inside him increased. Emily's abduction of this little child—no matter how innocent—was causing untold sorrow and heartache to a sister in Christ and her other children.

"Patty Ruth," said Matt, running his fingers nervously through his hair, "I can't take you home tonight because Emily is not feeling well in her mind. It would make her worse if I took you home before morning. Will you not cry, since I can't take you home right now?"

The five-year-old looked at the floor for a moment. She felt like crying, but nodded at the man and bit her lip.

Matt smiled. "Thank you. I know you'll sleep good in this bed tonight. I'll take you home in the morning."

Patty Ruth raised trusting eyes to his.

Matt cleared his throat. "Patty Ruth, will you…will you keep this just between us? Don't say anything to Emily about my taking you home in the morning. It would just upset her, and we don't need that. Okay?"

Patty Ruth nodded. "Okay."

"Will you just go along with being Holly, like at supper, until I can take you with me in the morning?"

"Uh-huh."

"And you'll make Emily think you're just going to keep on living here?"

Emily's footsteps were coming toward the bedroom.

"Here we go, Patty Ruth. You are Holly till you're on my horse with me in the morning and we're riding toward Fort Bridger."

"Uh-huh."

Chapter Eighteen

Matt McDermott sat in his overstuffed chair in the parlor, watching the shadows from the flickering flames dance across Emily's face. She held Patty Ruth on her lap in the rocking chair. He had seen Holly in that position more times than he could count.

Matt had developed a tremendous admiration for this child. Although Patty Ruth was uneasy, she lay quietly with her head on Emily's breast while Emily hummed an old hymn in a low monotone.

It had been a long, tedious day for the little girl, and though she was lonely for her family, very confused, and in some ways, still fearful, the natural need for sleep began to prevail. The monotone of Emily's humming, the ceaseless motion of the rocker, and the crackling of the fire served to dull her mind, and soon her head began to loll.

When Emily felt the child giving in to slumber, she rose from the chair, adjusted Patty Ruth in her arms, and said, "Beddy-bye time, sweetheart." Then she said to Matt, "I'm going to brush her hair and put her to bed."

Matt nodded. "I'll be in to kiss her good night in a few minutes."

Emily carried Patty Ruth to Holly's room and sat her on the bed. She quickly unbraided her hair and ran Holly's brush through it. After washing Patty Ruth's face and hands, she undressed her and put a warm pink flannel gown on her. It fit her perfectly.

All the while, Patty Ruth was heavy with fatigue, and without any fuss she allowed Emily to tuck her into the strange bed and kiss her good night.

Matt was in the hall as Emily came out. Whispering to him, she said, "Leave the door open, won't you? In case Holly needs me in the night."

As Emily made her way toward the parlor, Matt moved into Holly's room. Leaning over the little lump in the bed, he whispered, "Patty Ruth, are you all right?"

She looked at him with droopy eyes. "I miss my mama."

"I know, honey."

"But you'll take me home in the morning, won't you?"

"Yes. You go to sleep now," he said, kissing her forehead.

When Matt returned to the parlor Emily was still in her rocking chair. He tossed a couple of logs on the fire and turned to look at her. There was a smile on her lips but a strange emptiness in her eyes as she said, "Holly's tired. She'll sleep well tonight in her own bed. I'm so glad to have her home."

Matt felt exhausted in mind and body. Although his energy was spent, he desperately wanted to make Emily understand that Holly was dead and the little girl in Holly's bed belonged to another mother, who by now was in a state of panic. But there was no way to deal with someone whose powers of reasoning were gone.

"Emily…"

She smiled at him vacantly.

"Emily, this has been a very strenuous day for you. I think you should take a sedative tonight so you can sleep."

She nodded slowly. "Mm-hmm."

"Good. I'll mix it for you just before you go to bed. You can drink it while I'm making up my bed here on the couch."

As Emily continued rocking, she stared at some faraway place that only she could see.

A little while later, Matt went to the kitchen and mixed the powerful sedative. When that was done, he tiptoed into Holly's room to check on Patty Ruth. She whimpered in her sleep.

Matt drew a shaky breath and said, "You'll be home in your own bed tomorrow night, sweetheart."

It was ten minutes past midnight. A crowd of women was gathered in the general store with Hannah Cooper, along with Jacob Kates and B.J. Cooper. In spite of the warmth of the room, Hannah looked pale as she sat by the potbellied stove.

Julianna LeCroix had reluctantly left the group to pick up Larissa from Mrs. Peabody's and put her to bed.

There was a low, steady murmur of voices as the women talked among themselves and did their best to stay optimistic for Hannah's sake.

"Listen, everybody!" a woman's voice said. "I think they're back!"

B.J. left his chair, ran to the door, and jerked it open. Peering into the glow of light produced by many lanterns, he called, "It's them, Mama! I don't see Patty Ruth. Colonel Bateman and Deputy Jack are comin' in. Chris, too."

Hannah's heart felt as if it had stopped in midbeat, and she held her breath. Glenda went to her and took her hand while Mary Beth gripped her other hand.

Chris had come in ahead of the two men. He bent down and hugged Hannah's neck, saying, "I love you, Mama."

Her trembling hands cupped his face. "I love you, too, son."

Jack Bower and Colonel Bateman somberly removed their hats and stood before Hannah.

"We've scoured the town and searched the surrounding areas," Jack said, "but we've found no trace of Patty Ruth. We've systematically made a circle wider than she possibly could have walked if she had simply strayed away from the front yard where she was playing."

"Wherever we've found footprints of any kind, Hannah," Colonel Bateman said, "we've made a thorough search. It helped to have snow on the ground. No footprints, no one's been there. We've come to only one conclusion, Hannah."

Tears filled Hannah's eyes. Her hand went to her mouth as she tried to keep her composure. Glenda joined Mary Beth in putting an arm around Hannah's shoulders.

"Patty Ruth wouldn't just take a walk," Hannah said. "It…it has to be that someone has…has kidnapped her!"

A loud sob escaped from Hannah, and she broke down and wept without restraint.

After a time she brought her emotions under control and said, "I'm sorry, I—"

"You ain't got nothin' to be sorry for, Hannah dear," spoke up Judy Charley. "Whut with yore tender heart, an' bein' a mother, yo're jist bein' normal."

"That's right," said Rebecca Kelly. "This world could use more tender hearts like yours."

There was a chorus of voices speaking their agreement.

"We love you, Hannah," said Loretta Noble, wife of the town's hostler.

"That's for sure," came the voice of Jacob Kates. "God never made a sweeter lady than Hannah Cooper."

The door opened, and Heidi Lindgren detached herself from the group, rushing to meet Marshal Lance Mangum, who was leaning on Andy Kelly and Lloyd Dawson. Doc O'Brien and Curly Wesson followed behind.

Mary Beth got up from her chair beside Hannah. "You can sit right here, Marshal."

Mangum smiled at the young girl and thanked her. He gingerly sat down with the help of the two men, then turned compassionate eyes on Hannah as Heidi moved up to stand beside him. "Hannah," Lance said, "I just wanted to say in person how sorry I am that Patty Ruth is missing. I'll be praying for her safe return. I'm not feeling too well, and I need to get back to my apartment, but I had to tell you how sorry I am that this horrid thing has happened. If I get my hands on the person or persons who—"

At that point, Mangum choked up.

Hannah laid a hand on his arm. "Marshal, I can't tell you how deeply I appreciate your joining the search party tonight. I hope you haven't overdone yourself."

"I'm going to the apartment to check him over, Hannah," said O'Brien. "I think he's all right. Just a bit exhausted from being in the saddle."

"I'm going along with you, Doc," Heidi said.

"Pastor Kelly," said Lloyd Dawson, "you need to stay here with Hannah and the children. Alex Patterson and I will get the marshal to his apartment."

When the door closed, all attention went back to Hannah.

"My troops and I are prepared to start the search again in the morning, Hannah," Colonel Bateman said. "And so are most of the townsmen. Every town, farm, and ranch within a radius of fifty miles will be contacted. It will take us several days, but somebody, somewhere will be able to turn up a clue as to Patty Ruth's whereabouts. We won't stop until—"

The door opened, and Captain John Fordham came in with Chief Two Moons and three of his braves.

"Colonel," said Fordham, "the chief would like to talk to Hannah. I already went over the situation with him."

"Fine," said Bateman. He nodded at Two Moons. "Welcome, Chief."

Two Moons paused to shake hands Indian-style with

Bateman, then looked around at the large group and nodded his silent greeting. He turned to Hannah and said, "Hannah Cooper, the hearts of Two Moons and his people are wrapped around you."

Hannah swallowed a hot lump. "Thank you, Chief."

"Soldiers of Colonel Bateman come to village at set of sun. Ask if we see Patty Ruth Cooper. When soldiers ride away, we have powwow. Braves and Two Moons agree if she not found this night, we help look for her when sun come up. Captain John Fordham say that is plan. Two Moons and many braves be back when morning come."

Hannah was overcome with the chief's concern and kindness. Her lips quivered as she said, "There is no way I can thank you, Chief. There are no words to tell you how much this means to me."

The chief's dark face was a picture of compassion. Thumping his chest with a fist, he said, "Two Moons understand language of heart."

Hannah managed a faint smile and nodded. "Yes. Language of the heart."

John Fordham spoke up. "Hannah, do you have reason to believe this might be a kidnapping for ransom?"

She shook her head. "It could hardly be that, Captain. Anyone who lives in this area knows that I am far from wealthy." She swallowed hard. "I...I just can't come up with any reason at all why someone would take or lure Patty Ruth from Julianna's yard."

"Jack," said Jacob, "I assume you looked for any telltale signs at the spot where the snowman stands."

"Yes. There are all kinds of footprints in the area because neighbor children often play in the yard. There was nothing that could give us any leads at all. There are wagon tracks in the street at the edge of the yard, but nothing unusual."

Pastor Kelly stepped to the forefront. "Well, other than the kidnapper or kidnappers, God in heaven is the only one who knows where Patty Ruth is. I want us to pray right now and once again ask Him to bring her back to her family safe and sound."

After he had prayed, Ross Bateman and Jack Bower assured Hannah the search would start at sunup. Two Moons affirmed that he and his braves would be at the fort gate at the rising of the sun.

One of the women suggested that someone stay with Hannah and the children overnight.

Glenda Williams spoke up instantly. "I'll stay with them."

"Me, too," said Abby, "if it's all right with Mom Glenda and Mrs. Cooper."

Hannah told Abby she was welcome to stay, and Glenda gave her permission. Mary Beth gave her friend a hug.

Heidi held the door open while Lloyd Dawson and Alex Patterson helped Mangum inside his apartment. Doc followed on their heels.

When Lance was comfortably settled on the couch, Dawson and Patterson said good night and left. Heidi stood by the couch as Doc checked his patient over and said it was just as he'd thought. The marshal simply tried to do too much too soon, but he would be all right.

As Doc prepared to leave, he said, "Heidi, I'll walk you home if you're going now."

"I think I'll stay for a few minutes, Doc, but thank you."

Lance expressed his appreciation for the doctor's care, and the short, stocky Irishman left.

Heidi sat down on the straight-backed chair O'Brien had occupied while examining Mangum. "Lance, that was a wonderful thing you did…going on the search when you knew you hadn't recovered from your wound and the surgery."

"I had to. I've come to love that Cooper family very much in the few months they've been in Fort Bridger. It was tough enough to have Solomon die on the trip here, but now they're staring this trial in the face. That sweet child is one special little girl. She's got to be found."

"We have to trust the Lord to bring her back," said Heidi.

"Yes."

"Lance, do you want me to help you to your bed before I leave?"

"No need. I'll just sleep here on the couch tonight."

"You sure? Wouldn't you rest better in your bed?"

"I'll be fine here."

"All right. But at least let me take these boots off for you."

Heidi pulled the marshal's boots off and brought him a pillow and blankets from the bedroom. When he was covered and comfortable, she patted his arm and said, "I'll say good night now."

He looked at her with eyes of love and said, "Heidi, a few minutes ago I said that Patty Ruth is one special little girl."

"And that she is. A little ray of sunshine."

"Well, you're a special little girl, too."

A smile tugged at the corners of Heidi's mouth. "I am, huh?"

Lance's pulse was racing. "Yes." He took hold of her hand. "In fact, you are so special that if you don't leave this apartment in ten seconds, I'm going to kiss you."

Heidi's heart lurched in her breast. Lance had never been this bold before, but she loved it. "How can I leave? You have hold of my hand."

Lance let go of her hand, keeping his eyes on her. "Okay. Starting right now, you've got ten seconds."

She did not move.

There was dead silence as Lance counted ten seconds in his mind.

"Time's up," he said softly.

"Good. That was the longest ten seconds I have ever endured."

Lance took her hand again and pulled her down to him. Their kiss was sweet and tender.

For a long moment, Heidi looked into his loving eyes, then said, "You need your rest, Marshal Mangum. I've got to go now." She left a moment later, feeling his gaze follow her all the way to the door.

More weary than she ever remembered being in her life, Hannah slowly made her way up the stairs with Glenda beside her. Chris, Mary Beth, Abby, and B.J. walked ahead of them.

Their little black-and-white rat terrier was at the door, wagging his tail. He rose up on his hind legs and yipped his welcome to the family he hadn't seen for hours. Though everyone was heavy of heart, they couldn't resist the dancing eyes and gaiety of the little dog. When everyone, including the guests, had petted him, Biggie looked around, ran to the door, then ran to the girls' room.

"He's missing Patty Ruth," said Mary Beth.

Biggie came running back, looked around the parlor again, and went to the door. Tail wagging, he whined and yipped as if to say, *Patty Ruth, don't play games! Come in the house and pet me right now!*

"B.J.," said Hannah, "he needs to go out."

B.J. opened the door, and at first the little dog moved about the landing, looking for the missing member of the family, then gave a whine and darted down the stairs.

Moments later, Biggie scratched at the door, wanting in. When B.J. opened the door, Biggie made the rounds of the people in the parlor, searching for Patty Ruth. After another dash to the girls' room he came back, looking puzzled.

Once Biggie was somewhat settled in B.J.'s arms, Glenda took over. She told the kids to hurry and get ready for bed. Abby would sleep in Patty Ruth's bed since it was the same size as Mary Beth's.

When the children protested, saying they wouldn't be able to sleep, Glenda told them they must try. They would need new strength tomorrow. Especially Chris, if he was going to ride out with a search party. Glenda's argument was sufficiently convincing, and the children filed off to their respective bedrooms. Hannah called out that she would be in to pray with them shortly.

"Now, best friend of mine," Glenda said, "I want you to get out of your clothes and ready for bed. While you're doing that and praying with the kids, I'm going to fix you something to eat."

"I really don't have any appetite," Hannah said.

Glenda stood with hands on hips. "When did you eat last?"

"I...I don't remember."

"Then you're going to eat something. Go on. Get into your robe and pray with the kids."

"All right, boss lady." Hannah gave out a sigh and headed down the hall.

Glenda smiled after her, then went to the kitchen.

Inside her bedroom, Hannah paused to lean on the dresser. Her body was so tired, and her heart was sore beyond belief, but she knew she had to go on. Mary Beth, Chris, and B.J. needed her. Suddenly she felt a slight stirring in her womb and realized that someone else was depending on her.

As she rubbed her midsection, she soothed the wee one

growing within her and sat down on a chair. She removed her high-button boots and her outer clothing. After giving her face and arms a quick washing, she donned a voluminous flannel gown, draped a heavy shawl over her shoulders, and put on her worn knitted slippers, then left the room.

When Hannah returned to the parlor, she found a cheery fire crackling in the fireplace. The pleasant aroma of hot tea met her nostrils as she entered the kitchen where Glenda was setting the steaming teapot on the table. There was a pan of something on the stove.

Biggie was eating something in his dish.

"How are Chris, Mary Beth, and B.J.?" Glenda asked.

"Quite torn up. My praying with them seemed to help. At least I think they'll sleep. I'm so glad Abby's with Mary Beth." She took a step toward Glenda. "And I'm glad you're with me."

Glenda wrapped her arms around her best friend and said, "I've got some nutritious bean soup on the stove and a big slice of bread all buttered for you. Come on. I want you to eat."

Hannah lowered her bulk onto the chair Glenda had pulled out for her. Glenda poured two steaming mugs of tea and sat down facing Hannah.

As soon as she took one spoonful of soup, Hannah realized how hungry she was. When she and Glenda had emptied the teapot and the food had been devoured, Glenda said, "All right, my friend, I want you to get to bed. I'll sleep on the couch in the parlor."

Hannah did not resist. She wasn't sure that she could sleep, but her weary body needed rest.

Glenda escorted Hannah to her bed, removed the shawl from her shoulders, and helped her get settled under the covers. Tucking her in as if she were a child, Glenda kissed her forehead and said, "Go to sleep in Jesus' arms, honey. I love you."

Hannah felt the warmth of tears fill her eyes. "I love you, too, Glenda."

Back in the kitchen, Glenda cleaned up the dishes with a prayer on her lips for Patty Ruth's safety and comfort, and for strength for Hannah and the other children. When she had the kitchen spotless, she snuggled down under a blanket on the couch and prayed again for Patty Ruth and her family.

Hannah lay awake in the darkness. Tears streamed down her cheeks as she whispered, "Oh, Sol, if only you were here, I know you would find our precious little girl. Whatever will I do without you?"

Suddenly a still small voice made its way into her aching heart. *I will never leave thee nor forsake thee. Lo, I am with you alway.*

Past the hot lump in her throat, Hannah whispered, "Oh, yes, Lord. You are my faithful and constant Companion and Guide. Please give me the grace to cast all of my cares upon You, and to accept Your will, whatever it may be."

As the stress of the day began to claim her, she closed her eyes and dried her tears with the corner of the sheet. She was well aware that the God of the universe—in His infinite wisdom—was in control.

"Please, please, heavenly Father," she whispered, "put Your loving arms of care and protection around my little Patty Ruth. You have said in Your Word that You give Your angels charge over us. May Patty Ruth's guardian angel help her not to be afraid and keep her from harm. Whoever has her, may they be kind to her. Please, Lord, do a work in their hearts and minds, and cause them to return her safely to us."

God brought peace to Hannah, and she went to sleep as Glenda had said, in the arms of Jesus.

CHAPTER NINETEEN

It had snowed a couple of inches during the night, and except for tracks made by horses and wagons that morning, a fresh, undisturbed blanket of white covered the ground.

Soon Matt was ascending the familiar gentle slope that would bring his farm into view. He hauled up at the back porch and entered the kitchen, leaving the horse untethered.

Inside, he moved into the hallway and paused in front of the master bedroom, taking a deep breath before turning the doorknob. The unmade bed was empty.

He crossed the hall to Holly's room. He had left the door open that morning and now it was closed.

"Emily, I'm home. Are you in there?"

Bedding was piled in tattered heaps on the floor. Blankets and sheets had been torn to shreds, and feathers from the pillow and mattress were scattered everywhere. A butcher knife lay on the floor.

Matt rushed to the parlor, but Emily wasn't there either. He hurried through the house, looking in every room, every closet.

He ran outside and scanned the ground to the right and left, catching sight of the footprints he had made that morning. Beside them were smaller footprints...Emily's size.

He dashed toward the barn. "Emily! Emily! I'm home! Emil—"

The sudden rush of air into the barn spun Emily's body. Beneath her feet lay the toppled step stool she had stood on after looping the rope over a rafter and securing it to the crude noose now cinched tight around her neck.

"No-o-o!" He sucked in a raspy breath, and the word came out of him again in a pitiful moan. "No-o-o-o! Emily...no-o-o-o!"

The breath locked in Matt's lungs and he found himself sitting up on the couch in the parlor, working his mouth soundlessly. Cold sweat beaded his forehead. He glanced toward the dwindling fire in the fireplace and looked around the room. Some of the tension went out of his body when he saw the first rays of morning light coming through the windows.

"Oh, dear God, thank You. It was only a dream. Oh! Thank You!"

He replenished the log supply to the fire then moved slowly down the hall to the master bedroom. He struggled to quiet his ragged breathing and looked inside the room to see if he had disturbed Emily.

There were two forms beneath the covers. Patty Ruth lay next to Emily, who had an arm around her. Both were sleeping soundly.

Suddenly Matt felt the impact of the awful nightmare and leaned against the wall for support as he made his way back to the parlor and sat down. He pulled the blankets up around him, trying to drive away the inner chill that claimed him.

He remembered Emily screaming at him, "If you don't bring Holly home to me, I want to die!"

If Emily woke up and found Patty Ruth gone, she might do exactly what he had dreamed of in his nightmare. Patty Ruth would have to stay here a little longer.

Patty Ruth sat at the breakfast table, eager anticipation exuding from her. Mr. McDermott had promised that she could go home this morning!

As they were finishing breakfast, Matt said, "Emily, I need to talk to Holly alone for a few minutes."

"What about?"

"Oh, just some Papa-daughter things."

"All right. I'll clean up and do the dishes while you two are talking."

Matt pulled up the room's only chair and sat down. "Sit there on the bed, honey, so we can talk. Patty Ruth, I've been thinking about this situation. I...I need your help."

A cautious look came into the little girl's eyes. "When are you gonna take me home?"

Matt cleared his throat. "Can I tell you a story? A true story?"

"How about tellin' me while you're takin' me home?"

"Well, you see, Patty Ruth, the story has to do with my taking you home."

Matt told of the McDermotts' journey in the wagon train, and about the Indian attacks. Patty Ruth listened intently as he told in detail how their little daughter Holly—who was Patty Ruth's age—was almost killed by the Pawnees.

When he began to cry as he told her about Holly dying of pneumonia, Patty Ruth tenderly patted his arm and told him how sorry she was.

Matt explained as best he could to a five-year-old about

what had happened to Emily's mind and that Emily was so affected that she could not grasp that Holly was dead. In fact, she thought Patty Ruth was Holly when she had seen her yesterday, because Patty Ruth so strongly resembled her own little girl.

"Patty Ruth, you know what it's like when we have colds, or our stomachs are upset and we're sick in our bodies."

"Mm-hmm."

"Well, Emily is like that in her mind. She is very, very sick in her mind. That's why she thinks you are Holly. She needs help right now that only you can give her."

"Grandpa O'Brien could help her. He's a doctor."

Matt wiped tears from his cheeks. "Please try to understand, honey. Emily's sickness isn't one a doctor can heal. Right now she needs Holly, and Holly is the only one who can help her get well. My little Holly is dead. You are the only one who can be Holly to her right now."

The child's lower lip quivered. "I'm sorry your little girl died, mister. I know it hurts your heart like it did mine when Papa died. But…but…I want to go home. I know Mama's worried about me. Please, please, mister. Please take me home."

Patty Ruth began to whimper, and tears brimmed in her frightened eyes.

"Honey, I'm sorry that your mother is worried, but she'll be all right when you do go home. My wife is very, very sick in her mind, and she might die if she loses Holly right now. Do you understand? I'm sure it won't be long till you can go home, but she needs you so desperately right now. Will you stay and help her a little while?"

"How long is a little while?"

"Well…just a few days."

Patty Ruth felt sorry for Mr. McDermott. He was a nice man, and he was very worried about his wife.

"Would you stay and help her, honey? Please?"

Patty Ruth nodded slowly. "All right, since it's only a few days."

Matt blinked as fresh tears surfaced and rolled down his cheeks. "Oh, thank you! Thank you! Could I hug you?"

Patty Ruth nodded again.

When he folded her into his arms, she thought of the strong arms of her father.

"Honey," Matt said as he released her, "it will help if while you're with us, you call Emily 'Mama' like Holly did, and in front of her you call me 'Papa.' Would you do that?"

Patty Ruth rolled her tongue inside her mouth, then with a deep sigh for such a little girl said, "Uh-huh."

"Good. Now let's—"

A tap on the door interrupted his words. From the hall, Emily said, "Matt, are you and Holly through talking?"

Matt got up from the chair and opened the door. A smile was on his face as he said, "Yes, honey. We just finished."

Emily extended a hand and said, "Come on, Holly. I want to hold you on my lap and rock you for a while in front of the fireplace. I'll read you a story. Okay?"

Patty Ruth flicked a glance at Matt, then said, "Okay, Mama."

Matt winked at her and grinned, and after a moment she winked back.

Matt announced that he needed to leave right away and do the cabinet work for Mrs. Mitchell. Both Emily and Patty Ruth hugged him before he left, and Patty Ruth pleased him by calling him "Papa" in front of Emily.

They watched Matt ride away, then Emily urged Patty Ruth ahead of her into the parlor. She took a book from a shelf, sat down in the rocking chair, and pulled Patty Ruth onto her lap.

When Patty Ruth caught a whiff of lavender from Emily's dress, a huge wave of homesickness washed over her. Her lips began to quiver and she almost started crying.

At the same time that Patty Ruth was eating breakfast with the McDermotts, Hannah watched the search parties ride away. She was touched to see Two Moons and his braves. Included in the Crow search party was Broken Wing, Two Moons's son. Chris Cooper rode alongside Broken Wing and his other good friend, Luke Patterson.

At midmorning, the stagecoach from Cheyenne City arrived, and shortly after it left, Curly and Judy Charley Wesson came into the store with two boxes from Ben and Esther Singleton.

That night, after a fruitless day of searching for Patty Ruth, Chris came home, and with B.J.'s help carried the boxes upstairs to the apartment. Inside were brightly wrapped packages, one for each member of the family. When they came upon the package with Patty Ruth's name on it, Mary Beth burst into tears.

Hannah lay awake in bed that night, thinking of sweet times with her precocious and demonstrative youngest child. Patty Ruth gave so many hugs, and she was so free with words of love.

Suddenly the scene at Julianna's house two days ago came back to Hannah's mind. She recalled the last time she had seen her little daughter while standing on Julianna's porch.

At the memory, Hannah broke down and sobbed. For the very last words she'd heard Patty Ruth say were, "I love you, Mama."

After Matt and Emily kissed Patty Ruth good night and left her room, the child lay awake, looking at the soft shadows on the ceiling.

She was sad at the thought of her mother and siblings worrying about her. On the other hand, she had a warm feeling inside knowing that she was going to help the poor lady whose little girl had died.

Since there was no one to pray with her, Patty Ruth talked to Jesus, asking Him to help her mother not to worry, and to help Chris, Mary Beth, B.J., and Biggie not to worry, either.

Before dropping off to sleep, she said, "An' Lord Jesus, please give the poor lady another baby so she won't miss Holly so much. An'…it prob'ly would be best if You make it a girl."

The days passed slowly as the search went on. Hannah tried to trust the Lord but couldn't help feeling that with each passing day the chances of getting Patty Ruth back grew slimmer.

Special prayer meetings were held at the church under the guidance of Pastor Kelly, and Hannah also knew that people in the church were holding other prayer meetings in their homes. No one had given up hope. They were asking God to bring the sweet little child home.

One afternoon, when Hannah was doing some minor tidying up in the storeroom while Jacob worked the counter with Glenda Williams, she heard a child's voice in the store. She jumped up from the chair inside the storeroom just as the little girl was saying something.

All eyes went to Hannah as she stopped short when she saw it was Belinda Fordham.

Patty Ruth's five-year-old best friend ran to Hannah, opening her arms. Her mother, Betsy Fordham, followed behind. Hannah burst into tears when she folded the child into her embrace.

"Honey, are you all right?" Glenda asked, laying a comforting hand on Hannah's shoulder.

Hannah spoke haltingly as she clung to Belinda. "I...I heard Belinda's voice from the storeroom and...and forgetting how much she and Patty Ruth sound alike, I thought—"

With that, Hannah wept so hard she couldn't speak.

Belinda started crying, too, and Betsy gently released her from Hannah's grasp.

Glenda embraced Hannah as Jacob and several customers looked on, their hearts going out to the young widow whose life had sustained yet another heavy blow.

When Hannah's crying subsided, Glenda said, "Come on, honey. I'll take you up to the apartment."

When they started to leave, Hannah looked at little Belinda and said, "I'm sorry, sweetheart. I didn't mean to upset you."

"She understands, Hannah," Betsy said. "You go on with Glenda. We're praying, and we love you."

Inside the apartment, Glenda guided Hannah to the most comfortable overstuffed chair in the parlor and gently guided her to sit down.

"Can I get you something, honey?" she asked.

"Just a little water."

"All right. Would you like to go in and lie down on the bed?"

"No, thank you. I...I'll stay here. You need to get back down to the store. Jacob needs you."

"But I can't leave you now—"

"I'll be all right, honey. I...well, I really need to be alone for a little while."

Glenda nodded. "Of course. But if you need me—"

"I'll call."

"Okay. I'll get you some water and be back to check on you later."

When the door closed behind Glenda, Hannah covered her face with her hands. Hearing Belinda's voice had shaken her to the core. Grief flowed over her like cold water as memories of Patty Ruth came alive in her mind, making her miss the child even more.

Hot tears welled up at the memory of Patty Ruth talking about her papa in heaven and asking if Jesus and Papa sat down and talked. When Hannah told her she was sure they did, Patty Ruth was glad because when she talked to Jesus in prayer, she asked Him to tell her papa that she loved him. Hannah recalled how amazed she was at the sweet child's perception of heaven and that she would think to pray such a thing.

The thought that Patty Ruth might never be found made Hannah feel as if she were sinking into a well of horror blacker than night and colder than Wyoming's winter wind.

She slid from the chair and fell on her knees, sobbing in agony, "Please, God! Please! You took my husband from me; please don't take my little daughter, too! I need her, Lord! I need those precious little arms around my neck. I need to hear her say she loves me! Please, dear Lord! Give me my baby girl back!"

After several minutes, Hannah said, "Oh, dear Lord, I'm sorry! Please forgive me! I'm sorry for having doubts about Your goodness. Forgive me for bringing up that You took Solomon from me. I...I know my wonderful God always does right. It's just that my mortal eyes don't always see it that way."

A measure of peace settled over Hannah's heart. "Thank You, Lord," she said, wiping tears. "Thank You for Your forgiveness, and for the peace that only You can give."

There was a knock at the door.

"Hannah!" came Betsy's voice. She entered the parlor and came to help Hannah to her feet.

"Is Belinda all right?" Hannah asked. "I'm so sorry I upset her."

"She's fine, Hannah. Don't feel bad. You and I have commented that our little five-year-old daughters have voices that sound very much alike. I can understand why you would jump at the sound and think it was Patty Ruth."

Hannah hugged her neck. "Thank you for coming up to see me. Please tell Belinda I love her."

"She knows that, honey, but I'll tell her."

Betsy had been with Hannah only a minute or two when there was another knock on the door.

"Miss Hannah...it's Jacob."

"Come in, Jacob."

The little man looked at her tenderly.

"What can I do for you, Jacob?" Hannah asked, rubbing her swollen eyes.

"It's something I'd like to do for you," he replied. "Things are slow down there right now, so Glenda said she'd handle it while I came up. I'd like to show you something in the Bible."

For a brief moment, Hannah's mind went from her missing daughter to Jacob's need to be saved. She so desperately wanted him to understand that Jesus Christ was indeed his Messiah, and that he needed to open his heart to Jesus. She had talked to him about it many times and prayed daily for his salvation.

"Certainly, Jacob." She glanced to her left. "There's a Bible right there."

Jacob picked up the Bible from an end table and turned to the first book. "I'm sure I'm not going to show you something you've never read in here, but I want you to see something that came to my mind this morning. I've been waiting for a chance to show it to you."

He sat down in front of Hannah on a straight-backed chair. "It's here in Genesis. Begins in chapter 37."

"Joseph and his brothers," Hannah said.

"Mm-hmm."

"Joseph was seventeen years old at the time."

Jacob smiled. "Know your Bible, don't you?"

"Not as well as I should."

He smiled again and shook his head. "Anyway, let me read a portion of it to you."

Hannah listened as the little Jewish man read to her of Joseph being taken by his jealous brothers and sold to the Ishmaelites, who carried him into Egypt. He paused and said, "Now, we could say that without question that Joseph was kidnapped by his brothers, right?"

A tiny smile touched Hannah's lips. "Most certainly," she replied.

Jacob read on as the chapter told how Joseph's brothers put goat's blood on his coat of many colors and took it to their father, Jacob, and showed it to him. Jacob assumed exactly what his sons wanted him to—that Joseph had been killed by a wild beast.

The little Jewish man then took Hannah to Genesis chapter 46 and read the passage where after many years, Joseph went to meet his father in Goshen, and father and son had a wonderful reunion.

Jacob Kates's voice trembled as he said, "Hannah, somehow I believe your little Patty Ruth is as alive and well as Joseph was, and it won't take years, but one day soon she will be back in your arms."

Hannah felt a wonderful hope rise in her. The story of Joseph's kidnapping and ultimate reunion with his father had not entered her mind as she had daily sought strength from the Word of God.

"Jacob, dear, thank you for being such a good friend and a source of great encouragement." She planted a kiss on his wrinkled cheek and smiled as his face turned pink.

CHAPTER TWENTY

It was snowing lightly when Matt McDermott crossed the back porch and entered the kitchen. He could hear Emily laughing toward the front of the house. The sound thrilled his heart.

He found Emily and Patty Ruth sitting on the parlor floor in front of a crackling fire, playing a game that involved clapping their hands together.

"Hello, ladies," he said.

"Hi, Papa." Patty Ruth played the part perfectly. She jumped up and ran to Matt and hugged him.

There was still a slight glaze in Emily's eyes as she looked up and said, "Hello, darling. You're home earlier than I expected. I haven't started supper yet."

"I finished today's job a little early. Sounds like you two are having fun."

"We are," said Emily. "Aren't we, Holly?"

"Uh-huh."

The sound of a horse blowing came from outside, accompanied by the rattle of a wagon. Matt peered out the window past the edge of the curtain. Turning back, he said in a low tone, "Emily, it's Dr. Garberson. We can't let him see Holly." To Patty Ruth, he said, "Holly, go to your room and stay there till I say you can come out. Close the door and be very, very quiet."

Emily frowned and got up from the floor. "Why shouldn't

he see her? He won't need to come for his visits anymore. I'm doing fine since Holly is home."

Matt gestured toward the parlor door, where Patty Ruth had paused. "Hurry, Holly! Do as I said. Be absolutely quiet, and do not come out until I tell you to."

The doctor's footsteps could be heard on the front porch as Patty Ruth scurried down the hall, went into her room, and closed the door.

Matt gently took hold of Emily's shoulders. "Honey, you must not tell the doctor that Holly is back."

"But—"

"Listen to me! It's best if he doesn't know it."

Matt pasted a smile on his face and opened the front door. "Hello, Doctor. Come in."

While Matt was taking Garberson's hat and coat, he said, "Looks like it's going to keep snowing for a while."

"So what's new?" the doctor jested. He turned to Emily. "Well, how's our girl doing?"

Emily regarded him with her glassy gaze and said, "I'm just fine, Doctor, now that Holly's back home. You won't need to come anymore."

Matt's pulse quickened as the doctor turned to look at him.

"Emily, dear," Matt said, "why don't you sit down there in the chair by the fire while I talk to Dr. Garberson a moment?"

"Well, if you two are going to talk, I'll go start supper," she said flatly.

"No, no," Matt countered, not wanting her to go anywhere near the door to Holly's room. "Just sit down and rest, honey. You can start supper after Dr. Garberson leaves."

"But—"

"Please do as I say, Emily."

She turned and slowly made her way to the chair while Matt took the doctor to the kitchen. Matt explained to Dr.

Garberson that Emily was merely having some of her hallucinations again.

The doctor told Matt to up the dosage of the sedatives, left him more powders for his supply, and departed, saying he would check on her after Christmas.

By the time the doctor was out the door and climbing into his buggy, Matt was in a cold sweat, but was greatly relieved that the doctor was none the wiser about the "guest" in the house.

That night, Matt found sleep elusive as he lay on the couch in the parlor. He was deeply bothered about keeping Patty Ruth from her family. The little girl had told him much about her mother, and how ever since her papa had gone to heaven she often heard her mama crying at night.

She told him about Mary Beth, Chris, and B.J., and talked a great deal about Biggie, saying that she missed her little dog and knew he missed her.

He would go to Fort Bridger tomorrow and find out how Hannah Cooper was faring.

The next morning, Matt left home as if he were going to one of his odd jobs. It had stopped snowing sometime in the night but was still cloudy.

When he arrived in Fort Bridger, Main Street was a beehive of activity, with people going in and out of stores and shops, and moving along the boardwalks. Wagons, buggies, and riders on horseback moved up and down the broad street.

The town was gaily decorated for Christmas, and many of the people on foot were laden with packages. Garlands of evergreen and bright red bows adorned most windows, and multicolored paper rings were linked together, trimming many of the doorways.

Matt had all but forgotten that it was the Christmas season. As he gazed at the beautifully decorated windows, he thought of Holly's death.

Not much of a Christmas for the McDermotts, he thought. *And not much of a Christmas for the Coopers either,* his conscience replied as he rode up to Cooper's General Store.

He dismounted at the hitch rail and wrapped the reins around it. "Dear God," he whispered, "show me what to do. Am I to return Patty Ruth and risk losing Emily? Lord, I know that someday soon I will have to bring that little girl back to her mother. Please let Emily's mind heal so I can do the right thing."

He released a heavy sigh and stepped up to the boardwalk. His eyes fell on the two big windows of the general store. A beautiful manger scene rested on a snowy white cloth in one of the windows. In the other stood a lovely life-sized doll clothed in a dark blue velvet coat with white fur trim and a white fur muff. Beside the doll was a pair of ice skates and a wooden toy train. Cutout silver stars hung in both windows, and like the other windows on Main Street, they were bordered with evergreen boughs and red bows.

Matt paused at the edge of the boardwalk while a few people walked past him. They spoke to him, and he returned their greetings with a forced smile. When he stepped inside the store, the tiny bell above his head made a cheerful jingle, and he was met with an array of pleasant odors and warmth from the potbellied stove.

Jacob Kates was alone at the counter. A middle-aged woman who had just laid her purchase on the counter said, "I'm wondering how Hannah is doing today, Jacob."

"Having a tough time," replied the small, wiry man. "There are a couple of ladies from the fort up in the apartment with her right now."

"Bless her heart. It must be horrible, what she's going through."

"Only God knows," he replied.

When the woman walked away, Matt approached the counter.

"Hello," Jacob said with a smile. "Welcome to Cooper's. May I help you, sir?"

"Just some information right now."

Jacob studied Matt's face for a moment. "Don't I know you? You look familiar."

"I was in here once a few weeks ago."

"I thought so. I seldom forget a face. Do you live somewhere in the area?"

"Yes. I have a farm near Mountain View. Just happened to be coming through Fort Bridger, and I wanted to ask about Mrs. Cooper's daughter. I heard that she was kidnapped several days ago, and I was wondering if she has been found."

"No, sir, she hasn't."

"I'm sorry to hear that. How's Mrs. Cooper holding up?"

"Well, sir, she's having a pretty hard time of it. And her troubles are compounded because she's expecting another child in March."

Matt was cut to the quick with this information. Patty Ruth had not told him her mother was expecting a baby.

"We're quite concerned," said Jacob. "Our town physician is watching her closely. He told me that the emotional trauma she's suffering could have a devastating effect on both her and her newborn child."

Matt felt sick inside. "That's too bad. Well, thank you for the information. My heart goes out to her."

A customer came up behind Matt as he was speaking and drew Jacob's attention. Matt quickly left the store. After waiting once again for people to pass so he could cross the boardwalk, he chose to duck under the hitch rail this time, and as he was mounting his horse, he heard two men talking. One man apparently had been out of town for a while. The other one was telling him about Patty Ruth's kidnapping and that many of the townsmen, the army, and even the Crow Indians were searching all over southwestern Wyoming in an effort to find the child.

As Matt rode out of town toward Lyman, where he was doing more carpentry work, his conscience was eating him up. He wanted to take Hannah Cooper's little daughter home, but if he did and Emily committed suicide, it would be his fault. He had no choice. Patty Ruth would have to stay with them a little longer.

The next day there was another light snowstorm, and when Matt drew near home in the late afternoon, he noted a unit of cavalrymen from Fort Bridger pulling out of the yard of a neighboring farmer.

He put his horse to a trot. When he arrived home, he quickly put the horse in the barn and went to the house.

"Emily!" he called from the kitchen. "Where are you?"

"We're in the parlor, honey," came her reply.

Emily was sitting in the rocking chair with Patty Ruth on her lap and an open book in her hand.

"Have some soldiers been here?" he asked.

"No. Why would soldiers come here?"

He ignored her question and said, "I want you to take Holly to her room, and both of you stay there till I tell you to come out."

Emily set her jaw, and her eyes took on a stubborn look. "Why do Holly and I have to hide just because some soldiers are coming?"

"No time to explain," said Matt. "Come on, before they get here."

Emily still did not move. "They're looking for hostile Indians, aren't they? Why would they come to our house?"

The sound of blowing horses and tinkling metal came from the yard. Matt's heart was pounding now. "Emily, come on. Do as I say. I—"

Heavy footsteps were on the porch.

"You keep Holly in here, and neither of you make a sound." Matt closed the parlor door and went to the front hallway.

He took a deep breath to calm his nerves and waited till the knock came, then paused a few seconds before opening the door.

He estimated there were a dozen riders, including the two men who stood on the porch.

"Good afternoon, sir," said the man with captain's insignias on his campaign hat and heavy overcoat. "I'm Captain John Fordham from Fort Bridger. This is Lieutenant Dobie Carlin."

"Matthew McDermott, Captain." Matt smiled at Carlin and nodded. "Lieutenant. What can I do for you, Captain Fordham?"

"Just a few questions."

Matt's stomach churned as the captain explained about Patty Ruth Cooper's abduction and the extensive search being carried out. "Have you seen a little red-haired girl?"

Matt's tongue burned when he lied. "No, sir. I sure haven't seen a little girl of that description."

"Well, if you should spot her, Mr. McDermott, please contact the town marshal's office in Fort Bridger."

"Sure will."

As Matt stood at the open door and watched the cavalrymen ride out of the yard, the Holy Spirit convicted his conscience. He closed the door and leaned his head against it, saying in a whisper, "Lord, please forgive me. I'm sorry for lying. I'm at my wits' end. I can't let anything happen that would take Patty Ruth away from Emily. I'm afraid, Lord...of what she'll do if she loses the little girl she thinks is Holly."

When Matt finally went to the parlor door and looked in, Patty Ruth was on Emily's lap in the rocking chair once more. Both looked at him as Emily said, "What did the soldiers want, Matt?"

His tongue burned again as he replied, "Just wanted to know if we'd seen any hostile Indians around here."

On Wednesday, December 21, the prayer service at the little church building in Fort Bridger was packed with people. Patty Ruth Cooper's abduction had touched many lives and tugged at hearts.

Several farmers, ranchers, and townspeople who seldom attended church were there, and even some who had never been through the church door were in attendance.

Since it was the Christmas season, Pastor Andy Kelly preached a heart-gripping sermon from James 1:17—showing that Jesus is God's perfect gift to the world, and that He is the only way of salvation from sin and its eternal consequences. A few people received God's perfect gift into their hearts that night and were saved.

While the church members were rejoicing, Pastor Kelly said, "Our marvelous God can use the sorrows in the lives of His born-again people to bring joy to our lives. None of us rejoice in Patty Ruth's abduction, nor the grief and sorrow her mother and siblings are suffering. But God has used this tragedy in the lives of the Cooper family to bring souls to Himself...souls who will be in heaven forever because they sat under the gospel tonight and responded to it."

Hannah Cooper, who was flanked by her three older children, nodded her tearful agreement.

"Before we dismiss the service," said the pastor, "I want to remind you that Christmas is next Sunday. Services will be at their regular times. The best place to be on the day we commemorate our Lord's marvelous virgin birth is in His house."

There were amens throughout the crowd.

"One other thing," said Kelly. "As the Coopers' pastor, I want to thank all of you who have been praying for them. Please continue to do so."

Kelly saw Hannah motion to him from her pew. "Yes, Hannah?"

"Pastor, would it be all right if I say something to the people?"

"Of course."

Hannah rose to her feet and looked around the congregation, then said, "I want to express my deep appreciation to every one of you who have held us up in prayer. It has been your prayers, your loving words of encouragement, and your kind deeds that have sustained us."

Her lips began to tremble. "The Lord has used a couple of very special Scripture passages to speak to my heart. Through them He has impressed in me that Patty Ruth is still alive. Someone took her for some unknown reason, but I know in my heart that she is alive."

More amens were heard throughout the crowd of people.

"We heard a wonderful sermon just now on God's perfect gift, the precious Lord Jesus Christ. And when we exchange gifts with our friends and loved ones this Sunday, we are picturing that perfect gift. There is none like Him, nor will there ever be. With that truth clear, let me say that the perfect gift I could receive for Christmas this year would be to have my Patty Ruth back."

There was not a dry eye in the building.

Hannah sat down with tears seeping from her closed eyelids. Chris, Mary Beth, and B.J. put their arms around their mother and wept with her.

After praying with her children and putting them to bed, Hannah lay in her own bed with pale silver moonlight flooding the room.

She looked toward the photograph of Solomon and herself that was taken when he was a Union soldier in the Civil War. "Oh, Sol, I miss you so much. If only you were here to hold me in your arms.

"It hurts so much to have our little Patty Ruth gone and in unknown hands. Maybe it was someone just passing through, and for some reason they happened to be on West Street as our little darling was playing with the snowman. If that's the case, they could be many miles away by now, and all the searching in the world would be to no avail."

Hannah gritted her teeth at the thought and swallowed the hot lump in her throat.

"Lord Jesus," she prayed, "You said in Your Word, 'Whatsoever ye shall ask in my name, that will I do, that the Father may be glorified in the Son.' I'm asking in Your precious name that no matter where my little Patty Ruth is...no matter who has her...that You will bring her back to me. I promise that when You do, I'll tell it to the glory of God, with all that is in me."

She wiped her wet face on the corner of her bed linens. "Thank You, Lord, that my other precious children are here with me, safe in their beds."

Hannah prayed for quite some time, and when she was finished, she still was not sleepy. She rose from the bed, lit the lantern, and picked up her Bible. She had lost count of how many times she'd read the passages in Genesis since Jacob had drawn her attention to them. She read them again, and once more her heart swelled as she considered Joseph's abduction by his own brothers; of the heartaches suffered by Jacob; and the happy ending to the story when Joseph appeared to his father alive and well many years later.

As before, Hannah gained strength from Scripture. She closed her Bible and held it to her breast for a moment, then laid it on the nightstand and doused the lantern.

When she was back under the covers, Hannah pictured Patty Ruth's precious little freckled face. Her heart was brimming with love for the child. She closed her eyes and imagined her child's touch, the smell of her hair, the feel of her soft skin, the warmth of her little body held close to her mother's breast.

So great was Hannah's longing to hold Patty Ruth that she threw back the bedcovers, put on her robe, and made her way to the boys' room. She awakened B.J. first, and hugged him good with hot tears streaming down her cheeks. He sleepily hugged her in return, and when she covered him up and kissed his forehead, she went to Chris's bed. B.J. was asleep again before his brother was awake.

When she left Chris and went to the girls' room to awaken Mary Beth, the sweet girl stayed in her mother's embrace for a long time, then said, "Mama, you're hurting way down deep inside. Would it help if we talked for a little while?"

Mary Beth could feel her mother's tears against her cheek as Hannah said, "I don't want to keep you awake any longer."

"It doesn't matter if you do. I love you with all my heart, and I know that sometimes a heart is made lighter when there's someone with whom to share the hurt."

Mother and daughter stayed awake until dawn as Hannah shared with Mary Beth the thoughts she'd had earlier in the night about Patty Ruth. The softhearted girl offered all the love and encouragement she could give.

The search went on, but to no avail. There was no trace of Patty Ruth Cooper.

Late one afternoon, when all of the searchers had returned to town, Colonel Ross Bateman and Deputy Marshal Jack Bower met with them at the church.

Standing before the seated group, which included Chief Two Moons and thirty-three of his braves, the colonel said, "Men, I appreciate your faithfulness to stick with this search for so many days. And in spite of our failure to come up with the slightest clue as to Patty Ruth's whereabouts, not one of you has even hinted that you're ready to give up."

"We can't give up, Colonel," said Pastor Kelly. "We must keep on till we find her."

Voices throughout the group spoke their agreement.

Chief Two Moons stood up.

"Yes, Chief?" said Colonel Bateman.

"Colonel Ross Bateman...Deputy Marshal Jack Bower, Two Moons suggest the white men go back to every house in town, and in country. Go inside all buildings. Look for Patty Ruth Cooper. White people would strongly object if Indian do it, but white men should look in every room of every house, and in all barns and sheds. Patty Ruth Cooper may be captive of someone lives close to Fort Bridger."

Bateman and Bower exchanged glances. "Your suggestion is good, Chief, but there is a problem with doing that."

Two Moons waited, keeping his dark eyes fastened on the colonel.

"You see, Chief, unless we have solid reason to believe that certain persons are the abductors, such a search would violate people's privacy. This privacy is protected by the law. We cannot do a search unless there is some kind of evidence that tells us the child could be in someone's possession."

The chief nodded. "Umm. Two Moons not understand white man's law. Just want to find Patty Ruth Cooper. Take her home to mother."

"We do too, Chief," said Bower, "but we have to do it within the law."

The chief nodded again and sat down.

Deputy Bower ran his gaze over the solemn faces of the group. "So we're all in agreement to keep up the search?"

Every man agreed to stay with the search until Patty Ruth was found.

"Good," said Bower. "I believe that somewhere, at some time, somebody is going to have seen Patty Ruth or something that will give us a clue to indicate her whereabouts."

CHAPTER TWENTY-ONE

The sun was shining on Friday, December 23, and the air was not as cold as it had been for the past several days.

Matt McDermott had driven his wagon to Lyman. After he finished up a repair job on a merchant's storage shed, he would do a bit of shopping and pick up some items Emily had requested to carry out her plans for Christmas. Then, on the way home, he planned to go into the nearby forest and cut down a Christmas tree.

At the McDermott farm, Emily and Patty Ruth were eating lunch together while two large pans of water heated on the stove. Emily had brought in the galvanized tub from the back porch and placed it in the bathroom at the end of the hall, across from the kitchen, so it could warm up.

As they were finishing their meal, Emily said, "Holly, I'm going to bathe after we eat. You go play in your room while I clean up the kitchen, then take my bath."

Patty Ruth sat down on the bed in Holly's room and pondered the fact that Mr. McDermott had told her he would be coming home with a Christmas tree. That meant it was almost Christmas, and she wanted to go home more than ever.

A few weeks ago, Chris had said that because he was the man of the house, it was his responsibility to go out and cut down a Christmas tree. He planned to do it Christmas Eve morning, and Mary Beth, B.J., and Patty Ruth could go with him.

Patty Ruth wanted to go with her sister and brothers when they made the trip into the forest to find the perfect Christmas tree. She closed her eyes, remembering the Christmas trees they had decorated in Missouri. No doubt this year's tree would be just as beautiful with its shiny decorations and the candles glowing.

Tears of frustration filled her eyes. She missed her mother and her sister and brothers, and a lonely ache filled her confused little heart.

"I wanna go home," she whispered.

Patty Ruth thought about it some more. She had done what Mr. McDermott asked, and she knew her mother would be proud of the way she had tried to help the poor sick lady whose little girl had died. But Mrs. McDermott was well now and didn't need her anymore.

An idea came to the little redhead.

She had seen neighbors driving their wagons and riding their horses along the road. If she were to go to the road, somebody would come along who could take her to Fort Bridger and her family.

By the sounds coming from the rear of the house, she could tell that Emily was pouring the hot water into the galvanized tub.

Patty Ruth dried her tears with the back of her hand, then went to the door and listened. She opened it a crack and peeked out just as Emily went into her bedroom. Patty Ruth waited until Emily came back out and entered the bathroom.

When she heard water splashing, she tiptoed down the

hall and carefully climbed up on the straight-backed wooden chair beneath the pegs where hats and coats were hung. She lifted her red coat and hat, put them on, and with shaky hands she reached in her coat pockets and pulled out her mittens.

Her heart was racing as she turned the knob on the front door and pulled it open. She cast another glance down the hall, then darted down the porch steps and ran toward the road.

Suddenly her feet slipped and she fell headlong into a snowdrift. She scrambled out of the drift, wiped snow from her face with mittened hands, and plowed ahead.

When she reached the road, she could go faster because horses and wagons had pressed the snow down.

Soon the McDermott farm was almost out of sight. Patty Ruth was panting now, and her little heart was beating like a trip-hammer as she pressed forward.

When a backward glance showed her only the very top of the barn, Patty Ruth slowed her pace a bit. The freedom she felt caused tears to well up in her eyes. She brushed them away and said, "I'm comin' home, Mama. I'm comin' home!"

Emily climbed out of the tub, dried herself off, and dressed. After emptying the tub with a pan and tossing the water out the back door, she hung the tub on the back porch.

She stopped in front of Holly's room and said, "You can come out now, Holly. Mama needs you to help her make some nice things for our Christmas decorations. Holly, did you hear me? You can come out now."

When there was no response, Emily opened the door. "Holly, I said— Well, where—"

She moved through the house, calling, "Holly, where are you?" There was no sound or movement.

Anger flared within Emily, and she shouted, "Holly! Where are you?"

The dead silence that answered put her into motion. She rushed through the house, looking everywhere, calling Holly's name. When she could not find her inside the house, Emily went to the front porch and scanned the area. She hurried to the back porch and called for Holly again, then dashed to the barn, not bothering to put on a coat. By the time she came into the house after looking in all the outbuildings, she was chilled and her teeth were chattering. Her anger had turned to panic.

Emily wrung her hands as she paced back and forth in front of the fireplace, mumbling to herself.

Her mind flashed back to the day when the Pawnees attacked the wagon train on the Nebraska plains and it appeared at first that Holly was dead. The same kind of terror gripped her now, and she sobbed and wailed, crying out Holly's name.

Patty Ruth plodded along the snow-covered road, doing her best to walk in the ruts made by wagon wheels. She squinted against the sun's glare off the white mantle surrounding her and studied the road ahead. It made no difference to her which direction someone might come. Certainly, when they found a little girl all alone who was trying to get home, they would be nice and take her there.

She had gone quite a distance when she saw a wagon coming toward her. Her heart picked up pace. She hurried to meet the wagon, her little feet slipping some on the snow. She would be home soon now.

Moments later, Patty Ruth's heart seemed to stop when she recognized the man on the wagon seat. It was Mr. McDermott.

When Matt and Patty Ruth pulled into the yard, they could hear Emily's wails coming from inside the house.

Matt jumped down and took Patty Ruth from the wagon seat, keeping her in his arms. He hurried up the porch steps and through the front door.

Emily's tortured cries were coming from her bedroom. He set the child down and found Emily lying facedown on the bed, screaming Holly's name.

Matt took hold of her and shouted, "Emily, it's all right, honey! It's all right!"

"No-o-o!" she wailed, turning over to look at him through a wall of tears. "The Pawnees have taken Holly, Matt! They took my little girl-l-l-l!"

Patty Ruth stood wide-eyed at the bedroom door as Matt attempted to get through to Emily and calm her. The child thought back to the moment when Mr. McDermott had found her out on the road. Patty Ruth had explained that since Mrs. McDermott was well now, she wanted to go home...

But Mr. McDermott had said it only looked like his wife was well. She really was not well at all. He had told her that Mrs. McDermott might die if Patty Ruth went away right now. With tears in his eyes, he had begged her to stay a little longer.

Patty Ruth's tender heart was touched by his tears, and she agreed to come back with him.

Her thoughts returned to the present as she heard Matt say, "No, Emily! The Pawnees haven't taken Holly. Look right here!"

Sniffling and gasping for breath, Emily let Matt help her sit up. When she saw Patty Ruth through her tears, she cried, "Oh, Holly! There you are!" She got off the bed and fell on her knees before the little girl, sweeping her up in her arms.

Emily smothered Patty Ruth with kisses and said, "Darling, Mama thought you were gone forever. Mama thought those bad, bad Pawnees had taken her precious baby, and she would never see her again! Where were you?"

"She just went for a little walk, honey," Matt said.

Emily's eyes were vacant and glassy as she turned to him. "She shouldn't have done that. The Pawnees are everywhere! They kill people—even little girls!" She turned to Patty Ruth. "You won't ever do that again, will you, honey? You remember those bad Indians, don't you? Remember? They killed your little friends who were in our wagon with you."

Emily hugged Patty Ruth tight and said, "Tomorrow is Christmas Eve. How horrible Christmas would have been if those Pawnees had taken my little girl!"

As Matt heard Emily's words, he thought of poor Hannah Cooper. How horrible Christmas was going to be for Hannah without her little girl...not knowing whether she was dead or alive.

Early on the morning of December 24, Hannah stood at the door of the general store and watched Chris, Mary Beth, and B.J. walk away with Jacob beside them. Chris carried an ax, and Jacob carried a length of rope they would use to drag the tree home.

"We'll find a real nice one, Mama," Chris called back over his shoulder.

"I'm sure you will, son. Jacob, please don't be gone too long."

"We won't, Miss Hannah," Jacob assured her.

Hannah closed the door and returned to the counter. She gave Julie Powell and Mandy Carver a grateful glance and said, "I appreciate you ladies helping today so Jacob could accompany my children to the forest."

"We's happy to do that, Miz Hannah," said Mandy. "'Sides, this is gonna be a very busy day. Julie an' me had planned to come together today so's you wouldn' have to be on yo' feet."

"Right," said Julie as the bell jingled, announcing the arrival of their first customers of the day. "You just sit down over there by the stove and rest yourself."

Hannah closed the store early, and the Coopers trimmed the tree together. When it was finished, Hannah stood with her three older children as they admired their work. There were strings of popcorn, glass ornaments, and candles set in holders fastened snugly to the branches. Later in the evening they would light the candles.

Mary Beth made her mother sit by the fireplace with her brothers while she cooked supper. When the food was almost ready, she called the boys to come and set the table.

While Mary Beth was dishing up the food, Hannah stared into the fire. It was wonderful to hear the three voices in the kitchen, but her heart yearned to hear the little voice that was missing. If Patty Ruth were here, she would be bossing her brothers in Mary Beth's place.

And another voice was missing.

"Oh, Sol," she whispered. "When you were taken last summer, I thought a lot about what Christmas would be like this year without you."

She swallowed with difficulty. "Sol, darling, you always made Christmas so special. You were such a delight. You always got as excited as the children. Remember how I had to be the calming element to keep you and the children from getting too wild?

"But it was so wonderful. I often just sat and smiled to myself as I watched my happy family make their secret

Christmas preparations. And when it came to the decorations and the meals, you used to tell me I worked too hard. But I wanted to make each Christmas a special day full of wonderful memories."

Hannah's attention was drawn to the kitchen as Mary Beth mildly corrected her younger brother for the way he had misplaced silverware at the place settings.

Hannah smiled as B.J. explained why he had put them that way. She whispered to Sol again. "Darling, I knew this Christmas was going to be hard. Very, very hard. But I didn't know that in addition to being without you, we would also be without our precious Patty Ruth."

She was trying to swallow the hot lump in her throat when Mary Beth said, "Supper's ready, Mama."

As the family sat down to the table and joined hands, Hannah looked at Chris. "It's your turn, son."

Her eldest child led in prayer, thanking the Lord for the food, but when he brought Patty Ruth up to the Lord, he choked up and paused for a long time before he was able to finish his prayer.

Though no one had much appetite, they slowly ate the delicious meal Mary Beth had prepared. While they ate in silence, each person eyed the empty chair with the dog sitting beside it. Biggie missed the little girl who often slipped him goodies under the table.

The meal was almost over when footsteps were heard on the wooden staircase outside, followed by a knock at the door.

"I'll get it," said Chris.

Lantern light from within showed Chris the cold, reddened faces of Colonel Ross Bateman and Deputy Marshal Jack Bower.

"Hi, Chris," said Bateman. "Are we interrupting supper?"

"We're about done, sir. Come in."

As they stepped inside, Bower said, "We just need to talk to your mother for a minute."

At that moment, Hannah and the other two children appeared.

Both men removed their hats.

"Good evening, gentlemen," Hannah said, giving them a wan smile. "Nothing today, I assume."

They shook their heads.

"Well, I appreciate the effort. I'll never be able to thank all of you properly."

"We'll get our thanks when that little redhead is back in this apartment, Hannah," said Jack.

Bateman cleared his throat. "We've called off the search till Monday. Jack and I felt that since there has been no trace of Patty Ruth in all this time, the men should be able to spend Christmas with their families. We hope you understand."

"Of course I do," Hannah said softly. "I want all of you to have your Christmas. I just appreciate what you've been doing."

There were more footsteps on the outside staircase. Chris rushed to the door and opened it before the knock came.

It was Chief Two Moons.

Hannah welcomed the chief in and expressed her thanks for what he and his braves were doing.

The stalwart Crow leader said, "Two Moons and braves very sorry Patty Ruth Cooper not yet found. We understand why white men not search tomorrow, but want Hannah Cooper to know we will look for her tomorrow."

Hannah nodded. "Thank you, Chief. Please hear the language of the heart and know how very much my children and I appreciate your help."

A smile tugged at the corners of Two Moons's lips. "Language of the heart is heard." As he turned toward the door, he said, "Will bring Patty Ruth Cooper home tomorrow if we find her."

"Nothing could make me happier," Hannah said.

When Two Moons was gone, Colonel Bateman said, "I

wish all Indians were like him and his people."

Hannah nodded.

"Before we go," said Jack, "I have one bit of good news for you, Hannah."

She smiled faintly. "I can use it."

"I stopped by Julianna's house as soon as we rode in. Heidi's there, helping her cook dinner for this evening."

"And you'll be eating there, of course."

"Of course! Anyway, my boss will be eating there, too." A wide smile spread over his face. "When I left the house, Lance and Heidi were holding hands and looking starry-eyed at each other."

In spite of her deep sorrow, Hannah grinned at the news. "That's wonderful! Those two were made for each other. The Lord just had to save your boss first. It probably won't be too long till we hear that Lance has proposed and Heidi has accepted."

"I'm sure you're right about that. Well, Colonel, we'd better get going."

At the door, Jack looked back and said, "I'd like to wish all of you a merry Christmas…but I'm afraid it would be a bit hollow."

"It's not going to be the same, I'll admit," said Hannah, "but we have a lot to be thankful for. Chris, Mary Beth, and I still have each other, and we have a lot of faithful, loving friends. Most of all, we have the Lord. So we will have a blessed Christmas."

When the two men were gone, Mary Beth said, "If you boys will help me, we can have the kitchen cleaned up and the dishes done in a matter of minutes."

Later, in order to try to bring some cheer into the home, Hannah had Chris and Mary Beth light the candles on the tree, which stood in a corner of the parlor across the room from the fireplace. When the candles were lit, the four of them stood back with their arms around each other and gazed with awe at their beautiful tree.

The Coopers had always opened their gifts on Christmas morning, followed by a hearty breakfast. Afterward, Solomon would read the Christmas story from Luke chapter 2, then lead the family in prayer. He always thanked the Lord for His bountiful blessings and for the greatest gift of all—the Lord Jesus, whose birth they were celebrating.

Each child had been taught from their earliest years that Christmas was the celebration of the birth of God's only begotten Son, and that the best gift they could give Him was to serve Him with all their heart.

Next on Christmas Day came a trip across town to Grandpa and Grandma Singleton's house. At that happy place, there were more presents to open, and always a big turkey feast later in the day.

As they stood in the apartment with their arms around one another, Hannah and her three oldest children were remembering those special times in the past. This year had brought a threefold loss—no Singletons, no Solomon, and no Patty Ruth.

After the presents were put under the tree—including Patty Ruth's—they sat down in the parlor and enjoyed the beauty of the decorations and the brightly lit tree. They talked of Jacob Kates and how much he was missing because he didn't know Jesus Christ.

Chris talked about the Crow Indians and his burden to see them saved, especially his friend Broken Wing.

Conversation dwindled, and the fireplace crackled as they sat in silence, each with their own thoughts.

When Mary Beth saw the tears in her mother's eyes, she took hold of Hannah's hand and said, "Mama, I know that our tradition has always been that no presents be opened until Christmas morning, but could I make a suggestion?"

"Of course, Mary Beth."

"Well...I would like to ask that tradition be broken for just one present. I think it would help if you would open your present from Patty Ruth now."

The boys exchanged glances, then looked at their mother and nodded.

"All right," said Hannah.

B.J. jumped off his chair, dashed to the tree and searched for a moment, then came up with the present and took it to his mother.

Hannah's face tightened when she read the tag on the package written in Patty Ruth's own hand, which had been guided by her big sister. *To Mama from Patty Ruth. I love you.*

Hannah tore at the wrapping paper with trembling hands. When the wrapping paper was folded back to reveal the handkerchief, Hannah studied the crooked and uneven lace border sewn by little hands of love, and burst into tears.

The siblings looked at each other in dismay. Mary Beth took hold of her mother's arm. "Mama, I'm sorry. I thought—"

"We're sorry, Mama," said Chris.

"Yes, Mama," said B.J. "We're sorry."

Hannah shook her head as the tears streamed down her cheeks. "No, no. Don't be sorry. This does help me, really. I can't help crying, but seeing the love that was sewn into this hankie by those tiny fingers goes all the way to the bottom of my heart. And that helps. Believe me, it really helps."

CHAPTER TWENTY-TWO

Patty Ruth Cooper stood looking at herself before the mirror in Holly's room.

Emily was in the kitchen, cooking Christmas Eve supper. She had insisted that Patty Ruth wear this red-and-green dress—the same dress Holly had worn on Christmas Eve last year. When Matt had checked on Patty Ruth a few minutes earlier, and she complained about how tight the dress was, he told her that Emily wasn't thinking clearly or she wouldn't have made her wear it.

The aroma of cooking food wafted through the room, but Patty Ruth just shook her head and said, "I don't want any supper. I wanna go home."

She heard footsteps in the hall; then Mr. McDermott appeared, saying, "I just thought of something that would really help Mrs. McDermott, honey."

Patty Ruth stared at him.

"Last year, Mrs. McDermott gave Holly a little necklace with a Christmas tree on it. Would you mind wearing it for her?"

Patty Ruth shrugged. "Okay."

Emily's voice called from the kitchen, and Matt said, "I've got to go help my wife take the turkey out of the oven. The necklace is in a small red box about the color of your dress. You'll find it in one of those top drawers in the dresser. It's made so you can slip it over your head. Put it on and surprise her when you come to the table, will you?"

Patty Ruth nodded.

When Matt was gone, Patty Ruth looked at the dresser. She had never opened any drawers since occupying this room. It wasn't nice to snoop in other people's things.

There were four drawers. She opened the one on the left and found some papers and an arm from a rag doll. The next drawer showed her a pair of baby shoes and some long stockings that Holly had worn when she was tiny.

Drawer number three held the little red box. As she took it out she found a photograph beneath it. Two of the faces she recognized. Mr. and Mrs. McDermott were sitting on chairs with what looked like a sheet hanging up behind them. On Mr. McDermott's lap was a little girl with dark red hair and long braids. Suddenly she realized she was looking at Holly McDermott. Patty Ruth could see a slight resemblance to herself, but Holly's nose, eyes, and ears were different. Especially the ears. They were very different.

Patty Ruth wondered why Mrs. McDermott couldn't tell that she was not Holly.

"Holly!" came Matt's voice from the back end of the hall. "Mama says supper is ready! Come on!"

Patty Ruth placed the picture back in the drawer and opened the small box. She took the necklace out and looped it over her head. The small Christmas tree hung to the middle of her chest.

When Patty Ruth entered the kitchen, Emily said, "My, don't you look pretty in that dress! Just like last y— Oh! Holly, you're wearing the necklace Mama bought for you last year!"

Patty Ruth got a big hug from Emily, then climbed into Holly's chair for supper.

After prayer, the McDermotts started eating, but Patty Ruth had no appetite. All she had was a deep ache in her lonely heart and a strong desire to go home.

She toyed with her food, half listening to Mrs. McDermott, who chattered happily about the wonderful Christmas they were going to have.

Patty Ruth thought back on the few Christmases she could remember. They were full of joy and laughter. *My papa won't be here this year,* she thought. *And it will be sad. And with me gone, too, what will my mama do?*

She knew that Chris had brought a Christmas tree home by now, and she pictured it in the parlor lighted with candles and decorated the way her family always fixed their trees. In her mind she could see her mother, Chris, B.J., and Mary Beth sitting in the parlor with sad faces. *I wanna go home,* she thought. *I don't care what happens here. I want my family!*

Her chin began to quiver as tears ran down her face and fell into her plate of food.

Emily talked on, not noticing that the child had not eaten a bite.

But Matt's attention was drawn to Patty Ruth's quivering chin and glistening cheeks. Her eyes were swimming in tears as she looked up at him and uttered one soft word.

"Please?"

Hannah Cooper and her three oldest children sat in the parlor, looking at the bright tree and enjoying the warmth of the fire. It was almost ten o'clock when they heard footsteps on the stairs outside.

"I'll see who it is," said B.J., darting for the door. "We asked Jesus to bring Patty Ruth home for Christmas. Maybe it's her!"

Mother and siblings left their chairs to follow B.J.

When he opened the door, disappointment fell over him

like cold water. It was Jacob Kates, not his little sister.

"My Sabbath was over at six o'clock, as you know," said Jacob, "but I couldn't go to bed without coming up to see my family."

Hannah smiled. "Jacob, come in. I'm glad you look at us as your family. Come and sit down by the fire. Do you want something to eat?"

"Oh, no, thank you, Miss Hannah. I'm really not hungry."

"Show him your present from Patty Ruth, Mama," said B.J.

When they sat down in the parlor, Hannah placed her gift from Patty Ruth in Jacob's hands.

His brow furrowed and tears filled his eyes when he read the tag, then studied the handkerchief sewn by Patty Ruth. "Miss Hannah, this is the sweetest thing I've ever seen." Jacob wiped the moisture from his cheeks and said, "Listen to me, all of you. Remember the story of Joseph in the Bible?"

They nodded.

"I know in my heart, just as sure as Joseph was reunited with his father, that Patty Ruth is going to be reunited with you."

Jacob and the Coopers sat before the pleasant fire, talking occasionally but mostly absorbing comfort from being together.

Not long after ten o'clock, Jacob stirred and told them he must get back down to his quarters and stoke up the fire. Jack would be coming home a little later, and he wanted to have the place warm for him.

Biggie had been asleep near the fireplace but woke up as Jacob left. When the door closed, the dog trotted down the hall and disappeared into the boys' room.

The Coopers remained in the parlor, discussing their love for Jacob and his need for the Saviour. To encourage her children, Hannah told them stories of people she had known who finally came to the Lord when it seemed they never would.

The children also brought up names, including Marshal Lance Mangum—the most recent person they had seen come to the Lord. Just talking about these people brought encouragement to their hearts that Jacob Kates would one day be saved.

Suddenly the clock on the mantel chimed twelve times.

"Well, it's Christmas," B.J. said.

"Merry Christmas, children," said Hannah.

She saw the strange look on their faces and said, "We all feel sad about our little one, but we must remember that we have each other."

At her words, all three children wished their mother and each other a merry Christmas.

"We need to get to bed now," said Hannah.

They all rose to their feet, though no one expected to sleep.

"I'll put out the candles," said Chris.

"No need," Hannah said. "I'll take care of putting them out."

Suddenly they heard footsteps on the staircase.

Hannah frowned. "Who could be coming to our door at this time of night?"

"Only one way to find out," said Chris, heading for the door just as a knock was heard.

The lantern light from within the apartment showed the face of a stranger.

Hannah took a couple of steps toward him. "Yes, sir?"

The man removed his hat, ran his gaze over the faces of the Cooper family, and said, "Mrs. Cooper...Chris, B.J., Mary Beth...my name is Matthew McDermott."

Hannah took another step. "Mr. McDermott, I don't believe we know you."

The children looked on curiously.

"No, but you know this person I have with me."

A little redheaded girl with long braids, clad in a red coat and stocking cap, stepped into the light that flowed onto the landing. There was a big smile on her face.

The soul-stirring moment seemed to be happening in a silent world of another time and another place. Patty Ruth stood there looking at them, but seemed unable to open her mouth. Just as speechless were her mother, sister, and brothers.

Finally, Patty Ruth said, "I love you, Mama."

Hannah Marie Cooper released her pent-up breath in a huge sigh and opened her arms wide as she dropped to her knees and folded the girl into her arms. Over and over, she sobbed her praise to the Lord and thanked Him for her perfect Christmas gift. Patty Ruth was home!

A yipping sound came from the hall, followed by the click of dog feet on wood floor as Biggie raced into the room.

Chris helped Hannah to her feet while Patty Ruth laughed in delight when the little dog stood on his hind legs and licked her face.

Biggie objected when Patty Ruth went to hug her sister and brothers.

Hannah stood, looking on, when suddenly she felt the cold air from outside and realized Matthew McDermott was still standing in the open doorway. There were tears streaming down his face.

"Oh! Mr. McDermott, please come in!"

As he stepped inside and closed the door, she said, "Please forgive my ill manners."

"No need to be sorry, ma'am. I understand your elation and joy. Go on. Hug your little girl some more."

When the emotion of the moment had subsided, Mary Beth helped Patty Ruth remove her coat, mittens, and cap.

"Mr. McDermott," Hannah said, "please come into the parlor and sit down. Mary Beth, there's hot coffee on the stove yet. Would you bring some for our friend here?"

Moments later, Matt was seated near the fire with a steaming cup of coffee in hand. He was chilled from being out in the freezing cold, but more so from the case of nerves attacking his stomach.

Chris, Mary Beth, and B.J. sat close to their mother, who was now in her rocking chair. Although Hannah's lap was almost nonexistent due to her pregnancy, she found enough room to pull Patty Ruth close.

"Now, Mr. McDermott," Hannah said, "tell us how and from whom you rescued our little Patty Ruth."

Matt almost spilled his coffee. "Well, ma'am, it's sort of a long story."

"Take as long as you want."

Matt sipped the coffee, then began his story. He told them he was a farmer from the Mountain View–Lyman area. His trembling hands gripped the mug tightly as he explained the loss of his and Emily's farm in Kentucky and their son's death not long before.

He told them all about the hard trials of the wagon train journey, and when he got to the part about the two Pawnee attacks, he struggled through it, having to stop several times and wipe tears from his eyes.

Each time he paused, Hannah waited quietly until he could collect himself and continue.

He explained that the stress of losing their little son and the farm, and then the trauma of the Pawnee attacks, had affected Emily's mind. When their little Holly got sick and died a few weeks ago, Emily's mind had gone into another reality, and she had not accepted the fact that Holly was dead. In her deranged search for her little girl, she had abducted Patty Ruth, thinking she had found Holly.

While all this information was sinking in, Matt told the Coopers that he and Emily were born-again Christians. Although the Holy Spirit had convicted him mightily, he had not returned Patty Ruth until now. With tears streaming down his face, he humbly asked Hannah's forgiveness for keeping Patty Ruth so long for Emily's sake.

Hannah's tender heart went out to this man and his troubled wife. Fresh tears stung her eyes as she realized the torment the poor woman had gone through, and the courage of her husband to risk her very life to bring Patty Ruth home. She reached out an unsteady hand and patted his arm. Her own horror and heartache seemed to pale as forgiveness quickly flowed into her soul. Although she would never be able to erase this awful incident from her memory, her overflowing heart wanted to help this desperate couple.

Hannah's children looked on expectantly as she said, "Mr. McDermott, I forgive you, and I know my children forgive you too. My heart goes out to you for the agony you have suffered."

Matt looked at Hannah through a blur of tears. "I wouldn't blame you if you didn't forgive me."

Hannah smiled. "Didn't our Lord Jesus forgive both of us for all of our sins against Him?"

Yes."

"And weren't our sins much greater against Him than what you did in keeping my daughter from me?"

"Well, yes."

"Then I would be wrong not to forgive you."

"There ought to be more Christians like you in this world, Hannah Cooper."

Hannah smiled at his words but didn't comment. Then she said, "Mr. McDermott, I want you to know that I am not going to press charges against your wife for kidnapping Patty Ruth, but I am going to be praying for both of you."

"Oh, thank you, ma'am. Thank you!"

Hannah hugged Patty Ruth real tight, then set her steady gaze on McDermott. "May I suggest something to you?"

"Of course."

"Our town physician is Dr. Frank O'Brien. He and his

wife are wonderful Christians. Dr. O'Brien knows a lot about mental illness brought on by stress...like Emily's. He was an army doctor for many years and was on many battlefields in the Civil War. He's handled hundreds of cases of soldiers whose minds snapped in the war. You should bring Emily to town and let Dr. O'Brien see her. With his knowledge and experience—plus being a Christian—I believe he can help her."

Matt had been staring at the floor as she spoke but now looked up and said, "I appreciate your telling me about Dr. O'Brien. I'll bring Emily to see him."

"Mr. McDermott," said Hannah, "how were you able to get Patty Ruth away from Emily tonight?"

"Ma'am, you can call me Matt. I'd like you to call me Matt."

"All right. And you can call me Hannah."

"Well, to answer your question, my guilt was too strong to ignore when I thought of you without your little daughter on Christmas Eve. I was having a real battle about what to do, when that sweet little girl on your lap looked up at me with big tears in her eyes and said one little word."

"What was that?"

"*Please.* It was the proverbial straw that broke the camel's back, so here she is."

Hannah kissed her daughter's hair. "Mama always told you to say *please,* and I'm sure glad I did."

"Anyway," said Matt, "I made Emily some coffee and slipped in a strong sedative. She will sleep till noon tomorrow. And I promise I will bring her to Dr. O'Brien on Monday."

"Good," said Hannah. "I'll tell him you're coming. Is it all right if I sort of fill him in?"

"Sure," said Matt, rising to his feet. "Well, it's getting late. Or should I say early? I need to get home to Emily. And all of you need to get some rest."

Matt's features looked haggard. Hannah focused on his

tired eyes and said, "You need some rest, yourself, Mr.— I mean, Matt. Hurry home and get to bed."

As he was putting on his coat, Hannah said, "It was a very difficult decision you made. Thank you for bringing Patty Ruth home."

"And thank you for your understanding and forgiveness, Hannah. God bless you." He ran his gaze to the three older children and said, "And thank you for your understanding and forgiveness, too." Chris and B.J. nodded silently, and Mary Beth gave him a compassionate smile.

Matt turned his attention to the child on her mother's lap. "Patty Ruth, could I have a hug before I go?"

The little girl slipped to the floor and ran to him. He scooped her up in his arms and held her tight while she wrapped her arms around his neck and squeezed hard. Looking at Hannah through misty eyes, Matt said, "Hannah, you have a wonderful little girl here. I've come to love her very much."

"I can understand that," Hannah said as she rose from the rocking chair.

As soon as Matt put Patty Ruth down, Biggie was there to get more attention from her.

"Matt," Hannah said, "I would like to meet Emily. Would you let me go with you to Dr. O'Brien's office?"

"Sure. We'll come by here first, okay?"

"All right. In the meantime, I'll talk to Dr. O'Brien about her."

"That will be fine. Thank you for caring about Emily."

Hannah smiled. "I'm a mother, too. Mothers understand things no one else does."

"I'm sure that's true," he said, taking hat in hand. "Well, I'd better be going."

Hannah stepped close to him, raised up on her toes, and

placed a soft kiss on his rugged cheek. "Go with God, Matt. And remember His Word. 'God hath not given us the spirit of fear, but of power, and of love, and of a sound mind.'"

Matt nodded humbly and donned his hat. "See you Monday." He stepped out into the frigid night.

While walking around the store toward the street, Matt paused and gazed up into the starry sky. Seeing one star shining brighter than all the rest, he thought back to that night so long ago when the wise men came from the east, guided by a star "till it came and stood over where the young child was."

"Thank You, Lord," he whispered, "for the perfect Gift of Your only begotten Son."

With his heart feeling lighter than it had in weeks, he climbed in the wagon and headed home.

Though the Cooper family was exhausted, they were at the peak of exhilaration. Everybody hugged Patty Ruth again, and Biggie got more loving from his favorite little redhead.

When Mary Beth noticed her mother gazing into space with a thoughtful look on her face, she said, "What is it, Mama?"

"I know it's late, but I think Jacob wouldn't mind being awakened to learn that his prediction has come true. Like Joseph of old, our kidnapped one is back with her family."

"I'll go down and get him!" Chris said.

After Jacob had spent a few minutes holding Patty Ruth and praising Jehovah God for her return, he thanked Hannah for letting him know the good news, and returned to his quarters.

Hannah looked at the bright but weary faces of her children and realized that sleep would be some time in coming.

She asked Mary Beth to prepare hot cocoa while she opened a tin of homemade Christmas cookies that "Grandma" O'Brien had given them.

As the children gathered around the table, Hannah produced the handkerchief Patty Ruth had given her for Christmas, told the child how beautiful it was, and with a big hug, thanked her for it.

They sat companionably around the kitchen table with Patty Ruth on Chris's lap. As they drank the cocoa and ate cookies, they could hardly believe the ordeal was over—that they were safely together again.

Patty Ruth had gotten her second wind now and told her family in precise detail all she had been through.

"Could Holly really have looked that much like our little sister, Mama?" Mary Beth asked. "I mean, could Holly's own mother mistake Patty Ruth for her?"

"Well, you heard Matt say that Holly's hair was exactly the same color as Patty Ruth's, and that Patty Ruth was exactly the same size as his little Holly."

"But what about her face?" B.J. asked. "Could Holly have really had a face like Patty Ruth's?"

The little girl's eyes widened. "Would you like to see her picture?"

"You have a picture of Holly?" Hannah asked.

"Mm-hmm. I brought it home so you could see what she looked like. She looked a little bit like me, but not a whole lot."

Patty Ruth slid off Chris's lap and dashed to her coat to reach into her pocket. When she returned to the table she climbed back on Chris's lap, unfolded the stiff paper, and handed the photograph of the McDermott family to her mother.

"I'll give it back to Mr. McDermott, Mama," she said. "I'm not gonna keep it."

Hannah examined the picture with Mary Beth and B.J.

crowding close to see it. "Honey, where did you find this?" Hannah asked.

"It was in one of Holly's dresser drawers, Mama. I din' snoop, though. Mr. McDermott tol' me to get somethin' out of the drawer, an' I foun' the pitcher. I jus' wanted to show you what Holly looked like."

"Well, we must certainly give this back to the McDermotts," Hannah said.

"Holly was cute, Mama," said Mary Beth, "but her ears were different than Patty Ruth's."

"Her nose, too," put in B.J.

"And her mouth," said Hannah. "I can see enough resemblance that from a distance you might think she was Patty Ruth. Especially with the pigtails, and the fact that they were the same size."

Chris reached out a hand. "Could I see it, please?"

When Chris had studied the photograph for a moment, he said, "Well, all I can say is, Mrs. McDermott's mind must be pretty far gone for her to look at Patty Ruth and think she's Holly."

By this time, the soothing hot cocoa was taking effect on everyone except Patty Ruth, who began to fill in some details that she had overlooked earlier.

The others were trying to pay attention, but their yawns grew wider and their heads were drooping.

All of a sudden the room was strangely quiet. Hannah and the siblings looked at Patty Ruth, who was slumped against Chris's chest, sound asleep. She had fallen asleep right in the middle of a sentence.

"All right," Hannah whispered, "let's all go to bed. Chris, will you carry P.R. to her bed, please?"

Mary Beth told her mother to go on; she would tidy up the kitchen. Hannah followed Chris as he carried his little sister to the girls' room and laid her on her bed. Hannah thanked him, and he headed for the boys' room.

While Hannah was removing Patty Ruth's dress, the little girl woke and put her arms around her mother's neck. "I missed you so much, Mama. I'm so glad to be ho—" This time, in the middle of a word, she was asleep once more.

Mary Beth came in and began to prepare for bed.

After Hannah put Patty Ruth's nightgown on and covered her up, she eased down on the edge of the bed and watched her little girl sleep. She was almost afraid to leave her. Finally, committing Patty Ruth into God's care, Hannah kissed a sweet little cheek and stepped over to Mary Beth's bed. Leaning over, she kissed her precious Mary Beth and told her good night.

After checking on the sleeping boys, Hannah went to her own bedroom. She undressed and put on her warmest nightgown. While turning the covers down on her bed, she was overwhelmed with the joy of answered prayer.

"Thank You, Lord, for being the same yesterday, today, and forever. Thank You for bringing my precious one home. Thank You that You never leave us nor forsake us. I humble myself in awe before You for Your goodness, Your grace, and the wonderful way You answer our prayers."

She paused to swallow a hot lump. "Thank You, dear Father in heaven, for sending Your precious Son, whose birth we celebrate tomo— Well, I guess it's today, isn't it? Lord, help me to ever be Your faithful, grateful servant."

She spent a few minutes praying for her children—as always—then climbed into bed.

As sleep pulled at her, Hannah said, "Sol, we have our little Patty Ruth back. God is so good. I love you, darling. Christmas won't be the same without you, but one day in God's will and time, we'll all be together again."

The emotions of the day overwhelmed Hannah. She gently

placed her hands on the babe resting beneath her breasts, closed her weary eyes, and allowed sleep to steal over her.

CHAPTER TWENTY-THREE

Because Christmas fell on Sunday, the Coopers had already decided to wait until after the morning church services to open their gifts. However, this did not keep B.J. and Patty Ruth from getting up extra early so they could sit and stare at the tree and the gifts beneath it.

Mary Beth and Hannah prepared a quick breakfast. While eating, Hannah reminded her children that Pastor Kelly was going to have a midafternoon service instead of an evening service so families could have Christmas night at home. Grandpa and Grandma O'Brien were expecting them for a big dinner at five o'clock.

When breakfast was over and the dishes done, there was much scurrying as the Coopers prepared for church. They were about to leave when there was a knock at the door. Chief Two Moons had stopped by to let Hannah know he and his braves were beginning another day of searching.

His heart filled with joy when he was invited in and saw a bright-eyed Patty Ruth smiling at him. Two Moons told Hannah there would be much happiness among his people when he and his braves returned to the village with the good news.

Hannah thanked him once again for all he and his braves had done, and with a smile, the chief tapped his chest with a fist and said, "Two Moons hear with language of the heart."

As Hannah and her children walked through the winter wonderland of sparkling snow and blue sky on Christmas morning, Patty Ruth skipped along ahead of them as though nothing momentous had occurred over the last nine days.

Pastor Andy Kelly and the people who filled the church building were elated to see Patty Ruth alive and well. Kelly put aside his planned sermon and preached on praising the Lord for answered prayer.

There was joy all throughout the town and fort as word of Patty Ruth's return spread as soon as church let out.

When they returned home, the Coopers entered their apartment with much anticipation, quickly ate a snack, then gathered around the lighted Christmas tree.

Patty Ruth and B.J. sat on the floor while Chris and Mary Beth handed out the presents. Hannah sat in her comfortable old rocking chair. She turned to look out the parlor window and announced that it had begun to snow. What a glorious sight! And what a blessed Christmas God had given them.

Amid squeals of delight and happy laughter, the four children made fast work of opening presents. Hannah made sure Chris, Mary Beth, and B.J. understood that she loved and appreciated the presents they had given her every bit as much as the one Patty Ruth had given her.

Soon the paper and debris were cleaned up, and the children wandered into their rooms to examine and enjoy their gifts.

Hannah listened to the happy chatter coming from the bedrooms. While she slowly rocked in her chair, a contented look etched itself on her face. She felt a small kick in her swollen tummy and patted her babe, whispering, "And a merry Christmas to you, too."

It was snowing slightly as the Cooper family and Jacob Kates trooped to the O'Brien home in late afternoon. Snowflakes stuck to their eyelashes, and the cold air made their cheeks rosy. The children carried packages for "Grandpa and Grandma," and even secretly carried one for "Uncle" Jacob.

The O'Briens met them at the door, and after a round of hugs, quickly ushered them into the cozy house. The Christmas tree was fragrant and aglow with what seemed to be hundreds of flickering candles. The delicious aroma of roast turkey and dressing and pumpkin and mincemeat pies greeted the group, making their mouths water in eager anticipation.

Edie O'Brien indicated that everyone should find a seat in front of the fire, and moments later, she and Doc came into the parlor carrying mugs of steaming hot apple cider, each decorated with a cinnamon stick. While Doc sat down with the guests, Edie left the room, saying she had some finishing touches to do on the dinner.

"Grandma, I'll help you," Mary Beth said, jumping up from her seat.

Shortly afterward, Mary Beth appeared in the parlor, telling the group that Grandma said to head for the dining room. Dinner was ready.

The table was resplendent with snowy white linen and gleaming candlelight, and the table fairly groaned with its load of bounty. When everyone was seated, they all joined hands. Jacob was used to this from eating meals at the Cooper home. He bowed his head with the others.

Frank O'Brien prayed, thanking God for the food and for the reason they were celebrating this day. He also poured out his heart in praise for Patty Ruth's safe return.

Jacob listened politely, though in his heart he still did not understand why Christians felt so sure that their Jesus was the promised Messiah.

Happy chatter filled the room as the meal began. Immediately, Doc and Edie wanted to hear the details of Patty Ruth's abduction and her return last night by the man whose wife had kidnapped her.

Instead of letting Patty Ruth give the lengthy version, Hannah told the story in brief, sharing her deep concern for Emily McDermott. She went on to tell the O'Briens that Matt was going to bring Emily to see Doc on Monday, and she would be coming with them.

When Doc informed the group how Emily's mind had been affected by all she had gone through, and that Patty Ruth's slight resemblance to Holly was enough to make her believe she was in fact her little girl, he told them he would need much guidance from the Lord to help bring Emily out of her demented state.

"Doc," Hannah said, "would it help if you had a picture of Holly to make Emily study the differences between her daughter and Patty Ruth?"

"It might help very much. Should we contact Mr. McDermott and ask him if he has one he can bring?"

"No need. B.J., would you go into the parlor and get my purse, please?"

When the photograph was in Doc's possession and he had studied it for a moment, he put it in his inside coat pocket.

Happy chatter continued around the table, and plates were filled and refilled until no one could hold another bite.

When the table was cleaned and the dishes done, everyone gathered in the parlor to enjoy the sparkling Christmas tree and to open gifts. Jacob was moved when he found that he had been included in the gift-giving by both the Coopers and the O'Briens.

After a while, the excitement of the day and the tension of

the last several days began to take their toll. The Coopers were trying to hide their yawns, but the O'Briens weren't fooled. Doc and Edie smiled at each other, and Doc stood up. "All right, it's time for the Cooper clan to head for home and get themselves to bed early. Doctor's orders! And the doctor is going to drive you home in his buggy."

"You don't need to do that, Doc," said Hannah, stifling a yawn. "It's only a couple of blocks. We walked over here. We can walk home."

"The kids and Jacob, maybe." A slanted grin captured his lips. "But not the two of you."

Hannah patted her midsection and said, "All right. I give in. These weary, swollen legs would be glad to ride instead of walk. You can drive us home."

The Cooper children bundled up against the cold and hugged Grandpa and Grandma O'Brien, thanking them for a wonderful time and all their gifts.

Snow was falling in fat white flakes from a dark sky as they rode toward home.

Everyone snuggled close together in the buggy, and the two youngest Coopers were close to being asleep when Doc turned into the alley behind the store.

Jacob said his good night, thanked Doc again for his gift, and went to his quarters.

Doc carried Patty Ruth up the stairs while Chris stayed at his mother's side, helping her climb.

"Hannah," Doc said, "when you come to the office with the McDermotts tomorrow, bring Patty Ruth with you."

After Hannah had tucked her children into their beds, she went to the parlor, where the only light came from the fire in the fireplace. Standing in front of the darkened parlor window, she watched the snow float down from the heavy night sky.

"Thank You, Father," she said softly. "Thank You for making this a perfect day. And thank You for my perfect gift—for bringing my little one home safely. And most of all, thank You for Your very own perfect gift. 'For unto you is born this day in the city of David a Saviour, which is Christ the Lord.'"

Monday morning came with six inches of new snow on the ground and a brilliant sun in an azure sky to accentuate the whiteness.

When Matt entered the general store to pick up Hannah, Jacob told him that Doc had come by earlier. He had decided it would be best if Hannah and Patty Ruth were already at his office when Matt brought Emily.

Matt pulled the wagon up in front of the doctor's office and took Emily's hand. "All right, honey, we're here."

She glanced up at the shingle above the door. "But this isn't Dr. Garberson's office."

"I know. Honey, I'm sorry I had to make you think you were going to see Dr. Garberson, but Dr. O'Brien is much better qualified to help you. Please. He comes well recommended. Do this for me, will you?"

Emily thought on it. "For you?"

"Mm-hmm."

"Will you give Holly back to me if I do?"

"Honey, let's see what the doctor says first. You trust me, don't you?"

"Of course."

"All right. Come on, let's go inside."

When the McDermotts entered the office, Edie O'Brien introduced herself as the doctor's wife, then said, "This is one of our expectant mothers in town, Mrs. McDermott. Her name is Hannah Cooper."

Emily smiled. "I'm glad to meet you, Mrs. Cooper."

Hannah noted the slightly vacant look in Emily's eyes.

Edie went to the door to the examining and treatment room, tapped on the door, and said, "Doctor, the McDermotts are here."

Immediately, the doctor came through the door. "Good morning, Mr. and Mrs. McDermott. I'm Dr. O'Brien. Mrs. McDermott, I'd like to ask you to wait right here with my wife and Mrs. Cooper while I talk to your husband for a few minutes. Would that be all right?"

"Yes, Doctor, that will be fine."

When Matt stepped into the back room, he found Patty Ruth seated on a chair. The little girl whispered a greeting.

"Hannah has already told me the whole story, sir," said Doc. "I just need you in here for a little while so Emily will think you are telling me the story. She needs to understand that I know all about it when she comes in here."

"That makes sense," Matt said.

Doc O'Brien took the photograph out of a cabinet drawer and showed it to Matt. "Patty Ruth was going to return this to you. She just wanted her family to see what Holly looked like."

Matt stared at it blankly. The photograph had never crossed his mind.

In the outer office, Edie and Hannah were chatting with Emily when Matt came out and said, "Emily, darling, Dr. O'Brien wants you and his wife to come back while he talks to you and does an examination. Will that be all right? I'll be right here."

"Of course," said Emily as she followed Edie through the door.

Immediately they heard Emily cry out, "Oh, Holly! Mama is so glad to see you!"

Almost an hour later, Patty Ruth came into the waiting room, closing the examination room door behind her. She smiled at her mother, then at Matt, and said, "She knows I'm not Holly now. Grandpa showed her the picture and let her look at me at the same time."

Matt took Patty Ruth on his lap and held her close, blinking at the hopeful tears filling his eyes.

Another hour passed.

Patty Ruth was still on Matt's lap when the door opened and Dr. O'Brien came out.

"Mr. McDermott," Doc said, "Emily isn't out of the woods yet, but I believe she will be in a few months. I want to see her at least once a week until I feel she's much better. She has made the big hurdle, though. By studying the picture and Patty Ruth at the same time, she now knows that Patty Ruth is not Holly. She has accepted my word that Holly has gone to heaven."

"Oh, praise God!" Matt cried.

Doc looked at Hannah. "I think it would be best if you and Patty Ruth leave now. Once Emily is much better, I know she'll want to see you. And I have an idea the two of you will become good friends."

"Wonderful!" said Hannah. "Come on, Patty Ruth. Let's go home."

Hannah and her little daughter gave Matt a hug, then left the office.

"All right, Edie," Doc called toward the inner door.

Matt was thrilled to see a smile on Emily's face when she entered the waiting room.

"Emily wants to tell you something, Matt," said Doc.

She moved up close to Matt and said, "I understand about Holly now. Dr. O'Brien says I'm going to get better."

Matt gazed into her eyes and nodded.

"And you want to hear something real good, Matt? I have to get better because of what Dr. O'Brien found out."

"Tell me, honey."

"We're going to have another baby!"

"What did you say? You...you mean it?"

"Yes," Doc said. "She's a little over two months pregnant."

"Oh, glory to God!" Matt shouted. "Glory to God!"

On Tuesday evening, December 27, Glenda Williams put on a big "welcome home" meal in honor of Patty Ruth.

Present among others were Pastor and Mrs. Kelly, Jack Bower, Julianna LeCroix and Larissa, and Belinda Fordham.

When everyone was seated at the table, Gary Williams nodded at Pastor Kelly, who rose to his feet. "Before we pray, I want to say something. Hannah told us at church that the perfect gift for her this Christmas would be to have Patty Ruth back. James 1:17 says in part, 'Every good gift and every perfect gift is from above, and cometh down from the Father of lights.' God gave His Son as the perfect gift in Bethlehem many years ago. He also gave Hannah and her other children the perfect gift for this Christmas by bringing Patty Ruth home."

Suddenly a small voice piped up. "Since we're talkin' 'bout gifts, don' nobody forget—next Friday is my birthday!"